BLOOD BATH

"You little bastard!" Scarlett leaped and shoved Gary hard, knocking him into the sizzling fire with another backhand. She held him in the licking flames as they surrounded her fingers, watching his flesh blister with satisfaction. She ignored the pain it drove into her, hating the smell of her own sizzling like a pound of bad meat. But the aroma of his cooking skin was a sweeter song, and worth it. Her own damage was not irreparable in undeath.

Scarlett turned her eyes back to a dazed Teresa as the woman struggled to get up, then back to Gary as the blood he'd devoured boiled in his veins and his dry flesh rose in tiny pus bubbles, popping in a hundred places with new sputters.

His screams were shattering wails of agony as the fury ate its Hell through him and his soul struggled to escape the steaming, deforming flesh. It was becoming the pungent, green smoke that swept around her.

"Too bad, Gary," she hissed. "Now you're really screwed. If you think it's bad being a vampire and sucking blood . . . try being a disembodied soul with no way to devour life at all!"

W9-AYA-860

NOW THERE'S NO NEED TO WAIT UNTIL DARK!
DAY OR NIGHT, ZEBRA'S VAMPIRE NOVELS
HAVE QUITE A BITE!

THE VAMPIRE JOURNALS (4133, $4.50)
by Traci Briery

Maria Theresa Allogiamento is a vampire ahead of her time. As she travels from 18th-century Italy to present-day Los Angeles, Theresa sets the record straight. From how she chose immortality to her transformation into a seductive temptress, Theresa shares all of her dark secrets and quenches her insatiable thirst for all the world has to offer!

NIGHT BLOOD (4063, $4.50)
by Eric Flanders

Each day when the sun goes down, Val Romero feeds upon the living. This NIGHT BLOOD is the ultimate aphrodisiac. Driving from state to state in his '69 Cadillac, he leaves a trail of bloodless corpses behind. Some call him a serial killer, but those in the know call him Vampire. Now, three tormented souls driven by revenge and dark desires are tracking Val down—and only Val's death will satisfy their own raging thirst for blood!

THE UNDEAD (4068, $5.50)
by Roxanne Longstreet

Most people avoid the cold and sterile halls of the morgue. But for Adam Radburn working as a morgue attendant is a perfect job. He is a vampire. Though Adam has killed for blood, there is another who kills for pleasure and he wants to destroy Adam. And in the world of the undead, the winner is not the one who lives the longest, it's the one who lives forever!

PRECIOUS BLOOD (4293, $4.50)
by Pat Graversen

Adragon Hart, leader of the Society of Vampires, loves his daughter dearly. So does Quinn, a vampire renegade who has lured Beth to the savage streets of New York and into his obscene world of unquenchable desire. Every minute Quinn's hunger is growing. Every hour Adragon's rage is mounting. And both will do anything to satisfy their horrific appetites!

THE SUMMONING (4221, $4.50)
by Bentley Little

The first body was found completely purged of all blood. The authorities thought it was the work of a serial killer. But Sue Wing's grandmother knew the truth. She'd seen the deadly creature decades ago in China. Now it had come to the dusty Arizona town of Rio Verde . . . and it would not leave until it had drunk its fill.

Available wherever paperbacks are sold, or order direct from the Publisher. Send cover price plus 50¢ per copy for mailing and handling to Penguin USA, P.O. Box 999, c/o Dept. 17109, Bergenfield, NJ 07621. Residents of New York and Tennessee must include sales tax. DO NOT SEND CASH.

DAVID DARKE

SHADE

ZEBRA BOOKS
KENSINGTON PUBLISHING CORP.

The characters, situations, conventions, and companies in this book, except for the cameo appearances of several real-life fans, authors, and editors using their *real* names, are not intended to reflect on any real people, situations, or companies, and are wholly of the author's imagination.

ZEBRA BOOKS are published by

Kensington Publishing Corp.
475 Park Avenue South
New York, NY 10016

Copyright © 1994 by Ron Dee

All rights reserved. No part of this book may be reproduced in any form or by any means without the prior written consent of the Publisher, excepting brief quotes used in reviews.

If you purchased this book without a cover you should be aware that this book is stolen property. It was reported as "unsold and destroyed" to the Publisher and neither the Author nor the Publisher has received any payment for this "stripped book."

Zebra and the Z logo Reg. U.S. Pat & TM Off.

First Printing: May, 1994

Printed in the United States of America

For Otto for allowing me to mold him into a character far from his own reality and mirror likeness (he wants to remain a wimpy book dealer) . . . for Lori, truly an agent and person without measure, for John, with thanks for trust and the license to kill, for Danielle for reading it time and again . . . and for all the would-be vampires out there . . .

this blood's for you . . .

Acknowledgments

Many thanks must go to many people, and I want to especially extend apologies to the real people and conventions I have depicted within these pages. Yes, indeed, these conventions are real, and except for Scarlett, can be much wilder than I have depicted. Also, I apologize for ignoring the growing antifilk movement in these pages.

Thanks especially to my wife, Danielle, again, and to Lori and John. More thanks must be addressed to my precious supporters, damn good writers themselves, who gladly gave me their ideas and critical assistance during the hellish weeks of my doubt: Bill Allen, P.D. Cacek (no relation to Carol Kacek), Mark Irwin, Rick Grant. And to all you others who may have suffered with me, thanks . . .

Finally, my greatest apologies and thanks to Otto Filip, owner of the real REALMS OF FANTASY in more or less the location I put it in Norman, Oklahoma. Although there are some very loose similarities to Otto's background and the background of my character, Phillip Ottoman, Otto is far younger, far better-looking, has no serious guilt or mental problems I am aware of, does not have a vampire problem or seriously believe in vampires, and is quite happily married to his wonderful wife, Doris, with a beautiful young daughter, Cassandra. Book buyers are welcome. Convamps, beware.

Part I:
Some Time, Last Month

Chapter 1

The music of Coppola's *Dracula* sent loud vibrations through the apartment. Dirk was still trying to find a mixture of face powders that would make him look good as well as dead. He was about to give up. The party would begin in another hour, at Amy's. All the way on the other side of Nashville . . . in the evening . . . on a weekend. During these summer months the visiting tourists drove like the drunken cowboy maniacs they were. He wished instead he were going to be at the convention in Tucson to greet Scarlett Shade.

But this was a helluva a lot cheaper, and since Amy was throwing it, it would be one hell of a party. She'd opened up and become a wild and crazy girl since she'd gotten so into the Shade books, and if there wasn't a party to go to, she threw one herself.

Like tonight, to celebrate Scarlett Shade's return to conventions and a more public life. Even if he and most of the rest of their group couldn't make it to the convention.

Dirk was almost as excited about it as Amy and the dozen others in their Shade fan club. He hadn't started reading the books until only four months ago, but after Tamara, the girl he'd been dating then, got him started . . .

He was reading all the books for the second time already. He wished they were real . . . liked the way they made him feel about himself and life. Life was a shit pit and instead of trying to cover that fact up, Scarlett's wonderful main characters, Count Downe and the gorgeous Countess Showery, freely admitted to it and were trying to do something about it, at least for themselves.

Their power . . . their love, of *self*. Not the pretense of altruism so many acted out. In Shade's world, there was no self-sacrifice or guilt. Instead, making your desires true.

Too bad it was only fiction.

Sometimes Dirk got so into the books he wanted to just close himself up inside them and become Count Downe . . . and that was who he was dressing up as for the party.

In the mirror, he looked pretty good. He tilted his jaw and slicked his black hair back, putting in his plastic fangs. The old saying . . . mirrors never lie. But Dirk knew he *could* lie to the mirror . . . could make it reflect him the way he wanted to be, at least to some degree. Just like the Count. He often looked into his reflection casually and pretended he was part of Scarlett Shade's ficticious world, and with this makeup, it was even better . . . except the goddamn powder color was still not right.

The doorbell rang.

"Who in the fuck can that be?" Dirk left the small bathroom and walked through his only slightly larger apartment, messy as usual, dirty underwear and shorts spilling out of his laundry basket, unwashed dishes on the chairs and kitchen counter. He wished he had picked them up as he peeked out the door's peephole . . . and gasped.

Countess Showery!

His breath was short and his heart light as he touched the knob. Of course, he knew it wasn't really her . . . besides being a vampire, she was merely fictional, but it sure as hell looked the way he figured she'd appear!

10

The bell rang again, and wondering who the attractive woman really was, Dirk opened the door. It couldn't be Tamara since the woman's blond hair looked very real and she wasn't at all plump. It couldn't be Amy, either, even though Amy's figure was just about that perfect. No way Amy would come here with the party about to start.

It wasn't Carrie, either . . . or Lesa. The other two girls in their fan circle were long gone to Tucson with George, but even if not, it couldn't be them. Neither was this gorgeous. "H-hi," Dirk said, entranced, holding the door open as the woman slipped gracefully inside. He wondered if this was a trick and one of the others had initiated a new member . . . and sent her over for a surprise. He gave her the once-over very carefully, suspecting a distant recognition. "Do I know you?"

She nodded, parting her full, red lips just enough so he could see the underlying fangs.

Okay . . . *so who was she?* He worked his memory harder. "Uh, so what's going on? Are you going to Amy's party?"

Again, she nodded, tossing her silky blond hair back and forth. Her gown was the only thing that spoiled her resemblance to fiction. Instead of a skin-tight or sheer outfit, it was a rather baggy black dress, not really short enough to expose what looked like well-shaped legs to Dirk.

So who cared *who* she was? He was pretty alone right now and could use a new face in his life. Dirk led her into his living room and gulped. "Sorry about the way things look . . . I . . . need to clean up."

She smiled silently, giving a faint curtsy.

Dirk's blush grew hotter and he waved a hand at a chair. "If . . . you want to make yourself at home we can go to Amy's together . . . I just need to work on this face powder one more time and get on my shoes, okay?"

Her red lips turned up as she nodded again.

Dirk waited for her to say something, hoping to identify

her by her voice, but she just stood there shyly. He inhaled her lusty fragrance, frowned, and looked right into her blue eyes, trying harder to place the familiarity of her features. "Hey, I'm sorry . . . what's your name?"

She closed the gap between them and circled him with her arms, and he was surprised that she was so tall . . . much taller than he first thought. She was right up against him and Dirk's face was full of her hot perfume. As she pressed closer, Dirk felt the interest below his belt . . . saw that fascination equaled in her eyes.

Dirk gulped. "I . . . I . . . uh . . ."

Then she laughed loudly and gracelessly. He jumped back.

"Boy, did I fool you, you *dick brain!*" came her bass roar.

A *man*'s voice. Dirk did a doubletake and dropped his jaw. *James.* He should have known with that long, blond hair! Dirk felt his heart in his throat, thudding with a big disappointment, but finally, he chuckled, too. "D-damn good makeup job, asshole. I thought you were a woman!"

"I am," James said in a high soprano. "I'm the Countess . . . here to drink your blood!"

"I mean it," Dirk said, walking back to the bathroom as his friend followed. "That's a great joke."

"No joke," smiled James. "Hell, you sure didn't look like you thought it was a joke. You looked like you were thinking about skipping the party. I was afraid you were going to throw me down on the floor and try to fuck my legs off."

Moving back inside the tiled room, Dirk poked through the powders open on the counter, shaking his head. "No . . . but you look damn good, I'll give you that. You've got a knack with makeup."

"Is that a hint you want my help?" James squeezed into the small space with him and looked at all the jars

12

and bottles. "Shit . . . what'd you do, raid a beauty supply?"

"These are my sister's." He fought a blush and put his fingers into two powder jars, comparing their tones, then streaked a mark from each on his pink cheeks, studying them.

But suddenly, his reflection looked perfect . . . like he really *was* Count Downe. He even felt like the Count.

"You already look fine, Dirk," said James, his voice high again, but this time almost as sexy as a real woman's. "Both of us. We look just . . . just like . . ." James began unzipping his dress, opening it on his pale, naked flesh.

Dirk gasped at James in the mirror, because now he really did look . . .

Like *her*. Dirk reached out to touch well-formed breasts that were *real*.

They were so close together in the confined room, sniffing each other like dogs in heat.

It *was* Countess Showery. He . . . *she* . . . had breasts. Dirk caressed them as the nipples stood, and pulled the Countess closer, not able to stop his frenzied tongue from licking the firm flesh. She shuddered and pulled his face to hers, his thighs against hers. Dirk opened his mouth to her, licking her fangs, their lower bodies rubbing together. His hardness crept into the crevice of her thigh and he dragged up her hem while she unzipped him, setting him free. Gasping, he slipped inside her hot, tight hole, forgetting all about his own appearance and the party, the way he had planned to seduce Amy and maybe Tamara, too.

Now he didn't need them . . . or want them.

He had the *Countess*. She had him. "Drink my blood," Dirk whispered.

"Drink mine!" she hissed back.

Dirk licked her neck, fumbling as he pushed in and out of her, her muscles pumping him.

The Countess!

She licked him back, unhooking his belt while their movements became faster.

Spitting out their plastic fangs, they both bit into the other's flesh at the exact same moment.

Chapter 2

Dan Rather was kind of sexy, Elaine thought, looking up at the TV from her book.

She saw him as a modern Count Downe. Stern, solid . . . sometimes gentle.

"Scarlett Fever was back in a fury this weekend in Tucson. Scarlett Shade chose that city to reemerge into the limelight and her appearance has brought back the full furor that surrounded her writing two years ago. The ripples are already spreading. After the two suicides at TusCon, one of the several science fiction and fantasy conventions that take place regularly across the United States, more reports of minor instances of violence have been reported. In Nashville . . ."

Elaine heard another voice, distant, but unfortunately much closer than Dan Rather really was. When it came again, far down the hall, she turned off the TV.

His voice: "Come on, Elaine, I'm tired! I have to get up early tomorrow morning. Some of us have to work, you know."

"Just a minute, dear."

When there was no reply, Elaine looked back down at the paperback she was so near to finishing . . . the latest by Scarlett Shade. She couldn't believe the way some of Scarlett's fans were getting so out of hand again.

It was crazy for people to get so caught up in fiction that they didn't know it from reality. Instead, these books gave her the meaning to a dreary life that had turned out far differently than she'd hoped. Through them, her fantasies *seemed* to become real . . . even the acts of pleasure previously abhorrent to her, something to be craved.

The books were a vacation from the horrible reality of life. Still, it bothered her that the suicides were always fans like herself.

Herself.

But she had no desire to kill herself.

"Elaine!"

Not yet.

She looked back down at the paperback in her lap. Ken always called her to bed at the most inopportune times. Now, here she was, about to learn if Countess Showery would find her lover, Count Downe . . . if they would once more end the book as they always did, coupling maniacally, bringing others into their knowledge and fold—

"Please, Elaine! It's almost *midnight!* You have all fucking day to read!"

She stood with the book unfinished, knowing she would return to it as soon as she let him think he'd given her another orgasm and she gave him his, and he fell asleep. They went through this routine almost every night.

Walking down the wide, paneled hallway of abstract paintings, full of bright yellows and orange, she began stripping as she soon as she entered the bedroom. It was dark, but he liked it that way when they made love, and she knew the floor plan well. He preferred not to actually see her when they coupled these days. Growing older, he claimed he didn't want her to see him wrinkled and paunchy, but she knew it was because he didn't want to see *her*. He rarely looked at her at all anymore, even when they talked at dinner.

When they made love—fucked—he probably fantasized that she was someone else . . . some firm, blond bimbo secretary.

Let him. She had her own fantasies.

"Suck me, will you?" He stood beside the bed, brushing his fingers down a hairless chest and past his lower stomach. "I'm real tired tonight. It's a lot easier to get up in the morning when you just suck me."

Tightening her lips against her teeth, Elaine passed the dresser mirror. She followed him to the bed and he sat. She hated fellatio. It was demeaning. Everyone in her therapy group last year had agreed that it was demeaning unless your partner reciprocated, and Ken was disgusted by her very smell. He hadn't put his face between her legs in five years.

But he seemed to think it was her duty.

A privilege.

"Please, Elaine. I work my ass off every day so you can go to your damn therapies and just sit around here reading those damn silly books . . . it's the least you can do for me."

She knelt before him and stroked his naked, spindly legs obediently, pretending, even though it was difficult with a flabby body like his, that she was with Count Downe.

She pretended with far more ease that she was Countess Showery, and she rubbed her tongue along his scrotum as he sighed: "That's it."

Yes. She paused, looking through the room's shadows at the mirror. She saw herself the way she wanted to be. Beautiful, with shiny, silk blond hair, her body firm and trim, her lips a full bow.

She *was* Countess Showery and he was Count Downe . . . or more believably, he was merely her *victim*. A man she had seduced with her great beauty and power and now could make her own . . . her slave.

The scenario was alive . . . *undead* . . . inside her.

17

Her tongue licked him with her giggle while she filled her mouth with his erection, almost enjoying this as she nibbled him and listened to his delight.

"You're great!"

She was. *She was the Countess, and her fangs brought unspeakable joy and eternity!*

Her eyes flickered back to the dark scene of herself and him in the mirror. Those shiny images always satisfied and showed her the truth of her desires, just as in the books. Her delicate mouth, filled with him, became the tool of her greatest lust.

Her reflected lips curled up and she saw her own sparkling teeth . . . highlighted by razor fangs.

At last, truly the Countess! But something was missing. . . .

Blood.

Blood.

She bit down hard, coming herself as the power flowed into her jaws with his salty spurt, coming so hard that the orgasm made her teeth close deeper and deeper into his tender flesh, sending hot blood, tastier than she'd ever imagined, shooting over her working tongue.

Drinking it all madly, Elaine didn't even hear him screaming.

Part II:
The Wings of a Bat

Chapter 1

Teresa Carson, doing her best to become a freelance journalist, had been wanting an interview with Scarlett Shade for some time. It had been hard getting the writer's San Francisco address and phone number since Scarlett hadn't joined the Horror Writers of America and wasn't listed in their directory, but Teresa had finally gotten to Shade through her publisher, Dark Descent Books.

After some persistent pestering and a lot of buttering up through letters and on the phone, Scarlett had agreed to meet Teresa secretly here in Amarillo. Secret because Scarlett didn't want to have to be fair and agree to other interviews.

So this would be an *exclusive!*

Teresa still felt tired after the jet ride from Denver. If she'd waited another week, she could have gone to the Denver convention to meet Scarlett . . . but she didn't want to take the chance that someone else might get to the writer first. Besides, it was a business expense and she'd never been to Texas before.

Teresa tried to show a professional energy as she led Scarlett past a dozen uniform doors to her hotel room. Scarlett was wearing one of her usual sheer black gowns that showed more than just the outline of her barely clad body underneath it. The neckline dropped low, almost to her very nipples, showcasing the antique necklace and its tiny mirror Scarlett always wore . . . just like the ones Scarlett described for Count Downe and Countess Showery. Her vibrant red hair hung in long wavy locks past her breasts and her needle-sharp fingernails were painted just as red. Still awed by the writer's beauty, Teresa was glad she had taken the time to dress nicely and get her hair permed. Maybe this would be the long interview she hoped for, and Scarlett would reveal things about her life and career she'd avoided since beginning her comeback circuit in Tucson weeks ago. Teresa was determined to give it her all to make that dream come true.

When they moved inside the room and shut the door, Scarlett went to sit at the small lounge table. Teresa nodded at the bathroom. "I'll be right with you," she said.

"Go right ahead."

Teresa closed that door, too, and faced herself in the wall mirror, fluffing her blond hair and adding pink rouge to her lips. For just a moment, her hair seemed to darken and she thought it was Scarlett in the reflection looking back at her. A quivery ice shot up her spine.

But she was just nervous as hell. She was the one looking in the mirror after all, and the person she saw was *herself.* She forgot it quickly. Stifling that unbusinesslike anxiety, Teresa squirted her naked thighs with a proven perfume. She faced the door, taking the tiny camera out of her makeup bag to check the film.

It would really be something if she could pull this off and get at least one photo of Scarlett . . . and hopefully several very candid ones.

Even if Gary and everyone else didn't think she could do it. Gary hadn't even come with her!

For reasons of her own, Scarlett wouldn't allow anyone to take her picture these days. Teresa had heard the rumor that Scarlett was now very superstitious about such images . . . that she had bought into the old Native

22

American belief that such an image would steal your soul, and that was why she avoided mirrors, too. It was well known that the reason for Scarlett's seclusion a few months back had been the tragedies surrounding her initial success.

There had been so many rumors . . . and now Teresa was determined to be the first to find out what was true and what wasn't. She would find out if Scarlett had really had a bad experience with voodoo rituals during her self-banishment and was afraid that images would be used against her. The people who believed it said that a new understanding of life through those rituals was what had convinced Scarlett to come out of hiding.

Then there were the old rumors that Scarlett was AC/DC in her sexual preferences, although that certainly had nothing to do with her photo phobia. Teresa intended for one hell of an interview . . . a pictorial like the one Scarlett had done for *Playboy* and *Penthouse* three years before. All she had to do was get Scarlett to take off her clothes. . . .

So she kind of hoped that last rumor about Scarlett's sexual preference *was* true.

Teresa slipped the Nikon back in her pocket, smoothing out the wrinkles in the fabric. She giggled at herself in the mirror, disbelieving those stories of Scarlett's superstitions. They were probably just another publicity angle for Scarlett's reemergence three months back. Some thought the whole seclusion thing had just been to let the bad publicity die and show Scarlett as a tragic figure, driven into hiding by forces she couldn't control. Just like the vampire heroes in all her wonderful books.

But the suicides were already increasing again, as though spurred on by Scarlett's returned presence.

Opening another button on her blouse, to set her subject at more ease and maybe attract her desire, Teresa smiled at the firmness of her own braless shape. She walked out and sat down at the room table across from Scarlett, laying her pocket cassette recorder between them. She switched it on.

Scarlett glanced at it. "You're a modern, I see. No pen or paper?"

Teresa shook her head. "I've got a photographic memory . . . this is just to help me make sure I don't put any words into your mouth."

Her eyes sparkled. "Photographic, huh? Well, the tape's okay, but you know I don't like pictures these days?"

"You've made that well known. Can you tell me the real reason you don't like photos and mirrors anymore?"

Scarlett's seawater eyes narrowed. "You're not going to get much of an interview by starting off like that, dear." She stared at the shape of Teresa's nearly exposed breasts. "Let's just say that all the rumors about me *are* true . . ."

"You were into voodoo?"

"If you like."

Teresa smiled. "Did you really go through rituals to free you of the blame for the fans who committed suicide in hopes of becoming vampires?" She paused. "How do you feel now that the suicides have started up again?"

Scarlett licked her lips and shook her head. "I don't accept that blame, dear. We're all responsible for ourselves. Life is a choice, dear. Life and death."

"But your books—"

"My books are fiction. They're about vampires. Okay? I can't help it that people get so wrapped up in them. Really, you're being awfully pushy." She frowned.

"But in your books," Teresa went on, choosing her words more carefully, "you show such wonderful truth to life. You show how none of us are truly responsible for the things we do . . . how we're all blameless of our mistakes

24

because of the things that happen to us beyond our control."

Scarlett studied her for a long minute that was becoming tense. "Then you've read my books?"

"Of course," Teresa blushed, working hard to ease up. "I love them! They've really shown *me* how to live—"

"Then you should know that you're misinterpreting them, dear. My stories are about *undeath*, not life. The wonderful thing about vampires is that they *can't* be held accountable. They're beyond life's petty priorities. They're dead. They're *undead*. Life itself is something too tricky to truly enjoy. Full of choices every minute." Scarlett settled back in her chair and folded her hands on the table. "The trouble with life is we didn't ask for it, but it's been given to us anyway."

"Yes," Teresa nodded. "I agree. You discussed that a couple of years ago in another interview. You talked about how bad your childhood was and how your father sexually abused you."

Scarlett frowned. "It was true. My mother died during my birth and my . . . father . . ." Her frown became deeper. "That bastard held me accountable and told me I owed him for it. They weren't pleasant experiences, but they taught me a lot about pleasure and how to escape the most miserable circumstances . . . through fantasy."

Teresa nodded her own agreement again.

"Pleasure is a truth we could all use more of," Scarlett sighed. "The responsibility thing comes from the fear of death and losing something we never even asked for. We're all afraid of death and we want to blame someone for it when people die, even though life is so often such an unpleasant misery. I like to believe that my books show others a freedom from that misery . . . in one way or another."

Teresa frowned back at her, not quite understanding even when she thought the words over again. Perhaps the rumor that Scarlett had gone deep into drugs was the true one, and that was why her books had become even more bizarre.

Maybe Scarlett was doped up now.

"Okay, we'll go on to something else," Teresa sighed, hoping to bring this interview back to her true purpose. "Do your own sexual experiences give you the ideas for the vivid nature of your work?"

"Everyone asks that. Doesn't anyone believe in imagination anymore? Lots of writers write about things they've never personally experienced . . . and that's part of what makes it *art.*" Scarlett sat back and frowned. "This isn't exactly the friendly interview you promised."

Teresa stood up and smiled. "Your fans want to know *everything* about you. Like . . . is it true you like other women?"

Scarlett was frowning, fingering her necklace.

"How friendly do you want this interview to be, Ms. Shade?" asked Teresa, posing like the model she once was. "I just want to let your fans know more about you, but I want to make you happy and work with you, too. And if all the rumors about you *are* true, I think I can make you very happy."

"Oh, really?"

Swallowing and nervous, Teresa took off her jacket and laid it on the chair. Her eyes studied Scarlett's carefully as she unbuttoned her blouse one button at a time, and she felt relief when Scarlett's face became a tight smile.

"Are you really a fan, or is this just a way to get into my good graces?" Scarlett asked. "Or just a way for a groupie to get into my pants?"

Teresa unzipped her short skirt and let it fall, then shoved down her skimpy panties the way she had when she'd worked as a stripper to help pay her way though college last year . . . after her own pictorial money ran out. "I'm more than a fan or groupie, Ms. Shade. I've read everything you've done. I want pictures of you, and if you'll let me, I'll sell a new photo interview and split the money with you . . . a *lot* of money."

Scarlett didn't move. She stared at Teresa without any expression at all. "I don't need the money," she said. "I can't allow you to take a picture, but if you just wanted to fuck me, dear, why didn't you say so? You're very pretty and sweet, and I love your smell." She stood and opened her nearly opaque dress at its side, letting it slide off her shoulders. She caressed her necklace. Her lips pursed.

Although Teresa wished that the author would be more agreeable to her plans, it didn't matter now. The situation existed and it was working out perfectly. She would give herself to Scarlett and use the talents she had learned in her experiences with the other strippers after hours . . . and in Scarlett's delight, she would never pay attention to Teresa's other intents.

"Well?"

Teresa smiled, locking eyes with Scarlett, moving her gaze down to the necklace and its hanging mirror. She saw herself surrounded in a gold frame, filled with the craving for success and a lust she rarely admitted to. Drawn to that hot emotion, Teresa bent down to her skirt and blouse, laying them over her coat and sliding the tiny camera into her palm. "I think you smell pretty, too," she whispered huskily.

Scarlett nodded, checking her watch. "How sweet of you. We have another half hour, so come on." She turned and backed to Teresa.

Teresa unfastened Scarlett's black bra and let it drop, then rolled down her own nylons as Scarlett sat on the bed. She reached out to unhook the nylons from Scarlett's belt and slipped them down, too, snapping a fast picture, unobserved, from her hand.

"Come on, dear," said Scarlett, spreading her creamy thighs, then moaning as Teresa pushed her mouth close.

Teresa darted a quick tongue, relishing the writer's loud groans of pleasure and snapping shot after shot when she paused. Scarlett was slobbering and hadn't noticed a thing.

"Oh . . . oh . . . you're so . . . good. You have me so excited . . . this is one for . . . my *books!*

Teresa licked her fast and furiously, then swiped the saliva running from her lips and put the camera to her eye, taking a really good photo of Scarlett lying so spent on the tan bedspread.

"You *bitch!*"

The cry welled in Teresa's ear as she clicked the camera again and again.

"See, it's not so bad," said Teresa. "We'll make a lot off these, and even *you* could always use more money . . . right?"

Much to Teresa's relief, Scarlett was smiling again . . . didn't seem angry. "It wasn't so bad," she agreed. "But now you've got to finish what you started . . . you've got to share it *with* me."

"You wanna do *me?*" Teresa asked with more than a little surprise. "You? Scarlett Shade?" She dropped her eyes and saw herself in the necklace again, wanting the satisfaction already showing in her face.

"Of course. It turns me on. We'll do each other . . . you in your way and me in mine . . . let's see who comes first!" She tugged Teresa close, back onto the bed, pressing her to the mattress, straddling her; pushing her cool cheeks between Teresa's thighs as Teresa did the same to her.

Teresa's heart pounded with excitement.

Scarlett's tongue was an expert, and in seconds she was leading Teresa down a pulsing path of joy. The surges crescendoed and exploded into a staccato repetition of blasting orgasms. In the intensity, Teresa couldn't stop herself from biting the soft flesh of her new lover, and she didn't at all mind the exquisite pain as Scarlett's teeth sank into her.

The minutes passed as the joy became so powerful Teresa was becoming numb . . . nearly blacking out from the incredible sensations.

A strange, lazy chill.

Scarlett stopped and looked up from between Teresa's quivering legs, her lips and teeth a slippery red. "So you see, my dear. You've had a better interview than you even dreamed for. You know all the truth now, but I can't have you spreading it around. You see, I'm not responsible. *I'm* undead. I gave you exactly what you wanted . . . and I hope you enjoyed it as much as I did."

Teresa was weak. She stared down at her unmarked flesh with astonishment, then back at Scarlett's dripping teeth.

Blood. *Her* blood.

She didn't understand . . . was too weak to feel the terror she wanted to feel. It was all like a dream, and she saw the ends to that dream in Scarlett's deep, dark eyes . . . in the strange necklace mirror and her pale reflection. She could barely keep her eyes open to see Scarlett stand and lick the spots from her lips.

Scarlett picked up the camera and pulled out the film cartridge, squeezing it in her long fingers until it cracked. Her lips fluttered over ghastly teeth as she drew out the slender length of film and dropped it all in the waste can. Teresa felt her nerves tingling, growing numb. "An image can be the mirror of our truth," Scarlett whispered. "It's not always wise to reveal the truth, dear."

It was so hard to breathe.

So hard to keep her eyes open.

Teresa didn't feel it when the author carried her convulsing body into the bathroom and laid her into the cold tub. She didn't feel it as Scarlett took a sharp knife and slashed her wrists, spilling her remaining life all over the porcelain walls.

She didn't know it when her heart stopped.

"Serves you right, dear." Scarlett kissed Teresa's pale forehead. She held up her necklace and looked into it, seeing Teresa's face and not her own.

Scarlett smiled, then went to the door and examined the hallway with her internal sight.

Empty.

She opened the door and placed the DO NOT DISTURB sign on the door handle. Laughing daintily, she reclosed the door, locking it from the inside with the bolt.

Becoming a green mist, Scarlett flowed under the door into the hall, forming herself once more.

Another suicide. Just like in the old days, but better.

Chapter 2

Fingering the key in her palm, Matilda snorted, glancing down her drab yellow hotel outfit to her pushcart of cleaning materials and brushes.

Do Not Disturb.

It was Sunday afternoon and the sign had remained on this door since Friday night. She remembered the state of the other conventioneers' rooms and shuddered at what this one must look like by now.

A real pit, no doubt.

Almost all of the convention's other guests had checked out at noon.

Matilda knocked on the door gently. "Maid," she called out.

No answer.

But she remembered what the hotel manager had warned her and the rest of the staff about possible suicides. Carl had instructed them all to check the rooms like this one.

She knocked again.

No answer.

Feeling funny, Matilda fit her key into the lock and twisted it slow. "Maid!" she called out again, louder.

She hoped to hell she didn't come in on the middle of a full-fledged orgy like one she'd barged in on yesterday.

But the door didn't open. It was bolted from the inside. "Is anyone in there?" Matilda called again, and blushed at her silly question even as she asked it.

Someone had to be. The door was bolted.

But no one answered.

She hesitated, then turned back around, leaving her cart. This was a job for the manager.

The manager and one of the hotel's repairmen worked to open the door as Matilda watched from her cleaning cart. The repairman's electric screwdriver was a loud whir as he removed the bolt and the door finally creaked open.

Inside the room, Matilda only heard silence.

And then, she smelled something strong and bad.

Carl, the manager, went inside, followed by the repairman. Matilda stepped forward, too, even though a shiver crawled through her limbs and she didn't want to. She stared at the unmade bed and clothes on the floor.

The bed was empty. Carl pulled away the rumpled sheets, and the repairman poked through the closet and under the mattress.

Forcing herself, Matilda went inside, too, wondering where the occupant was. She whistled. "Is anyone in here?"

Again, no answer. Carl, moving to the window, glanced back with annoyance.

The entry of fresh air from the hall made the bad smell stronger. Matilda pushed her heavy feet to the bathroom and rapped on that closed door, too. "Maid!"

Then, in the silence, she twisted the knob.

Goosebumps rippled her arms. She looked at the clean tile walls and the unused towels. Her eyes jerked to the counter sink and the open makeup jars . . . drifted past the toilet to the bathtub. Although it was empty of water, a naked blond woman lay there, her skin as pale as faded pink paint, a smile of immense satisfaction stretched her mouth into her cheeks. Her knees were bent and rested against the porcelain sides as though she were relaxing in a sauna. Her hands rested on her trimmed crotch. . . .

Matilda's eyes opened wider at the dried blood that hadn't made it to the drain . . . at the neat way the woman's wrists were sliced open . . .

The stained knife.

She screamed.

Chapter 3

"What if she *is* a vampire?" Phillip said.

"That's a question I always had about Dick Nixon."

Phillip Ottoman stared out the window at the growing Norman skyline hiding the Oklahoma plains, then through the simple office of file cabinets, the desk, and chairs. The musty smell of reality. He much preferred fiction to the reality . . . the rush of adrenaline from a scary horror film or book.

That was why he sold those books now.

"Look, Phil, everyone has nightmares, but you know they're nothing but a way to let off subconscious steam." Dr. Kevin Matthews looked up from behind his desk at Phillip as he finished reading Phil's notebook. The room was a mild green, the color for relaxation.

The color of Phil's fear. He looked down at the newspaper clipping: ". . . one of the suicides was Teresa Carson, a twenty-three-year-old stripper at the MileHiClub in Denver and a former *Gallery* model. Her body was found Sunday afternoon, an apparent suicide due to the new so-called outbreak of 'Scarlett Fever.' Her door was securely bolted from the inside and . . ."

"You just have to ease up on yourself, Phillip," Kevin said, handing the notepad back. "This is just another outlet for your other nightmares. Your old fears are becoming stronger because of your insecurity with the divorce. Being around all those horrible suicides has just made it worse."

Phillip looked at him, beyond him, at the framed certificates of psychology on the walls. He covered his face in his hands. "I know. I just want a normal life . . . to forget these damn dreams . . . But what about the marks I see in the mirror?"

"That's weird, Phil, but there's got to be an explanation. You need to have a GP check you out if they don't go away. Personally, I think your imagination's working overtime."

Phil touched his belt and started to stand, looking around the office. "You want to see? I'll show you . . . I got a bite on my dick, and you tell me it's all my imagination."

Kevin shook his head. "Take it easy, Phil. Look, you're just having bad dreams . . . and jumping to conclusions. You probably just got too drunk and the lady you were with got too excited."

"It was Scarlett Shade."

Kevin's lips twisted and he nodded. "That proves it was all imagination. Divorce delusions, Phil. I talked to Katherine and I know how bad the problems you two have are."

He bit his lip. "I can only see the bite in a mirror . . . figure that out."

Dr. Matthews, a younger man than Phillip's thirty-eight years, adjusted his glasses and smiled gently. He tapped his head. "Forget that stuff, Phil. Stick to reality. Just face it. You're getting divorced, not sucked by a vampire. This is probably just a fear of alimony payments . . ."

Phil snorted. "We can't wrap every problem up so neatly, Kevin."

"We can," he said. "Especially this one. Your night-

35

mares don't even hold together, Phil. Vampires can't even be seen in mirrors, so how could their bites? Assuming they actually existed." Kevin touched his head. "It's all up here, but you already know that, don't you?"

Phillip nodded. He didn't need this reminder of his own background to know that truth.

If it was the truth. But, dear God, he hoped it was.

Kevin walked to the windows. "I've known you since you worked here, Phil. I know why you had to leave. The old fears and pressures have built inside you . . . the troubles you and Katherine were having brought them back."

Phil scratched his beard and shook his head.

"Look, it's up to *you*, Phil. You've said it yourself. You've got to stop running in place and brooding about what might have been." He sat back down and their eyes met. "And as long as you're having these memory lapses again, and these delusions, you shouldn't be going to any more of these conventions for a while. The atmosphere of those things just make it worse, but you know that already, too, don't you?"

Phillip didn't answer.

"You're blanking out your guilt for something you can't be responsible for. These new nightmares may just be a way to try and clear yourself of the blame you feel. You're trying to take on the responsibility for every violent act you hear about. These nightmares are because of the interests—"

"My 'interests' used to take my thoughts off my problems!"

Kevin sighed and drummed his fingers on his own notebook, then opened it and flipped through its pages. "And now the cure has become part of your problem." He looked back up. "Meanwhile, your mind thinks it's protecting you from a knowledge that could hurt you, and every time your thoughts wander to the past, your defenses charge up and close your memory down. The delusions are even replacing your real memories." He smiled very softly, just as though he were talking to a state patient. "Phil, it's just your past. It *can't* hurt you, and it's the source of all your problems."

"Sure," Phil whispered, not meaning it.

Kevin walked to him and shook his hand. "There are so many artificial pressures . . . real and *imagined*." Their eyes met and Kevin winked. "Now get out of here. I've got real work to do." But he eyed him sympathetically.

This talk hadn't helped at all. Phil struggled with disappointment. "Thanks . . . I guess."

They stopped at the door and Kevin clasped his hand. "Come on, Phil. Stop taking everything so seriously and have some fun. Relax."

"I'll try," Phil said. He sighed. "At least I . . . I found a place to stay." He finally smiled back, but again, without feeling. "Wouldn't you know it, she's a Shade fan . . . a frigging *convamp*."

"They're pretty wild from what I understand," Kevin chuckled. "She'll take your mind off things."

"It's not like that with Connie, Kevin, she—"

"Connie?" He put an arm around Phil's shoulders. "The same Connie?"

Phil nodded.

"Well . . . no reason to feel guilt for her now, Phil. Personally, I'm glad to hear you've got company. But take it easy on her, okay? The Shade fans are just using fiction to hide from reality . . . a lot like you do. Hell, even I've read a couple of the Shade books. I liked them. You ought to try one, yourself . . . just remember that it's all make believe, though, okay?"

Phil nodded, starting down the checkered tile floor. "Make believe . . . right. Thanks loads, Kevin."

Chapter 4

Connie Sawyer was glad for the familiar sense of her old life being with Vicky brought back to her . . . that old life when she had actually had dreams that weren't just fantasies. Dreams she had believed would one day really come true. They'd given her an ambition she sometimes missed, especially as she stared around at the college students. The tables and booths were full of them.

Vicky had picked Connie up after work and driven her here to O'Connell's Pub, decorated in shades of green and leprechaun paintings. A cauldron of gold coins sat on a shelf with surrounding ceramic pieces of Irish flavor. After Connie and Vicky ordered dinner, Connie brought Vicky up to date . . . about Phil moving in.

"This is so strange!" Vicky exclaimed. "I never figured the two of you together after all this time. Not after he dumped you."

"He didn't 'dump' me. He just had enough problems without adding our affair to the list. It's not like that. His wife is divorcing him and he needed a place to stay for a while."

"Uh, huh," Vicky said knowingly. "Why's she divorcing him then?"

Connie shook her head, wishing she'd washed her hair that morning; it felt oily and stringy. "We had our fling a year ago, Vicky. I've hardly seen him with work and the conventions he's gone to."

"Well, at least he got to meet Scarlett Shade," Vicky said.

Connie picked at her ragged fingernails, wishing again. That they looked pretty like Vicky's . . . that she could stop biting them. "He won't say much about her, Vicky. Anyway, *I'm* going to meet Scarlett now. I took some vacation time and I'm driving to Denver tomorrow to sell some of my jewelry."

"Lucky bitch," Vicky snarled with a grin. "Is Phil going?"

"I don't think so. I'm going to be using the table he signed up for and take some of his books to sell. You know those dreams I told you he has? They've been worse. Now he's been screaming and waking me up at night." Connie frowned. "All the way down the hall."

"Down the hall? Sure he is." Vicky touched one of her curls with a finger that was as slender as she was. "*I* ought to go with you, then . . ." But she shook her head and molded her fine features into woeful seriousness. "But I have to take care of my daughter this weekend. I don't know why you ever let Phil move in, Connie. He really sounds like he needs professional help. Don't get any more involved with him than you have to, okay? I think he's just trying to get your sympathy and attention. A man on the rebound is all out to possess any woman he can." She paused. "I've had it up to here with them."

"I told you it's not like that with Phil, Vicky. We're just friends now."

Vicky laughed. "Whatever you say."

Connie crumpled a napkin and tossed it at her. They both laughed, then Vicky sighed. "I guess everyone's getting divorced . . . and if you ask me, Phil's divorce is probably his own fault. Men are selfish. That's the real reason I'm splitting with Rick, Connie. It's been over for a long time. We conned ourselves into believing we were in love in the first place."

Connie couldn't help feeling a little sad for her friend, but was pleased that Vicky was taking this so well. "Well, *I* thought you were in love," she said.

Vicky's slender, usually cheerful face turned dark with her surly smile. "Did you really?" Her laugh was nasty.

Connie felt a blush and glanced at the people in the booth behind Vicky, then the grinning businessmen at a table five feet away. "Why did you guys stay married this long?"

"Why not? Security's the main reason, I guess. I was scared shitless of the thought of being out on my own until I started to really get into Scarlett's Shade's books." Vicky laughed. "But why am I saying this to you? You're the one who got *me* started on them."

A waitress decked out in bright greens, complete with a sprig of shamrocks tied in her sandy hair, brought them their dinner.

Vicky watched the waitress go and dabbled long fingers through her own shorter sandy locks. "Maybe I should let my hair grow long again," she wondered out loud. "I want to start a whole new life . . . I want to act different, look different. I just want to *be* different."

"You *are* different," Connie said.

"You're just being sweet, dear."

The way Vicky used her words made Connie think of Scarlett Shade's books.

"No, you really *are* different."

Vicky toyed with a french fry as though it were something else, drawing brazen stares from the nearby businessmen. Vicky licked the brown fry with a lingering tongue and then slowly sucked it in between her lips. When it was inside her mouth, she chewed slowly.

Sexily.

One of the businessmen winked and Vicky gave him a forward smile.

"Stop coming on to every guy you see, Vicky," Connie complained. "You and Rick have been married for over three years. Do you just want to throw it all away?"

"In a word, yes." But Vicky ate her next fries more sedately and took a nibble of her hamburger. "I'm acting this way because I've finally found my real self, Vicky, not because Rick and I are splitting. I want to live for *me* and have fun like the vampires in Scarlett's books."

Vicky's words touched a chord in Connie's own readings and similar self-discovery months before. She stared into the brown eyes across from her.

"Look, Connie. There's no such thing as love for *others.*" She wiped her full red lips with a napkin defensively and took a drink from her stein. "We think that we love other people because we love the things in them that are *ourselves.* Didn't you get that out of her books?"

"Sort of," she admitted.

"It's like Countess Showery is telling the priest in *Mass Massacre.* 'If everyone were vampires, no one would be afraid of death anymore.' The frigging churches and TV ministers would go broke."

"Shh," Connie whispered, drinking deep from her beer. "Everybody's staring. God, Vicky, you don't even sound like yourself."

She shrugged as she finished her hamburger and popped the last few fries into her mouth. She lit a cigarette. "I'm just excited that I've found what I really want out of life." She tried a wimpy smoke ring. "Full circle. Remember our score cards back in college?"

Looking at her watch, Connie nodded again.

"*I* beat you, remember?"

"I remember," she confessed, dropping a tip by her plate.

They got up together and Vicky paid for both their

meals. As they walked out to Vicky's car, Connie thanked her.

"Just meet Scarlett Shade and tell me all about her. She must be a hell of a person the way she's got me going now." Vicky winked.

Connie looked across the street at the dark, scattered class buildings and tall dormitories for Oklahoma University. The sight of them made her feel the pointlessness of life. When she had entered those ivory towers, she'd left the yellow brick road. The more she'd learned about the world around her . . . the more she learned, period, the worse off the world seemed. Civilization was teetering on the edge; maybe the end would come from a nuclear holocaust by a madman posing as a Mid East dictator . . . pollution . . . AIDS . . . cancer caused by practically everything.

What was the point in living at all, especially when everyone else told her how she *should* live?

It was her life, wasn't it? But her illusions of that life had all crumbled in her education.

Vicky got in the driver's side of her Monte Carlo as Connie got in the passenger seat. "Hell, Vicky, we were just like Countess Showery back then. That's what I mean about finding myself. Having fun is what it's all about!" Vicky *vroomed* down Lindsay Street, past the university, with a cackle.

Connie watched the street's blaring restaurant lights blaze past. She tried to smile and feel as full of that fun as Vicky did, to let Vicky's words bring back the hypnotic fever she felt so strongly when she read Scarlett's words.

Vicky turned a corner fast. "Be careful," Connie said, holding tight to her safety belt as she strapped it on.

Vicky just slid her hand onto Connie's thigh, stroking the denim. "Remember those nights when we didn't have dates, Connie?"

Connie stared down, her throat suddenly dry as the reply froze in her throat.

"I sure remember those nights," Vicky went on. "We just *talked* a lot, afraid of what everyone else would think . . . about the taboos we'd been taught, but now we're *both* Scarlett Shade disciples . . ." She rubbed Connie in the right places, then reached up to Connie's hand and placed it firmly on her own thigh, sliding it slowly under her knee-length dress.

Connie's hand didn't even tremble . . . just froze. Scarlett's books had a lot of scenes of Countess Showery with women, and some of the passages made Connie wet . . . showing her the need of a forbidden pleasure.

Closing her eyes, Connie suddenly didn't want to stop her fingers from wandering up Vicky's hose. *Fantasy*. Reality had become a memory that was fading in the pleasure of Vicky's immediate strokes.

Pleasure. Her heart pounded, aching with the dreams and ecstasies of Scarlett Shade's books that always had left her somewhere between delight and lonely pain. Now they were demanding their fulfillment at last.

A few minutes later Vicky pulled up in the driveway of her home and stopped. She looked at herself in the rearview mirror and smiled, turning it so Connie could see herself, too.

Countess Showery gazed back from the reflection.

Vicky giggled. "I'm the Countess, and you're my maid, okay, Connie?"

Connie felt warmer than ever, cozy with the beer she'd drunk. She relaxed and shook her head, still staring at the beautiful features that weren't her own, but suddenly were, just like when she was alone. "No . . . I'm the Countess . . ."

Vicky eyed her with amusement. "We're twins, then . . . okay?" The two of them looked at each other, into the mirror, then back. Their flushed, sweaty faces moved nearer and nearer until they were hugging like they *were* long lost sisters.

When they kissed, their hands roaming over each other, it seemed the most natural thing in the world.

Chapter 5

Papa's hand dug deep into Phil's young shoulder, making him gasp.

The ancient street of Prague—the street he had lived in all his life, filled by smoke. The cobblestones half covered by torn papers and other litter . . . bricks from crumbling buildings, further demolished by the fiery explosions rocking them. Bodies of the dead and dying . . .

But those heartrending screams were dimmed to almost nothing by the sound of the approaching tanks and shrill, bulleting projectiles. They stuffed Phil's agonized ears with deafening impact.

"Hurry!" cried Phil's mother, clutching his other hand and dragging him and her husband into the burning rooming house down the cracked sidewalk.

Papa, red-faced, tears streaking his dirty cheeks as he shut the splintered door behind them. "There is no freedom!" he moaned in the native tongue that was as clear to Phil as English in his waking life. "All there is is hate!"

They forced their way through the building's wreckage and smoke into a back room crowded with neighbors, friends, and relatives.

"The revolution is already over," spat out Phil's middle-aged uncle, Ivan, wiping the blood from a gash in his ruined cheek. "The only freedom is in true death. We have been dead for years . . . living as Soviet slaves. Undeath!" He patted Phil's matted hair sadly, facing Phil's father. "But you must take your son and my children and escape. There is yet hope in other lands. We will die, but maybe *you and they can find freedom in life for a little longer. Maybe you will see the day when the world seeks love instead of oppression and killing—"*

Phil watched silently as his mother and father hugged Uncle Ivan and then some of the others. Uncle Ivan bent to Cousin Sonia and her brothers, whispering to them and holding them tight.

Then Uncle Ivan was lifting the cellar door in the floor and herding them into its darkness. He shone his dim flashlight down the creaky, railed stairs and gave it to Phil's father. "Go into the sewer and follow it until you're out of the city. A truck will take you to the border so you can get out."

Another blast shook the walls. They cracked deeper as more dust fell from the ceiling. Phil sneezed as he inhaled the particles. Papa pushed him past broken crates and a tall, cracked mirror to a chunky hole dug through the mortar walls. Phil looked into the blurry reflection of his cousins hugging Uncle Ivan through their tears—

New shrieks filled Phil's ears and he gasped at the now familiar whine of a machine gun . . . saw the reflections of Uncle Ivan . . . cousin Michael, and little cousin Montague . . . become twisting, gyrating figures that sprayed blood and intestines from the sudden gaping holes in their flesh. As they fell in their gurgling shrieks, a tall Soviet soldier grabbed cousin Sonia, the girl Phil learned the secrets of love with. Phil whined as the soldier began ripping off her torn dress and shoved his pistol up inside her. Sonia cried hysterically as the soldier bit her breast and fucked her with the gun's muzzle, faster and faster—

The reflection clouded.

Papa's strong hand pulled Phil into the wet sewer tunnel and its scurrying rats.

Sonia's screams—

A wet, muffled shot.

Phil shuddered when Sonia's shriek was cut off too abruptly. The sounds behind them faded.

Papa and Mother disappeared and Phil could only hear the splashes of his own feet through the dirty water. The flashlight was gone, too.

46

Phil knew he was no longer a boy when the tunnel ended and he stepped into a dry, barely lit room, teeming with more towering, cracked mirrors . . . their greenish fog the death of Sonia.

He saw those clouds part to a reflection of a perfect, red-haired woman's body, nearly nude, reaching her hands out to him.

But even though Phil knew that he was no longer as endangered by the wild death and despair he'd escaped from, it was still all around him.

The woman was whole physically, but he saw the open, spewing wounds like those ripping open his loved ones, inside her . . . as though he could see right inside her shapely body.

She wanted him. She wanted him . . . to make love to her, just the way Cousin Sonia once had.

She wanted him to make love to the death already filling her to the brim. Reaching out to Phil, she opened her arms and entreating hands. Her legs parted to desire, persuading him . . .

Then her mouth opened, too, showing Phil the fangs—

Undeath.

The reflections seemed to grow, looming, and Phil ran—

Phillip Ottoman felt as though he were on a hell-bent roller-coaster, plummeting fast. His throat was raw and he gagged out syrupy spit as he listened to the fading echo of his yells. He tossed and slipped off Connie's frayed, yellow couch, sprawling on the mildew-scented carpet, his breathing finally evening. He coughed, his lungs tight.

But once more, fear slowly backed away. Not far. Not nearly far enough, but at least he could think.

Sometimes, he just wished he had the balls to kill himself . . . just like some fucking convamp. Life was hell . . . worse instead of better.

What was the point?

A new shudder ran through him as he looked through the apartment. Raising a still jittery hand, Phil wiped the saliva out of his short beard and then onto his sweat pants.

He was weaker than ever from his new recurring nightmare . . . a nightmare recycled with a new ending tacked on like some cheap ass finale to a canceled TV show. It was a circle . . . leading him nowhere . . . always back into the hell of dreams he couldn't escape. Phil pulled himself up off the floor and held on to the couch with a shaky hand. His tomcat, Wolfgang, yawned, unconcerned as usual.

"Must be . . . nice to have such a lazy life," Phil accused the cat, shuffling past the stacks of his boxes into the kitchen. He found a coffee mug, his name emblazoned across it in chipped, black letters, filled it with tap water. He drank slowly, bringing it to the couch. His steps were stronger and he felt his heart pump in a gentle rhythm once more.

"Thank you, God," he whispered, relieved it was over again, that he hadn't been left to rot in that returned phantasm of his youth. One of his terrors was that someday he would die in the midst of one of the nightmares, and spend the eternity of an afterlife in it.

It was scary.

Sinking into the thin cushions, Phil tried to forget those images that were so familiar to his sleep. Sometimes it was hard to believe that any of them had ever been real. He hated waking up to these damn things alone, and wished again that Connie would hurry back. Solitude—loneliness—always dragged him back into the memories. Sometimes pleasant, usually not. Even the good things usually brought the bad flooding back, like remembering the youthful day his father had let him go with some friends to see *The Exorcist*. The intensity of that cinematic battle between good and evil still touched Phil deeply. He could remember the sweat on his brow as the child actress Linda Blair had vomited green bile and obscenities at the priests trying to save her life and soul. . . .

But now, recalling the film, she had Sonia's face.

48

The priests had died for their trouble, and what was the point? Life was a circular maze just like his dreams . . . its only escape in death.

Cousin Sonia had died. It stung him that she had not escaped. His nightmares were her haunting as she tried to find a way out of the hell he'd seen her suffer in the mirror. She'd made love to him less than a week before her brutal murder . . . before he even understood what love was. The nightmares of the crushed Czech revolution and the deaths of his friends and family . . . the desperation of his parents, melted into the cruelty of the world of hate shadowing this American society he'd finished growing up in. Serial killers . . . wars . . . the homeless . . . corporate brutality and capitalist mania . . .

And now . . .

Vampires.

Impossible.

It was the reason he wouldn't go the Denver convention with Connie. He knew he was close to crazy . . . knew Kevin was right and his fears couldn't be real and were only some new form of his inner torments. He didn't want to take the chance of acting as crazy as he felt.

The fears were too fucking real to *him*. The nightmares too fucking vivid.

If they *were* real, he didn't want to know it.

To lose those frightening afterimages, he studied the aged apartment. It was big like most older such places, but seemed small now that he had moved so much of his stuff here. His books covered the rug in their boxes and sacks. Connie's half-dozen mirrors made the number of his collection seem even greater with their duplicating reflections. The mirrors bothered him, reminding him of his dark memories.

The mess was already pissing Connie off.

Even when they'd all been carefully arranged on bookshelves, the number of these books and the space they took up had pissed off Katherine, too. Now, she was divorcing him. Only months ago he'd quit his psychology job to open the bookstore, and though she blamed that for their fallout, he knew she was more and more annoyed by his occasional memory lapses that were virtual blackouts.

But those attacks were nothing to what he was going through now!

Scarlett Shade.

Phil shivered.

And Connie was going to be there at the convention with *her.* . . .

But so were three or four hundred others.

It had only been a nightmare, anyway.

Hadn't it?

His headache thumped harder as the memories swelled . . . of himself mesmerized by Scarlett Shade when she signed his books in the Amarillo hotel's dealers' room two weeks before. It was the first time he'd met her, and her eyes had swallowed him, showing him his nightmare reflections. That night, he'd dreamed of Scarlett Shade the way her fans claimed to dream of her characters, even though he'd never even read one of her books. He heard her calling to him in his sleep . . . then dreamed he was staring into the mirror. His face faded and became hers.

A crazy dream.

Her watery image had reached out to him then, her fingers stretching right through the solid glass. He was afraid. The muddled images of her teeth, sparkling with his blood . . . the knife in her hand . . . images throttling him until the other nightmares broke in through the fantasy. More horribly than ever before.

He woke with a scream, in that hotel bed, alone. To someone banging demandingly on his door. He opened it to an uneasy security guard investigating his cries.

In the morning when he faced himself in the bathroom

mirror to trim his mustache and beard, he first saw the two tiny pinpricks on his abdomen . . . knew their prickling sting.

But they weren't there when he looked down.

He'd thought it was a marring in the glass until he had seen the two marks again . . . in the mirror in Connie's bathroom . . . and again, he saw nothing when he turned his eyes down. The pain was easy to ignore, but it scared him.

Impossible. Just as impossible as the way he sometimes imagined he saw his hideous past in the reflection of his *eyes*. The wound still hurt, be it real or imagined. When he returned to his store, he heard the murmurs of the suicides in Amarillo . . . the way that Denver stripper had killed herself in the room next to his.

"I've watched too many horror movies," Phil told himself bluntly . . . again.

Unfortunately, none of his denials helped him to get over these new tensions—now, not even his books and films helped him to forget as he tried to fight his own inner battles through them.

It was a long fifteen minutes before Phil could calm down. He took a sleeping pill, then relaxed in a short warm bath, ignoring the stab from the invisible red points under his pubic hair. As usual, after a few minutes, the pain went away.

He wanted to tell Connie, but she already thought he was crazy enough.

The gentle water soothed him. It was a passive purity, only marred briefly by his body's intrusion . . . only disturbed temporarily by *any* invasion.

Unlike himself.

But when he lay down in the wrinkled sheets after drying off, he tossed and turned, and it wasn't really relief when he finally slipped into sleep.

Chapter 6

Connie lay with her head on Vicky's soft shoulder, embarrassed . . . a little sick. The fantasy was over and the sweat and saliva covering her was a shroud.

The world was unchanged outside . . . still in shitty shape.

"That was *so* great, Connie."

"It . . . was *different,*" Connie said. She sat up and looked down at her body, then at Vicky's, remembering the fever of intensity that had burned so hot and hard in her that she hadn't been able to think of anything else.

Vicky licked her lips and sat back.

Connie turned to Vicky's dresser mirror and didn't see the Countess now . . . just herself, bare and pale-faced, covered in sweat, looking as lost and empty as she felt. "It's past midnight, Vicky . . . I have to get back."

Vicky giggled. "Amazing . . . doesn't seem like more than an hour's gone by to me. What are you worried about, anyway?"

"I—I told Phil I'd be back by ten."

Vicky narrowed her eyes. "So you two *are* back together?"

She shook her head and wiped her mouth. "We were never together . . . I just worry about him. Besides, I—I'm going to be gone all weekend."

"Why don't you invite him over for me to take care of, then?" Vicky laughed. She caressed Connie's hip. "I'm so glad we did this at last, Connie."

Despite the way Vicky had stirred her, Connie held tight to a guilt for the purposelessness of this escape. She looked at her empty face in the mirror again. "Look, I've got to . . . I . . . have to think—" She found her panties and jeans, socks, bra, and shirt and began to put them on as fast as she could. Her swimming head didn't know what to believe and what not to; what she wanted and didn't want—

"Slam, bam, thank you, ma'am?"

Connie shook her head and ignored Vicky, trying not to even think of how they'd spent the last three hours . . . in a fantasy world. This was the real world and she had to rest for her drive to Denver . . . and she wanted to check on Phil. He wasn't really her responsibility, but right now, he didn't have anyone else.

"God, my eyes are opened so wide now. There's just no limit to pleasure, is there?"

Connie slid into her shoes and began picking up Vicky's clothing, tossing them at her. Vicky slid off the bed and wiped her hand on a wet inner thigh, then licked those juices as though they were nectar.

"Vicky, please . . ."

Vicky merely pulled on a short bathrobe and tied it in the middle, then picked up her keys and purse. "Okay. Let's go if you *have* to."

Connie went outside and got in the Monte Carlo, shutting her eyes. The driver's seat rustled and that door clicked shut. The motor started.

She bit her lip and wiped her eyes, thinking of Phil.

At least they were still friends. At least he still *liked* her. That was what had drawn her to him in the beginning, that he liked her for just *herself.* But even if he was getting divorced now, she wasn't about to chance being rejected by him again. She'd needed a fantasy like tonight.

But Connie felt so empty . . . so drained.

When they pulled up at her red brick apartment house ten minutes later, Connie barely noticed it when Vicky leaned over to kiss her cheek.

At least Vicky couldn't get her pregnant.

Chapter 7

It had been a long drive to the mile-high city yesterday. All by herself, too. Phil still didn't feel well and planned to spend the weekend in the bookstore. He told Connie he didn't want her to go by herself, but after missing the first two conventions Scarlett Shade had gone to, Connie wasn't about to let it happen again. Besides, Connie knew the real reason he didn't want her to go.

His nightmares . . . and not wanting to be alone in the still new surroundings of her apartment.

But of course, he had all his fucking boxes of books.

Connie looked around the baize walls of the hotel room and took her red bikini underpants out of the dresser drawer. They reminded her of the excitement she and Gary had given to each other last night after she'd arrived and rested a few hours. He'd already left her for a panel he was on this morning, and he was doing a reading of one of his unpublished short stories after that.

She had to miss those activities these days, and it was already time for her to go to work, now, but these conventions were still a lot of fun. She grabbed her black slacks and matching shirt, then relaxed for a few minutes on the double bed, smiling into the opposing mirror. She knew the tricks to make herself reasonably attractive, but she was still nowhere near beautiful. Her straw hair was always limp, hanging down over a round face that would have been quite forgettable except for her unusually light base makeup and dark eye shadow and lipstick. It made her appear like a dead beauty queen, or at least a runner-up, which was just how she wanted to look. Better a dead beauty queen than not to be one at all. There were prettier women around these conventions. Some as pretty as Vicky, but with her makeup, Connie managed to hold her own.

It was one reason she still got into *fan*-tasies. Looking the part of a convamp helped her sell the jewelry she made, too. She'd earned almost two hundred dollars yesterday after spreading out her table in the dealers' room. Fans dressed as Klingons and in other trekkie costumes piled past her table and the others, and her jewelry and Phil's books especially collected the groups of women decked out in pale "undead" makeup. They dressed in dark, skin-tight clothing like she usually wore, too, and just like Countess Showery, they were always ready to "vamp" any poor unsuspecting male they happened upon. . . . Sometimes a willing woman. Male convamps were fewer, and dressed in capes and far less makeup, but had similar appetites.

These were the milder forms of the "Scarlett Fever." Fans who wanted to be vampires themselves . . . but for now, they satisfied themselves with sexual conquests. To that extent, Connie was still one of them. She was more careful these days, but old habits died hard . . . and she wasn't always sure she wanted them to die at all.

But now that she'd finally experimented with Vicky, she felt like she'd done as much as most convamps . . . and her life was still empty. Connie just wanted someone who would care for her. Maybe someone like Gary, even though he wasn't much of a future with his ambition to be a writer. He was as penniless a bum as the guitar geek her sister, Bonnie, lived with.

Bonnie was in love . . . and still miserable.

Did anything have meaning these days?

Phil.

She picked the lint from her pants and tried not let him into her thoughts, but as always, it was too late. She stretched out on the unmade bed with a sigh, feeling the hardened sticky marks her excitement with Gary had left. Her eyes were already damp. She couldn't help herself. She wished Gary had been Phil.

But even if Phil felt the same way, Connie was afraid of all his turmoils, and she would miss the men like Gary. Gary was tall and handsome, with beautiful, long black hair. Much younger and better-looking than Phil, and very available again, he'd told her yesterday.

She felt sorry for him. The girl he'd lived with a few months had been one of the suicides in Amarillo.

Connie sighed. She just hoped Phil would use the week-end to start straightening up all the books he'd moved into her place . . . or better yet, find his own apartment. She stared back through the hotel room. The desk attached to the wall and the TV beside it . . . the drawers . . . the round table and chairs. She glanced down at her low V-necked blouse, and putting on her convention name badge, stood and gazed into the mirror again.

The mirror. She remembered her pale complexion after Vicky. But now, letting herself drift, she looked past that, deeper into her own eyes. Empty . . . always empty. Hollow, like life itself. At least, *her* life. She remembered the way she would fantasize herself in her reflections, pretending she was staring into her soul. Now, she imagined herself and Gary in the glass instead of herself and Phil . . . herself and Gary as Countess Showery and Count Downe. Her fangs and his shining with blood.

When the mild trance ended, she shivered and left the room, hurrying down the hallway to enter the elevator with a group of usually attired people the con-goers named 'mundanes.' Connie poked a button, ignoring the low conversation, just watching the changing floor numbers.

She got out on the second floor, wincing as she approached the dealers' room. The nasal sound of filkers blasted out of another room across the hall as the folk singer wannabes sang songs about their favorite science fiction and fantasy heroes.

They were a lot like the convamps. Like *most* convamps, Connie amended to herself. She was doing her best to outgrow that stereotyped image. Hurrying down the hall, Connie looked at other people with the yellow badges like hers. She checked out the colorful, handmade posters declaring parties for tonight. In the dealers' room she passed a table of posters, bumper stickers and message-buttons. Messages like CAPTAIN PICARD IS WITH ME IN MY DREAMS—NOT YOU or FREDDY KRUEGER ATE JASON FOR LUNCH.

She moved between other dealers until she was behind her own table. Voices grew louder as customers arrived. She removed the black cloth covering her jewelry and the books she had brought along for Phil.

Scarlett Shade's paperbacks were still positioned in front . . . the few that were left. Their bright cover colors of excited women in Count Downe's clutches, dazed men hypnotized by Countess Showery's scantily clad figure, immediately drew stares of interest.

Three teenagers came up, two boys and a girl in squirrelly haircuts that inferred some kind of a gender trade-off. They sifted through the rings, stones, and books. Connie watched them as the girl in the buzz-cut picked up Scarlett's novel, *Blood Shower*. Connie caught the girl's eye. "Good book—I read that one twice already."

The girl opened the pages delicately. "I've got most of her books . . . I just wish they were true. I love the way the Countess and Count use mirrors, entering them like doors and coming out another mirror miles away, don't you?

" 'Reflections are the doorways to other souls,' " Connie quoted her favorite passage in the books. " 'Mirrors are the doorways to pleasure because they contain our true selves.' " She picked up a gold necklace she'd worked hard on. Connie held it up, dangling its tiny round mirror bordered by imitation rubies. "Look at this piece—it's just like the jewelry Countess Showery wears in that book. I'll let you have the book if you buy the necklace . . . special one-time deal."

The girl grinned wide, showing shiny braces, bumping her thigh into the shaggy-haired boy next to her. "I told you I wasn't the only one with fantasies. Will you buy it for me?"

"Shit," he answered, bumping her back. "You can't be a vampire with braces anyway . . . it's impossible." He touched the chain ringlets that linked to the shiny glass, appraising himself and rubbing his jaw with his other hand. "How much?"

"Thirty," Connie said.

He shook his head as his girlfriend tugged at him wistfully.

"Okay, for you guys . . . twenty." Connie tapped the book as she said it. "But you'll have to pay at least half price on the book."

The two whispered and Connie saw that she had them. The girl smiled as he reached for his wallet.

Connie took the cash and bagged the book. The boy linked the necklace around the girl's neck as the other boy with them looked on and whistled. Connie would work out what she owed Phil later. But actually, he owed *her* for even taking the books along.

The rings, pendants, key chains, and necklaces disappeared from her table as her wallet got fatter. Nearly all of Scarlett Shade's paperbacks were gone, too. When the red-haired writer appeared late in the day, wearing a necklace much like the ones Connie sold, Connie caught her breath. Scarlett stopped by each table selling her novels, fans surrounding her.

"Hello, dear," greeted Scarlett, speaking over the admiring voices as she finally stood in front of Connie's merchandise. "Got some books for me to sign?"

The writer's presence gave Connie a thrill of the mindless freedom she relished. She bent and picked up another stack of Phil's books from a box under the table. "Oh . . . I've wanted to meet you so long, Ms. Shade," she gasped, not believing this was actually happening . . . that Scarlett was merely an arm's length away.

Scarlett just smiled coolly and Connie pulled herself together, becoming more businesslike. "Uh, I've almost sold out." She spread the remaining titles across the table and handed Scarlett a pen.

Scarlett eyed Connie as though sharing a secret . . . and Connie looked back into the dark, dark pupils that seemed to hold the ultimate meaning for life itself. Then Scarlett dropped her head to begin her delicate scrawls on the title page of each book. "I hope you'll order a lot more"—she glanced up at Connie's badge—"Connie."

Connie shook her head, remembering Phil and wishing she'd called him this morning . . . worried about him despite herself. "They're not mine . . . Ms. Shade. I make and sell this jewelry. I brought these along for a book-dealer friend. He wasn't feeling well and couldn't make it."

"Please, call me Scarlett." She closed a book and opened another. "That's too bad about your friend." Her pen continued as she spoke, then, facing Connie again, she met her eyes once more.

Connie felt the strength of attraction grow . . . a secret. A secret that soothed every worry out of her.

"Maybe I'll teach you the method to peaceful living someday," she said, as if reading Connie's thoughts.

Blushing, Connie lowered her eyes to the necklace mirror poised between Scarlett's breasts . . . saw herself independent and self-satisfied, the way she wanted to be. Careless and free.

Then Scarlett turned away.

Connie blinked, suppressing her shudder at the returning emptiness.

But before Connie could think about it, a tall woman with short black hair came to the table. Although she was older, the purple fringe mini looked nice on her. She and a man moved from the studded anklets to the books . . . the most expensive of Phil's hardbacks. Connie tried to bring her attention back to sales.

"Boy, we ought to just buy all of these, Mike," the tall woman said to her companion, holding up a book and a gaudy necklace.

He rubbed his whiskery face. "Right, Trish."

But all they bought was a small hammered ring for her, the Ray Garton hardcover, *Lot Lizards*, two out-of-print Ron Dee paperbacks, and three by Scarlett Shade.

"I guess you two like all kinds of vampires," joked Connie, taking their dollars.

Mike shook his head. "We just like the sex scenes."

Trish punched him. "But not until you shave again."

By six, Connie had made two hundred twenty-five dollars. She was pleased, even more when Gary showed up to take her to dinner.

Chapter Eight

". . . we could live together and you could find a job out here, Connie, and you could still sell your jewelry on the side. I bet Doug at the bookstore would be glad to do it. We could share an apartment and I could write full-time. If I could do that, I'd have my novel finished in a month . . ."

"But then, how long would it take you to sell it?"

Gary shrugged, finished with his steak. He picked at a pea, cornering it and squashing it with a fork. "I bet it wouldn't take long. You really ought to read it, Connie. It's a psychological horror piece and it wouldn't even scare you."

"I thought horror was all psychological . . . and if it won't scare me, what's the point?"

"I didn't think you liked scary horror?"

"I don't . . . but . . ." She remembered the last time she'd read something of his and of the arguments her critique had caused. "Tell you what, I'll read it when it's published."

"You're a lot of help." He sighed, looking at her empty plate. "Ready to go?"

Connie nodded.

"I'll get the tip . . . uh, I'm a little short right now. I bought a guitar."

"How's a guitar going to help you get published?"

Gary shrugged. "It was too good of a deal to pass up. I can always sell it."

"That's my advice," she said, counting out her money and leaving it on the ticket, watching Gary drop a single bill as a tip. As he walked off, Connie dropped a five after it, then hurried to catch up. "You owe me big time," she told him.

"I'll pay you back, Connie, don't worry about it. When I'm rich and you need some cash, I'll drop a couple a thousand in your lap . . ."

"You owe me *now* . . . but I'm going to let you work off your debt, okay?"

Gary grinned.

"Great. I've got a lot of Phil's books he wants me to get autographed, and you're my assistant." She grinned now as his grin faded, leading him to the elevator and her room to get the bags of books she'd set aside.

When they got back downstairs with the books, it was a madhouse of fans and authors in the three rooms, their walls removed to make them one. Especially lunatic near Scarlett's long line.

A long-haired Ed Bryant signed several of the anthologies his stories appeared in and three copies of his book, *Fetish*. He chuckled at his groupies as they stared at his eye patch, centered by a realistic mouse that seemed to be crawling out. Connie smirked, but began to wish she hadn't volunteered to do this for Phil. The minutes were slipping by too fast.

Really, too slow.

But it was for a good cause. With signatures, these books would earn a higher price, and Phil would be able to afford his own place all the sooner. Sighing in that hope, Connie passed the time by scanning the seated authors and their fans.

None of them had anywhere near the number sucking

up to them as Scarlett Shade did, not even Dan Simmons.

Connie moved out of the way for the next autograph hound and found Gary standing in line for Tim Powers. Tim was jovial and talking to each fan as he signed, and ten minutes passed before Gary had gotten all four of the books Connie had given him autographed.

"That's it," Connie said, adding the Tim Powers books into one of her stuffed canvas sacks. Now their sales would really bring Phil a pretty penny, especially the uncorrected proof of *The Dinner at Deviant's Palace*.

She and Gary left the noisy crowd and walked together back to the elevator, up to Connie's room on the next floor to put away the books. She slid her bags to the carpet when they reached the door, ignoring the wildly costumed people swarming around them . . . another man dressed in Klingon uniform and makeup, a woman dressed to the teeth in Countess Showery garb and pale face powder . . . a man in hand-tooled armor like he was one of King Arthur's knights. The masqueraders filed down the hall to the convention contest. Connie watched them and took Gary's bag, lowering it, too, pulling his face to hers. They kissed. "Really, thanks."

Reaching down, he lifted his bag again, then hers. "Let's continue this inside," he said, stepping out of the way as more costumed guests walked around them, all of them loud and laughing.

She laid her hand over Gary's as he carried all the books inside. She lifted a sack onto the table when he put down the load. He winked and crossed by her to shut the door. She looked at him and herself in the mirror, wishing. . . .

But she shook her head as she examined the pocket program in her hand. "We can have our fun anytime, Gary," said Connie, holding him back. His eyebrows knotted as she held up the list of the weekend's activities and showed him the items she'd circled. "But I can't always see Scarlett in action, okay?"

Frowning, he finally shrugged. "You just wait until I'm more well known than she is. I've got a helluva book going now. You'll be begging me after it sells."

Kissing his cheek, she led him back into the hall and closed the door. "I'll beg you tonight after a few drinks. Wait until then, okay?"

He took her program and nodded absently. "Promise me you'll beg me all night long, okay? Hell, Connie, I haven't even seen you in months. I've really missed you. I keep telling you that we ought to move in together."

"And raise a family?" She smiled, remembering the old Carly Simon song.

"Neither of us is ready for that."

"You really missed me, huh? That's what you always say, but last time I called you a very sexy woman's voice answered your phone . . . not your mother, I hope?"

He blushed and looked sad. "That was Teresa."

Connie caught her breath.

"I don't know why she did it, Connie. I wasn't in love with her or anything, but I can't believe . . ." He huffed. "That was a lousy way to get me out of the mood, Connie."

"I'm sorry, Gary," she squeezed his hand, feeling insensitive. "I—I promise to make up for it, okay?"

His grin slowly returned and he reached down to his belt buckle.

"Not now . . . later, okay? You can pick a page from Shade and I'll do whatever Scarlett wrote, I promise."

"What if I pick a page with two women and Count Downe?" he said, his voice already lighter.

Connie did her best not to remember Vicky and shrugged. "What if you pick a page with two *men* and Countess Showery . . ."

"No way. The only way that would happen would be if you were really the Countess!"

"Coming back at you, Count Downe!" They laughed and continued the banter until they got back downstairs to another meeting room of bare white walls, full of chairs and somber people where a panel of authors was about to commence.

Sex and Horror. An open forum where the personalities would discuss the subject and how it pertained to their work and the work of others, with comments and questions from the audience.

And of course, Scarlett Shade was one of the participants.

Gary and Connie got quiet as they found chairs near the long table. It was at the front of the noisy room and the authors sat behind it, their name cards in front of them. A balding, bearded man in a black suit and blood red tie was in the seat next to the empty one. He glanced at the others seated on either side of him. Two men and an older woman. He peered at his watch and cleared his throat through the noise of the room's conversations.

After a moment, everyone was quiet. The chair in the table's center was still empty. Gary put his arm around Connie.

"Oh, shit," Connie said, "where's Scarlett?"

The bearded man glared at her, then smiled smoothly. "Welcome to the Sex and Horror panel," he said. "As you can see, we're missing one of our star attractions, but we'll try to—"

Someone booed.

Loud squeals outside the door interrupted.

"Close those—"

Connie turned back just in time to see her enter. Scarlett smiled, but said nothing in response to the cheers and greetings that rose up from the audience. With a faint curtsy, she walked to the table, around it, to the vacant chair, facing the writer who had spoken.

"Uh, looks like I opened my mouth too soon," he said thickly. "Hi, Scarlett."

She leaned her face to his and kissed his lips lightly, then faced the shouts still coming from the room. She raised one long finger until quiet reigned once more, then nudged the author next to her. "Thanks for the intro, Ron. I'm glad to be here." She winked, already very much at ease. "This is the Sex and Horror panel and I am the moderator. The thing about combining sex and horror is quite simple. Everything hinges around the reader's pleasure and willing participation with the characters. It must be unexpected. You have to get the reader hot and then surprise them, just like a vampire is able to use pleasure to weaken a victim . . . by getting *them* hot—"

"You've already got me hot!" called out a blond man sitting in front.

Scarlett smiled, showing ivory white teeth behind her red lips. "Good. Vampires hate cold meals, darling. But beware the surprise."

Connie was delighted, laughing hard.

Everyone was laughing.

Chapter 9

People were already lining up outside the door for the next panel when the Sex and Horror discussion ended a few minutes ahead of schedule. Connie nudged Gary. "I'm going to try and talk to Scarlett again."

"You and me both," he agreed.

Connie eyed him as they passed sci-fi buffs with pocket savers coming in for the next session. Scarlett, still surrounded by admirers, walked past them. "I thought you didn't want to come to this panel?"

"Temporary insanity brought on by the sight of you," Gary explained. "But since we're here, I want to see if Scarlett might give me a tip on marketing my stuff."

"You wish!"

As the science fiction audience began to sit and become quiet, Connie and Gary left the room for the busy hall. They followed Scarlett's flaming hair that was already several yards away. Excitement boiled in the others around them.

A young woman, convamp to the teeth, her middle obscenely rolling under a sheer outfit too much like Scarlett's, stood next to the writer at the top of the stairs in the upper lobby. The light from the crystal chandelier beyond the stair's rails made her seem even larger than she was. Her eyes gushed and her fanged mouth was a bulbous circle of delight as Scarlett signed a book and handed it back with a wink.

Connie heard them as she reached the outskirts of the human circle.

"I wish I were a vampire like your Countess, Ms. Shade," the chubby girl beamed, reopening the paperback to read the inscription. "God, then I could have any man I wanted! I wish at least that some sexy male vampire would come after *me* . . ."

Scarlett's smile was forced. "Being a vampire doesn't always give you that kind of power, dear . . . believe me. I'm afraid vampires are usually attracted to the same types of women *live* men are." She touched the woman's shoulder delicately. "Do yourself a favor and lose of some of your weight . . ."

The woman blushed. "I—"

"No offense," spoke Scarlett.

"None t-taken . . . but"—she closed the book again, bright pink as all eyes turned to her—"It'd sure be a hell of a lot easier to lose my fat on a strictly liquid diet—"

Connie chuckled. Everyone did. Scarlett just smiled demurely, scratching her signature on another title page. Others held out their books to Scarlett . . . *Blood and Death* . . . *Vampire Bordello* . . . *Blood of the Month Club: The Interview with Count Downe* . . . *Count Downe, Vampire Detective*. All of them with lurid, wicked covers of near naked men or women . . . their fangs dripping in sex and blood. Victims anxious for those shiny teeth.

It went on for fifteen more minutes before most of the people began to slip away. Scarlett signed one more book and turned away politely, brushing past an ecstatic man in a cape. She swished her way to the stairs.

Connie used the moment to press in closer.

But Gary got to Scarlett first, his voice high among the murmurs. "I don't know if you remember me. I was at this convention three years ago and you really inspired me. I want to be a writer like *you*—"

Rolling her eyes delicately, Scarlett leaned close to him. "Just like *me?*" She tossed her head smartly, dropping her eyes to the soft bulge in his slacks. "That *can* be arranged these days, you know."

His face was growing as steadily bright as the fat woman's had. "Well . . . I—Jesus!"

Scarlett winked, ignoring a teenager trying to thrust another paperback into her hands. *Death's Sweet Door*, her first big title, blazing in shiny, drooling red letters. "Maybe you'll get your chance. Have you written anything? Ever tried to get published?"

"I haven't had a damn bit of luck," Gary replied.

"Well, if I inspired you, maybe I owe you some tips . . . stick around the bar later tonight . . ."

"Th-thanks!" he said, grinning wide, heading there now. Connie frowned after him, but he looked right through her when he turned back around. "Hey, really . . . *thanks!*"

Scarlett continued downward, and this time, no one but Connie followed.

Halfway down the stairwell, Scarlett glanced back. "You're a patient girl. I saw you in the dealers' room, didn't I?"

Connie gulped hard. "I . . . I just wanted to talk with you again. I . . . you write the best books!"

Scarlett's smile barely broadened. "That's what they tell me . . . are you wanting to be a writer, too?"

"Oh no!" Connie gasped. "I just *read.*"

Scarlett smiled, her teeth gleaming. She was wearing the realistic publicity fangs she was rarely seen without.

And now, Connie was near enough to touch them! "I . . . I understand how hard it must be for you to come to these conventions after the terrible things that have happened."

"I'd rather forget the unfortunate parts of life. I've been afraid I'd have to stop meeting my fans. Everyone seems to hold me responsible."

"I sure don't," Connie said.

She touched Connie's wrist with fingers as cool as her demeanor. "I'm glad you like my books."

A moment later they were standing on the main floor, watching more conventioneers pour in the doors to register at waiting tables . . . drawing the stares of a mainstream public that only thought they were jaded.

Scarlett was walking away.

"Wait," said Connie, reaching out to her and stopping herself instantly.

Scarlett turned back, a sultry eyebrow raised.

Blushing, Connie shook her head and dropped her eyes. "Nothing . . . I'm sorry I bothered you."

"Fans like you are never a bother," laughed Scarlett. "Inconvenient sometimes, but never a bother. Why don't you join me in the bar tonight, too?"

"Really?"

Scarlett winked. "You seem like an interesting woman, dear. I'm always on the prowl for interesting people, it keeps me in touch. Who knows? You may wind up as one of my characters someday."

Connie felt a grin merge with the warmth in her face. She saw her own pleasure shining once more in Scarlett's tiny necklace mirror. Again, independent . . . satisfied with herself and life. She wished it were true. "R-really?"

"Really," Scarlett replied. "After all, I don't get my ideas out of thin air. Everything has to be reflected in reality." Scarlett stepped into the increasing crowd. "Catch you later?"

Still smiling, Connie watched her go. "You've caught me," she breathed.

And although she couldn't have heard her through the noise, Scarlett looked back and winked.

Connie moved to the bar, hardly believing that she had actually talked to Scarlett again and that Scarlett had invited her for a drink! She was glowing as she joined a group of convamps well dressed as characters from Scarlett's books, others like Scarlett herself. All of them wore fake fangs that didn't come close to equaling the writer's, long gowns . . . brazen, sheer negligees over red and black underwear and too many flabby shapes. Connie huffed, wanting to break in as they discussed Scarlett's books. She finally ordered a strawberry daiquiri and resigned herself to merely listening as she waited for Scarlett. Her eyes wandered the blue-and-white checkered walls, past other tables and booths.

People with convention badges everywhere. It was really getting crowded in here.

She finally peered at a mosaic of tiny mirrors on the nearest wall, seeing herself a hundred times in its connected squares. A hundred different Connies, because it was as though her expression was changed in each of them, revealing her life from a happy child to her current confusion and dissatisfaction.

With herself. With life. Even with all the men.

"I wish I could be a vampire," said the pudgy brunette next to Connie, drawing murmurs of agreement from the others. "I'd go back and show my ex a thing or two. Can you believe that he left me for another woman?"

"The same goddamn thing happened to me," spoke up the older woman on Connie's other side, a cigarette hanging past her fangs ridiculously. "But my ex left me for a man! He said women were too crazy for him . . . just because one night last month I tried biting him and sucking some blood. I was Countess Showery in the mirror, and I just wanted to see what it was really like. I thought he'd *like* it—"

"Oh," another woman chimed in. "When I look in the

mirror I pretend I'm the Countess, too, and sometimes I really see her there instead of . . ."

Connie sighed and looked around for another place to sit, knowing the direction of this conversation too well. These so-called fans didn't really care about the sacrifice Scarlett was making to be here with them. They didn't care about the way Scarlett braved the stares and comments from her critics. Connie was just glad that at least no one mentioned the suicides.

But she knew no one at the conventions ever did. Real life was what everyone came to these things to forget. Except for the convamps, and *they* only wanted to complain about their own screwed-up lives . . . just like Connie herself once had . . . and sometimes still did. The knowledge made her more uncomfortable than ever, and when Connie saw Gary across the room, she got up fast, snagging her drink from an approaching waitress. She stood just behind him.

". . . maybe I'll finally get a break," he was saying to a stout man.

"Congratulations, Gary," Connie broke in. "Maybe I really will be reading *your* stuff someday."

He looked her up and down, then shook his companion's hand and led Connie to an empty booth. "Maybe you could start reading some of my stuff *before* I publish it and let me know what you think."

"Maybe I will if Scarlett's going to look at it." Connie smiled.

Chapter 10

Connie was feeling very slopped after two hours in the hotel bar. Gary was still so starry-eyed he didn't need his drinks, but guzzled beer after beer anyway. His every other word was Scarlett.

"She's really going to talk to me . . . to help *me!*"

"Shh," Connie whispered. "You're not published *yet*, Gary."

Her words were unheard. Connie saw it in his dilated eyes, and finally, bored again, she moved around the crowded barroom of conventioneers and scattered "mundanes." She'd spent the last hour with Gary and had slurped up two more daiquiris. When Connie returned to the table of Scarlett's more mindless fans, she found she enjoyed them a lot more. She downed a marguerita and heard herself slurring her words. After that, she forced herself to slow down and switched to beer, hoping that her mind would stop buzzing soon.

She moved back to sit across from Gary.

"You could just stop drinking altogether for a while," he said, but without a true concern. It was as though a wall had sprung up between them.

But it wasn't a wall. The very problem was that there was really nothing between them. Like all Connie's relationships, their friendship was based only on what they could offer each other, until something better came along.

Only Connie's friendship with Phil seemed to be different. She still didn't know what interest he offered her or what she offered him . . . except that he sold some of her jewelry for her at his store, and now she was giving him a place to stay.

And he treated her like a person . . . as an equal. He looked right at her when he spoke to her . . . and just as herself, he didn't seem to know what he wanted out of life. He seemed afraid.

Connie sipped her Moosehead slowly. "I could stop drinking. I could stop breathing, too . . . but I want to have *fun*. These conventions are for fun, Gary. A vacation away from life's problems and *business worries.*" She locked eyes with him, hoping to see some interest for herself. "Away from life." But she wasn't in his eyes at all. Like his words, they were only full of his own hopes, and he turned away.

She bit a too-short nail.

"We all need vacations." Gary grinned, showing her his false cheer as they clinked bottles and made it a toast. His teeth gleamed as brightly as his glittery earring, but he didn't catch her hint. Or ignored it. "I sure hope Scarlett shows," he went on immediately. "I hope she wasn't just putting me on. This could be my big chance. If someone like Scarlett Shade helps me . . ." He touched the dark bags under his eyes. "I've finished three novels and all I ever get are fucking rejection slips from publishers and agents . . ."

"Aww." Connie mocked his familiar whine.

Gary turned red.

She didn't care. He was acting and sounding just like the would-be rock star her sister lived with, especially with his guitar purchase, probably as something only to impress her and other lonely ladies. Connie finished her bottle and started to move to another group.

Gary blushed and took her arm:. "Look, Connie, give me a break. I never really knew before what I wanted to do with my life until I met *her*. When I look at myself now, I know I could be just as successful. Scarlett's got so much power with her words, but I know I can write with that power, too! I can start my own plague of 'Scarlett Fever'!"

Connie circled her mouth. " 'Gary Fever'?" She snickered. "I've heard all this, Gary. But is that really what you want—to inspire your readers to kill themselves?"

"Well," Gary said, "I guess I wouldn't want to go that far."

"I hope not. I've wanted to be a character in her books, too," Connie said. "But I draw the line at suicide."

"You know, you're not a true convamp anymore. Hell, you're just playing the part to sell your stuff." He took her hand and shook his head. "Look, I'm sorry, Connie. I'm just so excited. This could really be it!"

Screams broke through the bar's noisy hubbub as a new group poured in. The convamps at the table were out of their chairs and waving their hands, pointing into the lobby. The bar's other patrons shook their heads, clapped hands over their ears, and rolled their eyes. Scarlett came up the short steps . . . all her fans scrambling up to surround her like a group of slaves before their master.

Connie couldn't resist turning back to Gary, still miffed. "Here's your big chance to be a star, Gary . . . good luck!"

His face twisted nervously and his skin paled. He downed the remainder of his bottle and didn't say a word.

Connie's heart fluttered, too. She stared at the older woman's timeless beauty. Scarlett had changed clothes and was wearing a clinging, one-piece pants suit. Black, of course, and it brought out the beauty of her very pale skin. The open neckline dropped almost to her navel to prove the truth of her firm, braless breasts. The ever-present necklace mirror flashed between them. Her body was as flawless as a statue's, her face as mysterious as Mona Lisa's smile.

Scarlett slid through her admirers, whispering to them softly as she nodded them back to their table. She stopped at Connie's toes and Connie dropped back onto the bench. "Hope I haven't kept you two waiting long," she spoke, her dark eyes twinkling a merry beat. "I had to check out a couple of readings. Friends, you know."

Gary scooted over so she could sit beside him. "I was wondering if you were really coming." He squiggled his eyebrows down, as though remembering something sad, lowering his voice. "Uh, did you meet Teresa Carson in Amarillo? She told me she was going to try to interview you."

Scarlett pursed her lips. "I don't give interviews anymore."

He shook his head. "But did you see her? She . . . she was one of the suicides and I thought—"

"I don't remember her . . . and I'd rather not discuss that sort of thing, please. I'm hounded enough by the press." Scarlett's lips tightened. "Let's find something more pleasant to talk about."

He paused, blushing, and waved at a waitress. "I'm sorry. I just thought . . ." He shook his head. "Teresa really got into reading your stuff, Ms. Shade."

"Well," Scarlett sighed, "that's very nice of you to say." She squinted at his name badge. "And of course, I feel bad about her, but I can't spend my time feeling bad about every fan I lose." She smiled impishly. "Thanks, Gary . . . and call me Scarlett, okay?" She waved at a watching, forlorn fan and showed him her teeth. He showed her his.

The waitress, thirtiesh and dark-haired, short and kind of dumpy, came to the booth. Her eyes got huge when she saw Scarlett. "Are you *her?*"

Scarlett nodded slightly. "Yes, dear. Now, please, another round of drinks for my friends here and for my fans at that far table . . . yes, them."

The waitress, her eyes still bugging, went back with the order and kept looking over her shoulder.

"I . . . I really appreciate you taking the time to talk to *me*," Gary said, his tone still apologetic.

"And *me*," Connie spoke up. "I just enjoy listening to you,"

"Ah . . ." Scarlett beamed. "This is why I came back to conventions . . . there's nothing so fulfilling as glowing fans . . ."

A few minutes later, the waitress returned with their drinks, her face still creased in a wide smile. Scarlett flashed her fangs and turned back to Gary. "So this kind of notoriety is something you want for yourself, too?"

"I wouldn't mind it, but I guess I have a long way to go."

"That depends on the quality of your writing. Did you bring any material with you?"

His lips twisted down like he was sick. "Uh, no . . . but I could drive home real quick . . . or I could bring it with me tomorrow. I live in Aurora and it's not far."

"I'm a night person, Gary. If you'd like to do it now, that would be fine." She stood up so Gary could get by. "I'll meet you at your room, okay? What's the number?" She batted her lashes.

Gary's face sagged. He glared at Connie. "Uh, Connie and I are in the same room."

The smile on Scarlett's full lips was saccharin. "How sweet," she said.

Sweeping his narrowed eyes back to Connie, Gary was gone.

Connie rubbed her stomach, trying not to think of the rebuff he'd just given her. She turned back to the table of Scarlett's awed fans. All silent now, staring at their idol.

Connie felt their rejection bitterly. "Shouldn't you go over and talk to them?"

Scarlett didn't even glance, instead she looked down at Connie's name badge again and lowered her voice. "I've heard it all before . . . Connie. They're not the kinds of fans I appreciate as much as the quieter ones like you. It's fans like them who cause all the disturbances, and I don't need any more of that kind of attention. They're just looking for a guru who can magically transform their lives." She sniffed. "They all *think* they want to be vampires . . . but they wouldn't even enjoy the gift if they had it. It takes a special kind of person."

"Like the characters in your books?"

Scarlett made a faint smile around her straw.

"So how do you know I'm any different?" Connie asked, feeling her new empathy for the convamps grow.

"You haven't asked if I could tell you how to become undead, for one thing." She laughed gently. "Are you done with your drink?"

Finishing it too fast, Connie nodded dizzily. "Done," she swallowed. "Do you have to go?"

Picking up the ticket and leaving a large tip, Scarlett led the way to the cashier. "I thought we might talk more privately . . . something you can brag about to other fans. After a while, all this attention bothers me."

A chilly uncertainty stabbed into Connie briefly. Scarlett was staring her up and down. Connie remembered the stories she'd heard of Scarlett and tried not to show her nervousness. But it was mixed with a peculiar eagerness . . . despite the vacuum Connie had felt after Vicky . . . the way those moments had made her look so hollow in her mirror. Automatically, she faced her reflection between Scarlett's breasts, seeing only a bliss in herself now.

Between Scarlett's breasts.

"You're a very attractive young woman," Scarlett breathed in her disarming, husky tone.

The ebony pupils, shining, it seemed, with promises, flowed from their center in Scarlett's blue-green eyes.

Into Connie . . . *inside her.*

Connie's heart thudded faster . . . an excitement . . . anticipation . . . overpowered every other thought. Her thoughts of reality began to fade away with the chill of Scarlett's fingers around her damp palm.

"Come on, dear," whispered the hypnotic voice. "You're just feeling your liquor. I can see it in your eyes."

They stopped at the counter register and Scarlett paid their bill. Connie knew that Scarlett was right. But she was sober enough to know that now, unbelievably, she was standing right here with the world's greatest writer . . . a woman whose prose sometimes led her in romantic fantasies. Erotic dreams. Connie felt as though every eye in the bar's room was fixed on her . . . but it just made her hotter. Not just the blushes she felt in her face either. The expanding heat between her thighs was more real than life itself.

If only it could go on forever.

"It can, dear. It can. In a way, you remind me of myself," whispered the voice that formed her will now, and Connie was surprised she had spoken aloud.

Departing the room's slick black tile, Connie traded an accidental glance with an aging convamp and felt the jealousy. She felt very, very special.

Still holding Connie's lax hand, Scarlett rubbed her thumb against Connie's and guided her through the lobby's green plants to a hallway of closed doors . . . passing a mirror.

Connie breathed deeply as she saw Scarlett in the reflection, but not *herself.* She went cold.

But it was *herself* as Scarlett. Scarlett in *her* clothing . . .

How . . .?

Scarlett stopped at the tug and faced Connie. "Don't be shy, dear. You've read my books . . . you *love* them, remember? This will be just like getting to read one of my books I haven't even written yet. One about you . . . and me. I see your fears and believe me, I can sympathize. I can take them away. Life is cruel and destructive."

The eyes stroked her, easing her, fogging her brain and the memory of what she had just . . . seen.

Or *thought* she'd seen. Maybe she was drunker than she knew. She'd mixed her drinks horribly . . . maybe the mirror's false reflection had been a trick of the light.

She knew she was really plastered. "I," Connie sighed, sweating. "Are . . . are we—"

Scarlett rubbed her thumb. "I don't have any of the popular diseases, darling. Just . . . *trust* me."

Scarlett's touch returned every desire. The hall's doors blurred as they passed them. Connie could barely read the hand-lettered convention posters on the walls or even the room numbers.

Then her hand was clutching the empty air.

Scarlett was gone.

"Je-Jesus!"

She shivered, very alone in the quiet hallway.

She *was* drunk.

Chapter 11

Connie yawned deeply and shook her head back and forth, pacing back and forth through the hall, her mind clear one instant and a layer of deep fog the next. . . .

Where had the night gone?

Scarlett Shade.

Connie was uncertain of everything, now. Talking to that beautiful woman . . . had it been real?

But Scarlett was more a part of her than ever. So if the past hour was true and not a drunken fancy, how had Scarlett gotten away so fast?

Strange.

But not really. Connie sighed with the newest pain, knowing that the bar conversation must have happened.

But the writer had ditched her. After all, Connie knew she wasn't even particularly interesting when she was sober. She wasn't very pretty, either.

Connie passed two older women dressed in white, shoe-length gowns . . . back into the plant-and chair-filled lobby. The bar's crowd was fading. Half a dozen voices combined into one low murmur of nonsense.

Connie remembered waiting for Scarlett Shade in there, but it seemed like that was hours ago.

Days.

Had she seen her?

Hadn't she?

It was too hard to remember . . . but a strange peace covered that curious confusion with mildness, and she turned to the elevators . . . feeling a furious desire. Craving circled her as the elevator moved up, then Connie stepped into the third floor hall, hearing the voices around her as though she were at the bottom of a deep, dull abyss.

She was. The abyss was frustration. She knew Gary was hoping to spend tonight with Scarlett instead of *her*. Connie slid her feet across the thick carpet slowly. It seemed that everything was really just part of a dream . . . that she *was* the young female convert in Scarlett's book, *The Sucking*, leaving Countess Showery's quarters to walk down the corridors of the castle . . . to bring the man who had jilted her into the ranks of the undead, enjoying the gift of pleasure that never had to be paid for.

Her own pleasure as she drank him dry, making him hers.

She pricked up her ears at approaching murmurs . . . a group of young men in chilling, pale-fleshed zombie makeup coming down the hall. They opened a door and filed into a room with two young women. The dwindling, off-key voices of filkers somewhere nearby made her shudder.

But Connie's face was flushed and damp with excitement when she stopped at the white door. She squinted at the gold numbers until she was sure they matched her key, all the while imagining Gary deep inside her throat, nibbling him until his blood flowed into her swallows.

She flipped on the lights and peered into the empty room. "Gary?" But Gary had left to get his manuscripts. She knew the disappointment he would feel in Scarlett's disappearance. But at the same time, it gave her relief.

She was too wasted to wait on him, though. Her eyelids sagged and she yawned, tasting her tongue sickly. After shutting off the light, throwing the room into near blackness, she pulled the shirttails out her slacks and slid out of her clothing. She fell onto the mattress. Only the city glow showed through a crack in the window curtains.

Connie relaxed, her head raised on two pillows to study her dim reflection in the big mirror above the desk. The light's trickery made her face a disembodied mask. Balling the sheet in her fists, Connie felt the world closing in, unwanted, just as it had been closing in when Robert had used her and gotten her pregnant the first time, in high school. She'd learned to be careful to take the pill and make her different partners use rubbers. Now, she called the shots.

Her lips turned up in a new strength. When Gary came back to her tonight, it would be over. She'd ditch him for good this time and never have to feel rejection from him again.

It would be over.

Just as over as it was with Phil.

She tried to forget that bad part of her past again, thinking instead of all the Scarlett Shade novels she'd read to escape it . . . the way they'd eased her frustrated guilt.

Pleasure . . . without guilt.

Connie tossed and turned, wanting the hypnotic effect of Scarlett's words, for their desire to rush back and eclipse her frustrations. She tried seeing Countess Showery and Count Downe the way she used to . . . fantasizing herself as their lover.

Connie . . . dear, sweet Connie, a dream voice seemed to speak through the half-hidden memories of Scarlett's books . . . memories of Scarlett, now. Connie visualized her face in Scarlett's necklace. She stared into the shininess on the wall and threw off the bedspread, then watched her hands as though they were someone else's, caressing her breasts. Gliding her fingers over hardening nipples, the goosebumps made her sigh. She parted her thighs with a gasp as her face blurred to become an imagination of Countess Showery's. Her fingers rubbed down into her damp hair and her excitement grew stronger. The strong fog of the evening returned and Connie reached out dreamily.

The reflection mimicked her. But it wasn't Countess Showery or herself.

Scarlett.

Connie gasped.

Scarlett's face . . . Scarlett . . . as foggy as Connie felt, floating in the glass, as though she were somehow *inside* it.

Connie held her breath as the image became clearer . . . nearer. The luminous green haze seeped from the frame into the room as Scarlett seemed to come right through the glass, just like a character in her books.

Scarlett . . . the dream of her . . . eased onto the bed's soft mattress, her contralto low and mellow. The bright glowing mist surrounding them drifted, disappearing. "Nothing to be afraid of . . . nothing at all," Scarlett whispered. "You're very pretty . . . full of life and fun you don't even know about. As I said, *not* like the others."

"H-how . . . ?"

Cool fingers combed Connie's hair from her face and lingered on her hot cheeks. "I never left you, Connie. I never will. You *are* mine. This is the best way for us to be together . . . because I am your reflection. I'm part of you."

"B-but I . . ." A fear crept through Connie as Scarlett's cool hands cupped her breasts and drew her into a new world—

But this was only a dream. Not real. Scarlett had come out of the mirror. She wasn't really here. "M-Ms. Shade," Connie heard herself.

"Scarlett," the dream said, reaching behind herself. "Sweet Connie. Don't be shy. Pleasure is the name of the game. Let yourself go . . . drift . . ."

Connie listened to the slow sound of a zipper as the

pants suit became loose around Scarlett's shoulders. A dream that felt and sounded very real. Connie's teeth chattered as Scarlett stood naked, an image of rich, pale flesh, and tossed the garment aside.

"You look so delicious," said Scarlett, reaching to pull the sheet away from Connie. "This will be the moment of your life."

"Life," Connie heard herself say, her lips forming the word on their own.

"Undeath," replied Scarlett, like a promise. Their lips touched, the frigid feel spreading numbness. "Please," Connie moaned, reaching up to Scarlett's standing nipples. "Please—"

Scarlett's icy tongue stroked inside her mouth gently, and Connie's eyes closed as her mind fluttered, every wonderful scene in Scarlett's books unleashed in her at once . . . siphoning away her own frustrated turmoil.

But sudden rapid knocks on the door drove them away.

Connie blinked . . . gasped . . . as though suddenly awakening from a long sleep. Her heart was a battering ram against her ribs . . . the naked beauty still poised above her. Connie felt Scarlett's cold, bare flesh with confused unbelief.

Still a dream.

The knocks from the door became louder . . . more insistent.

Scarlett's dry red hair tickled Connie's face. She shook her head and sighed. "Just a minute," she called out, then moved her eyes back to Connie's. "You're such a sweet girl," droned the reassuring voice. "We have a lot more to talk about . . . come to me when I call you, Connie . . . will you?"

The drunken peace returned to flood Connie, replacing the excitement with promise again . . . a promise to be kept.

Very soon.

Then Scarlett dropped her face to Connie's excited breast—teasing it with tongue and teeth. Connie moaned in rapture as the teeth pressed into her. The pinch *wasn't* pain. . . .

"Yes . . . please," gasped Connie, committed to Scarlett as she watched herself inside unfathomable pupils, safe and more than satisfied.

But Scarlett backed away, licked damp lips, and stood beside the bed. She helped Connie put on a T-shirt and slipped on her own pants suit that clung like a second skin. "Come to me when I call you," she repeated. "Obey me . . . okay? Don't let me lose you."

Connie nodded, and those words rolled on forever.

The door cracked open and Scarlett chuckled lowly, pushing it wide. Gary stood there, carrying a bulging briefcase, flushed with excitement and embarrassment as he studied them both. "I hadn't expected you so swiftly," Scarlett told him.

A tall blond man stood behind Gary with a heavy sack. Connie recognized him from the Sex and Horror panel. "Uh . . . sorry," he spoke up. "Are you busy, Ms. Shade? I wanted you to sign a couple of my books—"

Scarlett's eyes twinkled brightly as she held out a slender hand. "Just a couple?"

"Uh, my name's Mason," he said. "I've got all of your books and you only signed three of them earlier."

Gary nodded. "I told him you'd be up here. I didn't think you'd mind."

Scarlett lips twisted this way and that, finally a mirthless smile. "Of course not."

Connie waited, the intruders' words sounds of annoying insects . . . for Scarlett's next command.

Gary looked at Connie, then at the fan. "Maybe we ought to go somewhere else. Connie looks sleepy."

Scarlett took Connie's hand smoothly. "Yes. Sleep, Connie. Rest well." Scarlett sighed. "We'll get together some other time . . . privately. For now . . . forget. Forget it all."

Gary winked at Connie as he went into the hall. "Bet you never thought I'd ever be so lucky, did you? I'll see you a little later, okay? Keep it warm."

Connie saw the promise of earlier flicker in his gaze, and tried to smile back. Then she blinked as the sound of the shutting door made her feel stranded and lost.

Cold. Tears flooded her lashes. She stripped off the shirt and lay in bed, snuggling in the blankets until sweat plastered her hair, so fuzzy now that she was having trouble falling back asleep. She huddled like a fetus around Gary's pillow.

Scarlett Shade . . . a wishful fancy of Scarlett appearing from the mirror . . . "Ohhh!" she sighed, feeling it now as her breast ached and pulsed again. Connie's heart pounded in rhythm. She waited impatiently for Gary to come back to this room and want her, to give her what she needed.

Connie wanted to drink him. His *blood.*

Then the thought made her shudder. She stared into the mirror groggily, knowing she was still drunk. She threw off her covers and spread her legs wide. This time, she pretended her fingers were Gary's.

But the image with her in the mirror was Scarlett.

Wait for me, dear Connie. Dream of me. The future will be ours soon enough.

The voice caressed her, leaving Connie dead asleep and tossing in dreams of the pages of Scarlett Shade's books: Count Downe, ravishing her as she became Countess Showery . . . as they both slept in plush coffins to rise from the grave and continue a lust that drew them even closer together.

That dream merged with another . . . a lush vision of herself in Scarlett Shade's arms . . . Connie was Countess Showery come to life . . . to undeath . . . and loved approvingly in the embrace of her creator. Scarlett, naked, pale, beautiful . . . clutching Connie tight, their likenesses sucking the blood from one another through exquisite fangs that gave pleasure and not pain . . . life and not death. Connie gurgled sleepily as Count Downe swept into that vision and it became a lusty threesome . . . and then as they all went into the night to find others.

Other lovers . . . other pleasures . . . new ecstasies to share.

To devour.

The dream-orgasms became real in her head.

Chapter 12

Mason Hood opened one of the books when he returned to his hotel room. He sat down at the desk heavily. The hall outside was still alive with drunken voices and squeals. He put fingers in his ears to shut out the noise while trying to keep the book open. With difficulty, he reread Scarlett's scrawled promise to him. Her pen marks made him feel disembodied . . . floating in the air.

He had actually met Scarlett Shade. She had *touched* him.

He still felt those icy, soft fingers against his. He looked at the book's cover wishfully.

Blood Shower . . . by Scarlett Shade. Below the name and title, a distorted and softened photo of a beautiful blond woman, her nudity fuzzy, her mouth full of dripping red teeth.

Below her, a bare-chested man, ecstatic.

Himself.

"Boy," Mason whispered. "If only such things were real."

But they weren't. He knew that. Nothing cool was ever real. Like Dad and teachers from long ago said, the only sure things in life were death and taxes. Responsibility.

And real death wasn't cool like in the Shade books. There was no undeath.

Mason got up from the chair and looked out the window at the hazy Denver night, the mountains dark in the distance. The foreign solitude of being far from home was heavy on him. Voices and closing doors in the hallway were loud as the last retiring conventioneers dispersed for the night. Shaking his head, Mason flipped on the TV.

He was so exhausted after just meeting Scarlett. He was addicted to her books, and now, to Scarlett Shade herself. He'd felt so free near her . . . just like when he read her novels. He wanted every sound he heard to be her calling to him, because he was fantasizing *her* instead of just her characters now.

She'd met his eyes like maybe she wanted him, too. Her inscription told him that she wanted *him*.

But he would never know if those words were genuine. That other guy had been there, eager to show Scarlett the manuscripts he'd written.

Scarlett had excused Mason. It was already over.

Tomorrow, back to the mundane world, life's misery. His boss would know he'd skipped work to go to the convention, so Monday morning, he was certainly out of a job.

"Fuck work," Mason sizzled, using the remote to scan channels. As usual, he lingered when he got to the sample of Playboy programming. That was too painful, though. It reminded him that his girlfriend had dumped on him.

He wanted to see Scarlett Shade again; let her bite him and drink his blood the way he imagined in his dreams. He felt more alone than ever now that he'd actually met her.

He hoped . . .

But that would never happen. Like everything else he wanted, it was only a wish.

This was the real world.

Finally, reaching beside him, Mason picked up the phone and dialed Angela's number back in Kansas City.

"Hello?" spoke her soft voice.

But what could he say to her? "Uh . . . hi, Angie . . ."

"Mason? Where are you? Your boss has been calling here to find you!"

"I'm in Denver. I was, uh, thinking about you."

"Another convention?" She sighed. "It's over, Mason. Get with the program. You'd better get yourself together or you're going to lose more than just me."

Her flat tone wasn't at all what he wanted from her. "Hey, be nice to me, Angie." He rubbed his slacks and remembered the times when they'd been together very informally. It hadn't been that long ago. "Don't all those nice times we had together mean anything to you?"

Her tone was dull and sharp at the same moment . . . a two-edged knife. "What nice times? Look Mason, it's embarrassing to be dating a guy whose only ambition in life is to die and be a vampire. A crotch-crunching vampire at that . . . That's just about all you ever talked about. And I don't call trying to imitate the sex scenes in your goddamn books making love. Now fuck off. Don't keep calling me, okay? It's over . . . and tell your boss we're not together anymore, okay?"

"But—"

The tone of disconnection buzzed in his ear.

"Bitch." He slammed down the receiver, throbbing with the need under his slacks. *Disconnection*. "I don't need her," Mason spoke loudly to the TV set, finding the soft-porn again. "I don't need anyone but myself." For a moment, he watched the teasing scene of two couples as they moved back and forth over each other and into each other, then when it faded, he flipped to another hotel channel with its tame monster feature. Closing his eyes with the laser rays blasting in his ears, Mason tried to replay the pages of the novels, pretending he was the downtrodden lovesick wretch Countess Showery had found outside her castle. She had reached out to that poor bastard and brought him into her realm of undeath, giving him the joys life had denied him. Giving him herself . . .

Mason had even enjoyed the scene where Count Downe entered grandly, his cape flowing, joining them in a full-fledged ménage à trois!

He licked his lips and brushed the tips of his fingers over his crotch. His other hand rubbed her signature. All he could think of was watching Scarlett's fluid hand scrawl that inscription, and how she'd licked her lips, gazing into *his* eyes.

He'd seen himself . . . and her, together . . . in the jewelry mirror around her neck.

He just wanted his dreams to become his life. Nothing wrong with that. Nothing wrong with a few daydreams.

Dropping his pants to his knees, Mason fondled himself, pretending his hand was Countess Showery's, as he stared in the mirror and visualized the perfect lines of her trim figure there. With him. "Dream on," he told himself, adding as many details as he could to the hopeful fantasy.

Someone knocked on the door.

Mason pulled up his underpants as though his mother had just caught him at this when he was much younger. He went to the door and opened it slowly, dropping his jaw.

Gary. The writer, the wonderful man who had introduced him to Scarlett!

From behind, Mason heard Scarlett. "Aren't you going to ask us in?" hissed her sultry voice.

He looked back to the empty room with a grunt. "Where . . ." Then the mirror moaned as if alive, filled with a luminous green mist, and he saw her, more beautiful than ever, in its glass.

Not knowing . . . or caring . . . if this was real or just

another dream, Mason stuttered, inviting them both, holding his breath as Scarlett floated out of the glass.

Gary shut the door.

Mason felt only his urgent desire . . . lonely need. His heart was pounding as reality and fantasy combined . . . as the long-haired man stripped. Gary kicked his jeans away and lowered his bikini shorts, pressing a thick pole into Mason's shivering palm.

Mason stroked the tight flesh guiltily, not resisting as Gary tugged off his clothes, too. He shook his head. No . . . no guilt. Like Count Downe said, "there is no grace . . . nor guilt . . ."

"Do what thou wilt," Scarlett finished the thought aloud on Mason's bed, watching them.

But Mason wanted *her*. He pulled back and shook his head.

Scarlett purred. "There are no rules in *my* world. None but pleasure. I've come to give you freedom . . . and freedom *is* pleasure. You must lose self-control . . . why should self be controlled, Mason?" Her eyes drew him inside . . . and so suddenly that Mason *knew* that this was only another dream, Scarlett was naked, too. She stood and poured her smooth, milky flesh against him, drawing Gary into their circle . . . a smothering of lips and saliva, firm breasts, hard cocks, and a dripping cunt. The fantasies of Mason's desire all flooded together as ecstasy and pain merged, becoming one.

The lust and death they created united into the biggest orgasm he'd ever known.

He slurped thirstily at the blood and semen dripping into his mouth.

Chapter 13

Her head was aching—swimming in a muddy bog, when Connie realized she was awake. She sat up with a knot in her stomach. The pillow beside her was still empty, untouched.

Through the curtain's crevices, the sunlight was bright. "Gary . . ."

But the room felt empty. Connie didn't expect an answer . . . was not surprised when it didn't come. She leaned over the side of the bed, dizzy, holding to the mattress under her with both hands so she wouldn't fall to the shrinking floor. The gold carpet pulled away as if she were being shot into orbit.

"Help," Connie whimpered, clenching her eyelids tight and falling back just as quickly . . . a thousand miles . . . all the way to the cuddly, soft-warm blankets.

Suddenly, she wanted to sleep forever—to rest beyond the pull of another hangover. She moaned when her eyes turned to the room clock. *Eight-fifteen!* She shot back up, so fast it made the room's walls and their forest paintings spin into a surge of browns, greens, and yellows. Her acidic stomach was bitter and tossing.

She had to get to the dealers' room. Connie doubled over. Why had she drunk so much? She was unable to remember much of anything. Only a voice, calling her name, over and over. A voice familiar . . .

Whose?

A woman's voice. Husky.

Connie.

This time it was only her damp memories. The tones that had called out to her so long were gone. A throb in Connie's breast erupted in a pang that was both joy and pain. She grunted.

Scarlett Shade? Connie seemed to feel the woman all around her until her divisive blend of emotion pulled down a dense curtain to seperate those memories from the present. The thoughts disappeared as Connie sat back up, doing her best not to feel the stabbing wrench pounding her nipple. She slid out of the bed onto weak legs.

Where the hell was Gary? "Gary?" She sighed. What had happened to him? Her heart fell as she wondered if he'd spent the night with Scarlett. She knew he'd wanted to.

Or maybe he'd found someone else . . . maybe he'd really tried to find another woman for the Manwich Sandwich Connie half promised. Maybe he'd decided to take a solo flight with that unknown volunteer instead.

That bastard. She studied the mirror . . . herself. Alone.

Anger sagged in life's irrelevance . . . back to the lush fantasies that had accompanied the strange voice all night long. A tone that brought peace from these frustrations. A *dream* voice.

Connie couldn't stop a sudden shiver, but the glass still showed only *her*. "It was really weird," she muttered, holding to the wall as she forced her steps to the bathroom. She knew Scarlett could not have come through the mirror. Such things only happened in her books . . . *in Connie's dreams*. It had only been a *dream*.

Gary had intruded on that fantasy.

Connie gritted her teeth and climbed into the cold

bathtub. She stopped the drain, then switched on a mixture of hot and cold water, but mostly hot. She stretched out on the tub's warming bottom and tried to let the steamy water relax her aching, chilly bones, enjoying its soothing, the pure, spiritual peace the water gave her, *until the wetness reached her breast*. She hissed at a pinch, seeing nothing that could have caused it, then forced herself back into the warm wetness until the sting began to fade.

At last, the balmy ripples made her feel better again, comforting her against the newest rejection with a strong revival.

She got out, wishing she could stay in the reassurance forever, and wiped herself furiously with a towel, drying off fast as she saw her wristwatch on the counter.

But when she faced her naked body in the steamy mirror, she felt sick.

Her breast!

No wonder it hurt so bad. The red mark looked almost as though she stuck her convention badge right through her skin. She wanted to retch at the sight of two bright red marks, festering sores . . . just noticeable inside the ring of her aerola. . . .

Very tiny.

Connie held her breast as though it were a broken treasure. *How had the ugly punctures gotten there?* She circled a finger over the mild swelling . . . her wide eyes still held to the reflection, following the dark ring that wasn't all her own.

"Yuck," she gagged, reaching for a washcloth and soap, massaging the wound tenderly . . . not admitting to herself that the injury was starting to look like something beautiful. The red marks were like a seal of new confidence . . . the deep holes like a pathway into her very soul.

But . . . how . . . ?

There wasn't time to wonder how it had happened.

Connie dug through her makeup case and found a Band-Aid kit. Squirting salve on her finger, she looked down.

And saw *nothing. No marks.*

No wound.

Her brain pounded as she still saw *it* in the mirror.

"I'm not drunk now," she whispered, staring from herself and the undamaged flesh to the mirror and its brand. Gargling soured spit, Connie kept her eyes on the reflection and covered her nipple with two of the adhesive strips. She bit her tongue and bent over the toilet, choking and spitting out a drool of puzzled illness. When she finished, she looked down at the bandage uneasily, visualizing the impossible reflected imprint . . . seeing again her dreams of Count Downe and Countess Showery . . . Scarlett Shade coming out of the mirror.

Biting her.

Making the marks.

Staring into the mirror, Connie looked into those fantasies again. Closely.

Herself as the Countess.

Forget it all.

Connie closed her eyes, slowly reopening them.

She sighed when she saw her own pale face, and shook her head, going back into the room to get dressed and avoiding its mirror.

The illusions in her memory faded . . . disappearing completely.

Chapter 14

The convention petered out quickly after noon. There were still a lot of people tagging after favorite authors and going to final panels, but the buyers were gone. Connie had a surge of customers between eleven and twelve who bought the remnants of her cheapest wares and a few paperbacks, and then everyone but a group of gamers just disappeared. The gamers had little interest in anything not pertaining to role games.

Connie didn't mind. She had sold more jewelry than ever, and Phil's books had sold well, too. Especially the Scarlett Shade stuff. When the word came that Scarlett was seen leaving the hotel just before dawn, most of the remaining autographed copies sold like the proverbial hotcakes.

Last night's dreams and this morning's mirage seemed less and less real. Connie knew for sure she'd just had way too much to drink. She felt like Ray Milland with the D.T.'s in that movie, *The Lost Weekend*. He'd been plastered even when he thought he was sober and hadn't had any booze for hours. The alcohol was so deep in his blood it caused him to see all kinds of crazy shit . . . bats coming out of bloody walls.

"I think it's time to call it a day and get on the road," Connie told herself tiredly, not rested at all. She crated her remaining wares into cardboard boxes, clearing the table as wanderers passed. Several other dealers were closing up, too. With the drive ahead, Connie didn't want to wait, and with everyone else going, she doubted she would catch much flak over leaving early.

Gary had not shown back up, and she wasn't going to go looking for him. He'd sure put her in her place. She didn't care if she never saw him again.

Doug Lewis, the local dealer who owned the Little Bookshop of Horrors, waved at Connie as she passed that table to get a two-wheeler.

Connie stopped and smiled. "How'd you do?"

"Sold a load of Shade's books. I tried to get her to stay and do a reading at the store but she said she had to clear out. She promised to make it back by spring, though. I just hope she doesn't go back into hiding before then."

Connie smiled at Doug's wife, Tomi. "I sold most of my stuff, too."

Doug nodded as Rose Beetem, one of the convention's chairpeople, brought a customer up to his table.

"You leaving?" Rose smiled.

Connie nodded. "I'm so exhausted I'm seeing things."

Rose winked. "Stay out of the bars."

Finding a feeble laugh, Connie went on to the loading dock warehouse. She rolled a two-wheeler back and got all her boxes piled on. The unsold quantity only made one load. The joy of success helped her to forget Gary while she lifted the boxes into her Ford Escort.

When she stopped and reached for her car keys, she bumped her chest and winced. "Screw you, Gary," she choked, getting in and backing her car out, driving home.

Back to a mundane life.

Back to Phil and his problems, but she was ready for a vacation from this vacation.

Part Three:
Inside a Bat's Belfry

Chapter 1

Phil awoke late in the afternoon. He was glad it was Sunday and he wouldn't have to open the store. His eyes were sore, his muscles stiff and achy.

But although he didn't want to leave it, the room, his bedroom in Connie's apartment, was like a prison cell. He clenched his fists together until his fingernails stabbed the soft flesh of his palms deeply. The prison cell of his life, a circle of death and nightmares. Real horror.

He grunted.

The dreams of the tanks and the machine gun sound-track as he watched his uncle and cousins become bloody dancers in a rap-minuet of death still blared through his thoughts. It made him want to scream, but despite the tremble tugging his lips, he kept them shut tight.

Sonia.

Phil lay in the rumpled sheets for two more hours. Every muscle and bone in his body seemed to ache worse and worse. The memories of the Amarillo convention continued to rattle him. The suicides. All of them Scarlett Shade fans. Bloodless bodies. Fans who hoped that taking their own lives would make them vampires. The nightmares kept getting worse . . . just like when he was a boy and spent two months in the psychiatric wing of a hospital.

With that background, he didn't dare give voice to the fear of his new nightmares. Kevin was right about that. Phil studied his wall posters of a dozen horror films, clawed his pillow, stood with a wobble, then was plodding across the floor. He hesitated, then touched the poster for *The Fearless Vampire Killers,* no longer remembering the fun of watching Polanski's satire. Shutting his eyes, he tore it off the wall, cringing at the loud rip.

Out of sight, out of mind . . . he hoped. It was why he refused to watch anything on TV but pay channels like HBO. He didn't want to know the news of real life death and destruction. He'd seen enough for his lifetime already . . . and believed the news scenes were part of the fault for his memory lapses.

Phil went to a loud poster of *Horror of Dracula,* no longer liking the icy glint in Christopher Lee's vampire eyes that stared out at him. With a jerk, he tore that poster loose, too.

Suicides.

Mirrors. Scarlett Shade.

Vampires.

His brain was so wasted from exertion already that even the headache seemed to be gone, displaced in the poverty of any emotion at all. Phil focused on the bedroom as clearly as he could. Dropping the posters, he began tugging off the sweaty bed sheets.

It wasn't his problem. All he had to do, like Kevin suggested for a very different reason, was stay away from the cons, at least the ones Scarlett attended.

He dropped his damp clothing after the sheets, then went to the hall closet for clean linen. His legs slugged back to the bedroom and he laid his load on the mattress, then limped to the bathroom. He avoided a look at his reflection, filling the tub for another hot bath. Listening to the splashing water, he found the Tylenol bottle and swallowed three pills. The water had always made him feel better. The slippery moisture was so much like his dreams . . . formless and . . .

Like his life. It *was* his problem . . . if vampires were real.

If Scarlett could really come to him through the mirror . . .

He stepped into the tub with dread, knowing how this would hurt for a minute.

But then it would all feel so much better.

Water . . . a natural baptism in its cleansing.

He sank down, groaning as the water surrounded the mark . . . the bite.

It *was* his problem . . . because he'd been *bitten*.

When the stings finally ended, and the soothing began, Phil laid back and rested, not getting out until the water grew cold.

After drying himself, Phil put on his sweat pants and shirt. He walked through the disheveled apartment. For fifteen minutes, he rearranged the boxes of books, finding better places for some of the stacks in the hallway, but dizziness made him remember why he was here instead of driving back from the Denver convention with Connie. He stared at the phone, wishing he could call her, then picked up his personal phone directory.

It would be even better to talk to Kevin. He found the name and dialed. Kevin's wife, Denise, answered. "Hello? Matthews' residence?"

"Denise? This is Phil . . ."

"Good to hear from you, Phil! How's the book business?"

"Slow," he replied automatically. "Hey, I'm sorry to bother you guys . . . is Kevin around?"

She paused. "I think he's gone to the store . . . shall I have him call you?"

Phil's sigh was deep, as lonely as he felt. "Yeah . . . please . . . as soon as he can."

"Are you all right?"

"Sure," Phil said without conviction. "There's something bothering me, though, and—"

A crash sounded somewhere beyond her. "Crap—can you hang on?"

Phil let out a new sigh, more ragged than the last. "Just . . . just have him call me, will you?"

"Sure. Look, I'm sorry, I got to go. Our daughter—"

"Thanks," he said, hanging up. He stared at the phone. *Everyone* had problems, not just him. He held the receiver to his face again and dialed Katherine.

He was gritting his teeth by the third ring, about to hang up, when she answered. "Hello?"

His throat was so tight. "K-Katherine?"

She hesitated, her tone suddenly flat. "What is it this time, Phil?"

"I . . . I just wanted to talk to someone."

"So why'd you call *me?*" She sighed. "This is why I'm divorcing you. Look, Phil, don't pretend like you suddenly need me. Everything you do is pretend. You live in your own little world . . . the past. You don't want to talk to me or anyone else. You only want to talk and know someone is listening."

"Kathy, it's not that way. I do want to talk to—"

"Exactly, Phil. You want to talk, but hey, I don't want to listen. I don't know why I ever did in the first place. I've got my own life to live. Bye."

The dial tone hummed. Once more, he slid the receiver onto its cradle, feeling sorry for himself because no one else had time to. At last, Phil picked out the copy of *Death's Sweet Door* Scarlett Shade had signed especially to him in Amarillo, wondering for the thousandth time why he was dreaming of her the way he was, just as though he were one of her convamps.

Had it been real? He touched the spot under his pants. He'd never even read one of her books.

How could his dream be real . . . how could she really be a vampire?

He shivered, wanting Connie back, even if their short sexual relationship had only turned out to be a one night stand. Phil went to the coffeemaker and made himself a cup of Cain's. He dumped in a large spoon of sugar to help it down, carrying the cup and book to the divan. He sat beside Wolfgang, set the hot cup on the coffee table, and rubbed the cat's tummy.

Connie wasn't a part of the nightmare world that obsessed him . . . haunted him. Even though their past made it awkward sometimes, she still liked him and he liked her, and she gave him a feeling of peculiar peace. Thinking of her, Phil stared at the book's colorful front cover for a long minute, studying the arty Harry O. Morris working of doctored and bizarrely photographed nude maidens and men, half circling a handsome giant. His lush nakedness was covered by shadows, and pictured beside him was a voluptuous, breathtaking beauty.

DEATH'S SWEET DOOR
a supernaturally
divinely decadent
erotic novel by
SCARLETT SHADE

read the title above the artwork, and above that was the Dark Descent Books imprint of a squiggly Tingler-looking creature, like the one from the old Vincent Price movie, or maybe a French tickler, plummeting into a fiery valley.

"Very Freudian," muttered Phil, glancing at the blurb from Wayne Allen Sallee and a short one from Kelley Wilde. And an all-out encompassing blurb for the entire

Dark Descent line by Stephen King himself, probably traded for a six pack of Black Label.

Phil opened the book and skipped the full page of blurbs for the entire Dark Descent line from *Locus* and other reviewing magazines . . . the absurd editor's message on the next page, assuring the reader of fun and pleasure, not frights.

At last, he read Scarlett's inscription to him on the title page: "I want you very much, dear man. You have so much lust and hate in your veins it makes me wet just to think of drinking you . . . Scarlett Shade."

And below her signature she had sketched a cartoon heart, disembodied fangs sinking into it.

He turned to the dedication: "For Bram Stoker and Montague Summers . . . you guys just didn't understand at all."

Phil turned the next page to Chapter One.

Chapter 2

Mason woke up on a hard floor, blinking at the sights and sounds of the TV.

Still on.

Where the fuck was he?

But as his eyes focused, he recognized the hotel room . . . its dreary department store paintings. From the way the sunlight flooded the place, it must be afternoon already. He grumbled, wondering how he had gotten so drunk. His skull pounded.

He'd probably missed checkout time, too.

He wished he'd fallen unconscious on the bed instead of the floor. Looking down at his nakedness and shifting, he moaned. His rectum was on fire and he gagged in its growing agony . . . like someone had tried to give him an enema with a rough tree branch, or maybe with the open pocket knife beside his leg.

It was stained with a dried darkness. "Shit-fuck!" he winced, getting to his feet, investigating his asshole with probing fingers and a frown of distaste. But despite his raw pain, there was no blood, only a smeary white stickiness of something gross.

Thank God!

Still, he trembled at what he must have done . . . what had certainly been done to him. Everything looked so foggy in the mirror . . . *he* felt so soggy. Like he was still in the midst of his orgasmic dreamland.

Mason held to the back of a chair and steadied himself, gazing into the mirror now filled by the reflection of his bare flesh and not Scarlett. In spite of his suffering and self-disgust, he wished last night's dreams had been true. He loved his dreams. In his dreams, he was everything he wanted to be. In them, Angela begged him to come back to her . . . apologizing for breaking up.

In the dreams, Countess Showery was real, wanting him as much as he wanted her. Scarlett Shade herself . . . the dream fuck of his imagination. He fancied her and himself as he had in his drunken sleep, wishing she really *had* come to him.

But he knew it hadn't happened. She had signed his books and he had come back to fall asleep. The rest was vivid wishfulness.

But he was so fucking *sore*. He knew he'd dreamed of Count Downe, too . . . and how that handsome vampire had seduced him with the Countess, and driven his vampirehood deep up his anus.

It felt like that part of the dream had happened!

That forbidden pleasure had been better than he could imagine . . . and in the dream Count Downe offered himself to Mason as a conquest. Scarlett looking on with approval.

Mason's first real taste of blood . . . *The best fucking bizarre dreams of Mason's life.* He looked at the sunlight flowing through the partially opened window. Mundane reality, once more. Daytime. Fantasy never seemed as real in light.

"Fuck life," Mason muttered, hearing Scarlett's voice moaning her desire for him through the visions of lust.

Mason.

Such a sweet voice, freeing him from the expectations of others that made life drudgery.

Working his tired and sore muscles, Mason yawned. He turned to the disheveled bed. . . .

To the silent body of a long-haired, naked man. The bed sheets were a muddy, dark red-brown and now he noticed the stink of a dirty copper pungency.

The dreams floated wildly around him as he went to the man and turned him over, and Mason began to giggle with new panic as he remembered.

The man's groin was a gnawed mass of drying flesh. His wrists were sliced open neatly to the bone, covered in hardening red goo.

It wasn't a dream, either. Last night *had* happened.

Mason steadied finally, and went to the window, staring out at a bright sun. Even though he'd chewed off the man's dick and guzzled his blood, assisted by Scarlett *herself,* Mason knew he wasn't really a vampire yet.

But right now, more than ever, he wished he was. He was in a shitload of trouble.

He came back to the mirror and flattened his fingers against it, hopefully seeking the entrance to his dreams, but the fantasies had grown dark and all he could see was the reflection of death on the bed behind him.

Someone tapped on the door. "Maid."

Mason stared at the pocket knife open on the floor, thinking of all the suicides he'd read of and never had the balls to imitate.

Until now.

Scarlett Fever.

Chapter 3

Phil sprawled on the divan, Wolfgang on his legs, and read:

Chapter One—Count Downe meets His Match

The castle walls, majestic, glorious, golden in the moonglow, rose up from a grassy ground. They were as firm and unyielding as Count Downe himself.

Multicolored banners fluttered joyously from the highest towers . . . proclaiming to the night sky the jubilance Count Adolph Downe felt within his quivering soul.

Tomorrow. Tomorrow, O day of days and joy of joys . . . For tomorrow was his long-awaited wedding day to his beloved golden-haired cousin Elizabeth Showery . . . the Countess of the palace beyond. The very sight of it on the distant, jagged horizon, gleaming like the love they had known since childhood, made his heart overflow.

"My love of loves," Count Downe uttered the sweet words and laid the back of his hand majestically to his forehead. "Oh, how sweet will be my life now . . . with you at last at my side forever . . . my wife most truly upon the sun's rise . . ."

Then the words froze on his lips as he spied the billowing, white cloud of dust that was approaching faster and faster.

And then, the quick cloppety-clop of noble hooves.

Count Downe's jubilant heart crested and fell when he saw that the stallion . . . and its tall rider . . . were garbed in the rich red-and-blue colors of the crest of Showery: A noble lineage bathed in shame since Elizabeth's long-dead grandmother had cleansed herself in the blood of virgin boys and girls. A hopeless act to hold on to her youth.

As the valiant steed and rider galloped nearer, Downe shuddered with dismay, dreading evil news.

With that paralyzing ice almost solid inside him, he strode to the archway and stairs leading down into his velvet, luxurious rooms.

There, amidst the jewelry of his heritage, he went to the golden couch always ready for him, and lay upon it with a creased, damp brow, facing himself in the gilt mirror across the room.

Waiting.

At last, a knock on the ornate door.

"Enter," spoke Count Downe.

Elegantus, Downe's gifted Latin slave, slid the door to and entered with a deep bow, nearly burying his long face in the golden carpet. "Pardon, Your Majesty," Elegantus cried in virtual agony, distressing Count Downe anew. "I bring ill tidings."

"Speak, Elegantus," Downe whispered in a voice still powerful and deep, not betraying his innermost fears.

Elegantus, now a frail, elderly creature after these years of faithful service to Downe's father and himself, dared to show Count Downe a rheumy eye. His voice, shrill, was yet heavy in his own betrayal of joy. "Your cousin . . . the ravishing Countess . . . your bride in the next day's time . . . is slain, O Count. A messenger has come with this ill news and begs your mercy and forgiveness."

Count Downe stood slowly, the weakness overtaking him even as a hellish fever burned hot on his handsome face. "Slain? O, be it not so! My cousin . . . my lover!" His long fingers overtook his tearful eyes to hide his weakness.

"It . . . it is true, O glorious Count!"

The ecstasy of the future he so anticipated . . . the life he had craved . . . dashed so cruelly in an instant by the fates. The pain of life was too much.

Too cruel.

"Kill the messenger of these evil words," spoke Count Downe, facing his sudden suffering that was yet swelling greater and darker within his heaving bosom.

"It . . . shall be done," obeyed Elegantus, bowing to the floor.

"And," Count Downe found a new strength to utter, "slay yourself, good Elegantus. I would spare you in the future of such a dark service as you were forced to bring to me."

"Kind lord," whispered Elegantus, and as Count Downe wept for all his loss, his faithful servant departed to fulfill the royal directives.

The great door shut solidly.

Count Downe stared into the big mirror with abandon, dreaming his cousin there with him, alive.

The howls, constant, of weeping, echoed hauntingly through Castle Downe all that night . . . into the next day. The mourners beat their breasts in eight-hour shifts to insure that they did not become too weakened to show Downe's unceasing sorrow.

Downe attired himself in sackcloth and covered his royal self in ashes. So many times, his hand strayed to the jeweled dagger at his belt . . . to end this ghastly misery.

But he knew he must live, even in this new vacuous darkness of useless life, to rule as his beloved father had ruled. He did not dare betray his own people as he had been betrayed by the finger of fickle fate.

The night and the wedding day now never to be, passed, but Count Downe did not emerge from his apartments. He did not touch the feasts brought to him, and they were taken away uneaten, thrown to the paupers and dogs.

The dark night fell again. Darker even than the raging sorrow in Count Downe's unending, furious nightmares . . . of himself and his lost love in a life stolen from them.

A joy never to be theirs.

The moon, like his beloved Elizabeth, was no more.

Oh, if only she, like the moon, could yet return to him! Whole and beautiful, and his once more!

114

The torment of this delusion . . . of his need . . . was so heavy over Count Downe's broken heart, he could bear his life no more.

Half mad, Count Downe made himself naked and strode out onto his high roof that overlooked the mourning castle grounds. He stared up at the naked flag poles no longer floating the joyous banners, and then out at the dark shadow on the craggy horizon that was Castle Showery, shamed again, and all but demolished in its terrible loss.

Downe strode back to his apartment and gazed at himself in the gilt-framed mirror, seeing the hollowness of his face that reached deep inside his soul. He raised the glittering dagger before him, aiming its sharp, gleaming point toward his empty heart.

His heart . . . his soul. So filled with love and excitement only two nights before, now dashed to pieces by the torrential, unbending waves of nightmarish fate.

But as he slowly and with urgent precision, slid the blade to touch his fair chest, he saw—

Could it be?

His own countenance was disappearing, replaced by a green mist, and beyond that wispy cloud. . . .

Was it indeed dear Elizabeth's comforting specter, coming at last to strengthen his soul against this evil deed he neared?

The white-clad figure in the shiny glass wafted gently closer, as though floating into his empty soul. The figure, clad deliciously in the loveliest robes Elizabeth had ever worn, grew magically to life size, elevating his crushed heart.

And indeed, it was Elizabeth, her face wondrously pale and perfect as it had always been . . . still filled with the promises of eternal joy, now the reflection of his own desire.

"I'm . . . mad," choked Downe, turning away from her impossible splendor.

And her sweet voice spoke to him: "Nay. Madness is not for nobles as ourselves, dear cousin. I am true. I am truth as you have never known or dared to imagine. Your truth . . . of your desire. We have been trapped so terribly in the drudgery of responsibility not even of our own making! The tradition of life has shackled us from our joys. Even as children, our love and its making had to remain a secret until

115

we were of the age tradition had set upon us. We were not free to seek our desire . . . our pleasure. Life itself was the fearsome chain binding us from one another, and mercifully, life from me was taken, but not so treacherously as it might have been. My dearest grandmother has come to me from the beyond, giving me the secret! I live now, dearest cousin, unhampered by life's wicked lies, to be the fair vision you behold . . . to be the maid I craved to be."

Count Downe gasped, his eyes full of her as she was suddenly as naked as himself . . . her dear body the greatest delight he had ever known. Her slender hand slipped out from the watery glass, eager for him. The cool fingers touched him in his most private places, and he filled them with his own long need.

"We must live for ourselves, dearest Adolph. We must throw aside these burdens which now stand between us forever, and spread our newfound rapture to all who will join us. I am the mirror of your lust. Ours is a new royalty that cannot be touched by death and despair. The blood we spill will not be wasted in the grave, but will feed us as we build a new world of pleasure and self-fulfillment not possible in mere life . . ." She stepped all the way out of the frame, impossibly, but with a gentleness he could not, and did not want to, deny. She bent before him like a slave, and her raised hands slipped the dagger from his, letting it fall with a loud clatter beside them. "There is no love but what is ourselves, dear cousin. Our life is our love . . . and if you would give that love to me, I will devour it and give you the death that is more than life itself. More than love. The end of self-deceit and the beginning of a pleasure and every desire that will be yours for the taking. Undeath."

Count Downe, still stunned by her soft tone and the extravagance of a beauty even more than he could recall in his former days with her, laid his palms upon her silky, white-blond locks. She bent forward, her hair brushing between his thighs, gliding her mouth over him until his hardness increased in her jaws.

Her lively tongue, cold, but so delicate and masterful, filled him with a greater warmth than he had known from her as even a youth. Not even in those times when they played this very game in the hiding places, far from watchful eyes.

116

Shuddering, biting his lips against this building storm of the greatest ecstasy he'd ever known, Count Downe shoved himself deeply into her hot throat, and did not flinch as her teeth closed tight around his thickness . . . as her fangs bit deep and a hot suction dragged the very blood of life and love from his veins.

At last, so weak he could no longer stand, Count Downe fell into her comforting arms. She turned his face to the mirror and he saw the room, empty of him or her. He held in his gasp as she laid his head upon a pillow, whispering: "You have departed from the life you have served, cousin. But you will rise again as I. You must come to me in the darkness and we will build our kingdom of fantasy. You will have a thousand wives and I a thousand husbands, because two cannot fulfill the truest joy alone. Undeath is so sweet, my dear, and we must rejoice that we have escaped the rigid confines of our ancestors. Death and life are meaningless without love, and in our acceptance of undeath we reject all limitations of love . . . of life . . . of death. To love is to serve. To live is to serve. Undeath is to command . . . to revel . . . There can be no loss once we have rejected life."

Phil put down the book and shut his eyes. The written words of Scarlett Shade made his heart tight. A sorrow was in them for himself and his long-dead cousin, Sonia, back when he was a mere boy and she was but thirteen. He looked into a mirror, seeing her death . . . the reflection of that moment still inside him and feeling the guilt of lost love that had trapped him.

She would never be older. He would never see her again.

The scenes reminded him of the way Sonia had taken off her old, patched dress, parading before him as he fought the buttons of his pants.

Her young breasts and body mesmerized him as she flowed into his arms, as she guided him inside herself. She told him she loved him.

117

And he still loved her.

But the next day, the tanks had come. Death had ended their courtship. Phil tried to stop the shudder of his spine and picked up the phone, calling Kevin again, this time only getting his answering machine. He felt like the character, Neville, in Matheson's *I Am Legend* . . . the last human being on earth . . . and if Scarlett Shade was really a vampire like the ones in her books, if his dreams were real, he wasn't even that.

Because he, too, was infected.

It was a long fifteen minutes before Phil could begin reading again.

Chapter 4

"Phil called again. He left a message on the answering machine."

Kevin didn't smile. "Again?"

"Second time today. Don't you think you ought to call him back?"

On a Sunday, no less. Kevin still liked Phil, even though Phil had always kept an inner distance from everyone for as long as Kevin had known him. He didn't mind a call from a friend even on the lazy weekends as he recuperated from listening to the wackos he dealt with during the work week, but Phil was rapidly becoming an unofficial patient himself, and a nonpaying one at that. He looked from his book to Denise, a pretty woman, even dressed in her "Sunday sloppies": torn jeans and a paint-stained work shirt he'd cast off long ago. Her short brown hair was mussed beyond repair, but that was the price of marriage and love . . . it replaced the fantasy of romance so many of his patients felt they couldn't live without. "What did Phil want?"

"He said he had some kind of a problem or something and acted like you knew something about it . . . he sounded pretty depressed. Depressed and *desperate.*" Denise glanced back at their five-year-old daughter as the dog howled. She was pulling its tail. "Stop that, Karen!"

Kevin felt a smile tug at him as Karen stared blankly at her mother and began to cry. The terrier high-tailed it to safety, coming to crouch at Kevin's feet. He dropped a hand and stroked the fur. Denise picked Karen up and consoled her . . . the wrong thing to do, but Kevin didn't tell her again. "So what's Phil's problem?" Denise asked.

Kevin shrugged, closing the book and putting it down, feeling guilty just looking at it. It was the rare collector's piece by Stephen King, *Dolan's Cadillac*. Phil had loaned it to Kevin last year before he left his job at the state hospital, and Kevin was just now getting around to reading it. He knew he could probably keep it forever if he wanted to and Phil would never remember, with all his other worries. Kevin even felt he'd earned the book by trying to help Phil out lately.

"Kevin?"

"A patient's problems are supposed to be confidential."

"You said he wasn't a patient because he wasn't paying you . . . I won't tell anyone." She put Karen down and the dog cringed.

Kevin watched them both carefully. "Phil closes out the world because it scares him . . . just like a lot of others. Just like all those damn Shade fans."

"Is Phil suicidal, too?"

"Maybe," Kevin said, looking back down at the unjacketed, signed book. "I think Phil's struggling to find a purpose now that his wife is divorcing him . . . now that he's working for himself and not someone else. I believe he feels he's losing his motivation, so he's developing some pretty absurd fantasies to keep going."

Denise sat beside him, close, laying her head on his shoulder. "We all do that, Kevin. How do you think you convinced me to marry you!"

He chuckled with her, but didn't feel the laughter at all. He stared at the book. "Phil's fantasies could become dangerous," he told her. "They're already close to that for

120

himself . . . but they could get that way for other people, too. He needs some real help . . . and he's broke."

Denise picked up the TV remote and turned it on. "Money." She flipped the channels, one after another. "Nobody cares . . . unless they're getting something out of it themselves."

"Well . . . I care. I've been helping him for nothing, okay? I just don't feel up to him right now. I'll call him tomorrow." But when he picked the book back up, the guilt for Phil grew. Then, in the pages of a fantasy, it dimmed.

Chapter 5

Another convention over.

Back in her dark basement office at last.

Scarlett Shade looked at the decor of her lair. More a lair in truth than many writers' work rooms, because now she often enjoyed picturing herself as a black widow spinning her sticky web for victims . . . the victims of life.

She could relate to them all since she was a writer and it was her business to relate to anyone, and it hadn't been that long since she'd been a victim herself.

Then, she'd been *turned.* Jeanne, still looking like a beauty queen despite her hundred years on the earth, had become her mentor, luring Scarlett out of a convention motel, burying her in secret, then meeting Scarlett the first night she rose from the unmarked grave. Jeanne had read her books and liked them . . . especially her literary discovery of mirror-travel. It had given her a wild idea for greater domination, and she herself taught Scarlett her tricks of seduction. Although Scarlett rarely saw her anymore, she still received occasional letters, sometimes even a phone call.

Standing, Scarlett picked up a thank-you bouquet of roses splattered in the blood of Jeanne's most recent satiation. "Dear Scarlett, A fan of yours begged me to bite her . . . Thanks, Jeanne, read the card.

So Scarlett knew that Jeanne's plan was working for others besides herself.

The computer screen lit up as Scarlett sat behind her desk and switched it on. Its glow filled the room, shining amber on the gray file cabinets. Behind her, the mahogany shiny in the rare absence of total gloom, was Scarlett's coffin. She didn't bring the wooden box along with her to the conventions, of course. A little pinch of her burial earth and a dark room did fine.

But here, the casket was out in plain view. One of the perks of being a horror writer. Along with the mirrors she collected and hung on the far stone wall, it was a natural for her setting.

The mirrors were like video camera monitors, looking into more than a hundred of the lives that fed her, and she could shift their scenes from one soul to another like flipping channels on TV. Sometimes Scarlett used the mirrors as investigative devices for the lives that *would* feed her. During her research for *Death's Sweet Door,* Scarlett had studied past the *Vampire* heading into *Voodoo:* sympathetic magic . . . the use of images to affect the reality of the self. She'd learned how mirrors reflected the soul and the desires held inside. Mirrors were a natural step and Scarlett had hypothesized that it was only misunderstanding that a vampire could not be seen in a looking glass: the undead gave up their souls for eternal physical pleasure without guilt, and that was why they didn't seem to be visible in a reflection.

But for a supernatural being, mirrors were a psychic *Star Trek* transporter system.

It had been a daring step of imagination for her as a writer, and after she was *turned*, she'd been overjoyed to learn that her conjectures were true.

Mirrors were everywhere . . . and just in case, Scarlett, like her characters, always wore her necklace. The devices made her secret convention work very easy. When she seduced a victim through the mirror of their lives, only the reflection of her bite was visible. After the voluntary suicides of her fans in the past, it was another natural step for her to make her intentional victims appear to be a resurgence of those suicides.

A supernatural step. Even more. For those in tune with her words, she found she could enter their souls without even drinking their blood, possessing them, using them for her purposes. The psychic connection to their lust and feeding fed Scarlett almost as well as if she were guzzling blood herself.

But it wasn't quite the same . . . not as fulfilling, even if safer. So, she flirted with danger and still seduced some choices personally.

But the fans and novice writers she occasionally invited by always admired her casket first. None of them ever guessed that she actually spent several of the day's hours *inside* it. Not until she proved to some of them that the fangs in her mouth were quite real.

Scarlett felt the power of undeath she had perfected under Jeanne's guidance. Her fingers hesitated above the keyboard. Besides its seductive uses for victims, writing helped her to fill the empty wasted period between the rising and setting sun, although her best work was still done after dark.

In the shadow of undeath.

Scarlett bent down to her travel bag and took out the three fat manuscripts Gary had delivered to her along with every ounce of his blood. She carried her load back to the computer and sat down, wondering if Gary or the others, including his would-be interviewer friend from Amarillo, would manage to rise after their autopsies and burials. But even if they did, they would go after their new blood desire with little idea of what they were doing. The confusion of a vampire's resurrection was strong . . . much like that of a newborn babe into life. It was hard for most to release the things of life that had been so important to them without guidance. It was nearly impossible for most to come to grips with the truth once they knew it. When the lucky ones figured out what had happened, if they didn't perfect their technique for seduction or get luckier, they would still be searching for a willing victim for days, getting weaker all the time . . . eventually, too powerless to materialize on the ground above their graves. When that happened, they were trapped within their coffins, alone and hungry, until the end of time. Jeanne had warned Scarlett to give the gift of understanding to only a few others. People who might not, at first, want to be vampires . . . who would carry on thoughtfully without drawing attention.

Like Connie.

Connie had been completely sucked in by her overly romantic prose, like all the others, but Scarlett planned better for Connie. She'd laughed at her own lost romanticism, but loved reliving its taste through that sweet little convamp. The memories had flooded her senses. Connie would make a wonderful vampire if Scarlett could seduce her to devotion.

She whispered her name, "Connie . . . dear Connie . . ." She knew Connie would hear her. Connie was already infected with the pleasure of her words, and now, her bite. She revered mirrors, too, and Scarlett was using the secret of those reflections better than Jeanne had ever planned. The fabricated selfishness in most such images were closely connected to her domain, and it was so easy to spread her influence through the glass, just as she did through her books . . . a thousand of them all at once. Soon, a *hundred thousand!*

Connie would soon be hers.

Sighing with anticipation for that blood, Scarlett felt her juices of dark creativity peaking in the lives she had consumed. She needed to write . . . or at least, rewrite, and then, she thought she might pop down to the old man in the rest home who had been feeding her the slight snacks between conventions these past two months.

But like so many others, he was nearly empty now.

Chapter 6

Teresa Carson closed and opened her eyes again and again. The darkness was the same either way. She'd already spent an eternity in the bleakness and was beginning to wonder if it would ever end. She had first figured that she must be comatose, lying unknowingly on some hospital bed while forever trapped inside her mind. Finally, she'd decided that this was the lonely afterlife of some hell she had never taken seriously. She felt the presence of others around her, heard the moans, but couldn't connect to anything but their despairs . . . to her own. The last thing she could remember with any confidence was the wonderful sensation of a mouth . . . knowledgeable lips, a tongue, and teeth, suffocating her, but bringing her the greatest excitement of her life.

Teeth. When she had missed the need to breathe, and touched her own, she'd *known,* and Teresa had wanted to groan and feel sorry for herself.

Because she was *dead.* One knowledge had led to another, but she still didn't know how to get out. She replayed it all once more, not liking the way it was getting harder to move in this confinement . . . the way she was becoming steadily weaker. The cushions sighed under her and Teresa raised her hands to the silky cloth above her face again. *How could she really be dead if she was moving? How could she be thinking if she was dead?*

How?

The Scarlett Shade books. Scarlett Shade herself. Scarlett and herself, naked on the bed, sucking each other like wild animals . . . it seemed so long ago through the dark hours she'd spent since. Somehow, she knew that days had passed. She couldn't forget the sharp pinch of Scarlett's teeth sinking into her, and then the sensation of weakness as every measure of her own existence was being drawn out of her by those teeth.

Every pain.

Teeth. The publicity vampire fangs in Scarlett's mouth were unbelievably *real.*

Teresa scraped her fingernails across the inside top of the casket surrounding her. She dropped those fingers to her mouth and felt her own sharp incisors once more. *She* was a vampire. "I'm a vampire!" Teresa muttered to herself for the thousandth time, "so why can't I get out of here?" She forced her memory back to Scarlett's books, knowing she had to imagine herself as nothing . . . a vapor. It seemed so easy, but it was really difficult to do. A vapor was merely an essence, nearly nothing, and to become that, she had to believe herself as that.

Nearly nothing, and then she would recreate herself out of the memories she had left, making a lie . . . a something, appearing as *something*. . . .

From *nothing*.

Teresa moaned. With all her concentration, she released her concerns for life at last . . . even her desire, hopes, for true love.

Until she was a vacuum sucking in the emptiness that surrounded her. She became a part of it completely.

Life.

Forever gone.

She felt herself a breath of shapeless mist and slipped

out of the coffin . . . rematerialized inside a damp, shadowed mausoleum, remembering the books to imagine her clothing as she did. Her remaining senses were more sensitive than she would have ever imagined they could be, full of the life no longer a part of her. It made her starving. She sniffed the air that was filled with a million scents . . . oil and gas, food of every kind, sweat . . . tears . . .

Blood.

That scent was the strongest of all. She licked her pointed teeth with continued amazement, and slid her feet across the marble floor. When she stepped into the moonlit grounds of a grassy, well populated cemetery, she glanced down at her black gown . . . just like the one Scarlett had worn. It was really fine on her, too . . . and she had imagined even that necklace. Teresa handled it delicately, looking into the frame.

She saw only the autumn trees and monuments behind her in the glass.

She *was* a vampire. "This would make a great story for the magazines," Teresa chuckled. "Really great."

But what was the point? With life gone, who cared? Teresa rubbed her middle automatically with a feeling of hunger, even though that feeling was nothing like she had ever known before. She sniffed the air again, trying to separate the various blood scents, but all of them smelled delicious. "No reason to be picky, I guess," she told herself, finding a brick path that led to a narrow road, then following that asphalt trail. She felt a little nervous at first, like she was still naked, and she wondered how she would react if the night watchman found her out here like this.

Remembering what she was, Teresa just gave a giggle. "I'd bite the dude." She thought of her new power, feeling better and better about this arrangement.

At last, Teresa rounded a corner and saw the gate and its decorative rose bushes, its iron-barred doors shut tight.

"So what?" she said, recalling another page from the Shade works and just following directions. This was easy once you knew what you were doing.

What you were.

Once you admitted to being nothing . . . a lie of life.

Teresa felt giddy, becoming a mist, and she slid herself through the bars, down a trashy sidewalk toward a gritty-looking wino, surrounding him like a puff of smoke. She wanted to laugh at her joke as he rubbed his red, pulpy nose and his bloodshot eyes went wide in terror.

But like this . . . she had no mouth. She couldn't even smile, and his blood-streaked eyes reminded her strongly of her need . . .

But not *him*.

She let the winds blow her down a winding street, leaving the wino still choking, and the familiar mountain-scape above city buildings proved to her that Mom and Dad had buried her in the family crypt. She had not been interested in her location in the relief of escape, but now, locale gave her a needed familiarity.

Mom and Dad.

Teresa reformed. They had disowned her after the pictorial she had posed for . . . stopped sending her money. They certainly deserved her teeth.

Gary, too. This would teach him to pay more attention to his writing than her.

But first . . .

She remembered her boyfriend from high school . . . the one who'd popped her cherry after leading her from her church background. Then he turned his back on her when he got Jesus. He'd told her he was too good for her . . . that a woman's virginity was her ultimate trust and that she had given hers up so he couldn't even desecrate himself by talking to her anymore. He refused responsibility for having been the one to take her innocence away.

Placing herself in the streets, Teresa followed her thirst

to Brian's apartment house. She looked at the old two-story structure, finding his door on the second level. Still licking at her teeth, she flowed up the outside stairway, her fingers gliding the smooth rail. She stopped, unable to enter.

Again, Teresa remembered. She had to be invited.

She knocked lightly, sensing him inside. Felt him get up out of his chair to answer.

The door opened. His face turned sheet white.

"Brian . . ."

The door slammed shut.

Not cool. Not cool at all. Teresa fought her frustration and started to knock again. She was hungry, and the odor of Brian's life was something she wanted to taste! Her hands clawed at her gown as she tried to think . . . to remember.

The mirror.

Teresa touched her necklace idly, wondering how true to life . . . to death . . . to undeath . . . Scarlett's books were. Would Scarlett's bizarre twist work? Desperate for his blood, Teresa looked into the circular glass and thought of Brian deeply, forming his face in her thoughts . . . then into the mirror, until his likeness filled it as if it were her own reflection.

Her lust. Belief in only that lust.

"Brian," she whispered, stroking the surface of the glass with a deft finger, just the way Countess Showery did . . . and as though he could see her, Brian's features edged tight . . . the image of his bulging eyes staring straight at her.

A moment later, she heard him unlock his door, and then she was looking into the reality of those glazed eyes. He made a choked noise, holding up his jittery hands, backing into his living room as she entered, trying to free himself from her gaze.

"Surprised to see me, Brian?" she chuckled, appraising

131

his simple new lifestyle of stick chairs and bare walls. "You've certainly humbled yourself."

"I . . ." He took his chance as she broke their contact and bent fast to the coffee table, lifting a Bible.

"You don't need that," she told him softly. "You don't even really believe in that stuff, do you? I can see inside you now, Brian. You're just afraid to die in a car wreck like your brother did. Fear of death isn't faith, dude. You rejected me . . . denied me your love, and I'm going to take your life for that. Life and love is the same lie to both of us. They're pretty and nice to imagine, and I bet they taste good, but I'm beyond all that now. I'm in a fantasy world . . ." And just like that, Teresa's clothes were gone.

"T-Teresa—" He dropped his Bible, open-mouthed, and she pushed him back to his couch. She opened his slacks as he sat still. "I . . . I can't stop you," he sighed, "can I?"

He wanted this as much as she did . . . an excuse for his own lusts. Teresa looked deep inside his eyes at the clash of fear and desire. "Especially not if you don't want to," she smiled, and clamped her teeth into his most sensitive flesh. As he trembled, hard in her jaws, she relished this first taste of another life, living his experiences. When he was empty, she remembered caution and knew from the thoughts she'd caught in Brian's head how Scarlett had made Teresa's own death appear a suicide. Teresa went to Brian's kitchen, took a steak knife, and sawed it sloppily across his wrists.

This wasn't so hard . . . it was kind of fun. Teresa's near perfect memory remembered *Blood Fever: The seduction is our greatest power. These confused humans want to believe in the pleasures and eternal existence we can bring them. None but a few truly believe in eternal damnation. It's too frightening. No one wants to deny the things they want for eternal life, and if we can give them a death that is existence as well, they will deny the fears they were taught as children.*

"Thanks, Scarlett," said Teresa. She turned back to Brian's white-gray flesh and collapsed veins, shaking her head. "This time, I popped your cherry, Brian, and believe me, you bled a hell of a lot more than I did." She saluted his death and opened his door, leaving the apartment more traditionally than she had entered it.

She was still hungry.

Chapter 7

Near midnight, Connie only wanted to find a cheap hotel and crash. But driving through Kansas was like driving through no man's land. There weren't many cars on the highway. The civilized areas were few and far between, so the night was a moonlit landscape of flat country farmland . . . a wasteland. She fit a tape into the player and smiled as the speakers sprayed out the loud buzz of a synthesizer, thinking of the frequent battles she and Phil had over music. He hated rock and only listened to soundtracks and light classical stuff. She kept her eyes on the highway and the rolling plains, fighting boredom by relishing the drum beat and frantic rolls of a keyboard.

Last night's dreams still bothered her. Scarlett's voice calling her . . . all night long, seeking her as she slept. Near visions of Scarlett and herself naked and kissing vague in those cobwebs. *Was it real or Memorex?*

Connie knew it couldn't have been real. It was just a dream linking fantasy to her inebriated fragments of reality. She *should* have stayed sober. Connie unwrapped a stick of gum and chewed it furiously. "God, it feels like the whole frigging weekend was a one-hundred-proof dream. No more booze for me!" She hesitated as though someone might be listening and hold her to the oath. "At least . . . not so much."

The car trembled as it jolted over a chughole. Connie yelped, her breast pinched by a hot needle.

For five more miles, the pain got worse, and finally, gritting her teeth, Connie slowed the Escort to a stop at the side of the dark highway. The bright reflection of a speed sign spilled over her.

The pain was a vibration of desire and dread all at once, titillating and frightening her at the same moment.

She turned on the dome light, then opened the buttons on her shirt, staring at the bandage. She pulled it loose and saw nothing.

"This is really *strange,*" she whispered, taking the compact out of her purse. She opened it, chilled anew by the shiny image of tiny holes around her nipple. They were still bright red, but the color wasn't spreading. Her eyes moved back and forth from the nipple to its mirror likeness and she gritted her teeth.

Now you see it, now you don't.

Impossible . . . and just looking at the impossible and dwelling on it was making her want to scream.

Dropping the compact, Connie sagged back in the cushions and replayed the moments in the bar after Gary had left her and Scarlett. A shudder shook her at the way Scarlett had disappeared.

If she'd ever even been there . . . maybe Scarlett was a ghost. . . .

"And maybe I'm a ghost, too." Connie recalled the blurry moment when she had been beside Scarlett and faced a mirror . . . and seen only Scarlett. She'd been completely plastered. Maybe she *was* crazy . . . maybe the whole weekend was a nightmare and she would wake up in her safe bed screaming. Just the way Phil screamed himself awake twice a week.

A nightmare?

Scarlett's lips . . . and teeth . . . around her nipple.

"Oh . . ." Despite the hot desire her thoughts woke, she

135

shook her head, not believing that nebulous green fog of memory. "Scarlett flew out of a mirror and bit me," she breathed sarcastically. "Sure thing. It happens every day." She sipped from her open bottle of orange juice, trying to clear her mind.

After a few minutes her breast felt better, barely throbbing.

She stopped in Wichita to use the bathroom and fill the tank with gas. The city's stench made her drive out of there fast, but she picked up a late dinner at a truck stop, far enough from the factories that she didn't have to hold her nose.

More hours passed before Connie was at last steering the expressway through a sleepy Oklahoma City behind a turtle-paced station wagon. Since she'd grown up here, she barely noticed the occasional oil derricks left standing. She sped up when she passed Moore and got on the exit lane to Norman, doing her best not to listen to the hypnotic rhythm of the Escort's rolling tires. Their gentle hum tried to lull her into the sleep she craved, almost like the voice of her dreams calling her.

Con . . . nie.

Ten more miles passed.

She looked out the windshield at the new dark flatlands full of warehouses and homes. The empty spaces they replaced since her youth were now busy with construction equipment and half-erected structures.

The world was changing so fast.

Connie heard a honk from somewhere behind and glanced up at the rearview mirror . . . *froze.*

"N-no—" Her left foot crushed the brake and the Escort's tires screeched. More honks blared and a yellow LTD shot into the lane beside her. It nearly nipped her back bumper as the driver shoved his arm out the window and gave her the shaft.

"Jesus—" But in the blink of her eyes, it was her face looking back at her once more, not Scarlett Shade's.

Connie shuddered. "Jesus," she groaned again, turning the Escort off on the exit ramp. Five minutes later, she passed Phil's small store and parked at her old red brick apartment a block beyond. She got out and walked to the scratched front door.

Connie heard the voice somewhere inside her head. *Connie . . . dear Connie.* Once more, Connie's sore breast seemed to throb.

She was *tired*. Being tired was like being drunk, sometimes. She held to that weak explanation, making herself forget Scarlett, even the scenes in Scarlett's books she'd wanted to enact with Gary.

Gary had shown how much he cared for her.

Fuck Gary.

She got through her door and grunted, stubbing her toe on one of the boxes inside. Connie groaned and flipped on the light, flinching at the bright reflections in the living room. "Shit," she whispered, looking at her face over and over, relieved, and at the same time strangely disappointed it was her own.

Her toe stopped throbbing as Connie slipped into the hallway and glanced into the spare bedroom at Phil. His slim face twitched under his beard.

She almost woke him to tell him she was back . . . complain about the boxes louder than ever. . . .

But for once, he seemed to be sleeping peacefully . . . and she *was* tired.

She wanted to relax. To dream.

Sunlight. Even though her body ached, especially her sore breast, Connie made herself get out of the security of the warm bed.

She stretched and wrinkled her nose at the sweaty musk

of her T-shirt. Her eyes moved through her bedroom from the double bed that looked as though it had gone through half a dozen garage sales . . . past the rickety night stand and its scarred wood-look lamp, her makeshift bookshelves created from cast-off lumber and bricks. The dresser mirror flashed in the morning rays of the sun and the two wall mirrors repeated that brightness.

She squinted at the stacks of Phil's books piled all over the dirty green carpet even in here. "What this place needs is a demolition crew."

This wasn't exactly the palace of her dreams, especially not now. She rubbed her still sore toe. It didn't look as though he'd done much to clean things up over the weekend, either.

She passed into the short hallway. Although narrow, Phil had still stacked more of the cardboard boxes all the way through it. She remembered the way she first chuckled when he'd put half a dozen boxes in the bathroom. Enough reading material to spend your life on the toilet.

But it wasn't funny anymore.

Phil was still snoring when Connie passed his door. Sunlight slipped in through the blue curtains. She yawned and studied his grisly posters walling the crowded room, surprised he'd taken several down. "No wonder you have nightmares, Phil," she whispered to herself.

The living room was more boxes, her ratty couch and coffee table, and, of course, some of the mirrors she'd begun collecting even before reading Scarlett. With a look at one of them, she touched her breast, but knew she wouldn't see anything crazy in them now that she was sober and rested. Phil's sleek cat arched his back and yawned when she came near, hissing a warning.

"Good kitty," Connie reassured it, keeping her distance from its place on the cushions. She looked at the videotapes Phil had haphazardly dumped around her twelve-inch TV set. Universal classics, Hammer flicks, Dario Argento. "What a life."

She needed to call Mom and let her and Dad know she was back safely. Her phone was on the floor . . . an old black rotary dial one. She stepped around more boxes and picked it up, but eyeing the wary cat, she decided not to tempt fate and just sat down on the carpet.

"Hi, Mom," she said a minute later. "I got back early this morning, and I made some good money. I—"

The excited, frantic tones of her mother cut her off and she stared at the exposed book titles all around her sightlessly.

Listened.

Chapter 8

The distant, static sound of the TV and noisy talk show conversations were *not* part of his nightmares. Phillip Ottoman blinked and groaned at the high-pitched voices that crackled as though in the midst of a fire. He stared through the still-foreign bedroom, flooded with his books, wondering what the hell was happening.

Connie?

He worked to make himself calm, and walked into the living room slowly, forcing a smile as his striped cat bounded up to him like a dog. It stood on its hind legs and he dropped a hand to stroke it. The voices assaulting him were from one of the network channels he tried so hard to avoid.

Just the thought of TV's violent news was bringing back his headache, bitterly reminding him of where the sewer tunnel led him in his nightmares. But he held his tongue, remembering that this was Connie's home, not his. "Good, Wolfgang."

Connie turned away from the snow-filled TV screen. Its human images and background was blurry and filled with lines, and the electronic crackle still fuzzed the voices from its speaker. "Good morning, Phil," Connie said, her voice tight.

"I . . . I'm glad you're back. When did you get in? I didn't even hear you."

Her round face was tense and her narrow eyebrows clenched. She shook her head back and forth. "Phil— listen to me! I called my mom and she was so worried— the police found three people dead at the hotel back in Denver! More suicides. God, I sure hope it wasn't anyone I know!"

"What?" he stared at her blankly.

"That's what Mom said. I'm sorry about the noise, but I just want to find out what's going on—"

Phil put his hand on the divan's arm and sat down on the wasted cushions heavily, his head awash in the pressure of violence long ago. He stared into one of the mirrors at the fuzzy, colorful likeness of Sally Jessy Raphael darting through her audience, glad when Connie turned down the sound of her sharp voice.

Pressure.

As though some giant, invisible hand were crushing his skull. He did his best to fight the approaching seizure.

"Hey—take it easy, Phil!"

The warmth of her hand on his helped drive back the iron grip, and he knew he was crushing her fingers. The strain worked its way into his every muscle.

Connie yelped and her face twisted, but she didn't pull away.

And that made it better. More and more quickly, the guilt force and inner fear eased, and he finally released her and dropped back to the cushion behind him, breathing deep and laboriously. "Th-thanks," he forced his trembly voice.

"Jesus, Phil. You had better take it easy . . . this is too crazy! What is it that sets you off like this? Is it Czeckovslovakia again?"

He shook his head, feeling the oily, limp hair smack up

141

and down on his low forehead. "I . . . I don't know. It . . . it just happens . . ."

She stared at him with sympathetic confusion.

Knowing that she cared helped, but already, the pressure was building again. He wanted to tell her what he believed . . . about Scarlett Shade . . . but what good would it do to tell her or anyone else?

Who would believe him?

He wasn't always sure he believed it, himself. "Please, get some Tylenol, Connie—"

She stood fast and nodded, hurrying to the bathroom. Phil flinched at the sound of a crash and heavy thumps, imagining the stack of books she'd just knocked down.

But they weren't important. When he got like this, nothing at all seemed important.

The sound of running water in the bathroom as she filled a cup for him was so distant, as though she and these surroundings were part of another world.

All Phil could think of was that more people had died. More senseless suicides . . . people rejecting life for death.

Scarlett Fever?

Vampires?

"And the earth is flat," Phil chided himself, his heart at last slower and steadier.

Connie barely spoke of the convention as she and Phil sat at her tiny kitchenette bar and ate breakfast. He was calm again and the TV was silent, but she avoided the subjects he told her he didn't like, her face a cautious mask. They drank coffee and chewed their food without trying to impress each other, both of them slurping and smacking loudly.

"I sold a lot of your books, Phil. I sold a lot of jewelry, too. Maybe I could loan you some money for a deposit on an apartment."

142

He glanced at her over the table and gnawed a rubbery slice of bacon, liking its deep smell more than the taste. "In a hurry to get rid of me, huh?"

Her lips turned down. "You know I don't like all the clutter. I stubbed my toe last night, and sometimes, I like to have the TV on, even when I'm not watching. Nothing personal."

Phil nodded. "You don't like the way I freak out sometimes, too."

Connie shook her head. "I don't like it, but that's because it worries me and I don't know what I can do about it."

"There's nothing *you* can do." He chewed and sipped from his glass of orange juice. "I've tried every therapy I could. It was better for a long time. I haven't had the damn nightmares this often in years. They're worse than when I was a kid now."

"You ought to go back to the hospital," Connie said.

"I don't even have the money for a place to *live*," Phil grumbled. "Besides, Kevin . . . other doctors, too, told me that there's not much they can do besides prescribe drugs that will just make me a walking zombie. This is something I have to come to grips with myself."

"I know." Connie wiped her mouth with a napkin and gulped. "I really can't stand you being here sometimes, Phil, but I do care. No matter what I've said when I was pissed, I want you to stay here until you feel better." She blushed. "I worry about you, Phil."

"Until I feel better?" He laughed, but it wasn't humor. "You could be stuck with me for the rest of your life . . . my life, at least." Connie's eyes were in his, but she didn't say a word. Phil blushed this time. "Well, I'm sorry I didn't straighten up much. I tried, but just didn't feel up to it. I took your advice and started reading *Death's Sweet Door* instead."

Her face barely twitched, but he saw the way her eyes perked up. "Really? What did you think?"

Holding himself back, he didn't mention the way the book had connected so deeply to his emotions, afraid it would lead to discussing his nightmares of Scarlett herself. He'd had enough serious discussion for today already . . . but this was just the ticket out if he steered his words correctly. Connie loved to talk horror literature, especially Scarlett's. "I haven't finished it, yet," Phil said with calculation. "Shade's 'purple' prose is just a bit heavy. The way she describes orgasms as tidal waves on the ocean and drinking blood as 'sipping from the fountain of youth' is a little too much."

"Well, she's still my favorite writer of *all time*. The reviewers all say she's the most promising new horror novelist in years! I think she's going to be bigger than King . . . and . . . *I* think she has really *nice* descriptions." Connie blushed. "I actually met her, Phil. I really met her and she bought me a drink. It was so nice." Connie leaned back in her chair and smiled. "I dreamed of her and her books all night long. I'd love to get nibbled by her Count Downe!"

Phil stared at her and made himself take a deep breath, drawn back to the dreams in spite of himself . . . the same way Scarlett's words seemed to encourage fantasies in Connie . . . in all her fans.

But they weren't fantasies to him—his nightmares stood in the way of her visions. All he could see was the horror of his past . . . how Scarlett Shade seemed to emulate that terror. In her books, in his dreams.

Undeath. Phil remembered his uncle's long-ago words . . . the way Scarlett's characters craved the slavery he had escaped.

Undeath.

"What's wrong?"

"Nothing . . . just . . . I don't think horror's supposed

144

to be pleasant," he replied flatly, refusing the other words that wanted to come out. "If someone or something makes evil seem like something to be desired and appealing, I think maybe they're only making the problems worse. I . . . I think some of those influences are the real reason for Scarlett Fever."

"Don't blame Scarlett for that again!" Connie frowned, but then she giggled. "Just listen to you, Phil . . . You sound like my father or something. That's just the kind of stuff he would say."

He shook his head and forced a new grin. "Don't make my hot European blood rise, Connie."

She cocked an eye at him. "Really, you *can't* blame Scarlett for any of what happened. She's had to take a lot of crap, and I was glad to meet her and tell her *I* don't blame her! Remember what good ol' Hitchcock said. You remember? People started blaming him for the shower murders that copycatted his movie, *Psycho,* and he told them that all he had provided for the murderers was a method for a motive and desire already there. He said that at least a murder in a shower was a lot easier to clean up after."

"Yeah. Well, Robert Bloch actually wrote *Psycho,* and Stephen King wanted to sue for plagiarism for murders ripped off from his plots, but at least all those guys show evil as something despicable. They don't show monsters and vampires as poor, misunderstood people who just don't know any better."

"That's exactly what happened in *Psycho,*" she said. "You *can't* blame Scarlett for any of what happened. She gave an interview in *Locus* and said she hated the way the nuts used her books in their crackpot ways. She's really had to take a lot of *shit!* Besides," Connie said, lowering her tone, "sometimes those books can cause influences that you might *enjoy* if you'd stop being so serious and just let up . . ."

"But we're talking about suicides and not murders, aren't we?" Phil felt the heat building in his face, his unsaid accusations for Scarlett growing stronger.

"Yeah," she said. "But it's the same idea."

"No. Believe me, Connie. Murder and suicide are worlds apart. It usually takes very different forms of mental illness to cause the two. They just seem similar. To generalize simply, murder is a hatred of others and self, and suicide is a hatred of self and others."

"A riddle? Don't get so heavy on me, Phil . . . I quit college, remember? Like I said, just lighten up."

Phil remembered Kevin instructing him to take life more gently, too, and he closed his mouth, letting her presence calm him . . . by looking at her. She really wasn't beautiful, but she *was* pleasant to look at. Her always braless breasts, not huge but nice enough, were clearly outlined by her T-shirt. They sometimes made him regret breaking it off with her now.

But he'd thought that Katherine had loved him. He'd wanted to build a life with Katherine and raise a child. He was responsible to her through their vows, first, even before a responsibility to himself. It was another reason he didn't care for Scarlett's untraditional stories with vampires as heroes. He *liked* tradition, at least to a point. It gave him something to cling to against his inner hell. That was why he had held to the Catholic belief against divorce and extramarital affairs . . . or at least, had tried to.

But it hadn't done any good. Maybe the divorce was the cost of his sin with Connie. Or maybe it was because he *was* crazy.

"Don't look so morose, Phil. You might like the influences in Scarlett's stuff if you gave them a chance, know what I mean?" Connie purred . . . a warmer purr than his cat Wolfgang had ever managed.

A purr of promise. Even though the moments between them were long since over, Phil squirmed. "You've been reading too many of those damn sex scenes in Shade's books, Connie."

She pulled back slowly. "You're right. And now you're getting divorced."

He shrugged, biting a lip. Connie sat back and straightened her blouse, winking. "Just kidding, Phil. We're just friends now, right?"

"Right," he said. He forced an unfelt smile he couldn't keep from going crooked.

She peered at him more closely. "Are you sure you're feeling okay?"

"I'm fine," he assured her.

"Bull. Look, Phil, I feel guilty about leaving you when you get like you were this morning. What if—"

"I'm all right," he said again, more gruffly. "I don't usually have this much trouble. It's just the divorce." He reached across the table and squeezed her fingers. "I feel much better now."

She made a face. "But it'll happen again, won't it? Phil, I *do* worry about you. I wasn't kidding . . . maybe," she paused, "maybe you really ought to just stay in my apartment . . . at least until you get over the divorce. I just don't see why we can't move some of this stuff to the store."

He shook his head. "It's my personal collection, Connie. If I brought it to the store I might end up selling some of it accidentally. I tried to warn you what you were getting yourself into. So don't feel bad about changing your mind. Katherine did, and you and I aren't even married."

She sighed and kept his hand firmly. "Huh-uh. You need me right now. Besides, you gave my stuff a space in your store. The least I can do was give you a place to live." She looked at her watch. "But after I help you dump off the books, I need to pick up my summer clothes at Mom and Dad's. Dad's throwing a fit . . . as if they didn't have plenty of space already. Then I have to go to work at my *mundane* job."

"Mundane is what life is all about," Phil nodded. "I could use a little of it. The old Chinese curse was something like: 'May your life be interesting.' "

"You're really feeling depressed, aren't you?"

"I'll be okay."

They finished dining and she went in for a shower while Phil scrubbed the dishes. He heard her squeal and something fall, and started to go back and check on her, but then he heard the water end and nothing more, so he dried the dishes instead. It was half past noon before he and Connie unloaded the boxes in her car back at the store. He was to have opened at twelve sharp, but he doubted that his tardiness had caused anyone disappointment. No one was waiting on him, and Mondays were always slow, if anyone came here at all. Tuesdays weren't much better. In fact, no day was much better. Connie held open the door while he carried the books in, wishing now that he had gone with her to Denver.

The conventions were still where he made his real money, and he enjoyed meeting the authors and getting their signatures. It helped him forget himself in all the excitement. Phil remembered the eight hours he had spent getting Stephen King to sign nine books, having to get back into line three times because of a three-book limit. But in time, those first edition copies had netted him almost two thousand dollars. Not bad . . . even if he'd had to spend four of those hours listening to an old bitch mutter her annoyances.

It had been no worse than listening to the inmates at the state center, although sometimes weeks and months went by before he earned out the wages of the time he spent. He liked hobnobbing with customers, too, telling them the stories that loosened purse-strings. He knew he would have made a lot more if he *had* gone to Denver with Connie.

With Scarlett Shade. It brought back the dread. What if he had had a blackout and freaked out . . . and maybe tried to douse Shade with holy water or put a stake through her heart . . . or cut her head off . . . or . . . ?

What if she had come back to him in the mirror? To drink his blood . . .

Connie was watching him carefully as he stacked the last box behind his long counter. She leaned forward to peck his bearded cheek.

The bell over the door rang and they broke apart quickly. Phil looked up as two women walked in.

Connie glanced at them and back at Phil. "Call me if you start feeling bad again, okay?"

He just waved as she reached the door, then began taking inventory of the unsold stock while the women browsed.

Chapter 9

Her mother was gone when Connie arrived at the two-story home she'd lived in during high school and some-times college. She felt a little bitter that her father had waited to buy it until she was nearly grown. Mom said he hadn't wanted her or her sister to tear it up like he claimed they'd demolished the previous home. The furniture was all new and expensive, and the walls were still spotless. It had always made her feel more like a guest than part of a family . . . an intruder on the lifestyles Dad and Mom wanted.

It felt more like the hotel she'd spent the weekend in, not cozy at all like her place . . . even with the size of its mess. But maybe the mess was worth it to keep Phil around a little longer. Since getting back . . . since Gary had rejected her, she didn't seem to mind it as much.

She walked through the richly decorated rooms. Hunt-ing and fishing trophies adorned every wall. Dead, dumb creatures Dad bragged of bagging, giving him a sense of importance and purpose. They alternated with Mom's huge collection of brass that gave her a similar self-impor-tance. Both her parents took great pride in appearances. Mom's immaculate kitchen would have swallowed Con-nie's twice over . . . the workplace of a Stepford Wife. More brass in the form of showcase pots and pans, and an old antique mirror opposite the kitchen table, framed in the polished golden metal. Connie kept her distance from it, remembering the shock of seeing herself before she took the shower . . . the sight of the injury still on her breast.

Still only in the mirror. In Scarlett's books, the showcase of the soul.

What did it mean? How was it possible? But she had relaxed as she studied it . . . feeling a strong connection in its strange beauty to the dreams she'd had of Scarlett. It was a part of the same fantasy she had when imagining herself as Countess Showery. When she entered her shower, she'd pretended she was that character again, the wet spray the warm blood of virgins. She ignored the sting it gave her breast for the first moments, but was glad when the pain went away.

Relaxing now, she smiled at her reflection, no longer nervous. She looked back at the familiar home that already seemed part of another life. Going to the kitchen table, Connie found the folded newspaper, sat down, and began to scatter it.

She found the comics section first, reading "Calvin and Hobbes," then scanning the rest.

After that, she read Ann Landers' column like Mom always did. Mom used to quote the bitch as though she were some kind of a prophet, trying to steer Connie's life.

Thank God she was no longer as forceful as Dad.

Connie's fingers flipped through the newspaper. She thought of Phil's pale face when she'd told him the news.

SCARLETT FEVER IN DALLAS read a headline. She went over that story about a divorcee meeting her friends for a card game that had turned into a frenzied scene. The divorcee had imagined herself as Countess Showery and taken that fantasy to the limit. It made Connie want to laugh and cry at the same time. This was the stuff Phil really hated to hear about.

151

Trying not to acknowledge the sliver of ice that crept into her spine with that story, she continued searching until she found a small last-minute bulletin, down in the corner of page one.

DENVER SCI-FI, FANTASY CONVENTION BECOMES A HORROR!

Connie bit her lip, and read:

"No end to 'Scarlett Fever?' Violence marred a weekend science fiction and fantasy convention once more as bodies were found in rooms early this morning. Police were immediately alerted. News and story on Page B-14."

Connie located that section and turned to the back page, her heart pounding.

It really *was* true.

And there, with a story that told little more than the front page bulletin, were pictures of the three suicide victims. Connie caught her breath hastily and heard her heart thud harder.

Gary.

Her eyes misted and she saw the wet drops spoiling the newsprint, followed by more . . . from *her.* "Oh Jesus," she whined. "Gary . . ." Her skin crawled as she thought of their on and off love affair. A love affair without love.

So why was her heart twisting as though Gary were a part of her?

She couldn't believe it.

The fury of the tears poured faster and Connie gave in to them, letting out all the confused emotions that boiled inside her. When the tears would no longer come, she stared up into her red-rimmed, bloodshot eyes and worked to pull herself together. In the brass mirror Connie saw a scared, confused little girl looking back at her. "Oh, Gary," she choked. He had seemed so hopeful and full of life. So excited. Why would he have killed himself? Why?

Maybe Scarlett hadn't liked his books. . . .

It was the only explanation Connie found close to believable, but even that one rang hollow because Scarlett was too nice to be so cruel.

Knowing the reason didn't do a thing to make her feel better, but at least now Connie knew why he hadn't come to her room. She rubbed her eyes until they hurt and laid her face on the newspaper for a long time. She stood up and drank a glass of water.

Wanted to spit it back up.

Poor Gary. He'd never become a famous novelist like Scarlett now.

Finally, letting shock go in favor of curiosity, Connie forced her eyes from his picture to the other two. They seemed very familiar, too. But after a long moment of concentration, Connie only felt definite about seeing the other man, Mason Hood. The dark-haired woman was just another convamp. Connie wasn't sure where she had seen Mason, but . . .

She sighed again and looked for the story: "Gary Wembley, an aspiring novelist who worked at Avis Rent-a-Car, was found with Kansas City car salesman, Mason Hood. Both were nude in Mason Hood's hotel room after having apparently engaged in sexual relations that became violent before they each took their own lives. Police conjecture that these two suicides may have been part of a secret love triangle and not connected to some of the previous convention suicides and related violence in other cities. Current official belief is due to Gary Wembley's relationship to Teresa Carson, who also committed suicide last week at a similar Amarillo convention. . . .

The clouds in Connie's mind began to part for a short second, and just as suddenly, became thicker than a lake fog. Connie wondered if Mason was the fan who had come up to her room with Gary to get Scarlett's autographs . . . it looked like him.

In her dreams.

Connie shuddered. It all seemed as if it had been real, but it hadn't. It was part of her strange dream. She wondered if Gary had ever found Scarlett, because that had been part of her dream, too, hadn't it? Those dreams were suddenly becoming nightmares. It was as though she were suffering one of the blackouts Phil had told her about.

"I had way too much to drink," Connie told herself. She sipped another glass of water, very slowly, putting Gary from her mind as best she could. She regretted her bad thoughts of him now, and didn't want to think of Gary or this weekend at all. It was like another life . . . another world. She only wanted to forget the unpleasant reality of events.

That was what she had gone to Denver to do.

Mom still wasn't back, so Connie got together the belongings she'd forgotten before, putting them into her maroon Ford Escort. She wanted to talk to Mom because that family tie still gave her a security she needed, especially right now. At last Connie wrote Mom a note telling her to expect Phil and her to be by tonight . . . and to please have Dad on his best behavior. She hoped Phil would come with her. Maybe it would make him feel better to get out of the apartment, too. She tacked the note on the refrigerator.

Calling the Waldenbooks she worked for, Connie explained her circumstances in a very abbreviated form, pretending Gary had been a closer boyfriend than he was. The manager sounded bored and suspicious, but gave her the next four days off. He told her that Phil had called.

Connie went to the phone, suddenly wanting to be with Phil and tell him about Gary and how that horrible news was affecting her, but it rang before she could reach it. Connie grabbed the receiver. "Hello?"

"Hi, Connie! When'd you get back? I called your apartment and got worried when you didn't answer."

It was Vicky.

Connie gulped, feeling a twinge. But despite last week, it reassured her just hearing Vicky's voice. "I—I got in early this morning. I drove for hours."

Vicky sounded disappointed. "Then you were long gone when they found the bodies?"

The reminder made her wince. "Y-yeah. Long gone. I . . . didn't even know about any of it until I called Mom about ten this morning."

"Ten? Did it take you that long to get back? Shit, girl, you're probably dead on your feet!"

"Oh no, I got back at about two this morning. I woke up at ten and called Mom—"

"Hmm?" Vicky hummed. "So how come you haven't called me. I'm still your best friend, aren't I? The other night didn't change that, did it?"

Connie sighed, shifting her thoughts to Gary again instead of that confusion. "Listen, Vicky, I really don't feel like talking right now. I knew one of those people in Denver . . ."

"Gary Wembley?" Vicky paused.

"Y-yeah."

"I thought you'd mentioned his name before. I'm sorry, Connie."

Connie sniffed. "I don't know why it's affecting me so much . . ." She hissed, looking down at the pictures of the victims, wanting to cry all over again. "It's terrible."

"Sounds like you and I need to have lunch. Get together like we used to. We were always there for each other, Connie. Maybe getting together will make you feel better." Vicky sounded glum. "I know it would make *me* feel better."

Connie recognized the tone of depression in her friend. She wrapped her fingers through the phone cord and twisted it. "What's wrong, Vicky?"

"I just miss you. That's one reason I was calling . . . and

I was thinking that maybe we might want to be roomies again . . . after I sell the house. I was hoping that you might want to share your apartment with me."

She shook her head. "I don't think so, Vicky. Phil hasn't found a place yet. My apartment is a shambles with all the books he brought with him."

"He won't be around forever, will he?" Vicky giggled despite a tone of disappointment.

Connie frowned, but felt better as she allowed the shock of Gary's death to move farther and farther away this time. There was still an empty pit in her stomach . . . but it was shrinking. "Listen, I've got to go. I'll call you tomorrow, okay?"

"Okay. But tell me first . . . did you meet Scarlett?"

Connie felt smug now, drawn back with the opportunity to boast. "I sure did. I even had a drink with her. She's everything we dreamed she'd be, Vicky. She's very nice and she's *beautiful!*" Just for a minute, Connie felt funny as the insides of her thighs tingled. The sharp needle stabbed back into her left nipple and she bit her tongue, her eyes drawn to the mirror. "Ev-everybody wanted to talk to her and *I* got to! It . . . it was great!"

Connie, dear.

Scarlett.

Connie hissed, her voice gone. Her reflection was fuzzy again, blurring even as she looked, becoming the image of herself, but also of Scarlett, as though she were studying a picture of herself with Scarlett superimposed. The voice in her mind held her tight. . . .

In her dreams. Suddenly, she felt tense that she had no control over her fantasy.

"Call me early tomorrow and we'll make lunch, how about that? I want to hear everything, maybe this weekend we can—"

Fighting a frightened fascination, Connie closed her eyes tight, trying to silence the eerie inner voice, too. Her own tone was a tremble, "I—I have to go to another convention this weekend, Vicky." She paused, reopening one eye slowly.

To herself. Only herself, pale and scared.

"Really?" Vicky paused again. "In Denver again?"

Sudden anticipation for another weekend made her anxious for that relief. Connie knew the shock of Gary's death was why her mind was betraying her and making her see things now. "I—I think . . . Scarlett will be there, too."

"Where at?"

"Oklahoma City." Connie kept her eyes on the reflection, dreading that it would change. Again.

"Oke City—great!" Vicky hummed once more. "Okay. Lunch tomorrow, okay? We'll get takeout and bring it over here. I bought a mirror like the ones you collect and I want you to see it . . . and maybe you can fill me in on this convention stuff. I'll go to this one, too. It would be good for me to get away from everything for a weekend and maybe have some fun! I really want to meet Scarlett Shade and—"

"I have to go, Vicky. I'm too dragged out. Bye—"

Connie hung up as the girl continued talking, not giving her the chance to reply. Vicky could talk for hours even if nothing at all was happening to either of them.

Connie backed away from the mirror until she could no longer see it, then shook her head and hurried back out to her car.

Chapter 10

Phillip studied the two young women who'd come in as Connie left. He was sure they were Oklahoma University students after listening to them whisper and giggle—back and forth through the store for an hour, whisper session after whisper session. They picked through Connie's shiny jewelry, then browsed through the fantasy and science fiction paperbacks quickly. Now they were pouring through every selection in his horror section.

It was the part of his store he felt very much a part of. *Sonia*.

He tried to call Kevin at the office, but Kevin was too busy to talk . . . too busy trying to help people who had already gone around the bend to talk to someone who was headed there now.

Everyone had problems.

Phillip looked at the rows of shelves crammed full of colorful new and used hardcovers and paperbacks. Every remaining wall space was covered by the posters he collected and sometimes sold, from an original Universal Dracula to a blood-drenched ad for the last Freddy Krueger flick that had not really been the last. He played a restful Ennio Morricone soundtrack through the store as he straightened his stock.

When the two women finally made their selections and

came to face Phil, he rolled his eyes at the paperbacks they each laid on the counter.

Of course, Scarlett Shade.

The tallest woman, statuesque with a slender face, long wavy black hair, and longer legs in tight slacks, tugged at her turtleneck while Phil added up prices and tax. "Were you up there in Denver where those people killed themselves?" she asked.

Phil swallowed and shook his head. "I didn't know anything about it until this morning."

"And Scarlett Shade was there, *too,*" spoke up the other girl, a shorter brunette with sparkly eyes. "Have you ever met her?"

Phil allowed a chuckle. "How do you think I got your books signed?"

"Oh, wow," said the brunette. "This is too strange!"

"She's strange all right," replied Phil.

The tall woman gave Phil her money and waited while he sold the other books to her companion. "I think it's just great that we have someone here in town who has actually *met* Scarlett Shade," she said. "All of us in my dorm want to be just like her."

Unable to hold back his frown, Phil reminded himself that she was a customer. He didn't hold to the adage that the customer was always right, but it didn't pay to piss off a customer with money, either. So he just said, "Really? All of you want to be vampires?"

The brunette took her change and nodded urgently. "It would be so much fun! You don't need a degree to be a vampire. All you have to do is party all night long and have sex . . . and vampires don't have to worry about getting AIDS 'cause they're dead!"

"Undead," broke in the tall one, brushing back her black hair.

"Sounds like a blast," Phil said, trying to keep his mind

off the recent nightmares. "But you'd have to drink blood."

"So?" The tall one fluttered her lashes at him and sashayed to the door with her bag. "It might taste good. Count Downe says that everything is wonderful when you're undead . . ."

Putting the money in his drawer, Phil just watched them go out the door, and flinched inside and out at the brunette's last remark.

"I'd love to be undead."

He went back to the tiny cubicle of a bathroom where he stored all his brooms and cleansers, then filled an empty Dr. Pepper bottle with water and drank it slowly. He stared at his haggard face in the mirror, trying to look inside his eyes and know what was behind the dark masking of the minutes when he didn't know what he was doing . . . the meaning of the dreams that haunted him . . . escaping from death and undeath in the sewers, arriving in a room of mirrors that had once reflected only Sonia.

Himself.

But since Amarillo, they showed the voluptuous red-haired woman of death.

Undeath.

Scarlett Shade.

Scarlett Shade was a vampire.

Her words . . . her teeth . . . Phil brushed his fingers over the sore mark. Maybe he didn't want to know what he was doing or what the nightmares meant. He knew that the guilt he felt was opposed to the craving of the two students . . . that although their simple view of life was primally appealing, the remorse he could not help but feel held him back. His teeth were clenched so fiercely he felt their enamel crunch.

He walked back to the counter and his paperwork, not looking up until the door's bell sounded again.

"Hey, Phil!"

He did his best to smile. "Hey, yourself." He scratched his forehead and closed his thin eyebrows. "Did you get fired?"

Connie stopped in the middle of the room, right between the hardcover and paperback shelves. Her weak smile disappeared, "No . . . Phil, I just couldn't go in and work. I—I don't feel up to it." Her face wobbled. "Gary . . . Gary Wembley was one of the suicides in Denver."

"Do I know him?"

"God," she sniffed, "don't you remember? He wanted to be a writer. He bought all those Joe Lansdale books from you last year in Denver." Her face darkened. "He was staying in my room."

"Shit." Phil reached for her hand with sympathy. "I'm sorry, Connie. Are you okay?"

"How—how can you handle news like that? I never would have believed it of him. I w-waited for him to come to the room but he never did." Her voice was damp and deep. "I thought he was . . . with . . . someone else—" Phil came around the counter and held her. She sniffed and choked, burying her face in his shoulder. "Something must have really freaked him out. The paper said he might be part of a triple suicide. They—they found him with a naked man who'd killed himself, too." She squeezed Phil harder. "Th-that's what's really weird. No way that Gary was gay, Phil. He wasn't into guys at all, not even for experiment."

Another bloodless body.

Phil just rubbed her shoulders, feeling every trauma of his nightmares. A responsibility he didn't want and *shouldn't* feel. His throat was too tight to speak . . . especially as the minutes dragged and she rubbed her pelvis into his, her sobs disappearing into sighs.

Connie finally released him and stood back, her chin still trembly. "Th-thanks, Phil. Friends really help. Vicky

161

called me and tried to cheer me up, too. Do you remember Vicky Cossiter?"

Phil shook his head.

"You'd remember her husband. He—he was always in here buying those *Conan* books a few months ago. Big, football-looking guy?"

"Yeah. He hasn't been in for a while. He owes me ninety bucks for some titles he ordered."

"That's Rick." She leaned on the counter and found his Kleenex, dabbing her eyes, her voice stronger. "God, Vicky could talk to a . . ." Connie squiggled her lips and sighed forlornly.

"Brick wall?" suggested Phil.

"Yeah. Anyway, she thinks she wants to come along to the convention in Oke City this weekend . . . to meet Scarlett Shade. She's really jealous because I had a drink with her. We're going to meet for lunch tomorrow so she can hear all about it. God, I'm glad it's going to be right here. I think it'll make me feel a lot better to go, but I sure wouldn't want a long drive right now."

"Scarlett Shade." He sighed, not liking his thoughts at all. "Yeah, and I just sold out of most of the books she signed to those two girls who were here when you left. I'll have to order some more and get her to sign them this weekend."

"I'll have to introduce Vicky to her, Phil. Do you think Scarlett will remember me?"

"No one could forget you, Connie."

"Except *you*," she punched him lightly. "Remember how you forgot our night in St. Louis?"

He blushed, remembering the way he'd blacked out into the nightmare as they made love. He'd come to with sweaty screams. She blushed, too. Finally, awkwardly, she kissed his fuzzy cheek. "Promise me you'll remember if there's a next time, Phil . . . and I warn you, I may need you tonight. You don't have any excuses to say no now, either."

"I promise," he agreed, liking the way she'd felt in his arms.

"Good." She pulled up a sleeve to her watch. "Good, and tonight, I want you to meet my parents, okay? How about it? I told them we're just friends and there's nothing between us, but Mom's been bugging me to meet you."

The pressure of her plans threatened him and he dreaded the headache always hovering. The pressure always grew with any new responsibility. But she took his hand and the vise beginning to squeeze him eased a bit. He felt the peace she seemed to give him grow stronger.

It was a nice feeling.

"I don't like you being in such surroundings, Connie, especially not now with all the violence," Mr. Sawyer muttered.

Phil turned to the kitchen. Connie ignored her father. Mrs. Sawyer was giving her a bunch of recipes and they were both whispering and giggling, just like the two students in the store today.

Phil turned back to Mr. Sawyer, a balding man with a huge beer paunch. But he still kept trying to catch Connie's eye as she sat at the table with her mother. The big house was so clean it was almost as if no one lived there. Connie's old room, naked in her departure, was still the one area that held an aura of real personality. The brass and trophies in these other rooms made them as false as the reflections in a fun house. The decorations were as hollow as Mr. Sawyer's faint manners.

"I don't wonder that the police think these suicides are connected," said Sawyer. He sucked on his cigar and directed the smoke right at Phil. "They sound something like the Jonestown suicides in a book I read."

Phil shrugged, not replying. Connie's father made him nervous. He didn't like the kinds of books Phil did, only nonfiction. Crime stuff.

"So you own the bookshop where Connie's working, is that right?"

Feeling ridiculous, like a very overaged college student dating a junior high school girl, Phil gritted his teeth and shook his head. "No sir. I own Realms of Fantasy on Porter Street, near the hospital."

"I work at Waldenbooks, Dad, remember?" Connie called in. "Phil lets me put some of the jewelry I make in his store and sells it."

Sawyer scratched his double chin. "On commission, no doubt . . ."

Phil nodded.

"Hmm. Realms of Fantasy, huh? Sounds like one of those porn shops to me, Phil. You don't have a back room where you sell porno, do you? I know how older men sometimes use younger women like Connie."

As Phil blushed and opened his mouth, Connie shouted, "Daddy! Stop it or I won't be home for Thanksgiving . . . *or* Christmas!"

"I'm just asking your boyfriend some of the usual parental questions," her father shouted back.

"He's *not* my boyfriend!"

Sawyer ignored her and grinned at Phil. "That was just a joke, son. You don't even look like one of those porn people. You need a haircut and shave, but every kid since Vietnam's needed that. Hell, I was proud to fight those damn gooks. If Nixon hadn't been run out of office, this would be a better country." Then he leaned closer and lowered his voice. "But what bugs me, Phil, is you got a bit of an accent. Are you an American?"

This time Phil frowned, the ache at the back of his skull growing and spreading. "I've lived in this country since I was ten."

164

"Can't place that funny accent," repeated Sawyer in his pushy whisper. "Europe? Russia, maybe?"

"Czeckovslovakia," Phil muttered, unable not to remember the scenes Mr. Sawyer was bringing back.

Sawyer's face was calculating. "I'm a good one for history. I guess that means you came to America about the time the Russkis squashed your revolution, doesn't it?"

Phil felt his nervous face and twitching fingers turn to stone. He saw the mirror, inviting him in.

The memories flooding him. The new ones of . . .

Scarlett. Red as Sonia's blood. Her sticky fangs, hungry for life.

Undeath. Phil gritted his molars. There was nothing he could do to push the past back into hiding, but as his voice stuttered snatches of words, Connie came to stand beside him and took his shivering hand. "It's okay, Phil. Daddy didn't mean it." Then she stared at her father. "That was cruel and mean, Daddy."

Mr. Sawyer chuckled darkly. "Well, it's the truth. A man's got to face the truth or he ain't even a man." But his voice became softer as Phil steadied himself through Connie's concerned touch. "Sorry, Phil. You were young. But what I'm getting at is that if some foreign country invaded America, none of what happened to your country would ever happen *here*. A man's got to take responsibility for his own."

Responsibility. Phil blushed, knowing it far better than he suspected Sawyer did. The sewer's revolving path in his nightmares dug at him.

Connie squeezed him tighter and the ghastly memories slowly faded. Phil managed a sigh. "My parents took me out of the country because it was hopeless."

Sawyer sniffed without sympathy.

Connie sat down on the chair arm and put her arm around Phil's shoulders. "I brought Phil over for you two to meet him and get to know him . . . not to upset him."

Mr. Sawyer was pacing back and forth between his chair and the coffee table. He stopped and pulled back the curtain covering the sliding glass door. The backyard was dark. Connie looked at her mother, at her father, then down at Phil. She tightened her hand on his shoulder. "Dad. We're just friends, okay? Phil needed a place to stay and he's going to get his own apartment."

He swung around. "Doesn't Phil have any male friends?"

The way Mr. Sawyer spoke made Phil feel like he was invisible. He pushed Connie away and stood. "Connie, I ought to leave."

"Okay," she whispered, taking his hand. But she turned back to her father first. Mom had come to stand right behind him. "Phil's going through a divorce, Dad. Just cool it, okay? I'm a grown-up now and this is my life."

His eyebrows were a single salt-and-pepper line under angry wrinkles. "Don't you dare——"

"Please, Ralph," said Mrs. Sawyer.

"Hush, Maggie. You're always taking her side——"

"Connie," muttered Phil.

She nodded and walked him to the front door. Sawyer just stared at them both and didn't say a word.

"I'm sorry, Connie," whispered Mom. "I told him not to act like this."

Connie kissed her mother's cheek. "It's just the way he is." Then she laughed brokenly. "But tell him—if he ever asks you why I don't want to live the way he does, *he's* a big part of the reason, okay?"

Mom nodded and then shook Phil's hand. "Nice to meet you, Phil. Take good care of my little girl."

"I think she's taking care of me," Phil replied.

They went onto the front porch and Mrs. Sawyer shut the door behind them.

166

Connie and Phil walked to his Dodge Caravan silently. She hugged him before she slid in. "I'm sorry, Phil."

The warmth of her words soothed him and drove the past even farther away. He held her tight.

Chapter 11

She lifted the coffin's lid and sat up, looking over her basement room.

Something was different. Scarlett felt a loss within herself through the blood she had consumed.

Someone had died . . . someone she drank. She sat up in the velvet cushions and studied the lives that were hers. Although there were thousands, it took her only a minute to spin the images through the frames and locate the one that had turned blank and empty. Her loss became greater.

The old geezer at the rest home. Stan Hodge. She remembered him like the grandfather she'd never known, except she didn't feel sad about his death except for herself . . . because she could never again consume her slight meals from his wrinkled flesh.

They would bury him and he would awaken in total confusion . . . to the eternal existence she had promised him for his favors, but it wouldn't be the new life he'd anticipated.

No. Like the others, he would be trapped inside the fear of death, just as he had been in life, not knowing the secrets she had promised but kept from him. His panic would grow in the hollow darkness that would be just like his life until he couldn't think at all. As the others, he would spend this new lease in terror and hunger, uncertain of what he was, not believing what he could be.

Too bad. Old Stan had tasted good with his long life and its experiences.

Scarlett flowed out of her casket and touched her keyboard, not up to even writing one page now. She stared back at the souls infected by desire . . . drawn to her by their want of her characters and the stories she wrote. Scarlett examined them with care for her new choice, as possibilities floated in and out of the frames by her growing will.

The apartment was in its best shape in months. Dirk scratched the scar on his neck where the stitches had been. The smooth rise of tissue fed him a mixture of disgust and thrill. It was still hard to believe that he and James had gotten so carried away a couple of weeks before, but for those moments, he'd really believed that James was Countess Showery, that he himself was Count Downe.

He'd even believed that fantasy when they had removed their clothing in the tiny bathroom, wrapping their arms around each other, delusion staggering them both. He'd felt himself deep inside *her*, their sweat mingling as they stumbled their way back to Dirk's bed, ignoring the phone that began ringing fifteen minutes later. Dripping blood from the gashes they had made in each other's throats, they took turns with each other's assholes and mouths . . . until the hallucination of their excitement abruptly ended.

They'd missed the Shade party . . . the opportunity of Amy and Tamara, and both of them required stitches. Their explanations for those wounds to the medics had been embarrassing, but Dirk wished the illusion of those hot moments had never ended.

He moved his eyes from the boxy console television to the plainly bordered mirror above it, wishing again that he were really Count Downe. He saw his face alter in imagination, looking far better than it had in his makeup, and he let the fabrication roll until Countess Showery was in the glass there with him . . . the real Countess, not James.

It was the truest description he had ever conjured up, exactly the picture in his mind drawn by Scarlett Shade's vivid words. The Countess was blond and delicate . . . her lips redder than red under her diminutive nose, and under them the glimmering teeth . . .

The sound from the TV speakers dimmed . . . an empty roar. He stood and walked to the set, shutting it off, and stretched his hand toward his lust.

As he did, his image in the mirror disappeared in a green-tinted haze.

The shiver that ran up Dirk's spine was another mixture of his emotions . . . fear and hope. He spread his fingers against the hard surface, skinning his fingernails over it. Countess Showery faced him and extended her hand to meet his, and impossibly, her palm felt soft and real.

Their fingers entwined.

Impossible . . . but not for a *fantasy*. Dirk stepped back, hoping this would continue and that he could draw her out of the mirror. He clutched her hand and smiled as her arm splashed through the glass . . . as she herself flowed out to stand opposite him. "Count Downe," she said, giving a curtsy just like the one James had made.

"You can't fool me this time, James," Dirk breathed. "Get the fuck out of this dream."

Her image blurred, her shape and colors swirling before his eyes, and he swallowed . . . seeing the foldout on his bedroom wall . . . the old one from *Playboy* of Scarlett Shade.

But in a 3-D reality! Her lush hair sprawled down her shoulders and firm breasts . . . her flesh tone pearly but with a strange underlying quality of life. She crooked her finger and posed with a hip thrown to the side, her other hand sliding through her pubic hair that was as red as on her head. "I'm not James," she hummed.

Dirk stood dead still, breathing so fast that everything was foggier than ever. She moved nearer, slipping her chilly skin to him as she examined the scar on his throat. "Tch, tch," she sighed. "What a waste. Some of you guys just can't wait, can you?"

"You're not real," he whispered.

"I am if you want me . . . do you want me?"

Her blue eyes were the mirror this time, showing him his life, which had been unpleasant and dreary, filled by the routine of going to work, watching TV, eating, sleeping . . . only livened by her books and the meetings of the fan club. The shiny pupils caressed him. Taking slower breaths, he dropped his gaze to her wonderful, perfect breasts, fingers itching to touch them.

"I'm yours," Scarlett murmured, "if you'll be mine. Don't speak of this meeting or everyone will believe you're crazy . . . just expect me every few evenings. Stare into the glass and . . . *want* me."

Now he was staring into her necklace mirror . . . a reflection of himself as Count Downe . . . even more powerful and handsome. "I want you," he replied.

"Then let's get down to business, Count."

He nodded and helped her unbutton his shirt.

Chapter 12

"Jeez. I can't believe Dad."

Phil looked up from the steering wheel. "It's okay, Connie."

She couldn't read him from the half of his face she saw. The look of his shadowed features . . . *Gary's face.* She forced her voice. "It . . . it's really terrible . . . when someone dies that you know, Phil."

He nodded.

"Yeah . . . why am I saying that to you?" She laid her hand on his arm, fighting the nearing tears, watching the shadows change him with relief. "I mean, hell, you have *blackouts*—"

The sharp intake of air and the way his eyebrows merged stopped her dead. The expanding shadows now made his eyes two orbs in a sea of darkness. She sniffed. "Look, Phil, it's really strange. It still feels like the whole weekend was an insane dream."

Phil grunted, then looked at her directly again, slowing the van. "A *dream?*"

"Yeah. I'm dreaming like a first-class convamp," Connie replied, adding levity she didn't feel. Shifting in her chair, her arm pinched her breast and she yelped.

"Are you okay?"

Her lips trembled. She didn't want to tell him that she

had fantasized Scarlett as a *vampire*, actually biting her breast. That would make her weird dreams stranger than his. "Yeah," she said, "just a pinch. I hurt my tit somehow." Connie sighed, changing the topic. "I am sorry about what Dad said to you, Phil. He really wasn't making fun of you."

Phil shrugged and his voice was higher. "Forget it. But I want to hear more about your dreams. What was it really like this weekend, Connie? You *do* feel that what happened to your friend Gary was your fault, don't you?"

After a moment, she shook her head. "It couldn't have been, but I still feel sick about it. I feel like I didn't really know Gary, and I feel so different myself."

"I always feel responsible for what happened to my family, too."

She moved a hand over one of his, squeezing him gently. "Yeah. Phil . . . do you want to sleep with me *tonight?* Just tonight, Phil?" She needed someone's arms around her . . . for someone to whisper in her ear. "We . . . don't have to do anything."

Phil didn't speak for a long moment as her warm breath lapped his face. Then he met her lips briefly, one eye still on the road. "I . . . I think I'd like that, Connie. Really."

She pulled back slowly and laid a deft hand on his hip, leaning closer again. Her lips nearly caressed his ear. "If you're sure I won't make you freak out this time."

"You won't." He turned his face and their lips touched. His hand reached down to stroke her thigh.

Connie sighed. The chair creaked as she sank back. "That feels nice. You know what you're getting yourself into, Phil?"

"You can show me."

"I will." She let him keep his attention on driving until they reached her apartment a few minutes later. The streetlights were like a slow strobe.

173

Connie. Dear, sweet Connie.

But this time, the memory of Scarlett's voice made her warm as she thought of herself and Phil as Countess Showery and Count Downe.

They both got out, stretching, and she met him in front of the van. They walked together to the front door. "It was really terrible to learn about Gary, Phil." She reached down to his hand and gripped it firmly. They went inside, walking down the dirty yellow hall to her apartment.

"I really do understand, Connie."

Opening the door, they went in, and this time she ignored the mess he'd made of her place. She hugged him. "I know you do. Good God, Phil, you must have been going through hell ever since I met you. I think your wife's a real bitch!" She kissed his forehead. "You shouldn't be alone, Phil. Maybe none of us should ever be alone."

He shook his head bitterly. "Maybe not." He went to Wolfgang and held the cat close. "But I'm always alone in my dreams."

"Dreams," Connie said. She looked at one of the mirrors as she said it and felt relief, and again, equal disappointment, that her own face looked back at her. She took his arm. "You know what, Phil? You're just like Count Downe. I'll take care of you . . . just like Countess Showery takes care of him. For a while at least. How about that?" She pointed at all the boxes, pushed up on her toes, and settled her lips on his. "And I don't want you to move right now even if you find someplace. After what happened, I need someone around."

"Okay," he whispered, setting down the cat.

"But let's find a better place for all these books, okay?"

"Okay."

She looked over his shoulder as they hugged. "That was easy."

He pressed her close. "I'm trying to be an easy guy these days. Doctor's orders."

It was still her in the reflection, but the tall brooding man with his arms around her suddenly wasn't Phil. The silky, flowing cape reminded her . . .

Count Downe.

She blinked and sighed as the broad shoulders became Phil's slump and the cape disappeared to be his checkered shirt and jeans.

What this time? She wasn't drunk . . . not really tired . . . her depression for Gary was ebbing fast with the touch of Phil's body against hers. She smiled uneasily, tilting her face again to meet his lips. Maybe the fantasies she saw were just a spiritual mirage. She had been like a woman in a desert, hallucinating that every shiny object she saw was water . . . her truest desires now . . . that she was the Countess and Phil was the Count.

She covered his mouth with hers completely, wanting him to satisfy her and take away the frustrations. She wanted *him*, and it drove away every other thought.

"Phil . . ." she mumbled. He held back for only an instant. Her hips rubbed into his as he brought her to the couch. She tugged off her shirt as the cat watched in boredom. They kissed, hugged, and made love for the next hour, going from the opening frenzy to a pace almost passive and calm, but it all sent the shock waves of a thousand joys through her. It was more than with the others because she felt the concerns they were sharing, too . . . an empathy for one another. Love. She loved their reunion . . . the feel of him between her thighs and in her soul, easily replacing the moments with Gary . . . with Vicky.

When she whined her delight, it must have affected Phil, too, because she felt his energy and excitement increase . . . felt him shudder above her and grunt.

They were both quiet in each other's arms for long

minutes. Finally, Connie kissed his cheek. "That was wonderful, Phil. The best time I've ever had with anyone . . . even better than the last time with you!" But as she said it, she wasn't sure it was the truth . . . fought back the dream of Scarlett.

That wasn't real, anyway.

Phil's face tottered, the same way his features twisted sometimes when she passed his door and looked in at him sleeping. "It . . . was nice," he said simply, his voice hollow.

"Just nice?" She moved a finger down his hairy chest. "Then we'll have to try it again."

He was frowning.

"What's wrong?"

Without an answer, he sat up, spreading his fingers through his pubic hair. She saw him wince and grit his teeth. "Did . . . did I hurt you?"

He shook his head . . . and the look on his face reminded her of her own when she saw her herself in the mirror this afternoon . . . the wound that wasn't there. All of a sudden, she felt it pinch like it was sore and raw.

But she didn't want to bring it up. She felt renewed. Safe. Not even thinking of Gary bothered her. Not even the revived soreness of her breast.

She shifted to the carpet and pulled him down after her, cradling him as they lay close together. His arm slid under her neck and hers sprawled on his hairy belly. Connie spoke warmly in his ear. "Maybe I really love you, Phil. My intuition told me I did a long time ago. I really want to help you—"

His face wobbled back into a smile. "Help me? You already are. If it wasn't for you I'd be sleeping in the store. Not to mention the way we spent the past hour."

Connie spread her fingers on his chest. "I mean with your more personal problems . . . hell, Phil, you're a soap

176

opera trying for prime time. Maybe this is what it's all about—people who need each other getting together."

He sighed. "It would be nice if that were all there were to it, but it doesn't do any good, Connie . . . the world's problems and our problems are still there. Now there's all these damn suicides, my wife . . . and . . ."

"It makes me feel better when there's someone else to face it all with."

He shut his mouth for a long time. "My life's not a soap opera," he said, pushing her hand away. "It's a fucking horror story."

She shook her head and took his hand again. "I feel that way sometimes, Phil. That's why I read and watch the things I do . . . to forget my own troubles. At least I can close the book or turn the TV off." She moved a finger across his lips. "Don't think about reality. That's why the news bothers you." Connie pressed their lips together lightly. "We can turn off life, too. You and I just did."

He shook his head. "We didn't turn life off, Connie. But life . . . is scary."

"Not if we turn off the *bad* things. That's why I like Scarlett's books, Phil. They turn horror into something *fun*. That's why I like the conventions . . . because I can just be crazy. *Everything* is crazy at the conventions."

"We . . . we can't just turn off the bad things, Connie. Everything is crazy, period. I feel like my life is the dream sometimes, and that my nightmares are the reality." His hand clutched hers and he looked deep into her face. "I wanted it to be more between us, Connie."

The unexpected words made her smile. "Really? That makes me feel good, Phil, because I've liked you for a long time." She rubbed a finger over his lips. "Don't look so morose, okay? God, you really are just like Count Downe sometimes, aren't you? He was my fantasy man for a long

177

time . . . but now, I think I want you to be my fantasy. Funny, huh?"

He frowned. "Fantasy is my whole problem." He picked up one of his business cards from the coffee table.

The look of his unrepentant hollowness brought back the weekend and its aftermath as if it were still now. She lowered her voice. "You wouldn't ever kill *yourself*, would you?"

He released her. "I'm too afraid of death," he whispered. "My nightmares . . . what I'm really of afraid of is that I'll die in the middle of one of them and be stuck in it forever."

She tensed. "Well, at least it makes you too afraid to commit . . . *suicide.*" She relaxed beside him once more. "Now I just have to get you to finish reading Scarlett Shade." She shook her head on his shoulder. She still felt lost in a desert, and she knew it was a lot of the same way for him, but at least now, they were lost together.

But for how long this time?

She rose on an elbow, feeling his stickiness inside her. The risk she'd taken tonight brought back all the useless precautions she'd taken before.

He'd made her pregnant, anyway.

"What's wrong?"

She took a deep breath. "I—I don't really know what you want from me. Men have always treated me like some unwanted toy except when they want something from me . . ." She stopped.

"What . . . are you trying to say?"

New tears waited just behind her eyes and the words were already feeding into her mouth, but Connie clamped her jaws tighter than tight.

"What, Connie?"

She took a deep breath, moving his fingers away and holding her sore spot. She squeezed gently, suddenly enjoying that pain that was less than the hurt in her words.

"I never told you. I just didn't think you really cared, Phil . . . and if you did, I thought it would make your life even worse. You . . . had so many worries already . . ." She inhaled deeply. "You—you got me pregnant, Phil. I know the odds on one time doing that, especially with all the precautions we took, but . . . it happened."

Phil's face clouded darker than ever and he held his face between his hands. "Connie." His fingers twittered like the cry of a bird and he stared at her through them. Like a little boy who'd just lost every hope of Christmas. "God, if I had known . . ."

"I . . . I'm sorry I brought it up." She started to touch him, but as her hand neared his, she felt a barrier just like the one Gary had put between himself and her at the convention. The barrier between herself and almost everyone, especially the men she slept with.

The barrier of self. Sometimes it was hers, but she had just opened herself up to Phil more than she ever had to anyone, even Vicky.

And the barrier . . . his tears, was just like a rejection. She just wanted him to hold her and tell her he loved her . . . at least that he cared. "Just a sec," she said thickly, getting up to go to the bathroom . . . to be by herself for a few minutes and let him sulk. Maybe she would cry, but she didn't want him to know he had that power over her. She walked straight ahead, the foggy image of herself in her mind. The straggly straw hair . . . her round, blotchy face.

Lost. Cold. Again.

Yes, she was lost . . . lost alone, just as she had been for years, and nobody really cared. Gary hadn't . . . none of the men . . . not even Phil. Sniffling, she hurried on until she was at the bathroom sink. She leaned on the green tile counter, trying not to look in that mirror, but . . .

She couldn't stop herself. She wished for her fantasies. In her reflection . . . the two holes in her nipple were not

179

much different than they'd looked before, but the problem was, they were still there . . . slightly darker and more inflamed. No wonder she'd felt the pain. Every pain of her life was inside her breast, as though drawn to the mark there. She wanted someone to take it all from her . . . the dream of Scarlett sucking all the pain of life right out of her.

As if bidden by Connie's worn thoughts, her face became Scarlett's. Beautiful and peaceful. The vision of her soul. Empty of hurt, craving only the pleasure she would find in others.

The image wobbled back into her own whitewashed complexion. Connie took a deep breath. She felt better . . . stronger. She wet a washcloth and dabbed her pale, sweaty face.

Chapter 13

Phil wiped his eyes, not wanting the new crushing guilt of another responsibility. This one real, very real. Not imagined.

How could he have known? How could he have guessed what he had done?

Those short moments of his pleasure months before . . . moments of escape from an empty relationship with his wife and inner turmoil. Using pleasure for that escape . . . using his desire of escape for pleasure. Forming a life, but as thoughtless and careless for its future as Dr. Frankenstein for his creation.

Forming and then taking that life. Death. A sacrifice to his past. To escape his past . . . and even at that cost, it hadn't worked, but made it worse.

The mirror showed his torn features, more ragged than they'd ever been. Sonia . . . Connie . . . Katherine, too. Death. Undeath. In the reflections, Phil saw himself fade . . . into the crushed moments of his youth . . . the fire and smoke and hell of responsibility that had never released him and that he hid from the rest of life in. The scene faded to become only Connie . . . beaten and inconsolable . . . to become . . .

Scarlett.

He grabbed at his abdomen, the invisible marks she

had driven deep into him. The pain spread into his soul.

You've lost meaning. Lost life. Lost love. You're a murderer as much as those you despise . . . thinking of self. Release those dreams and nightmares and let me give you the desire of your soul . . . guilt is meaningless. You can't change the past . . . you can only change yourself in a fantasy. We are what we are, but in our desires, we can be who we want.

Her face molded into Sonia's . . . into the memory of himself and Sonia.

Give me your pain and life . . . your empty love. Let me drink from you and make you like me . . . you are so near. Guilt is death and I can offer you undeath, freedom . . . and you will savor the joys you have never known and cannot know while you cling to your lonely self. You are so close. Self. The taste of another will fulfill you. . . .

Phil sagged, breathing fast, reaching out to the out-stretched fingers.

Love.

Fear.

The vision of Sonia became only himself, alone in the burning streets . . . disfigured by Scarlett's countenance under his own. Hot with fever, the fear of himself made him drop his hand before it reached its reflection.

As she took some Tylenol, Connie looked up. Phil limped into the room as though drunk. "I . . . I'm sorry," he said.

She swallowed the pills and filled a paper cup with water.

"Are you . . . okay?"

She shrugged.

His face was unhappy, and he hugged her more tightly than ever. *"Ow!"* she flinched.

Phil let go and backed a step, surprised.

182

She blushed. "It . . . it's okay. Just my sore tit . . . sore tits and . . . broken hearts."

"What happened?"

"It just hurts," she said. "I told you in the car . . . I pinched it or something." She moaned, a new careless confidence in this physical pain, so much more fleeting than the pang of her soul. "It's . . . sore."

"Did you bruise yourself?"

She shook her head. "I don't know what happened . . . forget it, okay?"

He frowned, reaching for her, then glanced at the mirror. "Connie—" Phil's face had gone pale and she suddenly wondered if he saw, too. "How . . . ?" He touched her nipple.

She dropped her jaw at the mixture of a new excitement and the pain of something like hot steel sliding deep into her flesh . . . reality slipping abstractly into the mirror. She shook her head hard. "It's . . . it's just part of . . . a dream," she finally whispered.

Phil looked at her breast intently, then moved a finger through his own sticky pubic hair. His face was as empty as hers in the reflection . . . almost her twin, the noise of his breath loud and hard. "Tell me . . . tell me about your dreams, Connie."

She swallowed a low gulp of air as she saw the marks on him, too.

Only in the mirror.

Chapter 14

They both sat at the kitchen table, still naked. Connie felt like a germ under a microscope every time Phil looked at her. "Maybe it's some kind of a new tattoo or something, Phil. Maybe I got it from the convention when I was drunk. Look, it doesn't hurt at all now."

He looked down at himself and she did, too, and he ran his fingers through the curly hair. "What about me, then? Don't you think it's strange that we both have these marks?"

She didn't *want* to think about it. "Out of sight, out of mind," Connie said. "Countess Showery always says we shouldn't spend our time worrying over spilt blood . . . we should *drink* it." She snickered to break their tension.

He didn't even smile. "Tell me about your dreams."

Walking to the fridge, she took out a bottle of Taylor Burgundy and unscrewed the cap, then poured a glass for herself. After a moment, she went ahead and poured him one, too. "They're just dreams . . . I guess some people might think they're nightmares, but I *don't*. I haven't had nightmares since I was little, Phil. My day life was so terrible, I had to learn how to control my dreams." She shook her head and laughed. "Sometimes I think *they* control me . . . but they're definitely not nightmares!" She thought of this afternoon at Mom's with a brief flinch. "Not . . . not really. Not . . . anymore."

"You're lucky." He took the glass from her and sniffed it, then sipped.

Connie sat back down and sipped from her own. "I dream a lot . . . even when I'm awake. I used to dream about the guys I wanted to fall in love with me . . . about dates I never had. I'd listen to the other girls talk about their dates and experiences with guys, and when I'd sleep, I'd put myself in their place." Her lips curled dimly. "It wasn't real, but it was nice, and then . . ." She shook her head.

Phil closed his eyes and took another drink.

Connie watched him. "Then I started to read Scarlett's books and I found out that Countess Showery was so much like me . . . so sometimes, I pretended to be *her*. It was fun . . . I fantasized about her and Count Downe, pretending I was *her* in my dreams. Vicky told me she used to do it, too. She . . . she still does . . . even though she's a lot prettier than me." She hesitated, waiting for him to deny her self-critique, but he said nothing.

She hadn't thought he would speak. Not really. Connie sniffed.

"So what about these dreams at the convention?" asked Phil. "Tell me, okay? I've been dreaming, too."

"You told me you've had your nightmares for years, Phil, what do they have to do with mine? I'm not having *nightmares*."

"You said you got that mark . . . *in a nightmare*."

Connie shook her head, stroking her breast. The soreness fell further and further away. "It was a *dream*. Like the others. I dreamed of Count Downe and Countess Showery, just like I used to. I don't do that so much anymore, but I guess meeting Scarlett brought them back." She hesitated and took another gulp of the tangy-sweet wine. "Don't laugh, but I dreamed about *her*, too. I dreamed she

185

came right out of the mirror like the undead in her books, that she wanted me and cared about *me* . . . that she sucked my blood to make me into a vampire like the Countess . . ." She giggled and sipped her drink faster. "It's something I always wanted. Pleasure without guilt . . . like . . . like fucking without ever getting pregnant . . . that would be great. I hate to be pregnant, Phil. It's not fair that it only happens to women."

Phil frowned, mashing his fingers together as his eyes twitched. "I . . . How . . . how many abortions have you had, Connie?"

For a minute, she wanted to throw the glass across the room to show her anger, but instead gripped its slick sides tight. She stood and slammed it down on the table, jarring him. Her breast was suddenly stinging all over, as though all her bitterness with life had seeped back into it at a rush. More than ever, she longed for Scarlett's dream teeth to suck it out of her again.

The pain. Her life.

His lips sagged and he held out his hands. "I'm sorry," he said. "I shouldn't have said that. Look, Connie, I've had your dreams, too . . . ever since I met Scarlett in Amarillo. I dreamed she came to me . . . like you said, out of the mirror—"

"Fuck you, Phil." Connie walked past him and into the living room, kicking a box of books. "Fuck you . . ." She felt new tears and the loss of Gary more strongly than before. At least he had never accused her like that—All the losses of her life. Now like they were like the loss of *herself*. She turned away from him. "Goddamn you!"

A second later, she jerked as he touched her arm. "Connie . . ."

"Leave me the fuck alone!"

He didn't. His hands squeezed her forearms to pull her around. "Look at me, *please?*"

186

"Why?" She felt her nose clogging as the hot tears streaked her face. "You don't give a shit!"

"Look, Connie . . . I do. I'm sorry I said that. It—it hurts me, too . . . But your dreams . . . they're just like mine are now. About *Scarlett*." He bit his lip, whispering. "I'm *not* crazy—you've got the marks, too. *You* can see them in the mirror, too!"

She shoved him away, wanting him to release her. "Just leave me alone, Phil!"

"No. I *do* care, Connie!" He paused and she heard the long intake of his breath. "What if . . . Scarlett really *is* a vampire? What if our dreams *were* real and she sucked our blood?"

The hysterical giggle caught her and juggled her, flooding and churning her stomach back and forth. "You *are* crazy! And you probably think the mirror travel is real, too, don't you?"

He flinched further back. "It . . . it happened to both of us, Connie."

The pale texture of his face and the earnestness in his eyes bored into her. She sighed, trying to release all the anger and frustration. "No, Phil. Nothing happened to me, or to *you*. We just had dreams and maybe these damn marks are some kind of stigmata or some shit like that. We were both at conventions and we both met Scarlett . . . and we both had similar dreams . . . it doesn't make vampires *real*."

He reached up to her breast.

She backhanded his fingers away. "The marks don't prove anything, Phil."

"Connie." He stretched his face painfully and shook like he always did before a seizure.

"Don't you dare have a blackout, Phil."

"Connie . . . I really care about you." He gulped. "But I'm afraid—"

She shook her head, leading him to her bedroom and

finding a rubber this time. She tore open the package and rolled the latex in her palm, getting into the sheets. She hurt, and she didn't want to think, just to feel. To feel *good*. "Don't be afraid. Is this what you want? I do. Experiencing pleasure, this is what it's all about, Phil. My hopes and dreams are just that—*dreams!* Love is the fantasy. You need to finish that book by Scarlett. Love is a fantasy we all think we need to make us feel better. So, let's fantasize, okay?" She kissed him deeply, mechanically, pulling him onto the mattress, shifting herself over him, reaching down to force his new erection. It took time, but his tongue rejoined hers, in and out of their mouths.

And finally, she wrapped him in the thin lubricated armor she wished they'd used earlier, and lowered herself onto him. She came like a volcano and he did, too. She liked the power it brought her. Thoughtless . . .

Power.

She lay down beside him, but neither of them spoke, then she rolled to one side of the bed and he stayed on the other, not touching.

Listening to her snores, Phil studied her, exhausted, fearing his dreams. He knew they would be worse than ever when sleep finally came. The ragtag confusion of his life tugged the darkness closer, leading to the familiar nightmares, while Mr. Sawyer's hard words came back to grate in Phil's subconscious.

This new frustration of guilt was real, more than the mere nightmares. Nightmares that had foretold his future . . . the nightmares of his own hell that he now knew he deserved. An endless circle from the death of his first love . . . the undeath of his life, into an undeath of memories that sucked the hope of life out of him. His problems were all of his making . . . in his fears. His mind.

His self.

Did he really care . . . even about Connie?

Unable to hold open his eyes, Phil slid helplessly into them, sucked into the dark hole in his center.

His soul.

The mirror of . . . his soul.

The tenseness rose fast around him, and this time, nothing could slow it. The peace Connie's nearness once gave him was only another memory . . . far more distant than those approaching. He was fighting tears of frustration while the knife in his skull split it apart. Phil could all but feel the fluids spurting out of his brain and drenching his hair, leaking down his face onto the damp pillow. He clenched his hands together painfully, trying to drive out the recurring headache.

The dark room and Connie's raspy breath disappeared into the blacker sheet dropping over him . . . all the chilling nightmares.

He saw his wound when he looked in the mirror, and now, its doppelgänger on Connie's reflected breast.

A man's got to face the truth . . . or he ain't a man.

The images swirled through him.

They slept. Connie awoke in the middle of the night, her nipple hurting, thinking she heard Phil calling her. She sat up in the bed and yawned, looking down at him. "Phil?"

He was asleep. She lay back down and snuggled close.

Dear Connie . . . I still want you.

She opened her eyes on the face an inch from hers. Her breast ached, and she remembered.

She scooted back from him, her heart pounding, sad.

You must overcome your thoughts of love, Connie. Love isn't real . . . it's part of life, and life is a misery. In life, you must take the good and the bad. You see that better than ever. Only in undeath is

189

there pleasure. The choice of taking only what you want. Only in self.

Staring up at the dark ceiling, Connie felt a misgiving, and wondered what had awakened her.

She closed her eyes.

Chapter 15

Eternity.

Slipping through the crevices of her casket and the smooth tomb walls to stand on the mausoleum's floor once more, Teresa examined that singular, encompassing thought that had taken up her resting hours. She was still a bit weaker than she knew she should be. She had spent way too much time in the dark wondering what the fuck had happened to her. All it had taken to be free was a little selfish self-denial. Now, she had a lot of blood-sucking to catch up on.

Teresa studied the names of her close and distant relatives on the wall's plaques. Alex Carson, born June 1, 1931 . . . died December 28, 1988 . . . June Carson . . . Samuel Carson . . .

On and on.

Eternity. So here she was for that long period, and where the fuck were *they?* Where were her grandparents and aunt . . . or any of these unknown ancestors?

Heaven or Hell? For the first time since a young teenager, Teresa wondered if either of those legendary places existed. Vampires existed. She *was* one, even though those fangy creatures were believed to be legends, too.

Teresa fingered her new necklace and looked into it.

Eternity . . . and for all those long, long years, she would never see herself again.

That was a long fucking time.

And where the hell *was* everyone else? If *she* could breech death to claim this form of an afterlife, there had to be others like her . . . and surely there were other forms of an afterexistence besides this one.

Ghosts maybe?

Again, Heaven and Hell?

The scents of the city night breezed in to her. She remembered the Shade books that hadn't dealt with her new questions.

Those books dealt with *blood*—claimed blood was life. The experiences of others in the blood. *Undeath.* Scarlett's only concerns through her characters was in having a good time. "Is that all there is to it?" Teresa asked, listening to her voice that didn't even echo. It bothered her. No reflection . . . no echo to her voice. Like she wasn't only dead, she didn't even really exist. "Wrong." She denied her wayward thoughts. "I think, therefore I am."

But there was no echo, only the crackling sounds of dead leaves in the breeze outside.

"I am, therefore I think."

The taste of Brian's worthless life was even fading inside her. Her hunger was back and stronger than ever. "Nothing lasts forever," she told herself.

Nothing but herself.

And others like her. Scarlett Shade.

The memory of Al Pacino in a gory gangster movie . . . *Scarface* . . . came back to her. " 'Is this all there is?' " she tried to quote his cocaine-blinded character. " 'Is this all there is? Just fucking . . . and sucking . . .' "

Sucking. She tried to hear an echo of the Cuban accent she'd imitated badly, but nothing.

Nothing. Nothing but fucking and sucking for eternity. *It could be worse.*

Teresa pushed her feet through the dust, looking down to see that she didn't even leave footprints. She *was* just like a dream.

Somebody's worst nightmare.

"Fuck, fuck, fuck," she said, leaving the building and studying the grounds . . . now her eternal home. "Suck, suck, suck," she breathed, pacing her words like a silly rhyme. "Sucking, fucking . . ."

And now Gary was dead, too. She'd gone to his place to make him like her, finding his wrinkled father and plump mother there. They'd answered his door with teary eyes, and the surprise of them and not him had stifled her hunger for a startled moment.

"Gary . . . Gary's left us," Mr. Wembley had sniffed to Teresa. "We're going through his things."

Mrs. Wembley looked up through the tears in her eyes, too, holding one of Gary's old shirts in her arms. "Didn't you used . . . to date Gary?" she had asked.

The whole situation of sadness and frustrated love had made Teresa feel very out of place. Although it was nearly impossible to remember those emotions . . . any emotion, Teresa knew *she* had once loved Gary.

Turning abruptly away from his sniveling parents, Teresa had hurried back to the street, glad they didn't remember she was dead, too. She tried to feel sad but wasn't able to feel anything except hunger.

For blood . . . for souls.

For life.

She did her best to recall her experiences and the sensations of life, but those distant memories . . . like her years in college, high school, and the distant times before that as a child . . . were gone forever.

Something she could never return to.

Flowing fast over the path to the gate, Teresa paid no attention to the wind-trembling bushes and trees. She just felt empty . . . worse than even the worst times of life. She knew why Count Downe and Countess Showery, and *all* vampires sucked blood. It was another question that had bothered her since her self-discovery. Why did a dead body need blood to exist?

She knew the answer now.

The old Bible verse she had been taught as a good little girl in Sunday school class . . . "the life of the soul is in the blood." It was true.

The life she craved . . . a vampire's sustenance . . . had nothing to do with physical existence. It was all a trick. All done with mirrors. The life of others was all that gave her her new meaning.

Mirrors. She looked into the necklace, letting it fall back between her breasts as she misted herself through the gate bars and rematerialized.

It was going to be a long eternity.

But as a strong scent of hot blood flooded into her immediately, Teresa shrugged. She planned to make the best of this. She'd always made the best of every situation. Following her nose, Teresa paced as normally as she could down the sidewalk, kicking aside torn newspaper pages and a pop bottle, chewed sucker sticks. At least she was real enough to do that. But the bright orange street-lights she passed didn't show her shadow. "Me and my shadow," she sang, the sound of herself like a shoe getting free of sticky mud. "What fucking shadow?"

Near the end of the cemetery block, the delicious odors drawing her were very strong. Teresa stopped and peered at the old blue-and-white VW van faintly squeaking and shaking at the curb. She stretched her novice powers toward the vehicle and examined the fucking man and woman inside, literally *fucking.* She formed a sudden smile.

"Cool," Teresa breathed. "This ain't so bad. I guess it just depends on who you have for dinner." After all, Brian had not exactly been filet mignon.

More like a stale McBurger.

This was the real thing.

Feeling a lot like Jimmy Stewart in his Hitchcock peeping-tom movie, but guiltless, Teresa studied the thoughts of the sex-starved housewife inside the van. . . . Sheila, married for six years to a man who was obsessed with his work at the accounting office and barely knew she and their young children existed.

Teresa identified with her easily, feeling emotions similar to those she'd once known. but that were now too distant to fathom on her own.

But she was overjoyed to remember them . . . life . . . through this Sheila.

Her partner, Patrick, was her husband's jobless brother. He had plenty of time for Sheila.

Before Teresa could examine him closely, she felt a change in the situation and faded into a mist. Just in time. The van's side door slid open with a slippery clash of metal. Patrick poked his square-jawed face out, looking back and forth down the street. He looked right into Teresa's cloudy disguise. "I think a fog's rolling in," he called quietly back into the dark van, clicking shut the door. He stepped onto the sidewalk, kicking a can, still turning his face from side to side furtively.

But there was little traffic at this time of night in the area. Teresa listened to distant honks in the stillness. She'd only noticed three passing vehicles in this whole time. The stone and brick business buildings across the street were now as dark and lifeless as the cemetery.

Patrick took a last glance, then walked right into Teresa's cloudy form, and she knew why as he reached the cemetery wall and unzipped his pants, rolling his sex-slicked dick out.

Before he could pee, Teresa regrouped and flowed up to the top of the fence, reforming seated atop it. A bare branch stroked her forearm. She uncrossed her long legs and hauled up her hem, inches from his nose. "I love golden showers," she said, wishing she could give him one.

But that was something else death had taken away.

His head jerked up. He stared into her naked shadows.

Teresa jumped, almost on top of him. She reached out to touch him, guessing him at seven inches, hard, and uttered a sound of admiration. "I guess you know how to use that?"

Patrick's open mouth clucked . . . dropped low as he saw the clarity of the air now around him.

Teresa filled his eyes with hers, knelt, and swallowed as much of him as she could, biting deep, sucking hard, and reveling in the rich memories of a bad-ass life.

It took two minutes to finish him off. He gasped and shook, and fell with a loud smack.

That was when Teresa remembered the need for caution. A suicide? But there was nothing around to cut his wrists and make this look like another one . . . and the coroner would wonder where his blood had gone.

Then Teresa saw the bite mark she'd left. Two deep holes and a speck of blood. She smeared the spot on her finger and licked its warmth, puzzled. There hadn't been any sign of her attack in Brian.

The mirror.

Teresa knew she'd fucked up . . . but who would believe it, anyway? She didn't plan to fuck up again. Checking out the housewife inside the van, Teresa looked into her necklace frame, seeing Sheila's oval face smiling with anticipation for her dead playmate. Teresa rubbed the glass and concentrated her will through it, into Sheila, relaxing and sliding forward to the van as the side door slid open once more . . . to Sheila's blank face.

"What—"

Teresa shoved her back inside and closed the door behind her with a quick thought. "Want to suck puss?"

she asked the stunned housewife, now having a pretty good time despite her earlier worry. She understood Count Downe's motto.

Live for the moment . . . let eternity take care of itself.

Chapter 16

Phil felt the soft mattress take form under his back. The artificial light hurt his eyes. Weakness made him like watery molasses . . . the way he sometimes had felt back during college after a boisterous and very drunken party.

Long ago.

He squinted at the familiar woman standing beside the bed. Connie.

The sight of her chilled him in the snatches of his nightmares. It all came stinging back. He pushed himself up on an elbow and stretched his right hand toward her.

Impassive, she met his hand and held it to her stomach. "How . . . are you feeling?" she asked.

"Dizzy." He welcomed the bruised emotion in her tones that betrayed her gaze. He lay back down and relaxed as much as he could. "What's wrong?" Phil looked at her.

She moved to the head of the bed and stroked the hair off his damp forehead. "You were screaming, Phil." Her lower lip hung low. "It must have been a real bad nightmare. But after the crazy things you . . . you were saying last night, I'm not surprised."

"I dreamed about Scarlett Shade," he told her. "It started off with Czeckovslovakia, but then . . . it was Scarlett and her teeth . . . and . . . she had a *knife*." He clenched his fists. "She—she was going to drink all my blood, Connie . . . just like she was going to drink *yours*." Knife. Why? His head buzzed, knowing Scarlett didn't need it with her teeth.

Were they real?

Bloodless bodies. Suicides. Tensing his muscles and making his stomach tighten, Phil sat up too quickly and the mush of his muscles wouldn't hold him.

But Connie caught him.

He pushed his face into her breasts, remembering her own pain too late as she flinched. She didn't pull away or cry out. Instead, gasping lowly, she pressed him closer. After five wordless minutes like that, she shifted him and he saw that her face was as covered in tears as his. The strength was returning to him again and he moved to the edge of the bed with her help.

She helped him stand. "What does this do to you, Phil?" her frightened voice slipped into his ear. "What's . . . happening to *you*?"

He didn't ask her what she meant and went to the window with her, peering out as dawn lit up a small row of businesses: a paint shop, diner, drugstore, and insurance agency. Early morning traffic already flew by on the intersecting streets. "You mean . . . to *us*." He rubbed his face and leaned against the wall. "It . . . feels like I'm living my whole life all over again," he muttered, nearly stumbling as he backed away from the window. "It was . . . awful. Look, Connie, I . . . I'm sorry about last night. I'm sorry I frightened you, but you saw the marks, too. You have them. We . . . we're both infected . . ."

Her eyes turned away. "The marks are just an illusion, Phil. A weird coincidence. We were both upset. We could have seen anything last night."

"But I saw them—*you* saw them!"

Connie shook her head.

"Why does your breast hurt, then?"

199

"I told you," she said. "I probably bruised it. I'll be fine."

"So you think that maybe I *should* go to a . . . a hospital for a while . . ."

She squeezed him close without a reply, but nearly lifelessly, her touch as distant as a nurse's. She helped him avoid the book stacks as she guided him back through the hall to the kitchen table. He didn't speak as she helped him sit down in one of the straight-backed chairs. She seemed to withdraw from him even more. Her expression hardened. "You can't afford to go to a hospital, remember?" Then, as if everything were quite normal: "Want some oatmeal?"

He stared at the pot she put on the stove and shook his head. "I'm not hungry, Connie."

"All right," Connie relented. "But you have to eat something, Phil. I want you to have some soup, at least. After that you can just stay here all day and take it easy. I'll open your store and take care of all that since I have a couple of days off." She rinsed out the pot and searched through the cabinets until she found a can of Campbell's Noodle Soup. "I'm going to call Vicky and invite her to come by, so I guess I'll just close up shop for lunch the way you always do. I need some time to be with someone who . . . *understands* me. I won't be gone long. If you get antsy in here all day, finish reading Scarlett's book, okay? Then maybe you'll understand me, too." She made a high, light laugh. "Maybe you'll understand yourself."

He flinched at what she said, but helped her as she made a pot of coffee. "But—"

"No use arguing." She poured the soup into the pot and added a can of water, waiting for it to heat up. "Scarlett Shade is just the prescription for you. You'll feel real good afterwards. Take it from someone who knows! She's not a vampire, Phil. Vampires suck the life out of others and Scarlett gives her life to others . . . through her books, and"—she stopped and shrugged—"it's just part of your crazy nightmare." Connie poured herself a cup of coffee.

He looked down at his feet. The smell of the soup drifted closer and he was surprised at the hunger it awakened. So much like the hunger he felt in Scarlett's words when he'd read her book . . . and . . .

Phil looked into the living room at that title on the coffee table. If that book could drive him deeper into his nightmares, maybe that was just what he needed. Maybe it was the tool he'd been searching for to end the fear of his past. Through it, maybe he could finally face that truth. Maybe it would lead him to the truth of these new visions.

Maybe it would end the never-ending confinement of his own, private undeath . . . an undeath he knew he'd chosen to escape his own truths . . . to escape his own life.

Hiding the emotions beginning to surge again, he watched Connie, missing the security she'd once brought him. He didn't want to face himself, but now, at long last, it seemed the only way out.

She made a painful face and rubbed her breast . . . smiling thoughtfully a second later.

Chapter 17

"What have I gotten myself into?" Connie whispered to herself, walking down the hall to leave the old apartment house. She sneezed at the odor of its rotting floorboards and ejected the calm demeanor she'd shown Phil, surprised she'd pulled it off. She knew that her half-remembered dream of Scarlett had helped. She was near the independence she wanted. At least, the independence she wanted to *show*.

But it wasn't real. Connie knew that.

Last night, the need to cling to him, just to cling to anyone, had been so strong. It had her feel better and those moments had helped drive the loss of Gary farther away, giving her a needed focal point.

But that point wasn't Phil. It was *Scarlett*. Scarlett had come to her dreams to give her the peace Phil had offered her, then taken away. Scarlett took the guilt and hurt in exchange for fantasy, making life and responsibility unreal.

Because of Scarlett, her breast . . . her heart underneath it . . . didn't really hurt, no matter the way Phil had crushed them both. Scarlett had emptied them of feeling. Connie felt *wonderful*, full of the careless desires in the innermost spirit she now chose. For just a moment of doubt, the nipple *had* stung, but Scarlett's light caress had driven that sting and doubt away. Connie stopped beside her car as she passed through the small parking lot, rubbing her fingers over its flaking paint, feeling an urge to just get inside it and drive. Maybe to Mom and Dad's . . . or Vicky's . . . or maybe she would just keep driving.

But Phil needed her. He'd never screamed so horribly, and last night, he'd been absolutely raving. It brought new goosebumps. When he'd opened his eyes, he'd stared at her for long moments before the taut expression in his face relaxed.

He'd called her Sonia . . . his murdered cousin.

She shivered.

His fantasies were hideous nightmares of pain. Hers, of Scarlett. Joy. Freedom.

His memory lapses were delusions.

The cars sped by with occasional noisy honks. Connie ignored the sound of rumbling tires and walked quickly down the sidewalk and past a 7-Eleven. The cool air felt good on her face. She bought a newspaper and walked on to Phil's store. The only real appeal to the simple concrete block structure was its brightly painted sign. Winged dragons and fluttering bats surrounded the name's blood-dripping letters.

Realms of Fantasy. At least her own fantasies . . . Scarlett's . . . weren't so horrid as Phil's.

At nine, she put up the OPEN sign and turned on the bluish fluorescent lights, staring around the big room of books defiantly. The Realms of Fantasy. She bit her lip. Her tit was hurting again, but the mark she'd avoided in the mirror this morning was a fantasy, too. It had to be.

Phil had a mark just like it.

Vampires . . . She rubbed her breast.

What if it was true? What if Phil was *right?*

So what? Being a vampire wouldn't be so bad. What did she have to lose? What was so special about life?

No one came in. There wasn't much to do. The place

203

needed sweeping, but it looked like she would just about have all day for that. Connie called Vicky, wondering where her friend was as she left a message on her machine. Connie was already bored and just thankful she'd bought the newspaper from the stand next door.

The news was sickening, though. No wonder Phil avoided it. Worse than any horror film or novel, because it was *real*. The people dying and suffering were people like herself . . . starvation in the Soviet Union, another skirmish in the Middle East. Closer to home, ritualistic murders and more suicides.

She didn't want to think about it. Instead, she considered how different life might be if only vampires *were* real. Like Vicky had said . . . like Scarlett's books said, if everyone were undead the fears and troubles of life would be over.

But first they had to die.

She went to the phone and picked it up, looking through the Oklahoma City book until she found the number she wanted, then dialed the state hospital. "Dr. Kevin Matthews, please?" she answered the questioning receptionist.

Three long minutes passed as the words she would say tumbled in her mind.

"Yes?" he finally replied. "This is Dr. Matthews."

"Doctor," Connie said, her throat dry, "you don't know me, but I'm living with Phil Ottoman. My name is Connie Sawyer."

"Yes?" he said again.

"Phil's having some real problems," Connie told him. "He"—she shook her head with a guilt she didn't understand and didn't want to feel—"he's bad off, Doctor."

"Connie? You're the woman he's living with?"

"Yeah," she nodded. "Doctor . . . he's talking about vampires . . . *real* vampires."

"I know," Dr. Matthews said after a long moment.

"He's trying to blame something besides himself for the guilt he feels. Thanks for taking him in . . . Phil told me you were helping him out and I'm relieved about it. Are you okay around him?"

"That's . . . why I'm calling, Doctor. He keeps going on about vampires—"

"Vampires are just something he's latched on to through his other interests. How's he doing?"

"I just told you," Connie said. "I mean, the poor guy is really going over the side . . . the next thing I know he's going to be arming himself with stakes and hammers and *garlic!*"

Dr. Matthews laughed gently. "Calm down . . . what was your name?"

"Connie Sawyer."

"Phil's always had a problem with paranoia, Ms. Sawyer. Putting off his fears on fictional vampires is just a step towards his recovery. If he can focus all his fears and delusions on them . . . something that doesn't even exist, then maybe he can be free of his confusion—"

Connie hung up. Phil was right. Nobody cared. The doctor's explanations were fine . . . probably looked just great on paper, but . . . She bit her nails again, wondering why *she* cared. She got out the broom, swept the store thoroughly, then found a rag and a bottle of Windex to scrub the big windows.

At half past eleven, a young man—a college boy—walked in and moved to the section of science-fiction paperbacks. Connie gave him a smile but he didn't bother to return it.

Nobody cared.

When she finished the windows, she walked past him to the counter.

"Where's Phillip today?" the young man asked, rubbing a high forehead.

"He's not feeling well."

He combed back his greasy black hair with a nod. He was wearing an O.U. sweatshirt under his suede jacket and looked the part of a typical yuppie freshman. "I'd feel sick if I was him, too. Hell, he was up there at that convention in Denver, wasn't he?"

"I was, but Phil stayed here," Connie replied. "Can I help you find a book?"

He finally smiled. "I was Phillip's very first customer . . . Brad Slade. He helped me finish up my first edition Koontz books." He put the book in his hand back on the shelf and picked up another, flipping through it until he found the signature. "Phil really comes through, doesn't he?" Brad grinned. "Almost every book he carries is signed."

It was one of Tim Power's hardbacks she herself had gotten signed.

No, she thought sickly. *Gary* had gotten it signed.

Again, why did she care?

Brad put the hardback under his arm and picked up another, coming to the counter and scanning the newspaper. He lowered his voice, glancing back through the empty store cautiously. "Personally, I think the suicides are really *murders*. I read about how all the bodies were drained of blood. It would take real guts to kill someone and then drain the blood out of them. All that time, and you would just be sitting there and watching all that red stuff seep out . . . be hard to do before the blood coagulated, too. I think it must be someone who really doesn't give a shit about human life at all. Maybe a cult. Maybe it's even Scarlett Shade herself drumming up publicity!" He shook his head. "But has anyone mentioned those ideas in the newspaper . . . hell, no!"

Brad's words bothered Connie more than she showed him. They reminded her of how hard it was for her to believe that Gary had committed suicide . . . or that he'd been into gay sex.

206

It was just hard to believe he was dead.

Those thoughts brought back the terror of loneliness . . . that life was all a big masquerade of lies people told to use each other . . . not like her fantasies.

Or maybe . . . *just* like her fantasies. But different.

Weren't they?

Phil.

Vampires.

Connie didn't want to care anymore.

Vicky waltzed into the store ten minutes later. Connie sold Brad the two books and walked out with him and Vicky, locking the door behind her. She didn't hear the phone ringing.

Chapter 18

Phil sat at the kitchen table for a long time after Connie had left and he'd finished eating. He had felt the change in her.

The unfinished Scarlett Shade book waited for him across the room. So did the mirrors . . . inside them, his memories. Every guilt and fear. A never-ending journey of undeath.

Around and round we go . . . where we stop . . . nobody knows. . . .

But he knew. He saw his fear reflected.

He didn't know what he wanted to do, but he dreaded the book and the pull of its words . . . the feeling of Scarlett it brought far too near. He went to the bathroom and washed up, neglecting that mirror when he changed his shorts and pants. The pain in his face showed more than enough of his wound. The hurt in his eyes, reflecting the mirror . . . reflecting his eyes, reflecting the mirror.

An infinity of pain.

The phone rang. Phil hurried to it and picked it up. "Hello?

"Phil . . . is that you?"

Kevin. Phil breathed deep in the receiver. "It's me. What happened to you, Kevin? I called Sunday and you never—"

"Phil . . . are you all right? What's going on, guy? I told you to keep quiet about that vampire shit, and now your girlfriend just called me up and—"

"Connie called *you?*"

"Just now. Is she there?"

Phil rubbed his lip, wondering if she had called Kevin because she cared, or if she was just scared of him. Care. Scare. His heart pounded. "What did she say, Kevin?"

"What *could* she say?" he asked. "She's worried about you . . . you've probably scared her, too, telling her your stupid stories. Look, I told you—"

"Kevin . . . she's been bitten, *too.*"

He sighed. "Okay . . . cut it out, Phil. This isn't helping you deal with anything. You're afraid, and now you're scaring everybody else. Look, vampires can't exist. That whole bit with the bites and the mirrors is just a lot of crap, okay?

Taking a deep breath, he felt his solitary responsibility. The loneliness. "Whatever you say, Kevin."

"Damn it, Phil. You're my friend . . . but if you keep it up, you're going to wind up in a padded cell. Vampires are dead, guy. They're dead people risen to life to suck blood. They turn into bats and fogs and . . . they're *dead,* Phil!"

Phil was silent.

"They're dead . . . they're just like your fantasies, Phil. These *fantasies* are vampires, because they're living off your life! Just like your goddamn nightmares!"

"They're not *dead,*" Phil repeated. He looked at two mirrors, side by side on the wall. He saw himself . . . and slowly, just as it always did now when he looked at himself for a little too long, his image began to alter into the scenes he most dreaded. *"Undead* . . . I—I'm sorry Connie bothered you, Kevin."

"Phil—"

He dropped the receiver in its cradle, staring into his past . . . the destruction of Prague and his mind.

Life.

Undeath.

Beyond those wasted streets, dimly figured, a woman . . . beautiful, full of every fantasy he could want . . . even Sonia.

Undeath. His reflection . . . himself. His very soul.

It took fifteen minutes for the surrealism to fade, and Phil sagged as the strength drained out of him. He struggled to renew his determination. In his youthful viewing of *The Exorcist*, the priests had given their lives to save the souls of others . . . opposing the way Scarlett's vampires gave away their souls to save their self-centered forms of life, to saturate themselves with the lives of others.

A twisted reflection. Maybe an exact reflection . . . mirrors showed, always, an opposite to their image. Life . . . death.

He was infected by death and had been since birth, but now he was infected with undeath as well. So was Connie . . . maybe thousands of others . . . through Scarlett Shade. Phil found his wallet and van keys and went to the door. This was something he had to do, and he didn't want to put it off now that he was actually overcoming one of his greatest fears. Curiosity and the need to know was overpowering his fright not to know. He walked out and got in the van, starting it and backing to the street.

The traffic of cars and trucks stretched ahead as he steered into their midst. He squinted in the flashes of shiny bumpers and windshields. Buildings and stores with hurried pedestrians became quiet residential blocks of older homes, grandmothers on porches in rocking chairs . . . young children darting through yards of fallen leaves.

Finally, majestic buildings of stone and newer concrete appeared from behind those houses and their trees. He steered to the university and its columned library, then watched for a parking space in the rows of cars. He pulled the van in fast as a yellow Impala backed out. Students carrying brightly colored tote bags, notebooks, and text-books walked back and forth between the cars and glanced at him with superior grins. Phil got out, listening to his shoes clap the concrete, trying not to blush as he followed the signs and other students to a sidewalk.

Their giggles and voices seemed so innocent and care-less . . . he envied them. When he reached the barely decorative building Phil was tired with an age beyond his years and more beaten than ever. Up the steps, a door slid open for him and he walked into the paneled lobby of dark red wood, smelling the familiar scent of fine binding and rich paper.

But he didn't go to the fiction section . . . not even to religion or occult arts. Instead, he passed the long infor-mation desk and its beak-nosed attendant as she checked students out. Then a reading area, to enter a glassed-in room full of recent newspapers hanging over a rack of poles on the walls. A young man in a red-and-white O.U. sweatshirt was the sole occupant. He sat on one of the two plaid couches, reading an Oklahoma City paper, glanced up almost sourly at Phil's noisy steps, then back down at newsprint,

Phil inhaled that pulp smell, too, and ignored the stu-dent. His heart was pounding as he located Monday's *Denver Chronicle,* then the previous weekend's *Tucson Star.* Gulping, Phil found Monday's copy of the New York *Times* and a *Newsweek* with an old picture of Scarlett Shade on its slick cover.

DREAM WRITER . . . NIGHTMARE OF SUICIDES, read the magazine's biggest headline. He saw a copy of the *National Enquirer* on the coffee table between the two couches, and started to pick it up, too.

"You going to read all those at the same time?"

The student on the couch looked up and back down at

211

the woman's stern voice, and Phil twisted to see her in the doorway. Her unmeant smile was as slick as her bright green business dress. Phil felt himself turning red. "Not at the same time," he said.

She walked in with a waltz and held out her hand. "Then let's just take one at a time, all right?"

"Yeah . . . I just . . ." He let her take all of them but the *Newsweek*.

She peered at the cover in his hand and dimpled, almost friendly. "Scarlett Shade. Are you a fan?"

Phil shrugged. "I just want to find out more about her . . . about these suicides."

Her smile slipped. "A young man was in here last week with the same ideas. He has the notion that these suicides are really murders . . . is that your line, too?"

Swallowing hard, Phil shook his head. "Not . . . not exactly. I . . ." He let his words drop off and sat down across from the student, hoping the woman would leave.

"Good," she said. "I'm a fan of hers. I think these suicides are terrible, but the way the government is using a task force to get her stuff banned is absolutely psychopathic. It's one of the first times I've ever seen government groups and church groups agreeing on anything." Her slender eyebrows closed together, taking the momentary charm from her smooth face. "You're not with any of them, either?"

"No," Phil said, picking up the *National Enquirer* from the table and laying it over the magazine.

BLOODLESS BODIES—THE VAMPIRE WRITER! screamed the *Enquirer*'s front page, showing another older photo of Scarlett.

Older because she wouldn't let anyone take her picture anymore . . . because vampires couldn't be seen in photos, could they?

Nor in mirrors. The image of Scarlett in the mirrors . . . if she was a vampire . . . was false. A lie to life as much as vampirism itself.

"I wonder who brought that trash in?" sniffed the librarian. "I can't believe that even the *Enquirer* would seriously accuse a writer of Scarlett Shade's stature of being a vampire . . . next thing they'll be saying she's from another planet . . . or that she's Elvis!" She shook her head glibly. "Anything at all is possible in this day and age . . . for a cheap tabloid, anyway. I can't believe people buy that stuff and read it."

At last, Phil nodded with agreement. "Anything is possible."

"Let me know if I can help you find anything." Her smile came back and she finally turned away.

Phil didn't even nod, but stared back at the paper, alternating its columns with the magazine's. The periodical's wild conjectures and the opposing concrete facts merged inside him as he poured through their words, merging again with the dozen vampire novels he'd read and the greater number of films he'd watched.

Bloodless bodies . . . suicides . . . fans who wanted to be vampires . . . a writer who avoided mirrors and pictures. But in her books, in his *dreams*, the mirrors were a point of contact between a vampire's lust and a victim's surrender. To a self that was false and hollow. The milling ideas grew. . . . merging once more with his memory and a legend Scarlett Shade had redefined. Mirrors . . . traveling through them from soul to soul . . . vampires without reflections overtaking the reflections of others and dominating them in their blood lust.

Fantasy.

Inside him, just as in his nightmares, fantasy was merging with reality.

Shuddering, Phil hated this news more than any other he'd ever read or watched. It boiled the brain fever through him and he wished he'd loaded his system up with pain reliever. His head pounded relentlessly. Finding a pencil and paper, he jotted down dates and names of victims, not knowing why, not really knowing how any of this was helping him against his past problems or those more immediate . . . except that he was facing one of those past problems now, overcoming it to read this news to try and face his newest problem.

His skull throbbed. The soreness under his jeans was burning, too.

Newspaper followed newspaper, and Phil put each one up carefully before choosing another. The librarian came back and out as if she would catch him doing something he shouldn't. The student who'd been in here first finally left. A middle-aged woman, probably a faculty member, relaxed in one of the single chairs while reviewing a feminist magazine for a half hour. Faceless students came in and out as the morning became midafternoon.

Looking down at his two pages of notes, Phil replaced the Tucson paper and all its too-near memories. He had already read it, anyway . . . had taken the suicide story with him to show Kevin. He picked up the last, *The Denver Chronicle*.

GAY SUICIDES CONNECTED TO STRIPPER.

Phil sat down with a new feeling of nausea, worse than ever as he finished all the related news stories and that one. He started to get up and put the paper back down when he noticed another story. SUICIDE VICTIM FOUND BLOODLESS.

Phil read about Brian Schultz. He took a deep breath.

"Although Brian Schultz's body was found as the so-called 'Scarlett Fever' victims have been found, his only connection to that writer's books seems to be through a relationship with victim Teresa Carson four years ago. There has been speculation on this suicide being connected to the 'love triangle' deaths of Gary Wembley, Mason Hood, and Teresa Carson, but officials now believe the incidents of that connection are entirely coincidental."

214

Phil's appetite was really gone now. But . . .

He replaced Monday's paper and checked for today's, but the only current daily news was in the local papers. Phil picked up the *Oklahoma City Times*, rattling it fast as he sped-read the headlines, drawing frowns from a husky jock misdressed for the cool day in a jersey and shorts.

In the paper's second section, he found what he dreaded.

WAYWARD WIFE SUICIDE IN DENVER, BROTHER-IN-LAW LOVER DEAD OF UNKNOWN CAUSES.

With a tight stomach that had started to toss, Phil read of how Patrick Leader had been found on the sidewalk beside a graveyard, dead and drained of blood, the only outward sign of mayhem a deep and ragged set of holes in his testicle sac. A rat bite, hypothesized the officials and news writer, but no blood had stained the pavement, not even a drop.

Inside the van, Sheila Leader was a suicide, her wrists torn open by a pocketknife. No bite marks, just cut wrists and . . .

No blood.

It bothered Phil that the man's wound had been found and no one else's had . . .

Reflections.

Reflections of Scarlett.

Standing, Phil hoped for the understanding of the Shade novel he'd begun . . . that what he might learn through it would be worth a new nightmare.

Chapter 19

Vicky, dressed to kill in a very short skirt and top unbuttoned to her bra, pulled in at Taco Bell and ordered a sackful of delights for herself and a smaller menu for Connie. At the drive-through window she paid the teenager a special smile, lightly caressing the young man's thumb as he handed her the change. "What time do you get off, handsome?" Vicky asked, twirling a lock of her hair.

Connie saw his uncertain smile. "Six tonight . . . uh . . ."

"Maybe I'll be back for a snack . . ." Without waiting for his reply, Vicky pulled away and back onto Lindsay Street, back the way they'd come.

Connie frowned at Vicky. "That wasn't very nice to do to that poor guy, Vicky. Now when you don't show up, he'll be disappointed."

"Get off it, Connie. We used to do shit like that to all the guys. I'm just having some fun. Besides, I may just be back." Vicky was driving fast again.

Connie had already fastened her seatbelt. She tried to ignore the confusion Vicky's already probing fingers were driving her harder with. She thought she wanted this, but wasn't *sure* at all she wanted this.

But this time, it felt right.

It felt good, and it would help her forget her life, which was growing more confusing. Connie emptied her mind and began to reciprocate, closing her eyes. Vicky cooed, "God, this feels fucking good! Let's pretend, Connie, just like we're kids . . . When . . . oh . . . we get to bed . . . yeah, right there! Rub harder—"

Losing herself in Vicky's panties, Connie obeyed.

"You're doing wonderful things to me, Connie!" Vicky moaned vigorously, driving faster. "Listen, this time I'll be Countess Showery and you're my new maid and you don't know who or what I am . . . okay? Then you can be the Countess."

Connie . . . dear Connie . . .

The sweet, lush tone in her mind suddenly seemed more potent than just a memory . . . more than her dreams . . .

I wait for your sweet lips . . . to give you all the joy you want. . . . Don't refuse me. Don't refuse yourself. . . .

It was as though Connie were dreaming now, wide awake. Her heart beat fast.

Scarlett. Scarlett wanted *her.*

Scarlett Shade. Countess Showery. Count Downe.

Pleasure is the antidote to fear. Lust is the answer to frustration. Fill yourself with these and worry is a thing of your past. . . .

Connie remembered the words from *Blood Shower* exactly, even though it had been months since her last reading. Those were the words Countess Showery had spoken to the young woman she was initiating into the glorious life of undeath.

It was as though Countess Showery . . . Scarlett Shade herself . . . were speaking them to Connie now, coming into her mind and releasing her into the freedom she so often craved.

Connie breathed faster, hearing but not understanding the meaning of the sirens closing in.

"Shit." Vicky looked up at the rearview mirror and

began to brake and pull over into the right lane. The sirens were hurting Connie's ears when the car stopped at the curb and Vicky parked. She took her license out of her purse wallet, then pulled her dress high up to the edge of her panties. "Have you ever tried this?"

Connie looked back at the police car behind them, its lights flashing bright even in the sun. She swallowed hard, turning back to watch the uniformed cop get out and write down the license tag. "Tried . . . what?"

Vicky giggled and fit the license inside her panties. "N-never. I've never even been stopped."

"I have, but"—her face turned a little pale as she winked at Connie—"but Scarlett says we should try everything, right?"

She didn't answer as the officer stopped at Vicky's window and tapped on the glass. Vicky rolled down the window.

The cop bent down and his flat face peered inside. First at Connie, then back at Vicky. "I pulled you over for speeding," he growled. "You were doing fifty in a forty-mile-per-hour zone."

"You . . . you want my license?"

"And your insurance verification."

Breathing deep, Vicky pointed at the glove box. "Connie, would you get my insurance papers?"

Connie leaned forward and held her breath as Vicky pulled her hem high again, exposing herself to the policeman, especially as she slowly dropped her hand into her bikinis and drew out the license card.

For a moment, the cop said nothing at all. "Do you have AIDS?" he asked lowly.

"No . . . no sir," spoke Vicky.

"Please hold the card for me so I can read it." But he squinted back down at her long legs.

"You . . . you're not going to give me a ticket, are you?"

He chuckled grimly. "Just be glad I don't haul you in for bribery. Come back to my car, please."

Connie handed her friend the verification form and clenched her jaw as the door slammed. She waited. Part of her began to want to just get out of the car and walk away . . . back to her apartment . . . maybe back to Mom and Dad's. The options were getting slim.

Despite the fantasies, reality intruded. She touched the door lever, the impulse to leave stronger.

Connie . . . dear Connie . . .

The voice held her there, but the white, blue, and red lights in the rearview mirror continued in her eyes, holding back a fantasy. This was *reality*. Five minutes later, Vicky got back into the car and slammed the door again. She stuffed the insurance form back in the glove box herself. "Faggot bastard," she muttered. "Goddamn fucking laws!"

Connie gritted her teeth. Laws. Despite her fantasies, the outside world was still there . . . despite Vicky's fantasies.

There were *laws*.

Vicky slid the car into gear and pulled away from the curb at a much slower pace. Vicky turned at the next light and drove through a neighborhood, pulling into her driveway minutes later. Connie suddenly felt dirty all over. The desires and satiation she wanted to be wrapped in dissolved completely. She blushed.

"The cop called in my license . . . and I just sat there like some dumbshit blonde." Vicky snorted, opening her door to the clean afternoon. "Fuck rules and laws. There are no laws for the undead!" She hoisted her sack of fast food. "Come on . . . we'll eat tacos . . . for dinner . . . and *dessert.*"

Connie followed Vicky to the blue-and-gold flowers surrounding the porch and then into the frame house much more slowly. They walked through the front room, between the TV and brown vinyl divan and two easy chairs. On the wall was an elegant, antique mirror, as big as Vicky's wide screen TV, rimmed by a reddish gold frame.

"That's it," Vicky said, gazing with her. "Good buy, huh? I found it at a resale shop for fifty bucks."

"Very nice," Connie spoke with a low jealousy, staring into the depths of a reflection already cloudy.

Her soul.

"Wine or beer?" asked Vicky.

"Wine." Then Connie shook her head, looking away from her worn face in the glass. "Maybe we—we shouldn't be doing this. This can't be right, Vicky. We—we're not acting like ourselves. There *are* laws."

"We're not breaking them now. This is the way we should act, Connie . . . the way we really want to be. We're independent and we can do what we want. This is the way people act when they don't have any guilt. Morality has changed, dear . . . that's the truth."

Connie bit a knuckle. "Truth can't . . . change. What about love?"

"Love, huh? Well, we're friends, aren't we? Truthfully, I felt real funny the other night after you left, but I went in and read four chapters of *Blood Fever* and I understood it all again. Love is for ourselves. I stared into the mirror in the bedroom and it was like you were still here with me . . . and you really were the Countess and so was I, and it was just like we were making it together again!" The refrigerator opened and closed and Vicky came back with a bottle of Reunite Rosato, and poured it into two glasses.

Connie caught her breath and looked across the room at Vicky's mirror, not at all surprised she saw Vicky instead. The image blurred and became Countess Showery, fading into a fuzzy portrait of Scarlett. Vicky took a sip of her drink and gave the other glass to Connie. "We're not hurting anyone. Phil's fine, probably jacking off to Scarlett now that you've got him to read her, and I know Ricky's fucking one of his bimbos . . . maybe even some guy." She sat down at the table. "Did I tell you about that, Connie?"

Connie tasted the chilly wine and suppressed a shudder, then nibbled a burrito. "About . . . about what?"

Vicky went to the CD player and slipped in a disc. "I got him to read Scarlett, too, and a few days later I came home and there he was, right there on our bed, with his cheeks spread wide while some big guy from his office stuck a big dick right up his ass. He said he just needed the experience . . . told me that it was my fault for getting him to read the books. Can you believe it?"

The stereo sounds, a whisper of soft, lulling piano and strings. Mood music . . . New Age stuff, mellow for the masses. The hypnotic breeziness began to take away some of her anxiety. Connie frowned faintly, then deeper at Vicky's eyewitness account. "Rick? He's gay?"

Stuffing her mouth, Vicky shrugged. "He says he thinks he's 'bi.' I was pissed then. It was driving me crazy that he rejected me like that for another man, and I felt pretty inadequate until I realized it wasn't *me*. Count Downe says that no one is responsible for their own failings, remember? It's life that fails us. That's why death . . . undeath, I mean . . . is supposed to be so much nicer. Rick was right. He needed that experience, and so do *we*." She chewed and swallowed, standing. A moment later she put her hands on Connie's shoulders and moved them down her shirt. Vicky licked her lips. "Want to save the rest for later, Connie?"

Connie swallowed the last of her burrito. "I . . . I don't know—" The strings got heavier, their mood stroking her deep. "Why don't we just *talk*, Vicky?"

"We've been talking. We talk all the time. How about some body language? I want to share fantasies with you, Connie. Like we used to. Like last week." She came closer. "I just want to have a good time . . . *that's what it's all about!*" She unzipped her dress and forced it down her ankles.

The bad feelings tugged Connie back.

"What's wrong, dear?"

"I don't . . . want to. I just want to . . . talk. We're friends—can't we *just* talk?"

Vicky sighed and nudged her cheek to Connie's, her tongue a slippery worm traveling Connie's neck. "You're so afraid to be yourself, dear, aren't you? But remember, pleasure overcomes fear every time. I'll give you so much pleasure that you won't be able to think for weeks, dear Connie. We'll just take from each other until there's nothing left, and then we'll move on to someone new . . ."

Nothing left. Connie tried to push her back, but Vicky seemed much stronger than she'd remembered.

As though understanding Connie's gasp of surprise, Vicky hugged her tighter and jerked the collar down her shoulders. "I've been taking aerobics . . . *dear.*"

The softness in Vicky's voice was gone.

"Vicky!" Connie hissed.

"I'm giving you just what you *want,* Connie. I know your secrets." To prove it, she dropped her mouth and hard tongue onto Connie's neck, massaging a tender spot that sent a shiver of need shooting into Connie's sore breast. "Oh—"

"Yes," whispered the voice, soft again, as Vicky unbuttoned what was left of the torn blouse. "I'm *really* seducing you, just like—" She licked Connie's burning nipple fast . . . removing the bandage and sucking that tingling injury that was aflame in urgent desire.

Spreading that desire all the way through Connie.

It was . . .

Ecstasy.

Give in to yourself, dear Connie, whispered Scarlett's

dreamy voice. As though Scarlett herself were here with Connie now.

As though Vicky were Scarlett.

Give in to me. Be mine. Forever . . .

The voice of the books . . . of their author herself.

Of herself . . . her desire.

Vicky's hands slid the jeans down her legs and Connie cried out, hot and moist already. "Please . . ."

She felt herself rise into the air as the strong hands wrapped her waist . . . eased her down on the table, and she moaned in the moisture of Vicky's tongue sliding up her inner leg to tease her—

Then she screamed as every flicker of pleasure disappeared just as suddenly as it had come . . . as hard, savage teeth bit into her—

Chapter 20

He hated to sleep on his back . . . especially in his clothes.

Gary Wembley awoke, his throat dry and his hand reaching out for the lamp beside his bed as he tried to turn on his side.

Thunk.

A solid wall.

He stared into the blackest darkness he'd ever known, trying to remember where he was. The last thing he could recall was Scarlett Shade, taking down his pants and offering to suck him off . . . then actually doing it while some faceless guy stuck a long dick up his rectum.

"Shit," Gary muttered, wondering if it had actually happened. He felt nothing now . . . not sore . . . he could only remember how he *had* felt . . . it was as if his nerves were dead.

But that sensation in his memory had been fantastic. . . . Scarlett drinking everything out of him, every problem, until finally, her teeth in his flesh had become painful.

He'd grunted. She had looked up, releasing him from her delicious mouth for a moment.

The sight of the dripping red drops on her lips and teeth had shot terror into him, but he couldn't even gather the strength to keep breathing. When the sharp pierce of teeth clamped around him once more . . . the man had taken her place. Gary was fascinated when he'd watched her pick up a sharp knife and could only sigh as she sliced it deep into his nearly unfeeling wrists. The man continued to chew into his numb skin.

"What a fucking nightmare!" Gary groaned now, reaching out for the lamp again and hitting a solid wall once more.

The nightmare wasn't over.

"Where in the fuck am I?"

He lay in the crushing blackness, struggling with impossible memories to know where he was, calling out against his wild, dry ramblings.

Gary? I found you. I heard you—I felt you. Come out!

"Who is it?" Gary groaned, shoving his hands into another solid wall above him. "Where the fuck am I? What kind of a joke . . ."

Cool it, Gary. You're dead. I'm dead, too. Scarlett got us both.

The words formed inside him like his own thoughts, but they sounded like a voice. Teresa Carson's voice.

"Teresa? What kind of a gag is this?"

No gag, Gary. We're really dead. Now, just disbelieve in your past and emotions, disbelieve in purpose and love, then think of yourself as a mist coming up through the ground, and you'll be right here with me.

"Don't fuck around, Teresa. Where am I?" He tried to feel nervousness and thought he should be breathing hard with panic—

But then he knew that he wasn't even breathing at all. Dead.

But it didn't even hurt. He just felt . . . empty. "Shit!"

Cool it and come out of there, asshole!

It was ridiculous, but he did his best to try it. It was nearly impossible, but she egged him on, and he resolved himself; if she had done it, so could he! Finally, he lost his small sense of love for others . . . even for the parts of himself he always hated in others, and imagined himself becoming a mist. A minute later, Gary reformed beside her in a moonlit, leafy graveyard. He smelled a thousand scents more vividly than he ever had, and they struck at his memories, making him more hollow than he'd ever been.

It was Teresa, right there in front of him, the moon-glow shiny in her golden hair as it overpowered the final rays of sunset. They looked at each other with less emotion than either of them thought they ought to feel.

"Thanks," Gary finally said, looking down at his clothing . . . the same wardrobe he'd worn at the con. An open collar plaid shirt and wrinkled slacks. "Shit . . . are we ghosts? We're really dead?"

She nodded. "Here's the deal, Gary. Scarlett Shade's a vampire, okay? She killed me and I guess she killed you. But she sure fucked you over in the way she did it to you." She smirked and handed him a wadded newspaper.

"I don't believe it," Gary said, sitting on his ground plaque awkwardly, his knees raised to his shoulders. He unfolded the paper loudly and his eyes kept returning to the picture of himself as he read the story of how he'd been found . . . with that fan, Mason. Dreadfully, he moved his hands to his crotch and felt—

"Oh, fucking shit!" Gary unzipped the pants and slid fingers across the stitched remnants of his balls and a stubbiness—all that remained of his cock! The nightmares were a fury as he understood that all of them had been hideously real. "Shit . . . now everybody thinks I'm a fucking fag! That bitch made me fuck him up the ass while she watched, and then he . . ." Gary tried to find saliva in his dry mouth to spit, then gave up. "I have no dick! I remember . . . and . . . and—"

"Take it easy." Her thin lips curled, showing him the tips of two fangs he found almost as sexy as her exposed leg.

226

He reached up and found his own fangs, rubbing them with amazement and nearly forgetting the terror of his loss. "Wow. It really *is* true. I just can't believe this shit!"

Teresa put a hand on his shoulder. "It's not so bad, Gary. You didn't have much of a cock, anyway, and you don't need it now. The pleasure is all in our mouths. I remember the stuff in the books exactly, so I know what we have to do. Shit, I just feel sorry for the guys who wake up vampires who don't have my memory." She was wearing a long, slinky gown of blue-and-white silk, slit temptingly up the side. Her long leg showed as she perched her hot butt on a tombstone across from him.

"What was wrong with my dick?"

She shrugged. "You did what you could with what you had. Forget it."

He reached into his pants again bitterly, then stared back at her. "Fuck."

Teresa walked in a prim circle as though modeling. "I can wear something new and expensive every night. *We* can do it, you know. You just have to imagine the way you look when you come up from the ground. Maybe you can even imagine a nice, long dick."

The idea made him grin. "Well, thanks, Teresa." Gary tried harder to believe in the inconceivable. "I probably would have been stuck down there for a few hundred years before I would have figured it out."

"Hey, bats of a feather got to stick together. Now, I'm hungry."

He felt a gnawing in himself. A really strange sensation. The emptiness wanted to be fed. "I think I am, too." Then he thought of his books and ambition of being a famous author. "God damn that bitch! No wonder Scarlett did this to me! She knew I was going to be a really hot author, and she probably didn't want to compete—and she . . ."

Teresa sighed and shook her head, reaching to pull him up. "I doubt it, Gary. I've read your stuff and hers."

"That bitch!" Gary ignored her, but followed Teresa past monuments and trees to the side gate. "I ought to go after her and kick her ass! Revenge! I'll teach her a fucking lesson! If she had a dick, I'd bite it right off! Maybe I'll just bite off her nipples!"

When they stopped at the gate, Teresa rolled her eyes. "Now cut it out, okay? Forget about being pissed. The first thing on the menu is blood. You can still write. She does, right? You can do just about anything you want to. And you'll have a really long career, now. I felt like you did at first, but what's the point?" She touched the tips of her fangs. "The only points are in our mouths. Just cool the revenge shit. We're all on the same side, the way I see it. The only thing that matters about life is that we drink it."

Gary looked at Teresa for a long moment, at her very pale complexion, and shook his head. "I *am* pissed. You should be, too. And we're not on the same side, either. She's on her own side and we're on ours, and since she did this to us, we're the good guys, and we owe it to ourselves and her other victims to kick her ass."

"It'll be hard to kill her since she's already dead," Teresa soothed him, looking down the street. "Come on, Gary. I smell blood."

Smelling the tasty odor crawling into him, too, his memories of the other feelings disintegrated fast. He followed her pointing finger to a group of teenagers coming out of a show at the Bijou Theater down the street.

But he still wanted to do something kind of nasty to Scarlett Shade. The least she could have done was tell him what she was up to.

But goddamn, she'd sucked him good.

Chapter 21

. . . Countess Showery looked into the eyes of her newest love, bathing her hot face with a damp rag. She tasted the sweet blood on her own glittering teeth. "And now, my dear love, you will never die. Undeath is already a part of you and courses through your lovely white flesh. You are blood of my blood forever. Seek life you need not pay for. All life is yours in undeath. You will find it in your lovers as I have known it again through you. All the pleasures of life and love are yours now, just as your life is mine. Drink deep for yourself. The only peace is the peace of self. The peace of death . . . of undeath."

The maid, Vermillion, flinching once more as Elizabeth Showery's delicate mouth found its welcome between her thighs, closed her eyes to circles of stars that led her into the future she was so joyously promised. The pain of the bite was overcome in that rapture . . . of death . . . of all life and responsibility eased away to give her the desire of her own self and the hidden pleasures she had always craved.

Vermillion was one with the Countess.

"How can we be damned when every experience in life is ours through blood, my dear? The priests have lied to you. There is no fear in pleasure . . . no pain in our undeath. We are vampires . . . living through others still existing in that physical realm. We have cheated the judgment and no door is shut to us . . ."

* * *

Connie woke to not only the sharp pinch in her breast, but a boiling hysteria of needles being thrust into the crevice of her thigh and lower abdomen. "Ow!" she whined, her hazy eyes finally making sense of the whirling room.

"I . . . I cleaned out the wound really good, Connie. I didn't dare call an ambulance—what would they think of us? I can't believe—"

Neither could Connie. The moments came back to her like another dream, but this one *was* a nightmare. The proof of it was right there. In her pain . . . the drippy warm blood covering her pubic hairs . . . staining Vicky's teeth and face. The dark red splotches were already drying into crusty streaks. "I—I'm so goddamn sorry, Connie! I—I must have gone crazy!"

Raising an arm underneath her, Connie propped herself up and remembered it far too vividly, but as though it had happened to someone else.

Like a dream. A fantasy. A fantasy gone bad.

Biting her tongue, she touched the gauze bandage taped to the center of her agony.

Shuddering so hard she felt ready to fly apart . . . half expecting her limbs to rip from their sockets and shoot across the room . . . Connie sat up and held tight to the table to keep from falling. The blackness tried to overcome her again. Her ears were humming seashells, stinging with the shallow sounds of the replaying CD.

Those notes flooded her with approving sounds even as her own sick masochism filled Connie's throat with illness. Dropping to her stomach on the table and shrieking as her wound slapped the wood, Connie slid over it with hard gasps, holding tight to keep from falling onto the carpet.

"Connie!"

Sinking to the floor, Connie shook her head, finding her clothing and slipping it on with weakness. After another moment, Vicky did the same. Connie refused to think of why she was here . . . what had happened.

Vicky's sobs, more forced and mechanical now, were still loud. "I—I just couldn't resist you. You got me too excited." Vicky went to the sink and washed her face. "Man, you really had some power over me, Connie . . . you did *make* me do it, didn't you? And I thought I was putting you under *my* power . . . It m-must have been the power of the blood like the Countess and Count always talk about. They can never resist the want of blood . . . the pleasure . . ."

Barely holding herself together, Connie said nothing for a moment. "I—I want to get out of here, Vicky."

Vicky stiffened. "Oh, fuck," she moaned. "I can't believe—"

"Forget it, okay? Let's both just f-forget any of this happened. Just get me out of here."

Vicky dressed quickly. "I didn't mean to hurt you. I—I'm your friend. The divorce is . . . affecting me . . . making me do things."

Connie looked down at her feet, thinking of her own excuses. "Are you going to drive me?"

Grabbing her purse, Vicky stared at the table and the mess of spilled food around it. She looked very lost. Her face suddenly blank. "Goddamn . . . what happened, Connie? I barely remember . . . it . . . it's like I . . . blacked out."

Blackout. The cure for bad memories. With a hiss, Connie faced her. "Let's go . . . please."

They went to the door. It was long past dusk. The movement of Connie's legs made the soreness between them stretch inward and she began to cry silently. Vicky helped her into the car, and Connie ground her teeth as she sat down uncomfortably. She jerked back to avoid Vicky's reaching fingers, which dropped to her crotch as though nothing had happened. "Don't touch me!"

231

Vicky sniffed. "It wasn't *my* fault."

"I hurt, damn it!"

Vicky got in and the car shot down the street. Connie blinked from the passing streetlights and the glare from opposing cars. "I didn't *mean* to!" Vicky cried, the tears on her face real.

The disgust Connie knew for Vicky and for herself was worse than even the sting of her flesh. She had wanted it . . . for a moment, she had even enjoyed the hot pain of Vicky's teeth breaking her skin . . . the way it flooded her with a masochistic delight that was even more a combination of agony and ecstasy. There had been no laws in those instants. No separation of life and death.

Undeath. No truth or absolutes . . . only the perceptions of fantasy. Its mutual insanity had overcome them both, pushing them into a frenzy for self-satisfaction.

"We didn't do it right," Vicky whispered. "The books say there's no lasting pain in pleasure, Connie. Don't be mad at me . . . just think about it. Pleasure, no pain. You have to believe in it and forget everything else. We just didn't do it right—weren't ready. We will be next time. Maybe at the convention this weekend . . ."

Connie shivered.

Dear, sweet Connie . . .

Silence stretched until Vicky stopped at the store. Connie opened the door and got out.

"Please . . . forget it all, Connie."

Forget it all. Scarlett. But something inside her held on to the memories . . . even those that couldn't be real.

Vicky grinned vacantly. "I . . . I think I'll go find dessert since we didn't work out too well. That guy back at the restaurant. I'm still . . . *hungry.*"

Connie clenched her teeth. Vicky *was* cracking up.

Maybe *she* herself was cracking up.

Now . . . back to Phil.

He was cracking up, too.

Vicky just waved as the car pulled away fast, and Connie waved back automatically, barely believing she was acting so friendly. So civilized.

To a long-time friend . . . who had just—

Headlights bathed her momentarily as Connie walked to the store and checked to be sure she'd locked it. After pulling on the door handle, Connie leaned against the plate glass window and touched the new soreness in her crotch, then the pain now throbbing violently in her breast.

Breathing deep, she walked to her apartment down the street.

What was happening to her? Why?

Everything will be fine soon, dear Connie.

Connie couldn't hold back the imagination of herself under Scarlett Shade as Scarlett kissed her and licked her just like Vicky had. Her breast pinched.

More than ever, that fantasy seemed to have been real.

What the hell was happening?

Chapter 22

Phil finished *Death's Sweet Door* an hour before.

He poured himself a cup of coffee, thinking and facing himself more firmly than he had in years. The past and his problems had come down on him hard through his continued uneasy identification with the story told in the novel: Count Downe and Countess Showery, lovers from childhood, denied the simple pleasures they so desired, even the pleasure of being together. Downe and Showery had chosen undeath as freedom, denying responsibility for themselves and others in the loss of their love. Denying love itself. The Count and Countess went from activity to activity to fill the hollowness they had made eternal.

The understanding burned inside him: no matter how they denied it, they were yet prisoners of the life they had rejected. No matter how they denied responsibility, it was still part of them. Their only true reality was in their empty reflections . . . the images of that life they devoured to replace their loss. In the opposition, Phil had struggled hard to hold on to love, gathering its guilt tight.

Vampires were no longer a part of things real . . . only memories and desires kept them alive through others. It was all they had left.

He himself had held tight to his memories, too, not

understanding the dependence he placed on them . . . and now, they were practically all he had left.

But unlike the vampires . . . the emotions he felt were still his own, and he could yet go beyond his memory.

The book had spoken to Phil's own emptiness . . . scaring him so that he had wanted to be a part of Scarlett Shade's world. As it was, he was barely more alive than the Count or Countess.

A person had to face the truth . . . particularly their own truth. Wise words from an asshole, Connie's father.

Phil made a new pot of coffee and sipped the brew as he sat on the couch and stroked his fingers through Wolfgang's silky fur. The cat's simple purr of pleasure made him feel better, and he tried harder to relax and forget the ideas that had delivered greater violence to his headache.

He wanted to ignore his self-discoveries and cover them back up . . . to relax in the peaceful, numbing mindlessness he accused so many convamps of. He wanted desperately to forget the news of suicide and death he had read this afternoon, and roll up inside himself. "What can I do about it?"

The cat continued to purr.

Phil stroked the warm animal, thinking of the convention suicides and his dreams . . . the invisible marks.

Bite marks.

Had he really used his guilt of a shame he didn't even have to hide from his true responsibilities? Had he really used his fears to hide from the world around him? He wanted so badly to deny it.

But it was a fact. He had tried to keep from caring because he cared . . . because it hurt to care. He'd used the wound of before to protect himself from new injury.

The fresh coffee was bitter as he swallowed. Phil put the cup down and shifted uncomfortably, biting a knuckle. The pounding headache became worse, but Phil didn't get up to find the Tylenol.

The visions in his head were no longer only those of his terrible memory of Prague and the deaths of loved ones. Vampires, seducing through fiction, rewriting legend and history just like modern Nazis . . . devouring the souls that begged to be eaten, and Phil was infected, too, but he had been for years. He shuddered at the sound of Sonia's long-ago, terrified death scream.

"Jesus," Phil whispered, feeling the wormy goosebumps slithering under his skin. "I'm really crazy!" He shut his eyes tight. Five minutes later, he reopened them at the sound of dull steps outside the front door. The lock rattled and it opened.

Connie, pale and timid, just as Phil felt. She stood, silhouetted in the hall light, then held out her shaking hands to him.

The sound of her trembly breaths sounded an alarm in Phil. Her shivering, shaking fingers looked just like Sonia's those two and a half decades ago as Sonia implored the advancing soldier . . . a loss of life he couldn't have changed despite the guilt he'd wanted to feel.

"Phil . . . please . . ."

Pressure rattled him and instinctively, he shrank back. "Phil—"

She needed him. Her hands were Sonia's, Katherine's . . . Every person he had ever known, especially those he had hidden from in his own self-pity for Sonia. In that instant, Connie became a hundred people from Phil's past, her features a montage of every one of them. Her voice a combination of every plea . . .

Driving back hesitation and self-preservation, Phil forced a new will into his legs and felt himself standing, impelled toward her.

Just in time. She sagged into his arms, clutching him weakly. "Connie," he wheezed. "What—"

She screamed.

Part Four:
Inside a Bat

Chapter 1

Saving the last computer file for her newest novel, Scarlett Shade laughed and made a backup on floppy disk, then fit it into a cardboard envelope and stuck on an address label for Dark Descent Books. To her editor, Carol Kacek.

Carol would love this one.

But Carol loved all Scarlett's stuff, and Scarlett trusted her to revise the words to their most profound witness. Even though Scarlett had not yet turned Carol, it was almost as if Carol understood what she was doing and was undead herself . . . perhaps it was her greed and lust for power that had made her so sympathetic to Scarlett's cause. Like the truest capitalist . . . a vampire, she had cornered the market on horror writers, forming Dark Descent as a powerful book line and using the power of the contracts she gathered. She timed the release of the books she controlled to propel the writers she chose for success to the top of the charts.

Writers like Scarlett. Scarlett herself. Carol wasn't at all like some of those other editor bastards who published for the sake of mere art and entertainment . . . the ones like those overly conscientious bastards, Wendy McCurdy, Dana Isaacson, and John Scognamiglio!

One of these days, Scarlett promised herself, she would

initiate Carol and give her the joy and promise of the words she loved so much in these books. Carol had proven herself worthy.

And with an editor even more in tune with her then, Scarlett knew she would never need fear censorship.

But now wasn't the time for business thoughts.

Scarlett was delighted with the progress Connie was making. She had touched that woman over the distance between them constantly these past nights, drawing Connie to a desire she would be unable to refuse from Scarlett. Scarlett had even been able to use Connie's friend, Vicky, through the power in her written words, then the mirrors, to urge Connie faster down the path of her seduction.

Scarlett had high hopes for Connie . . . for this weekend when she knew Connie would come to her again.

The way it looked, so would that failed seduction, Phillip Ottoman. She recognized him now through Connie . . . the book dealer she had been forced to leave in Amarillo. Not only because of the alarm he'd raised through his screams.

His blood terrified her. Her, a fright of the night. Every seduction she directed at him through the link of blood or through the mirror's windows was overcome by his fears and self-berating guilt . . . a twisted emotion of love he would not release. He was so close to her, but so opposite, and his selfish fear, not of death, but life and his own failings, destroyed her best ability to use her reflective powers against him. His irrational lunacy was as a lake of the purest holy water, so powerful and self-perpetuating that overpowering him was a challenge she wasn't ready to undergo again.

Not yet.

Scarlett closed her open casket and took the envelope of her manuscript to the stairway, floating up it without effort.

Making the memory of past failure fade, Scarlett stared

back down at her envelope. It was time for celebration, not recrimination. But rather than smoking a single cigarette and sipping a glass of champagne like some Stephen King character, Scarlett planned the best of both worlds.

A young man from the writer's group she had spoken to last month. She would let him drink and smoke, and enjoy those tastes in his blood. Through the senses of others the same sensations became completely different, exciting. It gave her the knowledge of every viewpoint she made her own. Even if she was unable to make much other use of those wonderful tasting treasures and pleasures, at least it now created her writing ability.

Opening the cellar door through her will the way Jeanne had long ago taught her, Scarlett drifted down the long, paneled hallway to her study and its shelves of books. She laid the envelope on a finely carved table for mailing tomorrow and admired the line of the two dozen paperbacks she'd penned. The first several had been all her own ideas, but it was so much easier the way she worked now . . . revising and restructuring the manuscripts of others that would never be published anyway . . . adding her own special knowledge gleaned from the experiences she made her own. None of those now dead amateurs had ever found the talent to rise from the grave and survive. They existed in a hell of the undead, weak and trapped forever.

But she didn't feel badly about it. At least their words, disguised as hers, lived on.

They should be grateful if they ever found out. They always acted grateful when she promised to help them achieve publication.

Those thoughts brought Scarlett back to the nights when Jeanne had still been showing Scarlett the ropes . . . that very first night when Jeanne had brought Scarlett to the home of her own fiancée. Adam had not been completely serious about loving Scarlett more than his life

241

itself. Not even the promises of fantasies and pleasure of the hours she would give him could demolish the solid barrier of what he thought he believed in. He refused the seduction in her eyes and touch, driving her from his bedroom with a cross she hadn't even known he'd owned.

At that moment, his faith in the reality of life's lie had been strong.

When Scarlett fled back to Jeanne, Jeanne had explained it: that the seduction of such a will was not only necessary, it was the fun of undeath!

Standing together in the overgrown dump that was Scarlett's secret graveyard, Jeanne, dressed in a sassy miniskirt and pullover blouse, laid her cold hand on Scarlett's. "The meals that willingly come to us are already all but ours, Scarlett. Like the fast food restaurants, they give us the sustenance that keep us going, cheaply and quickly, but we all want the blood that is like an expensive caviar. It's so much more satisfying, and each enemy we make ours adds to our strength . . ."

Scarlett remembered nodding, even though she didn't really understand it all then. No more than she could comprehend how Adam's fervent belief in a power she'd rejected could drive her away from him.

"That's trickier," Jeanne had answered her question. "Adam doesn't even really believe in a power of God. He's just watched too many horror films. The faith he frightened you with is shallow, based only in fear, and if you were more experienced, you could have overcome him. You're still a baby in death. You will grow . . . and you'll learn not to even flinch, and how to trick such an unwilling victim."

"How?" Scarlett had then asked. "Is there a power over us? Is his fear a power?"

Jeanne had looked across the dark dump at all the rusty cans and torn newspaper, leading Scarlett into the adjoining cemetery. She walked across the grass toward a monument shaped as a tall, stone cross.

Scarlett followed uneasily, averting her eyes from the shape that seemed to glow and vibrate with the life she'd rejected.

"Why do you fear stone?" Jeanne kissed the cross lustily. "See. It is only a symbol. Not even a symbol erected in faith . . . only in tradition. The God of this cross . . . His Son who died to shed His blood for the freedom of man, is nearly forgotten. His love was sacrifice, not for His own pleasure. He wanted to give love for nothing but our acceptance, but we'd much rather have lust. The very memory of such love is nearly dead. A symbol without living faith is nothing more."

The brightness Scarlett had seemed to see, the danger she felt in its proximity, faltered. Scarlett stepped nearer to the structure and with her hand led by Jeanne's, touched the cold stone.

"God is dead to us. Jesus Christ has no authority over us if we refuse Him. If you refuse His trickery of the gift, you are not obligated to the giver."

Her earlier life and its learning, still near to Scarlett then, wouldn't let her understand. *"But . . . but Adam—"*

Jeanne drew her from the cemetery and back to the dump, then to the house she'd fled, clutching her hand tight. "Your lack of faith in yourself and purpose made his sniveling fear, a weak faith in love and life, more than it was. I will show you how. Watch me closely."

They arrived at Adam's still open window and Jeanne had slipped in through his blue curtains like a fast fog. Scarlett stared after her from the windowsill and gasped as Adam looked up from the bed he lay on, dropping the phone receiver.

"No one will believe your story," whispered Jeanne, floating to him fast, her feet barely touching the carpet.

"Back!" Adam screamed, finding his tiny cross.

Jeanne paused, and as Adam and Scarlett both dropped their jaws, her clothing had disappeared. Not even underthings hid her sleek, perfect figure from their eyes.

Adam dropped the cross at Jeanne's feet.

Jeanne kicked it aside with a flash and smell of sulfur, then glanced back at Scarlett. Scarlett tried to climb inside the room as gracefully, failing even that.

A sound made Jeanne turn back to Adam as he bent to pick up the cross again. Jeanne glanced at Scarlett. "Get rid of the clothes, darling," she whispered.

Forgetting how her teacher had gotten out of hers so quickly, Scarlett touched her top blouse button.

"Just think them off," Jeanne sighed. "Disbelieve in them. Our domain and power is in the mind, dear. Use it fully."

And Scarlett did. Just like that, her clothes were gone. She later learned she could make them reappear at will. Adam's face churned with uncertainty and finally, his lust for life's pleasures rather than life itself won out. The cross slipped from his fingers once more and he welcomed them both, crying out his joy as they both sucked him.

Dry.

Unlike the memories of her life before turning, Scarlett remembered that evening well. All the victims afterward wanted her seduction. Few of them resisted as Adam had, and Scarlett longed for such a challenge again . . . to make undeath more interesting.

Phillip Ottoman was such a challenge . . . more than. But through Connie, Scarlett knew she could weaken him and make him more manageable.

The doorbell gonged.

Scarlett stopped dead, turning to the hall. Perhaps she wouldn't need to call anyone to celebrate after all, but who could it be at this hour?

She stopped in the bathroom and looked in the empty

mirror, squirting on an extra layer of perfume. It covered her taint of death quite well, and when anyone noticed that underlying scent, she dismissed it as a fragrance she called Grave Delight. Some people had asked her where she bought it so they could get some for themselves.

Gong.

Walking more normally now, no longer floating, Scarlett straightened her long, black gown, disturbed a little when she didn't find the scent of life and blood beyond her door. She unlatched and opened it slowly.

"Hello, Ms. Shade. I guess I may as well call you Scarlett though, huh?"

Her inner senses told her disbelieving eyes that she really *was* seeing Gary Wembley . . . and behind him, that damn snoop, Teresa!

"Speak of the devil himself!" But as she shoved the door to slam it, both of them rushed it, and despite Scarlett's greater power, their leverage proved her defeat. Gary bared his wicked fangs as he kicked at the wood and shoved hard with his shoulder, and Teresa flung herself against it so powerfully the thick barrier cracked. Flung back by the force, Scarlett retreated to the hall as they both came in and shut the splintered door behind them. Teresa's wired face was open-mouthed. The hate in it ebbing as she gaped around.

But Gary stared Scarlett down. "You *bitch!*"

Scarlett studied his thoughts and held out her hands peacefully. "I didn't expect you so quickly, Gary, but I'm glad you're getting the hang of undeath. I've been looking over your manuscripts and—"

Teresa was still taking in her extravagantly decorated home with a gasp of admiration. "Wow! This looks just like the insides of the castles in your books!"

"Yes," she nodded matter-of-factly as she slid into her convention mode, still holding Gary captive in her eyes. "Description is easier when you can do it firsthand. A lot

245

of writers go to visit the settings of their books, but I find it simpler to just bring the descriptions into my own setting. Of course, I still find a lot of interesting things in the cities I go to conventions in."

"Tell us about it."

She took a step toward him. "I really am glad you found me, Gary . . . you, too, Teresa."

"You *killed* us!" snarled Teresa.

"You enjoyed it," countered Scarlett.

"That's not the point . . . if either of us had known what you were doing——" Teresa's face lost its wonder and became calculating.

Scarlett took her hand gently, stroking and leading Teresa to the fireplace at the end of the room. She tossed a waiting log into its red coals. It was a big stone fireplace, fashioned like the one in *Citizen Kane* but a quarter of its size. Even so, it was ten feet across and filled up most of the wall. Above it stood a shelf of her awards from various writing and publishing organizations. In the center, the prized Stoker statue of a golden haunted house, a horror novelist's Oscar. Scarlett sat down on the furry bearskin carpet near the warmth and patted a spot beside her hip.

"Wow." Gary followed them, his eyes glued to the awards. His footpads had become soft and gentle . . . timid. She felt his admiration in her achievements.

"I've given both of you what you wanted. What everyone wants. The streak of vampirism runs deeply in everyone . . . to reap life without any self-cost or denial." She coaxed Teresa down on the hairy bear rug, still eyeing Gary.

Gary squatted beside them at last. Teresa still frowned. She pushed Scarlett's hand away.

Scarlett sighed with a mock-surprise. "I was going to come for both of you but I thought the autopsies would take longer." She eyed him carefully. "I've been reading your books . . . you're really a fantastically gifted writer."

She wanted to choke on her words but stayed cautious. "I was thinking that we might even . . . *collaborate.*"

"Wow," Gary whispered again, staring back up at her trophies, kneeling close against her as her fingers slithered over his face, reaching inside him. But his own supernatural abilities shielded him.

Giving up, Scarlett faced Teresa, appraising her with fondness as she remembered her sweet taste. "So . . . how did you two manage to get it together so quick and get here?"

Teresa rustled her gown. "I've got a photo-memory, remember? It took me a week, but I trust my memory more than anything, so I knew that no matter how unbelievable what I remembered was, it had to be real." She bared her new fangs in a proud smile. "I helped Gary out—"

"Damn good thing, too. I didn't have any idea what the fuck was going on!"

Scarlett raised a hand to hide her grin. "Congratulations."

Teresa's eyes shone brightly. "Thanks. It was a little harder changing ourselves into bats . . . especially for Gary."

He shrugged. "I always thought the bat shit was just a bunch of . . . bat shit." He chuckled.

Scarlett nodded, better understanding their abilities now that she knew how Teresa's memory had led them. "I see. And you managed all this without even drinking someone's blood?"

The room was silent. Since none of them breathed, it was far more silent than either Gary or Teresa expected. Those two looked at each other nervously.

"Well?"

Gary's eyes smoldered. "You bitch. That's why we're here. You *made* us kill. And they were just teenaged kids, too! And . . . and you had that asshole bite my dick off!

Everybody probably thinks I'm a fag and . . . and . . . If you hadn't done this to us—"

"Don't blame me," she hissed, facing Teresa with a gleam first. "You came to seduce and use *me*, remember?"

Teresa flinched and started to stand. "There's a difference . . ."

"Stay where you are!" Scarlett shouted, then faced Gary. "And *you* came to seduce and use me, too. Just to get yourself published! Both of you—you were vampires before I ever even set my teeth into you."

Gary stood up to her, his self-delusive rage so ridiculous in his state Scarlett wanted to laugh. Instead, she snorted. "It's too late to change things, now. You'd already made your choice. And Gary . . . I was lying. You're a shitty writer . . . a *dickless* writer. It's going to take a lot of work to uh," she snickered, *"revamp* your stories into one of my novels—"

The remnants of his human concern and pride made his eyes blaze redder than ever. "You fucking plagiarist! I knew it! And you made us kill those poor kids—and now they'll be vampires, too!"

"Well, hopefully they'll never figure it out. There's too many of us around already." She kept one eye on Teresa as she crouched uncertainly, the other on Gary, advancing. "So what the fuck do you plan to do about it?"

He lunged at her and she smacked him across the cheek with a lightning fast blow, knowing he couldn't hope to equal her hard-learned dexterity. Gary flew backward, crashing right before the rippling fire.

Scarlett flipped around to Teresa before the woman could move, letting fly a kick that flew into Teresa's jaw. Teresa jumped back with the force of the blow and her head slammed the wall with a splintering *crack*. Scarlett strolled to her and kicked again, smashing Teresa's dainty jaw askew and sending a molar and squirts of blood flying. Scarlett prepared a new assault, but stopped at the sound of a new crash and glass breaking. She wheeled to see Gary using the fireplace poker to smash her trophies.

"You little bastard!" Scarlett leaped and shoved him hard, knocking him into the sizzling fire with another backhand. She held him in the licking flames as they surrounded her fingers, watching his flesh blister with satisfaction. She ignored the pain it drove into her, hating the smell of her own sizzling like a pound of bad meat. But the aroma of his cooking skin was a sweeter song, and worth it. Her own damage was not irreparable in un-death. Scarlett turned her eyes back to a dazed Teresa as the woman struggled to get up, then back to Gary as the blood he'd devoured boiled in his veins and his dry flesh rose in tiny pus-bubbles, popping in a hundred places with new sputters.

His screams were shattering wails of agony as the fury ate its Hell through him and his soul struggled to escape the steaming, deforming flesh. It was becoming the pungent, green smoke that swept around her. "Too bad, Gary," she hissed. "Now you're really *fucked*. If you think it's bad being a vampire and sucking blood . . . try being a disembodied soul with no way to devour life at all."

Gary's struggling hands, boiling to his white bones, tried to circle her blackening wrists and make her release him, but she held him fast until her own arm began shriveling to underlying bone and her gown had become an eruption of flames. Scarlett let go, laughing at the sight of him, his beautiful long hair a sun's corona about his melting face.

Fingernails ripped down Scarlett's back and she swung to Teresa's snapping jaws. Scarlett removed her burning gown in a single thought and faced her new challenger. Even without Scarlett's dripping wounds, Teresa had no hope.

"Fuck you," Scarlett muttered, grabbing her with long

bony fingers and throwing her after Gary, knocking his struggling form deeper into the spitting, orange coals.

Teresa's shriek was more honey to Scarlett, and she lifted the poker Gary had dropped to punch Teresa deeper. Ashes flew, but Teresa's body was already becoming a blackened mass of scorched flesh and—

Quick as a flash, Teresa became a mist . . . a lighter shade of gray and green than the smoke raging into the room.

Scarlett swung the poker through the particles that came flowing toward her, past her . . .

The mist shot to the hallway, and Scarlett felt the wounded, reformed vampire's hatred . . . Teresa's threat of a real revenge.

"Like *you* can really hurt *me!*" Scarlett shouted, following the fog into the bathroom and cornering it. "Just because you've learned a couple of tricks . . ."

Without warning, Teresa's mist gathered suddenly, diving and splashing into the huge mirror over the sink . . . into a glass that reflected neither of them. The tunnel of souls.

"Fuck," Scarlett whispered, feeling the only true emotion she contained besides lust and hunger. She glared at the mirror that showed only the room.

Teresa had escaped.

Fear.

"Fuck . . . that bitch figured it out . . ." Then Scarlett reached inside the mirror, her hand disappearing into the glass. She groped her fingers through the cold, underlying emptiness, knowing it was useless to follow. Hundreds of thousands of mirrors everywhere . . . no telling where the bitch had gone. Scarlett backed out of the room and shut the door, then back down the hall to the living room and her rubble of awards. She looked in the fire at Gary's disappearing, skeletal remains. No more trouble from him.

But Teresa . . . Scarlett pondered the undead neo-phyte's wounds . . . she had a long fucking way to go to get back to her coffin before she could regain enough strength to take Scarlett on again. With her inexperience, Teresa most likely wouldn't even make it to a mirror anywhere near her grave. She could be lost inside the labyrinth forever.

At last, Scarlett laughed.

Chapter 2

An hour after she'd screamed and all but fainted, Phil finally managed to calm Connie down. He listened with a faceful of pity and disgust as she told him her terrible story.

When she forced down her jeans to show him the wound, she felt his emotions grow stronger . . . saw the rising pressure so familiar in his features. "Don't *hate* me, Phil! Please don't hate me! I don't even know—"

He clenched his jaw. "Why? How could—"

"I barely even remember what I was doing . . . much less *why*," Connie said, still weak. Her hand moved over his. "Look, Phil, you were *right*. There's something happening. Not just to you . . . not just to *me*. This thing with Vicky . . ." She clenched his fingers hard with her own, drawing his grunt. "It was just like Vicky and I were in one of the fantasies we always talked about. Just like the fantasies I had when I read Scarlett's vampire books! We were pretending that . . ." Connie began crying harder. "It wasn't *me* with Vicky tonight, Phil. I don't know what the hell happened to us, but we really weren't *ourselves*."

His arms were strong around her until she was lying silent. "Maybe . . . maybe that's really the answer, Connie. Shade's learned to use our fantasies. She's learned how to control us." He shook his head back and forth, then walked to a poster of Karloff as Frankenstein's creature . . . a duplicate of the one in his store. "I saw the terrible things going on around me. Life. It scared me—everything scared me. Just like *him*." Phil tapped the poster. "I've always wanted to get away from it all and just hide . . . and just like what happened to *him*, I've been letting it all drive me insane." He bit his lip. "I thought *I* was crazy." He brushed his slacks. "All these suicides . . . she's got it made, Connie. It's the perfect setup. Her fans all want to be vampires. They beg her to bite them . . . and she *does*."

Connie's hand was lax in his.

Connie. Dear, sweet Connie.

The sounds in her memory.

The sounds in her own dreams. She held her hands out to him. "In . . . in the reflection . . ."

Phil looked into one of her mirrors at himself and her. Behind them, around them, the shadow of Scarlett. "I know." He came closer, pressing his palms to hers. "She's killing people . . . her own fucking fans. They're supporting her in more than one way."

She mashed her fists against the turmoil inside her. "She *is* controlling me. God, Phil—what does it mean? I hear her now!" She shuddered, her lips tremoring, and the tears slid down her cheeks freely. Her mouth opened and closed in nonsensical sounds, but Phil soothed her as best he could, silently stroking her hair.

Her nails dug into his skin harder. She saw the impossibly real teeth in Scarlett's mouth. Those teeth that had pierced her nipple and stung her as they bruised her tender flesh. "She's *not* a fantasy! Oh, Jesus, Phil!" Her fingers unbuttoned her blouse. "But how . . . *how could it be real?*" She hissed lowly. "Oh, Jesus, Phil. Oh, no!" Her wound grew hotter and hotter—the pleasure now a fire of futility. Connie felt herself slogging through that bog of bleakness, falling. "It really *happened!* It *was* Scarlett, Phil!

I . . . can feel her in me now! She *is* a vampire! Her fangs
. . ."

She swallowed hard but couldn't speak. She reached out to him, knowing she was fainting. Blacking out.

". . . *are* real."

Chapter 3

Connie couldn't sleep.

The voice . . . Scarlett's . . . was silent inside her and she wondered if it had ever been real. Outside her . . . inside her. Confusion. A fear of life and her fear of death collided in the pains of her body, digging deep.

For long minutes, she just lay there on her bed, trying to find comfort in the sheets and blanket, in the smell of Phil's fear surrounding her.

Who was he really?

Who the hell was he?

She tried to drift, liking the way she'd dreamed and imagined him as Count Downe come to life. Mysterious, full of fun.

Yes, Connie, the voice returned. *Full of fun. Full of life and love. Just what you need. I'm going to give it all to you.* The image of Scarlett was overlaid by Phil. Her sore breast ached for Phil . . . for him to be Count Downe and to slide his long teeth into her flesh and suck out her blood . . . the life of her love and all the pain of reality. She wanted *him* to drink her. . . .

But the memory of Scarlett's soft mouth against her burning tit spread through her. Another furious orgasm.

The voice, rising . . . just as it had been during those murky moments of wonder.

You will come to me, sweet Connie. Give up to yourself, We will yet finish . . . together. Phillip doesn't want you to know that freedom. But we will find it . . .

Together.

Together.

The voice *was* her own . . . wasn't it? It reassured her and made her feel complete.

I want you, Connie.

Want. Yes. *Want.* Connie wanted, too.

She wanted Count Downe.

Phil.

Now.

An hour after leaving Connie to sleep, Phil finished his Banquet Enchilada Dinner and let Wolfgang pick at the remains. Phil wondered seriously if he had succeeded in driving Connie insane, too. The freedom he was trying to force himself into was a scary territory he had hidden from so long he was uncertain of a new path beyond the tired circle.

Now they were both talking about *vampires.* Connie had been screaming about them. Real ones and not just fantasies.

Scarlett Shade.

And he himself had tried to come to that certain conclusion only hours ago. His dreams . . . her dreams . . . *were real.* First blackouts . . . the past . . . now vampires. The nightmares assaulting him now had a face. Not Sonia . . . not even the world. Scarlett Shade, as a vampire, drinking blood, then taking the knife and making her victims look like they'd committed suicide. No one would ever guess or believe. *Vampires weren't real.*

He felt the sorrow and hurt in Connie's eyes, the responsibility. A real one he must make his own, for himself as well as her and others. He had trapped himself inside his own reflections until he was no more real than those one-dimensional images, and only by acting . . . interacting, could he regain vitality.

Cousin Sonia, a pistol up her cunt, screaming with terror that was schelched by a muffled *bang*.

What could he have done? People dying everywhere. Too many to care about and stay sane. But he *could* do something now . . . about Connie. Most of all, himself. Although Connie's clutching fingers on his back had spoken of her need . . . not his, through her, he would find freedom.

Pressure.

Phil rubbed his face tiredly.

Was there an end to it?

A noise from the hallway made him look up. Connie emerged in a shadow from the bedroom. He held back his seriousness for her sake, making his tone mild. "Can't get to sleep?" he asked. "Or is your stomach growling? I already ate but—"

She faced him, naked, more appealing than he'd ever seen her, her figure suddenly a shape of perfection. He took a breath of disbelief even as her slender fingers caressed her breasts, her thumb twirling around her badge of undeath. He saw into those deep holes, which seemed different, his eyes held to them with a shiver as he felt his will sink like a jelly down his knees. Slowly, he dropped his gaze down her stomach, to the damp bush her other hand caressed. "Take me, Count. Fuck me . . . *suck* me. Drink my blood and make me eternal. Eternity is *ours*."

He swallowed hard to retain himself and shook his head. "Not funny, Connie."

"Oh, but fun is what it's all about . . ." She stepped into the living room and her face changed . . . now slender, lush lips and golden hair. She licked those lips. "So I am Countess Showery, then. And I have come to drink *your* blood. I am the Countess, alive in undeath . . . to bring

257

you the freedom from the life that has cheated us both
. . ."

"C-Connie—"

It was as though she didn't hear. She shuffled forward on the carpet. They stood face-to-face, her eyes a depth that wanted him . . . in them, the mirror of his past.

"Let me . . . drink *you.*"

Phil grabbed her arm, holding her sudden strength back as she pushed her open mouth toward him. "Connie! Wake up—"

She struggled against him, licking his cheek with the end of her tongue, dropping her free hand to his pants zipper. "Let me lead you to pleasure, and save your life in undeath, dear cousin Adolph."

Death's Sweet Door. As he recognized the words of the book, he saw that door opening in her eyes. Battling himself as much as her, he saw deep into that darkness—

Sonia . . .

Himself.

The remnant of himself drained even from his knees, to his feet, and he felt himself leaking out of his own flesh like it no longer existed. In its place rose back his one-dimensional reality that was little more than nothing. His muscles were shrunken and quivering into their own nonexistence, the truth of fear and dread he'd clung to . . . in her eyes he no longer saw himself at all, only that fear.

Fear . . . but twisted in love. He was pulled to the lies . . . to release the guilt—*she was Sonia!* Thirteen years old, her young body his if he would only take it . . . *let her take him with her into the darkness she had chosen.*

Chosen.

The blackout exploded its full force into Phil . . . pulling him frantically back into the whirlpool. He felt his limbs jerk convulsively as he was dragged deep. Sonia disintegrated before his eyes. Connie faded completely from sight . . . instead, the fire of burning buildings and his father's urgent hand around his. Shrieks and the rat-a-tat as blood drenched the Prague cellar's stairs with the life of his uncle and cousins.

Death.

And then, he saw, more truly than ever, Cousin Sonia and the soldier. He smelled the scent of burning wood and flesh . . . the stink of fresh, spilt blood as the echoes died. Sonia . . . Katherine . . . Connie, begging the uniformed man . . . offering themselves to him.

Their reflection was himself . . . his love . . . his truth.

The smell of smoke stung his nostrils, the heat of the fire singed his hair, his younger self denying the truth it was seeing in the cracked basement mirror. . . . The faces of love in his life were all Cousin Sonia, the girl he first loved and who loved him, bartering her barely formed body for life.

Bartering her life for life . . .

For *undeath*.

The din became silence, the moment *now:* Sonia, standing in the center of the dead bodies of her kin, sprayed with their warm, drooling blood, clasping the soldier and ripping open her dress, forcing his hand to drag down her dirty cotton panties. The soldier's laughing comrades looked on, as she unzipped him and drew out an angry pistol . . . his cock, hauling herself up by his shoulders and impaling herself on him in surrender.

"I'll do and be anything! Just let me live," she whined, her plea a gunshot in Phil's ears as the soldier lowered her to the floor and fucked her hard in the sticky blood of her uncle and brothers.

Worst of all, he saw the gleam of life inside Sonia . . . the gleam of love he'd known through her . . . die in her self-sacrifice for existence. The terror of her empty pupils, a vacuum hungry to be filled, but lost in eternal hopelessness.

Taking a part of himself . . . the love he had given. Sacrificing that love.

Phil and his parents . . . cowering in the tunnel, hurrying away from the echoes of undeath. And then the real sound of a shot . . . Sonia's distant scream . . .

The orgasm of death . . . or undeath?

Phil ran into delusion to hide from understanding and its futility . . . into another form of undeath . . . into the room of mirrors . . . alone. The reflections of his past, his present, his future, all of them focused in the fantasy of the shapely body now opened before him in the mirrors, beckoning him to fuck life . . . death . . . undeath.

Scarlett Shade. The circle went around and around. An infinity of mirrors and himself . . . an infinity of undeath.

His life. A sacrifice.

And as he faced them, himself . . . the mirrors exploded with a singing blast.

Connie stared down at the floor and denied what she'd done. "Phil," she moaned, still tasting his blood on her tongue. She felt filthy . . . dirtier than when she and Vicky had coupled lustily . . . not with any feeling of love.

Dirtier than when she understood that she had aborted her own children, parts of herself and her life . . . out of fear for her own life and a loss of pleasure in unwanted responsibility.

Her children.

All in the name of her own life and self.

But at least she hadn't killed Phil. His chest still rose and fell. She'd wanted to take his life so badly. The desire of her teeth to just keep biting into his torn, bloody skin had been overpowering. She had been Countess Showery, after all, giving the gift of forever to an unwilling recipient.

Do it, sweet Connie, whispered the voice inside her that wanted to make her free. *Drink him and I will save you. We will meet as I promised. I will come to you, this weekend, and I will make you mine.*

But Phil's body shivered with a pain that shot deep into her. She felt and tasted it in his life.

His blood. *Not* hers.

It's yours if you take it. Drink him dry. Fill yourself with pleasure and life.

Instead, Phil's blood stirred her love and she forced her teeth back from the trickle begun. His inner lies and a hidden truth, stagnant and buried by fear. Staggering back from him, bumping unexpectedly into the divan, she'd blurted a new cry as sharpness clawed her back—

Wolfgang, hair raised and back arched, fangs bared, hissing. Her horrified hands flew up to her slick teeth that were *not* pointed fangs.

Because she *wasn't* Countess Showery. She *wasn't* a vampire.

Not yet, spoke the whisper in her soul.

The extravagant promise of eternity and false ecstasy couldn't displace the sorrow Connie had tasted in Phil's life. She stood like a sleepwalker, battling for control as her wounded breast screamed for her to kneel back down and finish. The wound under her pubic hair boiled as commandingly. The voice inside her an unceasing, shrill shriek.

"No!" whimpered Connie, "I'm not a vampire! I'm not! I'm Connie Sawyer . . . not some character in a book!"

You want undeath. To be free of your own life. You are a vampire, dear Connie. Why give when you can take? Don't fight yourself— accept your own truth. Accept your own lies and make them that truth. Guiltless.

"No—"

The knowledge of her own shame was a crushing weight Connie didn't want, but she would not deny it for a lie.

Seek pleasure. Not pain. Think of your own desires. . . .

Chapter 4

Friday night, Connie would come to her. Scarlett finished cleaning up the mess her unexpected visitors had left and felt the certainty in her veins. She used an old broom she'd found to sweep the ashes and glass from the scarred floor, kind of enjoying the simple action that brought back near-lost memories of life.

But not quite. Instead, it made her want to be sad, and she couldn't even reach that.

She *could* know anger . . . so that boiled in sadness's place. What use were memories without feeling them? Scarlett turned her concentration back to Connie, finding a powerful lust, because Connie was becoming the best kind of seduction. Her strong will was more difficult to control all the time. She was fighting, but losing. That challenge gave Scarlett a sense of greater and greater accomplishment. The taste of Connie was . . . delicious. Better than that spineless, dickless Gary or even Teresa.

The pressures of Connie's life were consuming her and she wanted to escape them and herself. Scarlett knew Connie would meet her Friday in the Oklahoma City hotel . . . and Scarlett wanted the man Connie thought she loved, too. Phillip Ottoman was becoming more than a problem. Now he'd become so distant in his warped frame of mind she could barely reach out to him. The beliefs he wanted to find didn't fit at all in her fantasy world . . . not even the so-called real world anymore.

But if she could release him into fantasy . . . make him think he was released from his bonds of chosen fear, he might be quite tasty . . . another prime seduction. Perhaps she could yet make him beg for the freedom of her undeath.

Picking up the broken Stoker award, Scarlett frowned, and tossed it into the crackling flames that stank of Gary.

Teresa was still free.

Scarlett hissed, glaring back at the hall.

Cold in sweat, Phil swam sluggishly back to consciousness. Empty.

Sick.

The blurry surroundings of his living room cleared far too slowly, but he sighed that he was not in a nightmare. That hot mental imagery was only in his thoughts.

Sonia had *chosen* undeath. This time he had seen the truth in the mirror, and knew the warped reflection had given him the blame for her destruction before. Her rejection of him and their young love, for empty existence. He had let her sacrifice him to undeath. His belief in the mirror's illusion through that youthful sacrifice of denial had created his guilt, and his fear of that image and of life itself had fed the lie of his sight, making it more and more real.

Undeath. Lies. Warped reflections of truth . . . false images . . . trapping victims deeper inside their own concerns and desires.

Focusing on the furniture of his apartment, Phil knew he was where the mirror led him, and he knew he would never leave despite understanding and knowledge. It was not enough until he acted willingly to leave the meaningless circuit he had walked again and again. Guilt through the lie he made himself believe was his undeath, keeping him distant from the forgiveness of life, love.

A constant sweat, colder than ever, drained out of him and chilled him even more as he felt the sharp pain in his crotch and the frightening wet sting of his own blood. The surge was a rapid whirlwind tearing open his stomach as the shaking fit finally left him weaker than ever, tears flooding his eyes.

Katherine's rejection had brought back the strength of delusion . . . of Sonia's sacrifice of him and life at once, and those fears had grown in his refusal to admit them.

Connie.

Sonia.

For half an hour, the agony of a thousand long-denied emotions split him into another thousand pieces, and he barely held himself out of the black abyss of self-deceit yawning to comfort him and make him once more forget.

Phil bit into his lip until it was bleeding, too. He forced himself to his feet and shuffled to her bedroom. Connie lay on the bed as if dead. Phil shuffled to her warily, listening to her ragged breaths.

Nearer. He touched her bare leg lightly.

She didn't move.

"Connie?"

As she trembled, he heard her throaty choke. "Connie?" he said again, moving up to her shoulders. He reached out and ran a finger under her shoulder blade, feeling her shiver. Connie's damp hair covered half her ashen face as she turned toward him, staring through her strands of straw. Her eyes empty pits.

Hungry.

"Phil . . . please, Phil." Her hands rose and reached out to him.

He didn't want to touch her. Instead, he wanted to run . . . to hide from her need.

His own.

Her face blurred. . . . Sonia's face. Undead. Katherine's . . . another illusive sacrifice of unrequited love. Both hers and his.

"Please . . . Phil . . ." Connie's fingertips stroked his and he started to pull further back. Noisy, guttural sobs wracked her, tossing her back and forth as she tugged at her hair, and the emptiness in her eyes became his fear. "Phil," she choked wildly.

He forced himself to bend down to her, his spine stiff as her arms wrapped around his neck and she pressed her mouth to his throat. He pulled away, afraid of the meaning he was so close to. "Please," he moaned, "don't."

"Phil," she trembled his name. "P-please . . . just . . . tell me. Tell . . . me you love . . . me. I need someone to *love* me!"

He lay down beside her and pressed his bare flesh to hers, fighting his fear. Love. Nothing else made sense. It was the reason his youth couldn't accept the truth of Sonia's end. "I love you, Connie," he whispered. Their eyes met, and he saw the fear in them become that love, feeling it grow. He pulled her closer.

"I . . . love you . . . Phil," she gasped.

He plunged his lips to hers and knew that their tears were mixing the way they should. It was the sharing of pain as well as pleasure.

Of self.

Of real love. Finally, *real* love.

Chapter 5

The black emptiness inside the mirror she'd escaped through still unnerved the slight rationality Teresa had left. This was a labyrinth of nonexistence—maybe Hell. A vacuum of pale ultraviolet flashes . . . The realm of the dead. A billion souls trapped inside the reflections of the world they were no longer a true part of. They were the memory. Death . . . the undeath of dreams.

But through the image of life she and other vampires retained, the emptiness was not yet eternal.

It could be *fed*.

Cries and moans of pain and frustration rang though Teresa, she tried not to feel the hungry emptiness of death that waited to devour her in just the way she wanted to take from the living. Those lost souls were just like her, but without her ability to reenter the semblance of life.

Truly, she *had* found Hell.

And some of those souls were more like her than others. She felt them, like her, hovering in an undeath made almost more terrible than death itself because of their confusion of existence . . . unknowing of the reality of their undeath. Vampire souls, still tethered to their lifeless bodies but without the understanding of how to reject the last lingering of life to leave their graves and reform themselves as she did. Lies . . . not even knowing they were lies.

For a moment, she wanted to dive into the suffering horde to find Gary, but the shivers it gave her, even disembodied, was too much. It was too late for Gary . . . his body was no more . . . his tie to physical existence severed.

Hell.

Teresa moved from portal to portal . . . the mirrors that looked in on life . . . constantly reminding the bitter, suffering dead what they had departed and could never return to . . . even the vampires, never completely. Hysteria was trying to dismantle the rationality she had left, but Teresa kept it back, examining the thousands of silvery windows that peered into locations of life . . . bathrooms . . . cars . . . stores.

Denver . . . twenty miles . . . and a moving terrain that was familiar.

Gathering herself, Teresa dove fast into physical reality.

Bruce Parker smoked a cigarette idly, his other hand on the steering wheel. It was late, he was tired, and he didn't know what the hell he was going to do with all the mirrors he'd bought at the auction. He didn't know what had possessed him to lay down so much of his savings, even though mirrors were a big thing these days the way all those Shade freaks were buying them. But how long would it last?

Bruce just hoped it lasted long enough to unload these mothers on the market. He'd sold out all the ones he had in his secondhand store and people still stopped in wanting them. The commercial hunger had grown since the convention last week. He hoped he could jack up the prices and make some good money . . . at least enough to make a small profit.

Looking back in his rearview at the back of the pickup, he sighed. Hundreds of different-sized mirrors. He stared ahead at the slowly cresting road. Denver's white-orange night glow came closer, but Bruce was not relishing the job of unloading this shit by himself . . . then going home to let his wife kick his ass for the money he'd spent. Krista would absolutely murder him!

A fast Mazda passed by on the side and he sighed again, wishing he had never read the details of the auction in the *Bargain Post*. He thought of the way all those frigging Shade fans claimed to see Scarlett Shade and her characters inside the mirrors. Everybody was always saying how Shade was so bizarre, but those fans were the fucking weird characters if you asked him.

Still, *he* wouldn't mind seeing Scarlett in a mirror sometime. Especially when Krista chewed him out for buying all this. He turned his thoughts to that *Penthouse* poster up on his office wall . . . the *Playboy* foldout, too. It would be nice. . . .

A sudden chill wrapped him and he flipped up the pickup's heater. The warm air rushed out and he chewed the cigarette butt, peering up at the cloudy moon. The cold seemed *inside* him as Bruce turned the heater yet higher, still shivering. He looked back in the rearview again at the barely visible image of his eyes a few feet behind him, then sucked smoke into his lungs faster as the image fogged. . . .

Cleared.

But the eyes . . . Soft and blue. *Not his.*

Wanting to crush the brake, Bruce stopped himself just in time, hovering his foot over the peddle, knowing what a sudden stop would do to his purchases. His breath whined as he clenched his knuckles and squeezed the steering wheel, gulping at the black pupils staring into him.

Not his own.

His foot pressed the pedal slowly and he felt the momentum decrease. His jaw quivered when he finally came to a halt, flashing his emergency lights. He forced his eyelids shut against icy curiosity.

One . . . two . . . three . . . Bruce forced himself to whisper the numbers up to ten, and reopened his eyes, looking from his hands and the glowing green dashboard to the rearview that seemed to radiate the same color.

This time. Nothing. Only himself. Fighting the shakes, he turned in the seat to the frames of square and round shiny glass . . . himself and his pale face. His savings.

Bruce sighed grimly and lowered his head, wishing he hadn't stayed at the auction so late on top of everything else. The need to whiz made his bladder tight after the fright and he glanced up and down the empty highway lanes, then creaked open his door and stepped out. The inner cold still made his limbs tingle and he was surprised the chill of the outside air wasn't greater.

Spitting out the smoldering cigarette, he walked around the front of his vehicle to the roadside, unzipping his jeans, pulling out his pecker and letting loose on the concrete. The sound broke the night's silence. Watery reflections of the moonlight danced around him as a breeze rattled his new stock. Finished, he folded himself back into his pants and glanced at them.

At a woman . . . He trembled.

A frizzy-haired woman, her red and darkened skin like . . .

"Where did you come from—what—what happened to you?" Bruce gasped.

Her blue eyes . . . *the eyes he had seen in the mirror.*

Her teeth flashed . . . and behind her, she was invisible in the reflections. "I've been to *Hell*," she said, reaching a scarred arm out to him, charred flesh hanging from her thumb and fingers. Her clothing, a sleek evening gown once, was as tattered and burnt as her hideous flesh.

"I . . ."

"Nice load of mirrors," grinned Teresa.

270

He nodded, edging back to the truck's hood. "Just bought 'em. Were . . . were you in an *accident?*" He gulped loudly. "Are you . . . okay?"

She shook her head. "Not a bit." She took a step toward him. "How about you? You look like you've seen a ghost."

A semi came rushing up and its loud honk made him jump. "Look, I got to get into town . . ."

"Want to give me a lift?"

Not able to stop himself, Bruce shook his head. "I . . . I can't—"

"Too bad," Teresa said.

He choked in disbelief as her clothing completely disappeared . . . as she fogged in his eyes the way the reflection had.

The burn marks covering her disappeared.

Bruce blinked and they were back . . . then disappeared again.

She disappeared.

"Holy shit," Bruce felt the words run down his chin with his saliva. He backed up, turning his eyes back and forth, his heart a jackhammer on high speed. He crawled into his front seat and bowed his head, rubbing his temples with his thumbs.

A sudden urge forced his eyes up to the rearview mirror and he saw himself . . . himself and that horrid-looking woman . . . in a green nightmare of bony and pained sex that turned his stomach inside out. Bruce threw the door open and retched, then sank back and groaned.

"Don't cry . . ." slithered a sultry voice.

He shrieked at the touch of her flaky, hardened flesh that broke off in little pieces. His throat was raw as she pulled him onto the pavement and against her and began to unbuckle his belt.

271

Chapter 6

When the sky grew pink and the sun rose, it didn't destroy Teresa like in all those dumb movies. But she had felt every one of her new supernatural powers shrink into nothing.

The pain of her burnt flesh was worse than ever. She walked, half naked, into the graveyard, missing Gary and her past despite herself.

She was pissed off. Why had Scarlett done that to her and Gary? Sure, Gary was being a prick just like he always was, but had that been any reason to fry him like Scarlett had?

There was no honor among thieves . . . or vampires. Maybe because they were one and the same . . . vampires stole blood.

Teresa didn't really feel sorry for Gary . . . the nice thing . . . the terrible thing . . . about being dead, undead, was that she felt only hunger.

Except she stung in the pain of her own damaged body.

Except she was pissed off. Kind of afraid.

Because Scarlett had tried to destroy her, too. Gary was truly in his own hell now, and she had almost followed him into hers . . . the hell that all the other Scarlett victims were unable to get out of because of Scarlett's deceptions.

It was scary. Maybe being a vampire wasn't all it was cracked up to be.

Eternity.

Teresa turned back to the nearly empty city street beyond the trees and fence. Far down it she had parked the laden pickup and its mirrors at Bruce's dilapidated shop. She'd parked a dilapidated Bruce, too. He was hers now . . . not turned but infected by her will. She'd used the power of illusion—what he wanted to see—to convince him she wasn't the tattered mess she really was. Tonight, renewed, she would return to use him and the mirrors.

The sun got higher and made her already stinging flesh burn as she reached the square mausoleum. It was still early, and she was glad she'd had enough strength and will to follow her sudden impulse into the mirror.

Pressed against the stone that hid her casket reinvigorated Teresa. She relaxed there, wanting revenge. Even knowing it was pointless, she pretended Gary had been right. She was still near enough to her living memories to regret what she had chosen . . . and in that hate that was really all she could draw from her own self, she wanted to make Scarlett suffer worse than *she* was suffering. Not for Gary . . . not for anyone but *herself*.

But Teresa knew she had to get back inside her coffin to rest and recuperate for tonight. Without her powers in the daylight, it was going to be difficult. She searched the building and found nothing to use as a tool, but outside, in a sunlight growing hotter and more uncomfortable, she found a pickax.

So she added grave desecration to the crimes of her life . . . death.

But fuck it, it was her own goddamn grave.

Chapter 7

"Shit," Phil groaned, seeing the clock beside the bed. It was after noon.

But it wasn't his clock. This wasn't his room.

It was Connie's.

She was lying in the bed right beside him. He gasped as he turned over and a stab poked his groin. His first thoughts of being late to open the store disappeared. "Connie?"

She didn't move. Phil swallowed, tensing at the pale glow of her skin.

She was breathing.

He sighed. He hadn't dreamed. Not about Czeckovslovakia, or even Scarlett. "Connie?"

Her eyes finally cracked open. She moaned. "Phil. Oh. Oh, Jesus, Phil. What are we going to do?"

"Did . . . did you dream?"

"All fucking night," she sniffed. "Scarlett. Everything. I . . . I'm afraid."

He shook his head. "We've got to stop it. We've got to take her out."

"K-kill her?"

Phil chuckled darkly. "She's already dead. She's been using all of us, making her money from us and infecting our minds, then she picks out the meals she wants. God, we're just fucking lucky."

"What stopped her from doing it to you, Phil?"

He clenched his fists. "My past." He faced her. "I remember everything now, Connie. Cousin Sonia . . ."

She stared at him.

He steadied himself. "I only know I've got to destroy Scarlett to destroy those memories, now."

"How can you, Phil? No one else will believe it—people are always around her."

"This is my chance to make up for all the years I've wasted. He stood up and walked to one of his cardboard boxes, opening it up and picking through the titles, bringing out a stack of novels. He held up *Dusk* by Ron Dee and opened it, then took out *Dracula, Salem's Lot*. "Unsympathetic vampire novels. Full of lots of methods to kill off the mother-fucking, blood-sucking bastards." Phil went through another box . . . one of his few without books, and took out the studded cross Connie had given him long before. "Rest. I've got a lot of things to read and do."

She sank back to the mattress as Phil left the room

Hours passed. Connie felt weaker than ever in her life, falling suddenly into sleep and waking up in nightmares. The day and another night passed and she screamed for an hour until Phil gave her two sleeping pills. She didn't want them and the dark visions they now brought, but she couldn't resist her fears and screams because they were all that kept Scarlett and her seductions away now, and that terror had become the worst of all. She knew its hollow emptiness too well, and kept that hideous memory as close as she could. As the hammering on the apartment walls and ceiling increased from surrounding tenants, she finally gave in and swallowed the tablets, letting them drag her completely into the new fright of her fantasies.

Finally, daylight again. Scarlett's voice was not so strong. The vitality it held in the night wasn't there. Worn from the restless sleep, Connie nodded off again and again, and woke dreadfully to the shadows of a dimming, orange sun. Night was approaching.

The convention was tomorrow.

Phil had read through every one of his vampire novels, reciting sections aloud to Connie as he made notes. She thought he might have left a dozen times this afternoon as she lay on the couch. She watched as he came back in the door with a small sack.

"What . . . what is it this time?" asked Connie.

He pulled out a large vitamin bottle that looked empty. "Holy water," he said. "The books weren't clear, but it may help us even before we destroy her." He glanced at a mirror and shut his mouth fast.

"I don't think she can hear us now," Connie told him, peering at the late sun shining in a mirror. He came to the couch and sat and she touched the bottle with a sense of danger. It felt like it contained molten lava. "I don't understand how you can touch that if she bit you, too, Phil."

He bit his lip. "I don't know." Then he got a strange expression. "Yes . . . maybe I do. The mirror thing. I told you when I look into the mirror I see myself and my past . . . not the fantasies that you see. She can't"—he swallowed—"couldn't possess me because I was already possessed with my past. She can't infect me or control me. I've already been sacrificed to . . . undeath."

Connie looked at his wet eyes and touched them with her finger. "Do . . . do we drink it?

He went to the kitchen and got two small glasses, nodding, then poured barely more than a sip inside each. He took his turn first and made a sour face, and she touched her glass, which felt hotter than ever, bringing it to her lips and feeling it sting, burning a swath of pain down her throat. It seemed to toss and turn inside her as if it were alive, bringing back a hot scream and a low moan as she fought to keep from throwing it back up. It burned her life with the memory of shame for every wrongful deed she ever took part in. Her face burned in that hell and an embarrassment she'd never before come close to . . . as though she were on trial before God.

But somehow, she knew the only end to suffering was in holding it down . . . keeping the living water inside until she accepted it and her guilt. Only in that acceptance could the guilt be taken away.

At last, the fire simmered and she fell back, gasping.

But it wasn't over. She still felt the pain in her nipple, worse than ever as the opposition of her acceptance inside and her other desires faced off. "C-can you get more of this stuff?"

"Holy water?"

Connie nodded.

"I can get some of it . . . how much do you need?"

Connie remembered the books . . . about how Countess Showery's grandmother had become a vampire through the damnation of bathing in innocent, virgin blood.

But even innocent human blood was filled with desire that became lust. The books hinted: water, the blood of life, was without its own lusts. Even polluted and refined by man, it was pure. That natural purity already stung her and tried to revive her, and maybe . . . Connie sighed, hoping. "Maybe this is enough. Start the bath water, okay?"

He nodded. "It sure wouldn't hurt. You're really sweating."

She shook her head. "I'm going to put some of this holy water into it. Maybe it will help."

He got a funny look on his face. "God, we sound crazy, Connie."

"Maybe we are." She gritted her teeth. "Maybe this is

just another fantasy." She shook her head at his sick look. "I don't know if this will work or not, but I really feel different. Almost clean. I've decided that I don't want to go through life, or even undeath . . . as a vampire. I just want to love you and know you love me. This time, I . . . I want to have your baby."

Phil took her hand and helped her up, leading her to the tub. "I have to get you pregnant, first."

He turned on the faucets and she tried to touch the vial in his hand again, but it was still so hot to her fingers. Connie said nothing as she pulled off the T-shirt and saw her marks in the mirror, redder and more viscous than ever. The lower marks were just red . . . barely visible behind her hair.

Phil's face was lined. "Oh, Connie." He took her hand and helped her into the bathtub.

She caught her breath at a sharp pain and pressed her fingers deep in his arm. The pain was greater than any ever before, entering her wounds like an acid—eating her. She stuttered her tears and looked past him at the misted mirror, remembering too closely the fog Scarlett created.

"How . . . how's the water?"

Her teeth raked together. "It . . . hurts . . . worse than ever . . ."

Shaking his head, Phil followed her glance, then picked up a dark shade of her lipstick, opened it, and rolled it out until a quarter inch showed. He pressed the color against the glass and made two intersecting lines. "It's the law. There *is* a law of the undead, Connie. They can't *cross* that law." He smiled grimly at his joke. "The law of Love. It's something we forget about too often, and it's not . . . a fantasy. My love was sacrificed in my nightmares, Connie. I see it more clearly than I ever did. My nightmares were a lie . . . only real because I believed in them, holding back my knowing the truth. The belief Scarlett gets from her fans . . . She works against the laws of life in her books, but no matter how she ignores them in fantasy, maybe the laws are still *real* . . . and maybe the laws of belief and love can used against *her*."

She began to relax in the water as the pain dimmed, becoming smaller than ever. It shrank . . .

And shrank.

Connie remembered the policeman who'd stopped Vicky as she watched Phil open his slacks, looking at his own mark. "There's got to be some kind of law of love . . . some kind of law of life and death that can be used against what she's done." He tapped the mirror. "Reflections look real, but they're only an image. Vampires can't be seen in reflections . . . because they're not there . . . but they *are* there . . . in our dreams . . . inside *us!* The image only shows one dimension of the truth it's reflecting!" He rubbed his face in concentration. "We've got to stop her any way we can. It'll be hard to do anything to her at the convention, but I've got to try."

The knife in her breast was completely gone, but left a memory . . . like the aftertouch of a ring worn for years and lost. Connie looked down at herself, seeing no difference.

But even before, there had been nothing to see. She reached up to Phil. "Help me up, Phil. Please. The pain . . . is *gone.*"

He walked to the tub and eyed her closely, then touched her fingers with his. "Gone?"

She nodded.

He nodded, too. "Scarlett sucks our real life out of us, leaving only the vampire." He wrapped his palms over her slippery hands and helped her rise, and they turned together to the mirror.

Connie's flesh under the hair between her legs was still red and open. . . .

But the imprint on her breast was gone.

Chapter 8

Teresa Carson was recovered. She felt almost alive. The power crept back inside her, much stronger tonight. She had been so damaged in her duel with Scarlett she had stayed in her coffin all last night instead of going out, but the rest had revived her. She slithered out of her coffin, out of the mausoleum, staying a mist until she reached the barred cemetery gates. She visualized herself as a prim businesswoman, then revisualized herself as a feminine Carl Kolchak . . . the TV Night Stalker of her childhood. She formed that appearance . . . a straw hat on her head, a pale, seersucker suit . . . all the way to the boat shoes that the actor, Darren McGavin, had worn. "Teresa Kolchak . . . vampire reporter!" she giggled.

It was early tonight. The sky was still coppery blue from the sunset, but the disarming sun's rays were gone. She passed men in jackets and suits leaving the business offices, ladies in smart dresses and their own suits. Several glanced at her more than once, but she was enjoying this. The buildings became older quickly as the trash increased in the gutter . . . warehouses, car shops . . . and she stopped at the barred door to Bruce's Secondhand, a gritty concrete block structure covered by lewd, spray-painted graffiti: FUCK ME UP THE ASS! Etcetera, etcetera . . . She wiped a dirty window and peered inside at the shelves of junk, from a rusty kitchen sink to a grandfather clock, suddenly worried that maybe Bruce had awakened in her recovery and gotten away. With a sigh, she felt his presence inside and knew he had spent until late this afternoon in a comatose state.

Although afraid, he was eager for her return, and his mind was a confusion trying to decide what he should do.

Teresa was invisible in the smeary window, but behind her, she saw a group of teenagers . . . boys and girls, in a vacant lot. They were hunkered around a sporty Camaro like the one Gary had wanted to buy when he sold his first book. "You'd have done better if you'd started off a thief, Gary," she spoke.

But Gary's problem was that he'd always been pretentious, in sex and writing, in life and death. Shade had taken care of that.

Teresa waited until the kids weren't really studying her and she formed into a mist again, then slipped into the door's keyhole and inside the store, which reeked with age and oil. She flowed to the counter and the door behind it, smelling Bruce in the back storage room. She recreated her form from the spiritual molecules of herself and reached down to the doorknob, twisting it open to a near darkness. The hinges were silent and so was she as she stepped in and saw Bruce at a work bench, surrounded by junk in worse shape than the stuff on display. Rusted pipes were scattered everywhere. He was still wearing his ragged jeans and work shirt. Teresa shook her head and moved behind him, reading the old, discolored pages of the book he was pondering over his shoulder.

. . . "many different legends of vampires, but their being seems to be the darkest lusts of desire. A vampire victim trades their soul for those desires that are at best a reflection of the life they once had. Their new shallow reality is false, merely perceived as physical by themselves and their supposed victims . . ."

Teresa laughed out loud, and Bruce slammed the book closed, wheeling from the bench with a wrinkled, pale face of terror. He shook his head. "I've . . . been reading—"

"I see."

"You . . ." His brown hair, flecked by gray, was practically standing on end. "You're . . . not even *real.*"

She flexed her fingers. "Maybe not . . . but I'm real enough to you, aren't I?"

He blinked, but his face stayed stricken. "I . . . don't believe in you."

Teresa chuckled again, even louder, and without the echoes, her sound was chilling . . . especially to him. "I'm real enough to anyone who believes in me, Bruce . . . and you can't help it. I figured a lot of things out last night. I told you I took a tour of Hell . . . don't worry, I'm sure you'll get your own chance. It's full of people like you . . . and me. Vampires. Full-fledged capitalists. Atheists. Those who believe in only themselves and the fantasy they want to replace life with. We all live off each other and that's the way we all like it. *Fantasyland.*" She curled her lips and almost hated the lie that had completely become her truth. "The only way you can disbelieve in me is to deny yourself . . . and where would that get you?" She cackled. "It's all you have left . . . all most of us have left."

He frowned, thick lips trembling above his double chin. "What do you want now? M-more blood?" Then he squinted and blinked again, showing surprise. "Well, shit, at least you look better."

She posed. "Just needed my beauty sleep. You look better, too."

He blushed, almost relaxing. "I—I just woke up. I haven't even called my wife yet. She's really going to be *pissed.*"

Teresa leaned on the bench, both arms around him,

boxing him in. Her lips were an inch from his. "So what's it going to be? I'll let you think about it . . . that's more of a choice than I had . . . life and death . . . or undeath?"

"Wh-why are you giving me a choice?"

She shrugged. "Just playing games . . . you've already made your decision."

He nodded and she stepped back. He didn't move away and try to run, just unbuckled his pants. "Not now." She tossed her head. "Work to do first, Bruce." She walked through the boxed and unboxed junk covering the floor . . . coat racks, microwaves, old clothes, stoves with colorful wires hanging out them. . . . When she got to the pickup she reached up and took hold of a mirror. A nice, big one. She set it down on the floor. "What a messy place. Come here and move some of this stuff out of the way, Bruce."

"I . . . want you to *suck* me," he whispered. "Look, my wife is going to kill me, and if she doesn't, taxes are. President Clinton has put me in a bracket I can't survive on . . ."

"Politicians are just amateurs! Everything in its good time, Brucie," she sang, her lips a twisted smile. "Help me and I'll help you . . . heartless capitalism, Brucie. One equal value for another . . . something for nothing. Or maybe *nothing* for something! We all have to pay for what we want, so if you *want* to be a vampire, then I should get more than just your blood."

"What are you trying to do?" he muttered, picking up a broom and using it to shove things out of the way, then, lifting the chairs and tables and chests of drawers. Dust flew and Bruce coughed.

She helped him take the mirrors down and they lined them up on the concrete floor. "You'll see," she promised him.

* * *

At eleven-fifty, all the mirrors were unloaded and Teresa had fulfilled her bargain with Bruce. He lay naked on the dirty floor . . , quite beyond caring. It hadn't been as good for him as it was for Teresa, of course, but at least he'd come.

Once.

The phone was ringing again. Off and on ever since Teresa had arrived. She picked it up.

"Bruce!" screamed a whiny, bitter voice.

"I'm sorry," said Teresa. "Bruce is unavailable right now."

"Who the fuck is this?"

Reading the thoughts of Bruce's wife, Teresa just smiled. "I'm his lover, dear. I just sucked the life right out of him."

"Who the fuck—"

Teresa hung up, then took the phone back off the hook. His wife would be seeing him again soon enough. Unlike Scarlett, Teresa had explained to Bruce what to do when he woke in the darkness. After burial, the profanity of his resurrection into unlife would be his!

But now, to work. Teresa felt like a vampiric Woodward and Bernstein out to crack the Watergate case, although that was probably a double negative. She was, rather, a nocturnal Abe Lincoln, here to give freedom to the Shade slaves . . . but for her own purposes. The same purpose Lincoln had . . . to confuse the issue and the war she was initiating. She brushed a layer of dust from her arms and stood before the hundred or so reflections of herself, clapping her hands briskly to get attention from the other side. She just hoped the souls she'd passed last night would understand. "Listen, anyone who doesn't know what's going on. If the last thing you can recall is a night with Scarlett Shade . . . she's done a really shitty thing to all of us, and I want to do something really shitty to her. We're all dead, and so is she, but I think we can

284

have some *fun*. Now listen closely . . . all of you are in your coffins, in your *graves*. No joke. Until you believe it, you're stuck where you are. You've got to fully accept it and throw off the delusions of life and love. Everything centers around belief, okay? You're all vampires. True blue. Try and remember Scarlett's books . . . what you need to do is think yourself into a mist and get onto the ground. First, go get something to eat . . . but remember, you gotta be cool. You have a lot of powers and you need to use all of them. Stuff yourself with some blood and come back to your coffins. You get back in the same way you get out. Do it before daylight or the sun will weaken you, okay? Then listen for me and don't go anywhere tomorrow. Come here to me . . . into these mirrors . . ." Teresa stopped, hoping that the lost souls she'd passed last night were listening and understanding.

But the mirrors were silent.

"Be sure to come," she said again. "We're all going to a convention, okay? A *party* . . ."

Again, silence. Teresa shrugged and covered Bruce with a bunch of old newspapers, then sat down to look at his vampire book.

After a bored hour, she went back to her grave.

There was going to be an eternity of this to come.

Chapter 9

Kevin Matthews looked at the telephone before going to bed, thinking of Phil. He was nearly afraid to call him.

"Did you ever get hold of Phil?" asked Denise again. Kevin turned to her on the bed. She was dressed in another of his old T-shirts, but this time with nothing underneath. "I want to get hold of *you*," he said.

"You always do. But I'm serious, Kevin . . . did you?"

"His girlfriend called me the other day and I talked to him for a few minutes."

"I thought he was married."

Kevin took off his shirt and stuffed it in the hamper, then gazed at himself in the mirror, thinking of Phil and his mirror illusions. "He is . . . but he's getting divorced, remember?"

"Seems like all your patients have that problem."

"A lot of them." Kevin continued to peer at himself, wishing he looked more manly . . . more muscular. He flexed an arm, imagining he saw some toning. "Phil's girlfriend was worried about him. He's really going wild in his vampire belief. I just hope he doesn't do something stupid."

"Like what?" Denise giggled, staring into the reflection at him.

He looked back. She was pretty, but he wished she was

as pretty as she had been when they married ten years ago
. . . maybe as pretty as Phil's obsession, Scarlett Shade.

That writer was a real babe. He imagined Denise with
that long, red hair, big tits . . . "I just hope he doesn't freak
out and try to start killing vampires," Kevin replied.
"He's close to a breaking point. He thinks that writer
Scarlett Shade is a real vampire."

Denise stood up and walked to him. "Scarlett Shade. I
read one of her books . . . and I read that she was going
to be here in the city tomorrow. Some weird convention."

"Here?" Kevin sighed. "Shit. I sure hope he doesn't go.
. . . I told him to stay away from conventions, but—"

"Maybe you'd better call him again and make sure he
doesn't. Better yet, why don't we go? If he's there, you can
keep an eye on him . . . and I can finally see what all that
crazy stuff is all about. Shade has got to be one really
strange lady from the books she writes, you know it?"

Nodding, he flexed again, seeing his muscles expand.
"Hey . . . look at this. Muscles!"

She shook her head. "Wishful thinking, Kevin. Come
to bed . . . I'll find a sitter tomorrow and we'll check out
the weird world of these conventions. I've heard they get
pretty bizarre."

"That's what Phil says." He looked at her in the glass,
and as he did, she seemed to become sexier . . . her breasts
seemed to become Scarlett-sized . . . her hair . . .

Red.

"Come on, Kevin. I like you just the way you are. I
didn't marry you for muscles or brains"—she glanced
down—"or even for *that*. I married you because I loved
you . . . something I can't even see or put my finger on
. . . just you."

In the mirror, Scarlett. On the bed, Denise. Kevin
began merging those images and then stopped and
sighed.

The falseness in the mirror faded. He turned around

287

. . . saw all of Denise's imperfections . . . saggy breasts . . . a tummy scarred by her weight problem after their child.

But she was *beautiful*. She was *real*, full of imperfections, but also full of *love*. The occasional fantasies he allowed himself never offered him anything beyond the moment . . . just as Phil's guilty fantasies had never offered him anything but a curtain over a difficult moment of his past. With a fantasy or a nightmare you couldn't reach past the momentum of life and its growth ended, leaving you running in place. No future.

"Come on, big boy," she smiled, holding out her arms.

Chapter 10

The implements of Phil's strategy lay all around him. The apartment's mirrors were all marked by crosses . . . all but the one he'd kept here in the living room. Phil sat beside Connie as they both stared into it. He felt good now that he was doing something, even if he *was* crazy. It kept out the bad thoughts, fears, and memories. Facing himself by forcing himself to read the newspapers had given him a new feeling that he *could* do something about his problems. About Connie's, too. Beside him, the bottle of the remaining holy water, the studded cross, and a short, round pole he had carved sharp with a hunting knife she'd been given by her father. "I hope she comes," Phil whispered. He picked up *Death's Sweet Door* and threw it at the mirror, cracking the glass with a sharp snap. "Here we are, bitch . . ." He glared, picked up the cross and waited . . . and slowly, a fog overtook the glass, spreading . . . clearing.

The face of Scarlett Shade, smiling. Fanged. She laughed, the silent sound horrifying in her glee.

Phil lifted the mirrored cross desperately, praying to trap her in an infinity of reflections like the ones he'd trapped himself inside for far too long.

Instead, the mirror's new crack rent it into a thousand

pieces that sprayed out and imbedded themselves into his skin. He yelped.

He heard the loud sound as the other mirrors cracked back where he'd hidden them in his room.

Phil fell back on the carpet, stunned by the glass darts that had entered his chest like pins into a voodoo doll. After a moment, Connie, still silent, stood over him and bent down, removing the tiny shards with a repugnance.

"Did," Phil gasped, "you see?"

The tears leaked from her eyes and she nodded. Phil pushed himself up and tottered to the bathroom, finding bandages and seeing his new wounds, *not* only in the reflection. "I have to really destroy her. She's *real*, Connie. It's all real. Tomorrow, we'll check in at the convention motel . . ." He sighed. "She's my past and yours. Everyone's. She's undeath. I'm going to destroy her."

Connie shook her head, following. "She'll know, Phil. She's not stupid. She'll figure it out." Connie looked down at the robe she was wearing. She was naked underneath. Her breast was still unmarred, even in the mirrors. She opened the robe and stared at its reflection. Phil had taken a bath after she had . . . a holy bath . . . and his mark had disappeared, too. She couldn't stop an outrageous giggle.

"What's so funny?"

"Us. We were so afraid of everything, Phil . . . of each other, life."

"Of undeath? Of Scarlett?" He didn't even grin.

"Of *love*," she finished. "Do you really love me?"

He nodded, one eye still on the mirror, then led her back to the living room. "I love you. Do you love me?"

"I just want a night without fear . . . a night of our love." She shook the robe off and lay back on the divan. "I don't know if any of it makes sense without love. It was a lie—no one could sacrifice you, Phil. You have the right

290

to life and love if you choose it. I think that life is one insanity after another without that meaning. Maybe it's *all* undeath without love . . . maybe it always has been."

Phil didn't think of her words. She was beautiful . . . more than any woman he'd ever seen in his life. More attractive than he ever knew . . . because now he was seeing *her* and not just the image she tried to present to the world. She was more than the memories of Sonia . . . as lovely as Katherine before he'd replaced her with the concerns of that past . . . more captivating even than Scarlett Shade. "You're gorgeous," he whispered.

"Don't tease."

"I mean it."

"Then make love to me. Really make love, okay? I've been fucked enough for a lifetime."

He felt his stirring and nodded again, moving toward her, taking off his clothing.

"I really love you, Phil."

Sighing deeply, filled by more peace from Connie than he had ever known, Phil stayed close to her and held her tight. The nightmares were far away, but the dread of their false truth was as near as the shattered mirror. Connie stared at it nervously. "Are you okay?" he asked as she frowned and rubbed her abdomen.

"I'm still sore . . ."

He looked at her bandage, smoothing it with careful fingers. "You really ought to check that out at the emergency room, Connie."

"Oh, right. I'll look right in the doc's face and explain to him that my girlfriend and I just got a bit carried away . . ."

"Just tell him I did it," Phil chuckled. "I don't mind."

"Thanks, but"—she shrugged—"I'm sure Vicky won't give me rabies . . ."

"I just hope she didn't have AIDS."

Connie mashed her eyebrows together. "Me, too." Then she leaned to him and kissed his forehead. They reveled in love, dreading the next day. Phil knew it would be the moment of his found truth.

Chapter 11

The changes in the fantasy fabric of her universe was like a million insects crawling all over Scarlett, and she stared up from her rewrite of Gary's ex-novel at her mirrors, flying through them with her vision and seeing nothing out of the ordinary despite her sensations. Nothing as jarring as the sense of changes in that fabric. It was like a sudden, rushing wind.

She let the scenes of her captives drift through the glass, and hissed at the blankness when she came to Connie.

That bastard . . . Phillip Ottoman. *He* was causing these disturbances . . . he had figured too much of it out. He knew too much about her mirror secrets and had somehow managed to shut her out.

It pissed her off. He would be an annoying problem at the convention tomorrow. She tried to fathom him and Connie through the link of their infections. . . .

Blank. Only a blasting hatred for her—from *him!*

Scarlett hissed. It was *impossible!* No power he had could equal hers! The fury boiled so fast in her veins she couldn't even think. Even if he had no idea what he was doing, he was really starting to endanger her.

How much did he know, or *think* he knew? Tomorrow, at the convention, it would be too late to find out . . . unless . . .

Scanning the souls through her mirrors faster than ever, Scarlett found Vicky Cossiter.

Vicky stroked herself with the ribbed vibrator faster and faster, gazing at herself in the mirror under a naked Count Downe and Countess Showery. The Eager Beaver attachment to the vibrator . . . a real beaver-shaped critter formed out of plastic, jittered fast, up and down, nipping her quivering clitoris, bringing the mushroom cloud of undeath closer.

But it was really Count Downe's huge dick inside her and Countess Showery's tongue lapping at her as *he* pushed in and out.

So close . . .

The picture in the mirror blasted with sudden lines and flashes of static like bad TV reception. Vicky shrieked, her excitement almost disappearing in the interrupted fantasy. She stared in disbelief at the snowy fog building inside the wood frame. Who would she call for this? A mirror repairman?

Then the fog disappeared to become a beautiful woman. . . .

Scarlett Shade.

"Yes!" Vicky shoved the dildo in and out of herself faster, trying to regain her lost stimulation.

But instead of obeying her imagination, Scarlett stood there silently, fully clothed. "Obey me and I will fuck you and make you what you desire."

Vicky kept fucking *herself*, lolling her tongue in a frenzy for the excitement that had disappeared completely.

"Obey me!"

Vicky stopped. Stared.

Listened. She understood the words, but they meant nothing. The importance was in the promise of her success . . . the unlife . . . undeath that would become hers more strongly than even now. Scarlett would drink her blood, taking pain and life far away from her. Only the reflection of pain would still run through her veins. The pleasure of pain like she had tried to give to that ungrateful Connie.

The mirror fogged again and Vicky saw herself on the bedspread alone, the vibrator half in and out of herself. She flipped its switch to turn it back on, but it was still. She tried to imagine Count Downe . . . the Countess, there with her, but only saw the shadow of Scarlett, her frown stern.

Vicky licked the vibrator, pretending she was tasting the Countess. Disappointment stung her, but she was craving the promise to come after she did what Scarlett told her.

Craving to come.

Tomorrow.

She diddled herself with damp fingers.

Part 5:
Shade of a Bat

Chapter 1

As usual, Scarlett used the airlines to travel from home in San Francisco to her destination. Mirrors were easier, but too suspicious. Normal actions helped cover her tracks and made one less question for her to answer . . . and, it was tax deductible.

She arrived at the Will Rogers Airport at two in the afternoon, still disturbed by last night. The peculiar vibrations bothered her.

Scarlett was surprised how far the book dealer had been able to go in his struggle against her will. The insanity in him, combined with her fantasies, must have driven him really crazy now . . . and as far as she concerned, he was holding her newest disciple hostage. He had even reversed Connie's education like some cult deprogrammer.

But Phillip Ottoman would pay.

That bastard.

The taxi wound around the Oklahoma City maze and stopped at the Central City Motel, and Scarlett sat, still lost in her thoughts until the tubby driver took her bags out of the trunk and opened her back door. "Help me get the bags to my room and you get a twenty-buck tip," she told him.

He nodded with a mumble and walked ahead, the big

gray suitcase bouncing against his left hip, the two smaller bags against his right. Scarlett turned her face this way and that, seeing the confusion of expressways and a half-dozen gas stations and restaurants. The sun was bright overhead, discomforting the bare skin of her hands. They had refleshed nicely but were tender. She wore a wide-brimmed hat and a black duster, and, of course, her mirror sunglasses.

Mirror shades. She didn't resist the smirk. When they reached the glass doors, she waited expectantly and he had to set down the big bag to open one. Scarlett ignored his new mutters and entered the dingy lobby. She turned her eyes, taking in the lobby chairs and their occupants, the usual potted plants, back to the bright gold curtains hanging over the far walls of plate glass. Badged convention workers were all over the place with their walkie-talkies, putting up signs and moving chairs around. Lots of mundanes standing around watching them and very few congoers yet. Scarlett led the driver to one of the long tables beyond the motel's wood registration desk and smiled at the tubby black man with an admiral's billed cap. CAPTAIN COCONUT read his badge. The skinny white dude beside him was grinning wide and punched Coconut with his elbow, and he finally gave her an even grin. "Name?" he asked, opening a metal index box.

The other man laughed. "Look at her, man . . . It's Scarlett Shade!"

She smiled at him, exposing a fang, and took the badge Captain Coconut handed over. Lime green, her favorite shade of life, full of the hopelessness she delivered. The only color better was red—the color of life and hope, from others. She pinned the badge to her duster and nodded the driver back to the hotel's front desk. Scarlett stared at the large woman there through her glasses and touched her badge, waiting as the woman looked through her reservation book and found a key. Scarlett took a pen and signed her name to the book, then led the laden driver to her first floor room. The hall was narrow and lackluster compared to most hotels, but, she reminded herself, this was Oklahoma, after all.

And the way it was shaping up, this would be Phillip Ottoman's last convention and the beginning of a wonderful partnership for her and Connie. Scarlett felt his threat through the vibrations threatening her world with collapse, but knew he couldn't pull it off. He was still too multidimensional in his thoughts, desires, and fears. After wasting him or letting him destroy himself, she could relax with Connie. Scarlett was finding she missed a companionship . . . even if Jeanne said that it was worse to be around another vampire than not. Scarlett knew Jeanne was right and that nothing would fill the emptiness always inside her, but the blood and lives of others was never enough. She wanted to try. After only two years, even the memory of love was all but lost. She could only taste it in those she drank, and too often, not even then.

It bothered her that it was so completely gone. . . . Just the knowledge of it remained. But she had traded her love . . . her life . . . willingly. She had chosen this eternal existence.

Damnation. Hell.

Was it? Had life really been better?

It was so hard to remember and know. Existence had become an eternity of never caring . . . something she had thought she wanted. Pleasure upon pleasure . . . endless.

But what did it mean?

Eternity. But with each memory of another's life, she missed the turmoil of her emotions . . . even the pain. Maybe not feeling was worse than feeling. Worse than experiencing only by proxy.

It was too late now.

"Here we are," mumbled the driver, eyeing her key

and the door number he stopped at. "Want me to open this door, too?"

Scarlett studied the hallway, which was so like all the others, swept off her hat, then inserted the key in its knob's hole slowly and sexily, drawing his uneasy stare. She took a satisfaction in his blush, glad for it, experiencing a vague memory of embarrassment through the sight. She pushed the door open to a room, again, just like the dozens of others she spent her weekends in. The two double beds were neatly made up and the static manufactured wall paintings were as empty of life as she was. The TV and desk. She dropped her hat on a plain yellow bedspread and removed her duster to a shiny black, tight mini.

The driver chewed his gum faster and brought in the bags. His smile grew despite the battle on his face. Scarlett reached into her handbag, glittery with tiny mirrors, and handed him the bill she'd promised.

He gazed into her eyes.

But he was already undead . . . damn close to it. "Thanks," she dismissed him, feeling his eyes on her back when she turned and began to unpack.

A moment later, the door closed.

Scarlett took out the baggy of her grave dirt, placing it under a bed pillow, appraising her new apartment. She went to the curtains and pulled them shut, sighing in the welcome dusk that fell over the room. She sat in the chair at the desk and studied the mirror behind it, unable to use her powers to *see* during the sun's hours, but viewing all the fantasies of her own . . . of herself and new lovers, their blood.

Connie.

And the memories . . . the past she had rejected.

For unlife.

Undeath.

* * *

Scarlett was crying.

Alone.

She had refused all the fans . . . groupies . . . who made themselves more than available. Avoided them like the plague she had unintentionally begun.

The fans and papers called it "Scarlett Fever."

How could she be causing so much turmoil? Just by writing a couple of books?

The air-conditioning vent sighed its sympathy with her as Scarlett stared through the hotel room. In the beginning, the news of suicides and occasional rapes just made her laugh, and she liked the way they bolstered her sales. But after the two suicides right here at this convention, Scarlett could not help but feel guilt.

She gulped at the sound of a knock on the door and dried her tears on the bedspread, then stood up and went to the bathroom where her beauty gear littered the counter.

She didn't feel up to a visit, even if it was God. When the second knock came, she pressed herself to the door. "Please. Come back later." She walked back to the bed, shivering as a chill surrounded her.

As she sat again, she blinked at the green mist coming up from under the door. . . .

"What—" The mist, a cloud now, shaped itself magically before her and she clutched the bed hard.

"Hello, dear," spoke a soft voice as a body formed around it.

Just as though this visitor were a vampire in one of her books. Scarlett stared at the lady in short-styled black hair and slinky gown and managed a smile. "Bravo," she whispered. "How'd you do it?"

The woman stepped close and held out a dainty hand. "Imagination . . . the same way you write your books, dear."

"Get real." Scarlett sighed. "Look, I don't feel well, so leave me alone, okay?"

The woman's clothing disappeared.

"Jesus!" Scarlett dropped her mouth, full of admiration for the new trick and the beautiful body before her.

"I'm Jeanne," she smiled, sitting beside Scarlett. "I noticed you were in town and I just had to drop by and tell you what a wonderful

303

job you're doing. Do you know that people actually want to become vampires now?"

That unforgettable knowledge and its frequent aftermath made her sniff again. "Are you another fucking reporter . . . some parent? I just write the books," she whimpered. "It's not my fault that—"

Jeanne laid a cool, almost cold, hand on Scarlett's shoulder. "I'm not here to criticize you, Scarlett. I'm here to thank you. For centuries . . . since time began . . . everyone has been so afraid of us. You've turned the tide. When I read your books, I even thought you must be one of us."

The voice, sweetly hypnotic, stirred Scarlett, especially as Jeanne stretched out on the bed seductively. The guilt she'd been so frustrated by seemed suddenly distant.

"But I guess you're not, are you? Still, you are one of us in spirit."

Finally understanding, Scarlett just shook her head. "God, you're another convamp, aren't you? I just write books, okay?"

"I thought you said you believed in us?"

A bubble of sour laughter escaped as Scarlett remembered the pictorial interview she'd done for Playboy. "That was just for publicity."

Jeanne opened her mouth to the most realistic-looking fangs Scarlett had ever seen at a con yet. "Really?"

"I'm going to have to find out where you get all this costume and magic stuff," Scarlett said, staring into her mouth.

"So you do want it?" Jeanne let her tongue graze each fang.

"Sure," Scarlett said. The woman was nuts, but Scarlett was enjoying the way this interlude was pushing the guilt she'd known farther and farther away. She touched a fang in Jeanne's mouth with more admiration. "You're selling this stuff, aren't you?"

"Sure," Jeanne mimicked her.

"How much?"

"Just your blood, dear. Nothing you'll miss I don't think. All I want is your life."

"What!" Scarlett shook her head nervously and swallowed, inching closer to the room phone. Her first impressions were right . . . this woman was a fan.

304

Like a lot of her fans, totally fucked up . . . a little further gone than the ones who wanted her to suck their blood and make them vampires.

Jeanne thought she already was one.

"I won't hurt you, dear Scarlett. I just want to take away your guilt. Don't you want to be a vampire?"

She picked up the receiver. "You're crazy."

In an instant, Jeanne was right in front of her again, so near they were touching, and the chill of Jeanne's flesh sent a shiver deep. Scarlett dropped the receiver as their lips met.

Desire exploded inside her.

Inside Jeanne's deep eyes, she saw the things she wanted . . . the freedom from living she craved. The pleasure . . .

"There's no responsibility in death, Scarlett. You can be free. Life is a curse and undeath is our release. We don't want to spread it around like you do in your books because we need living blood to survive, and there's a lot of us around already. But the more souls we can control, the more power we have. And even if you're not undead, yet, you have a lot of lives under your control." Jeanne undressed her. "We choose our disciples very carefully, and I've chosen you."

Moaning as those experiences became real now, Scarlett lay down on the bed, nearly crying as her dreams . . . the hopes she'd written of . . . became real. The guilt was leaving her, and she clutched Jeanne's shoulders, panting out her joy.

Because it was all true. Undeath was true and life was what she wanted to make false. . . . It was a muddled existence of pain. Scarlett's mother had died at her birth . . . a birth she never asked for and learned to regret . . . lived to regret. Her father abused her . . . sexually.

Life. Life was the true Hell.

As the feeling of her body slipped into Jeanne's slurping mouth, Scarlett only hoped that this wasn't a trick or some past drug's flashback.

The guilt for the lives and deaths of the others disappeared, bringing her a feeling of victory . . . of the power already inside her.

The power of undeath.

Chapter 2

Connie had not been able to fall asleep when they'd arrived at the motel early this morning. It seemed nearly impossible to her that Phil could. He was planning murder, even if his target was no longer truly human. It bothered her in the way that it bothered her for her father to go hunting.

The guilt of Phil's past had destroyed his rest for years, and now . . . he'd slept like a baby.

It made her uneasy. A baby. She had killed her unborn child. Two of them. For herself.

Connie tried to believe there wasn't a difference in Phil's plans and her past . . . staring with habit into the mirror on the facing wall. But he said there *was* a difference. She rubbed the soreness of Vicky's attack on her. The unborn had been innocent lives, not even begun, existing through her actions and not through some choice of their own. The way Scarlett explained: no one was given life by their own choice . . . the choice of death only came through consciousness. The choice of life, death . . .

Or undeath. Connie had chosen the end of two unbegun lives because they would be inconvenient to her. She had made their choice for them. For life . . . and death.

Phil planned to make Scarlett's choice of death . . . for *her*, but it was a choice Scarlett had made already. Phil was going to close her up in her own fantasy the way he said he'd been trapped in his. A fantasy she couldn't draw others into.

Connie sat up in the bed and tried to stop a yawn, shutting her mouth fast to keep her insides in when new sickness boiled in her stomach.

Despite the independence received from the holy water. It *had* freed her, but not taken away her ability to still choose. It was why Phil insisted on destroying Scarlett. He was wrapped up in revenge and the idea that his love and meaning had been sacrificed to undeath. But Connie knew neither of them would ever be free of the torture of choice. She looked at the empty bed on the other side of the bed table. Phil had left during a period of her near sleep. She had been conscious of his departure before she'd finally fallen into her own darkness.

Thank God, this time there had been no dreams.

She stared harder into the mirror that showed only her . . . no memories.

No fantasy.

No Scarlett. Connie shuddered.

The air in here was close, but as she slid out of the bed, she knew it was going to get a lot closer.

Something was going to happen . . . if it didn't, she knew Phil would make it happen. For the first time since she'd known him, he was showing determination for more than just getting his rare books signed. He'd always called himself a wimpy book dealer, but not anymore.

Connie finished her shower, enjoying the blinding splash of the water without a twinge of pain. Drying off, she found her black convamp clothes, but shoved them back into the drawer, choosing jeans and a white sweater top instead.

The door rattled and opened. Phil stepped inside without a smile. They had barely spoken since last night. His choice as much as hers. Now, his face was still stern and expressionless. "I picked up our stuff and set up the tables, Connie," Phil told her. "I tried to arrange your jewelry as best I could." He went to the bag he'd packed at the apartment and took out the stake.

Connie turned away, her stomach jelly.

He laid it on his bed and drew out the cross, then the vial of holy water. She flinched at the reminder of how it had removed her mark yesterday, and she felt her chin tremble when Phil stuck the vial in his pants pocket. "I've got to go back and sell stuff, Connie. Lots of people are arriving now. I checked at the desk and Scarlett's already here. Downstairs. It's going to be packed tonight and even worse tomorrow. This place is booked solid."

Connie shrugged and finished dressing, staring at herself in the mirror and suddenly wishing for the fantasies that were gone, wishing that all this were only one of the terrible nightmares she'd had yesterday. "Are you coming?" Phil asked, pocketing the studded cross and putting the stake into a plastic book sack.

"I . . . I'm not even breathing hard," she tossed the words back without feeling, passing him to the door and into the hall where men and women her age and older were carrying their suitcases to rooms . . . talking . . . laughing . . . having a good time. Not caring about anything but the moment. The fun.

The fantasy of herself . . . who she had been.

308

Chapter 3

The sun was setting. Teresa felt the power creep back inside her. Wishing she could just open a door, bored with her magic already, she became a mist and slid past the broken stone that had once hidden her casket. No one had yet noticed its destruction.

Showed how much her mom and dad and other relatives cared about her or any of her other dead kin.

Teresa reformed with the seersucker Kolchak attire of last night, adding the necklace. She gazed into the mirror and saw into the window of life's physical reality she wanted to enter . . . she was getting pretty good at this shit already. She willed herself into the mirror like someone swallowing themselves and materialized in a big, gaudy glass in Bruce's storage area. She stepped out of it onto the dusty floor, looking down at Bruce, still covered by the old newspapers. His ripe lifelessness wafted through the damp air. "Too bad you have to miss the party, Brucie." She stared back into the mirrors . . . none of them showing her. Her stomach cramped between hunger and a fear of a complete nonexistence.

But she wasn't about to back out now. What the hell difference did it make, anyway? Trying to square a round jaw that just wouldn't cooperate, she swallowed . . . spoke.

"Attention. This is a call to . . . uh . . . *teeth.*" She tried to giggle at the feeble attempt at a joke. "Anyone who listened to me last night, come to me through the mirrors . . . the portals. Now. Leave your graves and find a mirror . . . don't stop to feed, please. You'll spoil your appetite and it's banquet time. I'll be waiting right here for you."

The empty mirrors remained empty.

Like herself.

Teresa waited.

An hour passed before the first mirror flooded with a green mist that flowed into the room. As the clouds broke, a broad black man took their place. He wore a cape like Count Downe's pulled around him, and walked out of the glass with a surly grimace.

"Hi," Teresa said.

He sniffed and turned toward her, opening his cape, showing his T-shirt underneath. RACISM AIN'T DEAD . . . BUT I AM.

Teresa read the message and forced a grin she wanted to feel, but didn't. "Pretty funny," she said, finding the right words at last.

He nodded, but didn't even crack a smile. They both watched other mirrors cloud . . . more vampires stepping out of the doorways that ignored the rules of existence as they did. After another three hours passed, there were twenty-two of them. Teresa counted twice to be sure and waited for stragglers, wondering how many of the undead had gotten lost in the labyrinth. It was nearly ten.

"I'm starved," called out an older woman in a beehive of gray hair and dressed in a masquerade bikini that showed too much of her wrinkled flesh.

Teresa walked to the black vampire, facing the others, too. "Follow me. If you get lost, find Scarlett. She's still connected to us somehow, and above all, stay *calm*. We're going to a con and it's going to be a hell of a party. Lots

310

of blood for all of us. We'll blow Scarlett's cover and get a good dinner besides. This may be our blowout, okay?"

No one cheered.

She shrugged, not caring, but wanting to. She pointed at the mirrors and walked toward the nearest, turned back to the black man. "You want to bring up the rear?"

"Back of the bus?" He sighed. "Just call me Blacula, bitch. I don't know what the fuck you're up to, but you got some style. You lead . . . we'll follow. Bring us to the promised land."

The sense of unity she felt with him and the others almost made her feel alive, and Teresa tried hard to hold on to that departed emotion as it disappeared again. They all looked at each other blankly.

She stepped into the looking glass, feeling the movement of the others with her into the bleak tunnel between life and death. It would take a while to find the way, but she felt the direction between herself and Scarlett.

Between Denver and Oklahoma City.

Between undeath and death.

Chapter 4

Phil covered his books as the dealers' room closed at seven. He had seen Kevin and Denise earlier. They had stopped by the table and made small talk, and Kevin, mundanely clad in a blue business suit, had studied Phil closely, but Phil had not shown his friend the turmoil of his soul. They'd left to check out some panels and readings but Kevin's presence here gave Phil a new paranoia.

But it also gave him more determination. Phil knew that something had to be done . . . and he was going to do it. He was glad he had not ordered more Shade books as he'd first intended to, even though he was sold out of them already. Other dealers had stocked up, drawing the crowds he no longer cared about.

He felt guilt for selling any of those books. Even if he destroyed Scarlett, it bothered Phil that her words would live on. But without her supernatural influence, Phil hoped the power of her words would lose their seductive edge.

Full circle. Phil followed Connie into the hall teeming with people. He was finally becoming free of the perimeter he had followed all his life, but feared that now that he'd finally left the training track for the race, it would end up in the same location he'd begun on before. He wanted the love Connie talked of, that *he* talked of and had felt, but first, he knew he had to destroy his past . . . his nightmares, forever.

Through Scarlett. He had to sacrifice *her!*

He was still afraid and his past was still inside him. Now he had to face fully the shame for the way he'd misused his life. The power of that undeath wanted to drag him back into its protective hell and he fought the desire of that imprisoning with the understanding that in all the fantasies to escape life's hard truths, he wasn't alone. He peered inside the plastic sack he carried his weapon in, feeling the hunger of this hunt. He hurried to Connie's side in the hallway of pamphlets and jabbering people.

She looked up. "When . . . are you planning to do it?"

Still expressionless, he stroked the sack in his hand.

"Please . . . don't. We can be free without this—maybe we *can't* destroy her. We can't destroy them all. The power of choice is what brought us together, Phil . . ."

He met her eyes and moved a finger through his beard. "I have to, Connie. Scarlett is dangerous to others." His mouth twisted bitterly. "To you. She's still a danger to me. I . . . have to."

She tugged him to a glass wall that looked out on the motel's plaza center and its empty pool. A hundred conversations hid theirs and he didn't look at the eyes that looked at them but didn't see them.

They were alone.

"I love you, Phil. Don't take that away . . ."

"I love you, Connie. I won't stop. Nothing will change that now . . . but it's already too late to change what's happening. I have to do this for myself if for no one else." He lowered his head and sniffed, then looked up at smiling faces full of amusement, some showing him a slight, ignorant sympathy.

None of them knew . . . none understood. No one would want to. "Maybe I was born for this. All of us are

313

born to die . . . we just choose the way it happens." Seeing her pain, he shook his head. "If I don't do this . . ."

Reaching down, she tried to take his bag. "Don't talk about dying! Jesus, Phil, I just don't think we should rush into this. There's got to be another way." She spoke lowly, stepping aside as some costumed guests walked around them, their voices loud and laughing. Connie pulled him back in the direction of their room. "Look . . . I know it all seems real, but . . ." She fought the choke as he pushed her back and kept the bag close. "What if it's *not* real, Phil? What if it's just another fantasy? We've got a good fantasy going now, and you said it was *real*. I don't want anything but love . . . let's hold on to it, okay?"

His eyes were small. "Love isn't a fantasy, but I have to be worthy of love."

She tugged him with her. "You *are*. You chose it—you said you were free—"

"I have to stop her, Connie. If I don't, I won't stay free . . . I feel that deep inside me. I was *sacrificed*, Connie. I let myself be sacrificed by caring about Sonia, and it destroyed me! I've hidden from that knowledge all my life. We have to be a law to ourselves if nothing else, or maybe we're not real. And if nothing makes a difference . . . *if* nothing's real, who cares?"

"We're real! We've all been . . . sacrificed, Phil—but we can end it!" She pulled him through the crowd, remembering how she hadn't wanted to care in the past but couldn't ever stay free of that emotion. She felt a memory in her breast and knew very suddenly that self-imprisonment was the freedom she'd sought. Not caring . . . freedom that was a prison.

"*I'm* going to end it," Phil muttered.

Her voice rose urgently. "Phil—this isn't love! It's destruction! We've got to put it behind us and go on. We need to talk about it, okay? Think about it!"

He said nothing. One of the women who had bought

314

over a dozen high-priced books this afternoon passed and waved at Phil. He followed, leading Connie up the stairs at the end of the hall and onto the second floor. He unlocked their door as they reached it.

Down the hall . . . only five doors away. Phil stiffened and Connie took a loud breath as Vicky Cossiter came out of that room in full Scarlett Shade attire. A sexy mini gown exposing more of her than not. Her sandy hair was full and floating, styled the way she'd wanted it. Vicky peered around with empty eyes that Connie knew too well from her own face in the mirror, and Connie ducked herself and Phil into the room fast before her friend saw them. Connie was afraid of Vicky because Vicky was everything she herself might be. She dropped her hand to her wound, shut the door, and sat down on the made bed. Phil walked to the closed drapes and pushed one open, looking out on the setting sun as it glinted on the shiny car bumpers crowding the lot below. All the things Connie wanted to say to him were so heavy on her tongue that she couldn't form even one word. Instead, she got back up and went to stare at herself in the mirror, suddenly posing in her wrinkled blouse and faded jeans. "Do . . . do you still think I'm pretty?"

"Sure."

The mirror showed her. Scared. She looked away from herself. "Then . . . then why don't you take me to a party? There's parties all over the place."

He sighed and she followed him into the bathroom. Phil washed his face while she reapplied her makeup, but far more lightly than she had before. "I don't think I'm in the mood to be in a bunch of noise and around a lot of people, Connie. It'll just make things worse. I've got to be ready. I need to find Scarlett alone."

She finished with herself and picked up a brush to comb his hair. "You won't be able to, Phil. This isn't going to work. Please, for now, let's try to forget, okay?

Let's go to a party. I'll be right with you. If it starts to make you ill, I'll bring you right back."

He shrugged, uncertain. "Scarlett . . ."

Connie walked past him to the desk and read the convention program. "She has a midnight panel. Okay? We . . . we'll go to that."

"I want to . . ." As her hand caressed his cheek, he swallowed and nodded. "Okay."

The party in room 253 and the adjoining 255 was swinging when Connie and Phil entered. Booze made the excitement wilder than ever. It was so loud that the songs of the filkers down the hall were completely overwhelmed. Those minstrels of hell were even complaining of the noise.

To Connie, it was a case of the pot calling the kettle black.

But she wasn't paying that much attention to the fun and games. She was keeping her eye on Phil.

Phil was talking it up with two book collectors right now. The same two young men who had bought a couple of hard to find, signed, first edition hardbacks of Matheson's *Hell House* just before the dealers' room closed. Phil even had a drink, albeit a small one.

Connie relaxed and went to the room's bathroom, nudging by two men speaking loud over thirty other voices, reaching down into the ice-filled bathtub for her fourth beer, wanting to be drunk. With the fantasies gone, without them to turn to, she felt more hollow than ever . . . or maybe now she just understood how hollow she had always been. Only the thought of her love for Phil turned it away, and he seemed to be so distant again.

Even with the three bottles of beer she'd drunk, the more she thought of the things Phil had told her . . . about how he understood undeath and its danger because he had lived it so long by choice . . . the more worried she became. Although he denied it, he seemed to be welcoming undeath back by his unrelenting desire to destroy it. The shuddering thought made her sigh as she inched back around the two men.

All at once, it got even noisier. The people all around her, some costumed and most not, were raising their beers and glasses with hoopla. It was almost like some kind of a Halloween party.

Connie froze when Scarlett Shade came in the door, attired in a nightgownlike garb that was even skimpier and more revealing than the one she'd worn on that panel in Denver. The sight of her this close, not merely a reflection in a mirror, made Connie tremble. The dozen cheering men between them were elbowing each other to get near her and offer her their drinks. Several of them were dressed in capes, their skin powdered pale, screaming out to Scarlett how they wanted to be vampires.

Scarlett took a long-necked bottle from one of the men who'd been talking to Phil a moment before. She leaned forward as he beamed and kissed his cheek, her words unheard in the excitement. She opened her mouth wide to her set of vampire fangs, pretending to sink them into the bottle's neck.

Everybody laughed louder.

The fangs were real, but how could they be? Connie let that doubt in past her fog of alcohol. Was she crazy . . . was Phil?

Was Scarlett really . . . ?

Scarlett caught Connie's eye and winked at her.

The warmth in Connie's face burst into beads of sweat and the flash plunged down her body, tightening her nipples and making the left one blaze as if on fire again, hotter than ever, but this time, not with any pain at all. Connie's thighs rippled with a surging tingle and she felt her panties suddenly become sopping wet . . . so wet she had to look down at her crotch to be sure it didn't show.

Scarlett opened her lips and mouthed unheard words again, and once more, sound was lost in the flurry of laughter and loud snatches of conversation.

But inside her head, Connie heard Scarlett's unmistakable voice . . . uttering her own name:

Dear, sweet Connie.

Connie felt wet heat pour over her . . . as though she were fainting into Scarlett's arms.

But a second later, the feeling was gone and Connie was wiping the sweat from her damp hair and forehead. She remembered Phil and her eyes darted back to the rear of the room until she saw him, sitting passively on one of the beds and sipping from a Coke can. He was still talking with the other book collector, a man whose head flared in curly, carrot hair. His name tag read Charley Wise.

Connie looked back at Scarlett, feeling relief that Scarlett's attention was elsewhere now. She was busy fending off questions from her other fans as convamps poured in.

With a new sigh, Connie made her way to Phil. She touched his shoulder. "Are you feeling all right?"

He interrupted his sentence and looked up, then nodded. "A little tired, But pretty good . . . I'm glad you convinced me to come here and relax."

She laughed and tugged his beard, relieved he hadn't made a move toward Scarlett . . . hoping that all her worries . . . maybe the past week itself, *had* been a dream. A fantasy gone bad she had finally awakened from. She felt lighter in her soul, knowing it must be the truth. She tried discharging those days from her mind and disbelieving in them as the alcohol spun her senses faster. All she wanted from those harrowing hours was the love she had found, and she kissed Phil's cheek, lowering her voice. "Don't get too tired, Phil. You've got other coming to do before the night's out."

Charley laughed brightly. "Goddamn," he yelped, "where'd you find *her?* Sex *and* laughs, huh?"

Phil just grinned.

The young man wouldn't shut up. He nudged Phil. "No offense, man, but she looks like a reject from the Scarlett brigade without teeth . . ." He giggled and pointed at Scarlett. "Go ask Momma to sell you a new set of fangs, babe! Then you can make ol' Phil's second coming tonight more *pointed!*"

Charley laughed insanely, but Connie saw the good humor disappear from Phil's glance. She laughed this time, wanting it back. She thumped Charley on his head. "You'd just love to feel my teeth, wouldn't you?"

With a quick look at Phil, he nodded cautiously.

She shook her head in mock-sadness. "It's terrible to leave a fantasy con with a dream unfulfilled, but I like three-course meals, darling"—she imitated Scarlett's voice as well as she could—"and you don't look like you're even an appetizer . . ."

Phil flinched as though she'd struck *him,* and Charley turned a red much darker than his hair. "Touché," he obliged, then went back to talking books.

Connie waited until Phil's face relaxed again. When he was talking freely to Charley once more, she turned away, back to Scarlett, and once again, Scarlett was looking right at her.

Scarlett's face reformed, rounding, her hair becoming like straw . . . like Connie's.

Like looking into a mirror.

Connie shivered, blinking until she was only seeing Scarlett again, wondering if she'd really heard that inner voice . . . Scarlett's . . . a moment ago.

Had she ever heard it? Wasn't it just the fantasy of the books? She denied the voice, knowing she was just drinking too fast.

The past week *hadn't* been real. It had gone by so

quickly—just like a dream. All of it. She didn't want it to be true, now, did she? But she took another gulp of beer, almost wanting to hear the imaginary voice again.

Scarlett's mouth slithered.

Sweet Connie.

Dripping passion shot through Connie even harder than before with icy déjà vu. She felt a strange urge to go right up to Scarlett . . . and kiss her, full on the lips.

In her dreams . . . all this had happened before. She felt that hold around her tighten. Seemed to remember . . . a fantasy . . . of Scarlett naked above her, as she and Scarlett caressed and licked each other like only two women could.

As though they were . . . sisters.

Blood sisters.

And then the feeling and desire was gone, instantly, as Scarlett broke the bond of their eyes and faced another fan.

Connie's breast was throbbing like a second heart.

Before she even knew she was doing it, Connie was pushing through the men and women to the writer, reaching out to meet the fingers that drew her to them.

"Hi, Connie," whispered the shiny lips. "I hope you don't mind, but I've captured you again. Your boyfriend has really put some strange ideas into your head. He *is* crazy, you know. I'll take care of him, though, and I'll take care of you, too. Tonight. We'll spend eternity together. Don't bother to try and remember me this time, dear. I'll hold all your memories. You're *mine.*"

Connie pressed herself against the flimsy gown and felt the cool, gentle flesh underneath. Her own skin was throbbing with desire, wanting Scarlett . . . wanting Scarlett to take her for her own right now . . . right *there*.

Wanting Scarlett to be naked with her.

Scarlett's probing hand snaked down to Connie's ass as the others became a mass of cheering spectators in Connie's mind. Her aching breast throbbed for Scarlett's velvet mouth to embrace it.

And almost instantly, they were both out in the hall where the smokers congregated and continued the inner festivities more quietly.

Connie's hand worked itself through a slit in Scarlett's gown and rubbed the silky panties underneath, feeling the delirious swell of Scarlett's soft bottom.

"Not here," Scarlett whispered, tugging Connie down the hall and away from the others. The voices fell away from them, momentarily replaced by a repetitious song from the filk room, and then even that was behind them. Scarlett moved them into a side hall and stroked a button on the wall while Connie just stared at her beauty, wanting her and knowing that she was *chosen* . . . that Scarlett wanted *her*.

Again.

The elevator opened, empty, and Scarlett pushed Connie inside. When the door slid closed and the floor lights began to change, Scarlett opened her arms and Connie flowed into them, hugging the woman of her dreams.

No.

"Are you mine?"

Connie felt her will drain, shaking her head more and more slowly, finally turning it into a nod against the taller woman's breast.

"You must *say* it, Connie. Are you *mine?*"

Looking up into those seawater eyes . . . into the fulfilling ebony points they surrounded, she forgot all her hopes, nodded once more, and her voice pushed up through her lungs. "Yes."

As the floor buzzer rang, Scarlett kissed her quickly. The elevator door slid open.

Others, loud and happy conners in states of vivid inebriation, flowed in around them, and Scarlett pulled Connie into the lobby quickly, then into a quiet hallway.

Connie looked down it wantonly, wanting to go to Scarlett's room. With Scarlett.

"Not now," whispered Scarlett. "I'm saving you for the last, dear. I just want to be sure of you this time. I have to take care of your boyfriend. Did you hear my voice?"

Lost in the eyes holding her tight, Connie remembered nothing else. She was alone with her fantasy . . . her truest lover . . . swimming in a sea of Scarlett.

"Yes," Scarlett sighed. "Forget now, dear Connie. Go back to your party. I will call for you and you must come to me when I do."

Connie nodded.

"Say it."

"I will come to you."

They pressed close together and Scarlett glanced to either side like a motorist at a stoplight, then she met Connie's open mouth with hers, sliding her tongue into Connie and taking hers, wrestling for a moment that was all too short.

Then she was gliding in unequaled grace down the hall while Connie stared blankly after her.

When Scarlett disappeared a second later, Connie still stared down the hall, then into the lobby with that same blankness, wondering what the hell she was doing here. The voices came back to her ears as loudly as the passionate need blazing between her legs. Her breasts were aching in it . . . her left breast a spouting volcano. "Phil," she murmured, wanting him.

Almost wanting anybody.

Even the geeky guy near the front desk, sitting alone and—

Phil.

The sense of self-disgust battered her that she had forgotten him—that she had left him alone.

Despite her promises, she had left him alone.

Chapter 5

The headache mushroomed in Phil's head.

Though he was only two feet away from Charley's moving lips, he didn't hear a word the young man was saying now. The way Charley's cheeks bulged made him look like some kind of sea bass. Their conversation about rare books and how they each found those treasures was slipping further and further away. . . . Phil heard nothing but the noise and screams on that hellish day of his youth. A nightmare returning as he put off the moments of what he wanted to do. Scarlett had been right here, in this room, and he should have . . .

He reached into his sack and touched the rough wood. He was afraid. Not just of Scarlett, but still of himself. The undeath of that long-ago day of hate, humiliation, and the greatest fear he had ever known, haunting him once more. Undeath.

He would never be free. Never completely. The past would always be waiting to suck him back into it. He couldn't accept that past until he killed it, because he was so afraid he would have to face it again . . . and again. He had to stand up to it.

He would not be free now until he faced the woman his nightmare led to. He had to *kill* Scarlett Shade. Phil slurped the sharp, sweet taste from the can in his hand desperately, wanting its cool familiarity to bring him back to the present and sanity. Wanting Connie to speak to him in her soft tone, but he couldn't find her in the crowd.

Charley was staring at him with a raised eyebrow on his quizzical face. His lips mouthing new words . . .

A sudden chilling heat swept over and around Phil and he sucked in a breath as if it were his last, and the room's sound—the laughter, frenzied voices—was suddenly louder than the noise of his inner machine guns.

"—all right?" Charley was asking.

Phil threw out his hand, dropping his Coke and watching it fall in slow-motion, spilling its fizzy brown color on the yellow carpet. His fingers clutched Charley's wrist shakily.

"Hey!" Charley shouted.

Phil felt his limbs freeze . . . saw it all through a haze. "Con . . . nie," he gasped.

Charley stood beside him and held up his head, shaking him slowly. "Hey, take it easy, man. Hell, you haven't even hardly been drinking—"

And then, the haze disappeared. Phil breathed deeply, stood, and smiled, feeling good.

Feeling strong.

Charley sighed. "Are you okay?"

Nodding, Phil glanced down at his spilt drink.

"The maid'll clean it up, man. Hey, you looked pretty trashed for a minute . . . Are you really feeling okay?"

Taking his hand, Phil stood up and looked through the room at all the boisterous people, most of them younger than himself. Women in tight jeans . . . loose dresses, men in T-shirts and jeans.

Phil saw Connie on the other side of the room—*no, Connie's friend, Vicky*. He stared hard as she fogged in his vision, visualizing her naked through her Scarlett Shade gown. Just as he had seen her in a forgotten dream last night as she invited him into her room through a mirror in his mind, her thighs spread wide. She was smiling at him. Then and *now*.

Crossing the room toward him.

Like Sonia once had.

He *had* dreamed last night. It wasn't over.

"I'll talk with you later," Phil said to Charley, and went to meet her, just as he had once met Sonia in her room.

Vicky was happy and quite drunk already. Phil smelled her heavy scent of liquor as they shook hands clumsily. "Oh my," she giggled, "I haven't been this plastered since . . ."

Phil just turned his lips up gently.

She pressed her warm mouth to his ear. "I dreamed about you last night, Phil. You and Scarlett. Scarlett told me about your guilt and problems. I'm sorry for you. Scarlett told me to take care of you . . . she said Connie wasn't helping you at all and that you weren't helping her, either. Scarlett can give all of us our dreams, Phil. We just have to trust her . . . to let her take care of us. You're still afraid of yourself. So come on. Trust *me* . . ." Pulling Phil with her, she pushed through the others to the door. "Really and seriously. It'll be wonderful. I'm going through a real crisis with my divorce, too. My self-esteem's hit rock bottom!" As they escaped from the crowd and out the door, she lowered her voice and led Phil down the hall in a tipsy two-step.

He relaxed a little against his will with her invitation. "You came to me last night," Phil said, lazily dancing with her. "You . . . you're a vampire."

She guffawed and pounded his back. "There's no such things. Just experiences. Life is experiences . . . undeath is only their enjoyment . . . through their reflection." She laughed louder and pulled Phil along faster, past partially opened doors with smaller parties and doors shut tight. DO NOT DISTURB signs hung from several doorknobs. "You're getting divorced, too," she told him. "It's driving you crazy. You can't take care of yourself. Just let go of your guilt, Phil. Forget love . . . It means nothing. Only blood has meaning." She winked at him. "I never knew how bad my life was until I started reading Scarlett Shade's wonderful books. They really opened up my eyes." She stopped at a door and looked up and down the hall carefully, her eyes blinking. "Where's Connie?"

Phil barely remembered Connie now, his head was full of all the images and nightmares again. "I don't know," he admitted.

Vicky just grinned wider. "While the cat's away the mice will play . . . Shit, she's probably in some room gang-banging a dozen guys. I bet she is, and leaving you to wait and probably catch a disease from her when she gets back. That's the way she's always been . . ." Vicky opened the door with a shiny key and led Phil inside.

Closed the door.

The streetlight from the window filled the room with a sense of timelessness. She guided him to the bed and started unzipping. "Nobody cares, Phil. My husband sure didn't give a shit . . . and I bet your wife was just the same . . ." She dropped her gown on the bedspread. He stared at her large tits . . . at the slight stretch marks up her stomach . . . the green panties underneath as she shoved them down to her ankles.

Green. The color of his fear.

Then she sat down on the bed and gazed at him. "Aren't you going to take off your clothes?"

Through the screams and tanks, he barely heard her, but felt a gnawing anger.

At her. At everyone. Himself.

"Hey . . . this is just for fun. I've even got rubbers for you, okay? I just have to fuck you before . . ." She shook her head, "Scarlett *herself*, can you believe it? She told me not to tell you, but I'm so nervous. I need her books . . . I need *her*. Hell, I want her and she wants *me*. I can't refuse her. I need her pleasure to forget about life and death."

Phil said nothing.

She took his hand and pulled him closer.

He saw the shine of the tears in her eyes. "Please . . . this is . . . Scarlett herself!" She laughed raggedly as his fingers stroked her cheeks and touched her tears. She wiped her face with his hand.

Hate raged through him . . . but not so much for her as for—

"Shit—just a minute! We've got to put that rubber on you first!"

She stood up and started to the bathroom as Phil reached into his sack, taking out the stake. "Vicky," he said.

She didn't turn back until she reached the bathroom. He saw her at her purse in there, tearing through makeup, pulling something shiny out.

A *knife*. Her face twisted and she walked to him slowly, shaking her head. "This is our best chance, Phil . . . Fuck me. I'll be Sonia, okay? Just fuck me . . . fuck her. Let *us* fuck you . . ."

He stepped back, looking into the mirror she was staring into.

Scarlett. "You—"

She lunged at him with a wretched, warped expression that made her face become two red, glittering eyes and a mouthful of teeth. Raising the studded cross from his pocket, Phil hit her in the face with it.

She croaked as it glanced off her brow, not leaving a mark the way it always did in the books and movies. Phil felt his insides turn to Jell-O and wheezed, doubting himself. But she screeched and covered her face, cowering, backing fast. This time, he swung the stake, smashing it into her forehead hard, bringing a bloody bruise. She toppled in midleap and fell to the floor with a loud scream, sprawled out like a blow-up doll, her legs wide apart. Phil was already diving on top of her, ramming the stake between her breasts when he finally looked at her teeth—

He tried to stop.

But his furious momentum drove the sharp wood in, and he felt sick as the point ripped her flesh open wetly and shattered her rib cage, squishing and crunching. The blood squirted out of her like a dark fountain . . . a geyser, drenching him in hot stickiness.

She had no fangs.

Phil studied the dead body, then, shutting his eyes, he wrapped his fingers around the stake and pulled it out of her flesh. Vicky gave a final sigh, and he stared down at the last light in her eyes. He licked the blood on his lips, tasting her, revolted, and lurched into the bathroom.

Chapter 6

The room party in 253 and 255 was winding down already when Connie reentered. She looked through the stragglers three times before the dread that Phil wasn't among them made her cold. "Shit!"

A couple of people stared at her with slow grins, and she just wanted to hit them, imagining that the new laughter she heard was for her.

She walked to the carrot-haired man wandering through the room and pouring the remnants of half-empty glasses into his. "Where's Phil?"

He sipped from his glass of leftovers, replacing the confusion on his face with recognition. His mouth formed a crooked grin. "Phil left," he chuckled. "Everybody's leaving. This con is really going downhill. Used to be that no one went to bed before the sun rose . . ." He took a deeper drink and offered her the glass. "Unless they were going to bed to do something besides sleep."

Connie sniffed. "I need to find Phil. Please . . . I'm not kidding around. Phil really isn't well. I don't know why I left . . . I shouldn't have. I promised him that I'd stay with him—"

"He was looking kind of sick for a minute there," Charley admitted. "Like he was going to barf or pass out or something, but he snapped right out of it . . . and I don't think he'd want you with him right now . . ."

She frowned. "Where is he?"

Charley shrugged. "Then again, maybe he would. I wouldn't mind two women at once."

Connie flinched. "Who?"

"Just a woman. Some convamp . . . I talked to her earlier. Vicky, I think." He pushed the drink at her again. "You're more to my taste . . . Connie. And I bet I *could* show you a real feast of a meal, too." He squinted at her mouth. "Especially for a vampire *without* fangs."

She shook her head. "Look, I'm not fooling. Phil has really been ill. I've got to find him. Where did they go?"

"Goddamn, you're persistent. What are you, his mother?" He laughed hard. Connie slipped back into the hall. The fog of the earlier drinks made her forget the anxiety at the way she'd found herself downstairs just minutes before, not even knowing how she had gotten there. She stomped her way past the knots of people, refusing interest in the drunkenly profound snippets that came from a dozen mouths. She passed some loud talkers engaged in restructuring the world's future political system, and scuffed her feet, trying to remember the room she'd seen Vicky coming out of.

Goddamn Phil.

But she had left him.

She found their room and remembered, counting five doors down, moving to it. She stopped with her hand on the doorknob and looked back the way she'd come, imagining Phil and Vicky, together.

Right inside this room . . .

The idea made Connie's stomach do somersaults, and she pressed her ear to the door, half expecting pants and moans of ecstasy. It made her long for a fantasy . . . of . . . Scarlett.

The silence was more than a relief.

Connie sagged into the door. It opened. She hissed, entering the dark room, turning on the lights. The double bed was empty. But in front of it lay Vicky in all her gory glory.

"My God, Phil! You . . . you *are* crazy!" Connie held her lips together and went into the bathroom, making a wavy line to the open toilet. When her frenzy subsided at last, she wiped the cold sweat from her face and flushed, listening to the hollow, wet roar. In the echoes, she heard light groans almost beside her.

Icicles rippled up her spine. She wiped her mouth with a wrist and turned her hot face, staring at a hand hanging over the side of the bathtub. She touched it and felt tears, feeling the responsibility that was hers, too . . . because she had left him. "Phil?" Connie stared at his form sprawled in the muddy water half filling the deep porcelain tub . . . at the knife—

But his eyeballs were moving rapidly under his closed lids, making her skin crawl. His face was ashen, its features drawn together in a horrible grimace as bubbly saliva dripped from his open, hideously sighing mouth.

"Phil!"

As her shrill screech faded, his fingers clutched the slick walls on his either side, and his eyes half opened on blood-streaked slits.

Connie gasped and took a step back as he rose like a zombie and the water drops slipped down his skin. He reached out to her.

Swallowing hard, she made herself take his jittery hand, helping him onto the bathmat and hugging his wet body tight. "Phil—" Connie just gasped. *"Phil?"*

Deep sighs. She felt them as she heard them . . . his new tremble . . . the hard chokes of his throat. "Sonia," he groaned.

"Phil?"

He was suddenly sobbing. "... *kill me* ... *kill me, too* ..."

"Wake up, Phillip—*wake up!*"

In the dimness she saw the tears running from his eyes. "Sonia?" He spoke deeply and emotionally, his face a nightmare of shadows. "We belong ... *dead,*" he whispered.

"Phil—"

His mouth moved in indecipherable whispers. His eyes closed slowly, and when he was quiet, Connie touched him and then shook his arm. She still felt drunk. "Phil?" she whispered, speaking in his ear.

His eyes rolled under their lids.

"What—what's wrong, Phil?" But she knew he didn't hear. She looked at the shadows in the mirror ... at herself and Phil.

Scarlett. Her face there instead of the reflection Connie expected. Phil jerked and Connie knew he saw her, too. He gasped and shook his head violently. "Vicky ... she's *dead.* Connie, she was attacking me. Scarlett sent her ... this proves it all."

Connie sobbed, icy in the horror of her friend's death. Her fingers wandered to the bite marks Vicky had left in her, back to Scarlett's laughing face dimmed in the mirror, fading fast. Connie wiped her face, shaking her head back and forth wildly. "We—we've got to call the police ..."

His jaw clenched tighter. "No. I'm getting free, now. Connie, I'm getting free for the first time ever ... and I've got to make you free ... everyone free."

The tears leaked from her eyes and she looked back at Vicky's dead form, sniffing the foul taint of blood. "What ... do we do about her?"

Connie. Dear Connie.

Her left breast exploded into a deep new pain.

Come to me, sweet Connie. Now.

The inner voice began to scream through her . . . but now Phil needed her more than ever. The emotions staggered her back and forth—the dam holding back her self-control split apart so unexpectedly she froze solid in the mammoth aftershocks of the quake shaking her apart. She was too frazzled and weak to obey the imploring voice that clutched her very soul. "She's . . . calling me, Phil. She—"

"We're going to her," he growled, searching the bathroom and finding the bloody stake, his dripping clothing leaving a trail of water. He slipped the weapon back into the sack and held it close, clutching Connie's palm and pulling her behind him.

Connie was afraid, more than ever, of him. . . .

Scarlett.

The voice continued to call, and desperately, Connie denied it, reaching back into herself to all the past fantasies and denying them, too. No longer denying herself, but them. The long-lusted desires for Count Downe and Countess Showery beat at her but began to break up . . . disintegrating into the true parts of herself she had taken those fabrications from. Her real fears . . . real desires . . .

Love.

As she felt that strength she had finally accepted, inside her, love not only of herself but for Phil . . . for others . . . the pull, the voice, disappeared. Connie squeezed Phil's fingers tightly in her own. . . .

It all opened up in her mind. Her fantasies . . . created through Scarlett's words . . . made real. Like Phil's crippling nightmares. Phil had allowed the lie of what he believed to destroy his life, and she herself had fled so deeply into fantasy to hide from reality she had given Scarlett's words the power to make her own fantasies real!

Phil had touched that truth, but the anger and bitterness for himself . . . maybe for his past and Sonia . . . was holding him from complete acceptance.

Fear.

"Phil—"

He opened the door and tugged her into the hall.

"Phil! Stop! We don't have to—"

But he showed her a stare so full of his hate she shut her mouth.

Chapter 7

They both went down the hall, momentarily pausing to watch the group of a half-dozen young men and women raggedly clothed in medieval garb sitting in a circle on the hall floor, playing a role game fervently.

Phil's face had become a rubbery mask. He knew it was all a dream within a dream. Everyone played their roles in these conventions . . . in the larger world outside.

Wasn't it all just a game?

If it was only a game . . . why all the blood? Phil was uncomfortable in the wet clothes, remembered the way his father and mother had made him run beside him while Soviet soldiers marched down the streets, rounding up the dissidents. The guilt for Sonia was becoming the guilt for a death he had caused—Vicky. And he had to—He tugged at Connie's arm as they went down the stairs. "Come on, she has that panel . . . it's called Life, Death, and Undeath."

"Let's leave . . . just get away." Connie held him fast. "Far away. She's gone from me, Phil. It's not something *we* can destroy! We just have to deny her the power of our belief—just like you said! That's all it is . . . She can do it all only because we're desperate to believe in her!"

But he pushed ahead, no longer caring if that was the truth or not. His life had been drained out of him through lies, and he wanted to make up for his lost years—to kill a lie with his bare hands! He clenched his mouth tight, turning a corner to another hallway of doors. Connie dragged his arm, trying to hold him back as they passed the consuite. They stopped behind a crowd of male and female convamps just like the ones Connie had seen fawning after Scarlett in Denver. These fans were doing the same now as Scarlett pushed through them into the room, but before she disappeared inside, Scarlett suddenly turned her face back to Connie's and Connie felt the connection of their eyes . . . felt Scarlett's intensity flood her with an energy like before, but more strongly than ever.

Tonight.

Connie did her best to deny it again . . . and it worked, but Phil—

He pushed ahead of her and broke the contact physically, making her refusal easier, pulling Connie after him inside the room. Convamps filed in and found chairs, and Phil dragged Connie to the front row. They both sat in chairs opposite Scarlett's name plate on the table. There were no other authors scheduled for this panel . . . only her, and she took her place, brushing her slender hands briskly down her black gown. She touched her necklace with a wry smile and sat down. Connie pushed her mouth to Phil's ear. "Please—let's leave. Phil, that's all we have to do. Just turn our backs—"

"Welcome to undeath," greeted Scarlett, facing the ninety eyes that were on her, hushing Connie. "The con committee has given me this panel for my own, and I want to give them my thanks. Of course, I am Scarlett Shade . . . if any of you haven't read my books . . ."

There was a burst of loud laughter.

She smiled. "Hey, this is my shameless plug . . . I just wanted to remind you that my books are all available in the dealers' room." Her eyes turned to Phil, then to Connie. Connie shivered, remembering the tips of the teeth in her breast, fighting a new wish for the mark she had rejected. Denial. But here, faced with a lie that seemed so real and appealing, it was hard—Her fingers dug into Phil's arm but he shook her off.

The barrier Connie knew too well. "I'll be happy to sign anyone's copy . . ." continued Scarlett.

Several people clapped. Whistles, cheers.

"First, would anyone like to ask me a question? Anything anyone want to know about the nature of my books?"

From the hall, screams grew suddenly loud, as though Scarlett were being cheered out there, too. Connie pulled her eyes away from the author's and back to the shut door, frustrated both in love and desire, wondering what the hell was happening out there. The sounds became shrill and pitched, more of fear than excitement.

What the hell? But Connie and the others turned back to Scarlett as Phil cleared his throat and caressed the sack in his hand.

Scarlett was frowning . . . nervous?

"What is the nature of your books?" Phil spoke.

"That question is very general, dear man. Could you be more specific? Otherwise we could be here all night."

The audience laughed again, but the screams outside were becoming deafening, breaking against them. Now definitely screams more of terror and fear than of fun.

"Is there a place for love in undeath?" Phil kept his attention on her as his hand moved to his pocket and Connie saw him clutch the cross. It shone with the power she was drawn to and she prayed it would show him the truth she discovered . . . the truth he spoke but denied in his hot tone. "What is the purpose of existence without love?"

Scarlett shook her head, but her eyes looked beyond Phil, at the door. "Love . . . is an absolute, dear man. In my books, there is no such thing as absolutes. Just like real life. Absolutes are fantasies . . ."

"*Vampires* are fantasies," Phil shot back, his voice stretching as he forced it above the din from the outside hall. "Isn't everything a fantasy without an absolute to support it? Life and death are absolutes, aren't they? And undeath is a fantasy?"

Scarlett's gaze flashed back and forth between Phil and Connie to the door. "Death and life are absolutes only if we believe in them as such. Belief is the only absolute in my materials . . . something you don't believe in is the only lie. For total freedom, everything must be subjective."

Several of the fans applauded, glaring at Phil with anger for daring to take on their god.

"Truth *is* an absolute," argued Phil, raising the mirrored cross, his hand no longer calm. "There must be an absolute truth and not just varied perceptions of it. In order for it to be truth, all subjectivity must be eliminated."

She laughed nervously. "No, dear . . . your argument is based only on the idea that truth be an absolute . . . and truth doesn't allow lies. Truth ignores lies, denies them . . . it doesn't waste time to eliminate them . . . as you're doing!"

More applause and chuckles. But the laughter of the others was closed down by the still-growing screams outside. Scarlett's eyes flashed. "What the hell is going on out there?"

Connie turned to see someone at the back open the door. Curdling shrieks and cries exploded hysterically into the room with a dozen bizarrely clad people, all with fangs gleaming in their mouths. A black man in a T-shirt, his skin nearly a faded gray brown, grabbed a slender brunette decked out in a revealing negligee. She was giggling frantically but the wiry expression of her face was

338

flitting between fear and her now uncertain glee, and her mouth opened wide in a moan that became a scream as the man dropped his face to her breast. Connie felt her limbs go limp as she saw a spurt of blood shoot over his lips—the wet, red fangs.

An old woman in a bikini leaped inside as a plump man ran to shut the door, and she knocked him to the carpet in one easy swipe of an arm, pouncing on top of him with her own gleaming teeth flashing brightly in her wide mouth. The man's shriek was lost in the cacophony of other shouts and screams as the audience began to realize that things were amiss . . . as the dozen vampires all fought their way inside and chose a partner . . . two partners . . . three.

The smell of fear and blood collided with the screams and slurpy sounds of sucking, like a group of thirsty teenagers mouthing their straws at a malt shop. The people who weren't struggling for their lives against this fantasy come true were running to the door with waving hands. . . .

But some of the men and women welcomed the fangs, and Connie's stomach turned in the memory of herself as she watched a woman well over thirty throw herself into a scrawny vampire's arms and open her blouse, flopping out a flabby tit for his ready teeth. A young, pimply-faced man embraced a red-eyed vampire old enough to be his mother and cheered her on with a pained grimace as she took his wrist in her mouth and chewed savagely.

Chaos.

Connie jerked back as Phil began standing beside her . . . as everything became slow motion. "*You* must be eliminated!" Phil swept his eyes through the hysteria consuming the room and held up the cross. It flashed in the room's fluorescent brightness. Scarlett's eyes popped in wide, blank fright, and Phil crooked the sack in his arm as his other hand dropped into his other pocket to clutch the vial, pushing back a fan, then veering the cross into an attacking vampire's face and grinning darkly as it sizzled with a stinking flood of death and the vampire jumped back.

With a hand before her eyes, Scarlett stood and backed up, toppling her chair.

Connie jumped up against Phil, pulling from groping, sharp fingernails. "Don't! You said it, Phil—*she* said it! Believe it! She doesn't exist! She's only a reflection . . . the reflection of your hatred now! Deny her—"

The screams and jeers from the surrounding fans became a block of incomprehensible noise . . . practically overpowering the harsh tones of Phil's voice. He ignored Connie and advanced, pushing her back. "*. . . you believe in this truth and it scares you?*" he was screeching. "*And you deny it? You deny truth?*"

Scarlett's fangs drooled with a clear slickness. Her mouth became wide . . . her arms stretched forward, their sharp nails slicing the air in her scream, which was mixed in pounding pain and victory. She struck the symbol from Phil and let loose a bellow of laughter: "We *both* deny truth!"

Connie tried to deny it *all*, could not overcome the force of mindless hate possessing Phil—Phil's slow motion hands uncapped the bottle and he threw a stream of water through the feet separating him and Scarlett . . . the drops glittering like pure silver . . . slapping Scarlett like a knife, ripping bloody gashes into her skin. A man in a blue business suit was yelling at the top of his lungs as he pulled a woman away from two vampires chasing after them with sharp, bared fangs. He pushed the woman against Connie with a blind stare of terror, vaulting over Phil's fallen chair and trying to grab Phil, too. "Phillip!" Connie heard his scream.

Scarlett cowered back, her face streaming in melting flesh and spewing blood . . . her fingernails talons of death, still ripping the very air as the room's crescendo rose fifty decibels.

Her destruction in Phil's bitter hate.

The blue-suited man, his face ringed in panicked terror, grabbed Phil's arm as Phil emptied his plastic sack and brandished the stained sharp wood he'd killed Vicky with. The man ripped at Phil's shirt as Phil leaped atop the panel table and dove onto Scarlett with his own yell joining the room's screeching rage . . . and Connie watched it connect to the necklace mirror over Scarlett's heart, driving it inside her as blood flew and her pale flesh ripped wide . . . as she fell back to the wall, pinned, and Phil's fury shoved the stake deep in a bubbling spring of stinking blood.

Connie shrieked, because she knew it was too late. More dark blood squirted from Scarlett's mouth in an upchucking stream, covering Phil and the man still trying to drag him back. Connie felt her heart squeal and tear in the ghastly sight and flipped her face away to see the room of fans cheering and clapping and screaming and laughing and crying . . . vampires everywhere. Teeth, blood . . . She flinched and felt herself pulled back by the unknown woman beside her as a vampire lunged at her and sprayed his cold, stinking, and bloody repast all over her. Then the woman released her and went to the man in the blue suit.

Connie sagged as a blond woman in a straw hat and seersucker suit clutched her shoulder and grinned darkly into Connie's eyes, her fangs spinning light and dark . . . life and death . . .

Undeath.

"Please!" gasped Connie, the room and its violent fury whirlpooling.

". . . seen Scarlett?" the mouth with the incredibly real Scarlett teeth was asking.

Falling into the deep pit of madness, Connie tried to

shrink into the chair, throwing out her arm, pointing at Phil and the crumbling, disintegrating shape he bent over.

"Shit!" the woman snarled. "I wanted to do that!"

Everything went black.

Chapter 8

Phil stood silently beside the dust on the floor and the gown it covered.

Scarlett.

The handcuffs bit into his wrists. Kevin stared at him with pity and guilt, his eyes damp, but Phil's heart pounded with the purpose of his action. The purposelessness. The moment's ecstatic victory sank fast and he felt the tug of guilt and undeath still biting him. He had taken part in the lie to destroy it . . . made himself more a part of it.

"Twenty-five dead . . . we can't count the wounded," said a cop, entering the room. "A bunch of these nuts are saying the attackers were *real* vampires . . . and jumped into room mirrors and disappeared. These freaks must all be high!"

"These fucking cons always have some shit going on," said another cop.

"Do you think they were really vampires?"

"You really fucked yourself, Phil."

He nodded, not meeting Kevin's eyes, watching the policemen and then the paramedics. He heard their whispers, too, as they examined what remained of Scarlett. She was puffing with green smoke. Her outer flesh had become a powdery dust that made anyone close to it sneeze. . . . Now, her inner skin and her internal organs, stinking like waste from a meat factory, decayed at a fast speed. Her bones, brown and cracked where already visible, were dissolving into a slimy muck.

"What the hell did you do to her?" Kevin said, his face pale and lined far beyond his years.

"She was a vampire. All of them were." He said it simply, then looked for Connie where she stood just outside the doorway with Kevin's wife, Denise. Neither had been hurt, not physically. Another medic stood beside Connie and was trying to take her blood pressure in the dissolving chaos.

Phil looked back again. Scarlett *was* the dissolving chaos, now literally, but undeath was still real.

Inside *him*. He had accepted it and welcomed it more than ever before.

"You're really crazy, Phil. I don't know what the hell all this was about, but there aren't vampires . . ." Kevin shook his head. "I feel guilty I didn't call you, maybe I could have—"

"Don't feel guilt for something you couldn't have helped. I'm a sacrifice. I wanted to be a sacrifice." He spoke quietly, seeing Sonia turning to dust in his mind, too. Even handcuffed, he felt the freedom from that past, but it was replaced with the new iciness of a lie he still believed in. He heard Connie's plea for his denial that he had discharged.

He'd . . . fucked *himself*. "Believe what you want, Kevin. Everybody does, but it doesn't change what you see." He felt sorry for Connie and himself, but at least he'd finally done *something*. "Take care of Connie, okay?"

Kevin still shook his head with perplexity. "Keep believing in vampires, Phil. With your background and the shit that happened here tonight, maybe we can get you sentenced to an institution for a few years. . . . Shade was so big I know that the prosecutors are going to try for the

344

death penalty. At this point, the safest thing is for you to just stay crazy."

Phil nodded. That, at least, was something he did not need to deny.

Chapter 9

Kevin and Connie both sat opposite Phil in the visitors' booth, separated from him by the thick glass that was somehow less restricting than the barriers of his mind separating him from them both before.

It seemed a million years ago, but only eight months had passed. With a faint smile, Phil gazed at Connie and the part of himself he had made real in her the night before he took the wrong path and began his circle once more. At least the growing child within her was a true reflection of himself. Life. Not death or undeath.

Connie's mouth moved and he heard her words in his ears over the phone receiver, their fearful warmth. "Kevin's done a great job, Phil. He's given all your records to the lawyers and they think they can reopen the case . . . they . . . they think—" She broke off and he saw her tears as she clutched the necklace cross around her neck—made from the same cross she had made for him.

The cross Scarlett had rejected.

The cross *he* had rejected.

"Phil," Connie whispered. "Those people killed . . . a lot of them must have turned in vampires."

He nodded. Shade was gone, but her disciples continued her work. Connie had brought him updates on the unexplained murders every time she came to see him, and although she knew enough to protect herself, he was afraid that after the baby was born, she might try to do something about all those vampires herself.

Alone.

"Leave it alone, Connie. Someone will figure it out. You can't do it. I want you to get the hell out this state, okay?"

She shook her head wildly, tears still dripping from her eyes, covering her face with both hands. A moment later, Kevin picked up the phone.

"I think we can get you off on the insanity plea this time, Phil. Mr. Drummond will be in to talk over the strategy with you a little later. But it looks like at least we've got some hope. The biggest trouble is still Vicky Cossiter. The prosecutors are going to stick with the pre-meditation charge and a love quarrel and we won't be able to avoid the charges of at least your neglect. But I still think we can get you off by your agreement to spend a couple of years in psychiatric treatment."

Phil shuddered.

Kevin's eyes sympathized, and he lowered his voice with a glance at Connie. "Hey . . . it's better than the death penalty . . ." He grinned weakly.

Phil barely grinned back. It was the cost of truth. Life. Death. At least he had seen the miracle of truth, even if he had not welcomed it in his action against Scarlett.

Love.

He stared back at Connie's round stomach . . . their child. "Maybe I'm safer in here, Kevin. At least none of the inmates are vampires—"

Kevin's face became grim. "You are crazy, Phil, you know it?" As Kevin and Connie got up and he helped her out of the booth, Phil got up to go, too, but stopped when a young lady in an outlandish seersucker suit and straw hat appeared from nowhere and dashed in the closing

347

door. She grabbed the phone and nodded at him. Phil put it back to his ear. "Who—"

"Congratulations on the Scarlett job, Mr. Ottoman," she smiled, her face distantly familiar. "I was kind of pissed at first, but you did a great job . . . really. Sorry I haven't gotten in to speak with you before, but I think I can help you with your problem."

"Who—"

She shook her head, then held out a necklace . . . a round mirror attached.

"What problem?" asked Phil tightly.

She swung the mirror back and forth hypnotically and he knew it was Scarlett's.

Phil hissed.

"Death has always been a problem. Hey . . . I want to help you, Mr. Ottoman. One equal value for another in my book. Maybe you did me a favor, maybe not. So if you want, maybe I can do you a favor . . . or maybe not."

He shook his head. "What kind of a reporter are you?"

"Still an amateur, I'm afraid . . . but here's the deal, okay? You get the death penalty . . . or maybe you decide you don't like playing the lady to the strong arms. Anyway, you get tired of life and the way things are, you just look in your mirror, okay?" She smiled. "I'll keep my eye on you just in case. You want me, I'll be there, and I know that you've been thinking about it a lot lately . . ."

"What?"

Her lips curled up slickly to show her teeth. "You still have a choice, Phil. Remember that . . . you have a choice up to your dying day . . . maybe even then. There's a lot of us out here now." She stood up and closed her lips, pursing them playfully.

That night, Phil dreamed of Czeckovslovakia . . . Scarlett . . . then the visitor's fangs.

HAUTALA'S HORROR – HOLD ON TO YOUR HEAD!

MOONDEATH   (1844-4, $3.95/$4.95)
Cooper Falls is a small, quiet New Hampshire town, the kind you'd miss if you blinked an eye. But when darkness falls and the full moon rises, an uneasy feeling filters through the air; an unnerving foreboding that causes the skin to prickle and the body to tense.

NIGHT STONE   (3030-4, $4.50/$5.50)
Their new house was a place of darkness and shadows, but with her secret doll, Beth was no longer afraid. For as she stared into the eyes of the wooden doll, she heard it call to her and felt the force of its evil power. And she knew it would tell her what she had to do.

MOON WALKER   (2598-X, $4.50/$5.50)
No one in Dyer, Maine ever questioned the strange disappearances that plagued their town. And they never discussed the eerie figures seen harvesting the potato fields by day . . . the slow, lumbering hulks with expressionless features and a blood-chilling deadness behind their eyes.

LITTLE BROTHERS   (2276-X, $3.95/$4.95)
It has been five years since Kip saw his mother horribly murdered by a blur of "little brown things." But the "little brothers" are about to emerge once again from their underground lair. Only this time there will be no escape for the young boy who witnessed their last feast!

Available wherever paperbacks are sold, or order direct from the Publisher. Send cover price plus 50¢ per copy for mailing and handling to Penguin USA, P.O. Box 999, c/o Dept. 17109, Bergenfield, NJ 07621. Residents of New York and Tennessee must include sales tax. DO NOT SEND CASH.

GOT AN INSATIABLE THIRST FOR VAMPIRES?
LET PINNACLE QUENCH IT!

BLOOD FEUD (705, $4.50)
by Sam Siciliano

SHE is a mistress of darkness—coldly sensual and dangerously seductive. HE is a master of manipulation with the power to take life and grant *unlife*. THEY are two ancient vampires who have sworn to eliminate each other. Now, after centuries, the time has come for a face-to-face confrontation—and neither will rest until one of them is destroyed!

DARKNESS ON THE ICE (687, $4.50)
by Lois Tilton

It was World War II, and the Nazis had found the perfect weapon. Wolff, an SS officer, with an innate talent—and thirst—for killing, was actually a vampire. His strength and stealth allowed him to drain and drink the blood of enemy sentries. Wolff stalked his prey for the Nazi cause—but killed them to satisfy his own insatiable hunger!

THIRST OF THE VAMPIRE (649, $4.50)
by T. Lucien Wright

Phillipe Brissot is no ordinary killer—he is a creature of the night—a vampire. Through the centuries he has satisfied his thirst for blood while carrying out his quest of vengeance against his ancient enemies, the Marat Family. Now journalist, Mike Marat is investigating his cousin's horrible "murder" unaware that Phillipe is watching him and preparing to strike against the Marats one final time . . .

BLIND HUNGER (714, $4.50)
by Darke Parke

Widowed and blind, pretty Patty Hunsacker doesn't feel like going on with her life . . . until the day a man arrives at her door, claiming to be the twin brother of her late husband. Patty welcomes Mark into her life but soon finds herself living in a world of terror as well as darkness! For she makes the shocking discovery that "Mark" is really Matt—and he isn't dead—he's a vampire. And he plans on showing his wife that loving a vampire can be quite a bloody affair!

Available wherever paperbacks are sold, or order direct from the Publisher. Send cover price plus 50¢ per copy for mailing and handling to Penguin USA, P.O. Box 999, c/o Dept. 17109, Bergenfield, NJ 07621. Residents of New York and Tennessee must include sales tax. DO NOT SEND CASH.

YOU'D BETTER SLEEP WITH THE LIGHTS TURNED ON!
BONE CHILLING HORROR BY

RUBY JEAN JENSEN

ANNABELLE   (2011-2, $3.95/$4.95)

BABY DOLLY   (3598-5, $4.99/$5.99)

CELIA   (3446-6, $4.50/$5.50)

CHAIN LETTER   (2162-3, $3.95/$4.95)

DEATH STONE   (2785-0, $3.95/$4.95)

HOUSE OF ILLUSIONS   (2324-3, $4.95/$5.95)

LOST AND FOUND   (3040-1, $3.95/$4.95)

MAMA   (2950-0, $3.95/$4.95)

PENDULUM   (2621-8, $3.95/$4.95)

VAMPIRE CHILD   (2867-9, $3.95/$4.95)

VICTORIA   (3235-8, $4.50/$5.50)

Available wherever paperbacks are sold, or order direct from the Publisher. Send cover price plus 50¢ per copy for mailing and handling to Penguin USA, P.O. Box 999, c/o Dept. 17109, Bergenfield, NJ 07621. Residents of New York and Tennessee must include sales tax. DO NOT SEND CASH.

MAKE THE CONNECTION

WITH

Come talk to your favorite authors and get the inside scoop on everything that's going on in the world of publishing, from the only online service that's designed exclusively for the publishing industry.

With Z-Talk Online Information Service, the most innovative and exciting computer bulletin board around, you can:

- ♥ CHAT "LIVE" WITH AUTHORS, FELLOW READERS, AND OTHER MEMBERS OF THE PUBLISHING COMMUNITY.
- ♥ FIND OUT ABOUT UPCOMING TITLES BEFORE THEY'RE RELEASED.
- ♥ DOWNLOAD THOUSANDS OF FILES AND GAMES.
- ♥ READ REVIEWS OF ROMANCE TITLES.
- ♥ HAVE UNLIMITED USE OF E-MAIL.
- ♥ POST MESSAGES ON OUR DOZENS OF TOPIC BOARDS.

All it takes is a computer and a modem to get online with Z-Talk. Set your modem to 8/N/1, and dial 212-545-1120. If you need help, call the System Operator, at 212-889-2299, ext. 260. There's a two week free trial period. After that, annual membership is only $ 60.00.

See you online!

KENSINGTON PUBLISHING CORP.